Never Forget

Angela Petch

Bright Pen

Visit us online at www.authorsonline.co.uk

A Bright Pen Book

Copyright © Angela Petch 2012

Cover design by Liam Russell ©

All rights reserved. No part of this publication may be reproduced, stored in a retrieval system, or transmitted in any form or by any means, electronic, mechanical, photocopy, recording or otherwise, without prior written permission of the copyright owner. Nor can it be circulated in any form of binding or cover other than that in which it is published and without similar condition including this condition being imposed on a subsequent purchaser.

British Library Cataloguing in Publication Data.
A catalogue record for this book is available from the British Library.

ISBN 978 0 7552 1453 2

Authors OnLine Ltd
19 The Cinques
Gamlingay, Sandy
Bedfordshire SG19 3NU
England

This book is also available in e-book format, details of which are available at www.authorsonline.co.uk

Quant'è bella giovinezza
che si fugge tuttavia!
Chi vuol esser lieto, sia:
del doman non c'è certezza.

Lorenzo de' Medici (1449 – 1492)

How lovely is youth
Which is over far too soon!
Be happy while you may:
There is no certainty in a tomorrow.
(Author's translation)

In memory of Paul Francis Sutor

Chapter 1
February 1999

They say things happen in threes.

Later on, Anna will decide the arrival of the package is number three. On a dingy February morning in Camden she's still in bed, drowsy after a poor night's sleep. From under her duvet, she listens to commuters scurrying in the street below, gloating at not having to join the bustle, but feeling on edge. Life feels wobbly. Her mother passed away a month ago after a long illness and now she's been made redundant from the Estate Agency.

Just as she's nodding off, her door bell rings. Sighing, muttering, 'I'm coming, I'm coming,' she untangles herself from her duvet-nest and opens the front door of her second floor flat.

'Parcel for you, Miss.' A young postman smirks, looking her over with a grin as she wraps her dressing-gown tighter. Taking the parcel, she shuts the door firmly in his face, slaps over the kitchen floor in her slippers and flicks on the kettle switch.

The package is bulky. It's something she's been expecting but has relegated to the back of her mind. At the reading of her mother's will last week, the solicitor had mentioned she had been left a file of assorted papers, as well as the sum of £50,000. Harry and Jane had been given everything else. While Peregrine Smythe of Smythe & Sons, in his crumpled Savile Row pin-stripe, had been droning on about the minutiae of inheritance, Anna was watching a trapped fly batting against the windowpane. From time to time she'd glanced at her older brother and sister sitting opposite, thinking how fat and bald Harry had become, how Jane could almost be a stand-in for Hyacinth Bucket with her immaculate hair-do sprayed stiff and crisp.

She makes herself a mug of Earl Grey taking it back to bed with the package. Inside the brown paper wrapper is a cardboard box, the lid tied down with an old shoe-lace which she pulls open. Lifting the lid, she sees a brown envelope bearing her name written in her mother's flowery handwriting, as well as note-books, bundles of papers rolled up in a perished elastic band and folded fabric.

She withdraws a folded sheet of lined note-paper from the envelope, cheap and old-fashioned, with a spray of violets printed in the top left corner, probably from Woolworth's. Her mother has written in English, which she spoke with a strong accent, but wrote well.

Willow's End,
August 16th, 1997

My darling Anna,

As you read this you will have already been to my funeral. Maybe there were a few tears but I hope it was also a happy occasion, with some of my favourite Italian music played in church and a 'spaghettata' afterwards. I imagine there were a few stories shared about me. Maybe the family will have recalled my quick temper and my dreadful mistakes with English. If people were kind about me or harsh, then so be it. 'Pazienza!' as we say…

I have so much to tell you. Maybe this is the coward's way out – to write it all down instead of telling you face to face. It was hard to know what was for the best. If I had told my story when I was

*alive, the results might have been cataclysmic.
'Cataclismico, disastroso...' they are nearly the same
words in Italian. There are actually many
similarities but, oh so many differences between the
English and the Italians - as I found when I first
came over here. But more of that later.*

*When the doctors told me my cancer was inoperable,
I decided to sort out my papers and write you a long
letter before it was too late. Let us call it a kind of
diary. At the reading of the will, my solicitor will
have mentioned they would be coming your way. I
imagine you will have felt that, as usual, you were
being left out. Apart from the money, Harry has
'Willows End' - I know he will cope with the
draughty old place, he always loved it and it will go
with his new status as Company Director. Jane has
my jewellery. She always loved dressing up with it
when she was a little girl.*

*And you have this brown box containing my
scribblings. I hope that by the time you finish
reading, you will understand that I never intended to
make you feel left out, my darling. Maybe a few
details have been forgotten over the years but I have
tried my best to fill in wherever I could.*

*Read it when you have time. Do with it what you
will.*

It is my inheritance to you.
     Your loving Mamma.

She leans back against the pillows, intrigued but at
the same time angry at her mother for being so
enigmatic. Theirs had always been a difficult
relationship. Sometimes she'd be folded into her arms
and her love would be tangible but for the most part,
she was distant, undemonstrative. It didn't help being

constantly teased by Jane and Harry who were embarrassed teenagers when Anna was born. 'You were an accident, one big mistake,' they tormented her, not realising how near the mark they were. She'd grown up feeling less loved than them and nothing but a nuisance most of the time.

Strangely, she had felt closer to her mother when she was in Claremont Rest Home last year, where she died. When Ines was confused, Anna knew how to soothe her. 'Tell me about your life in Italy before you came to England, Mamma,' she would prompt. Sometimes Ines would oblige, although Anna couldn't follow most of what she was trying to tell her. It was all a bit of a ramble. Other times she would refuse to talk, content to sit staring out of the windows at the gardens and the sea. On one of the last visits, she was tired, lapsing into a dialect which Anna couldn't follow. She didn't mind when her mother was quiet. There was room enough for both of them in her silence and the pair of them would sit holding hands, Anna giving her mother space to wander through her thoughts. Sometimes a sound or a smell seemed to spark off a memory and she would start to talk as if an event had only just happened. Perhaps a motorbike would zoom by on the promenade and it was as if she was in the past again.

Her sentences were random. *'The others have gone down to the city today. It's too hot to dance but the 'Tedeschi' are in the next valley now. They've been clearing the hamlets…'* and Anna would humour her, treat her accounts as everyday occurrences, *'Really Mamma? And what happened next?'* But if she felt like an intruder, listening to what should really have been private moments: *'If they find out, I'll be in such trouble but it was so hot. My blouse clung to my body, my hair floated on the water like weed. I nearly drowned, he held me tight…"* Anna wouldn't respond. She'd change the subject or fetch her mother's box of photos from her bed-side cupboard and they'd look at the family snaps together. There were afternoons too when her mother would sit with tears flowing down her cheeks and Anna would gently wipe them away. She'd cling to her daughter, *'He came back Anna, he came back. But I won't leave you - you're a good girl, my special gift.'*

Suddenly her thoughts are interrupted by her mobile ringing, making her jump.

'Anna! I was only a bit late…couldn't get away any sooner. Where did you get to?' It is Will. And he is peeved.

An explanation doesn't readily come to mind. Right now she doesn't feel like telling him that, yet again, she'd grown tired of waiting for him in the restaurant; that she hates the way the waiters in there cast pitying looks as she drinks her wine, trying to make the glass last longer in case he eventually turns up.

'Can I come over?' he says, 'I'm in a taxi. Be there in, say, fifteen minutes?'

She glances at her watch. Seven thirty. No work to get up for. No reason not to have Will in her bed during the day-time – it would be an unexpected treat. But then again her appetite for sharing Will, for snatched evenings or parts of days, is dwindling.

He lowers his voice. The cabbie is probably eavesdropping on his famous passenger whose distinguished features are regularly seen on Channel

Four News. 'I could stay the whole night, darling. Tricia's away at her health spa for two nights.'

A whole day and night together would have been bliss a few weeks ago. But she's not in the mood. 'I'm not feeling so good today, Will, I've a bad migraine'. (She's never had a migraine in her life.) 'Look, I'll call you soon.' Before he has a chance to persuade her otherwise, she snaps her mobile shut and switches it off. She needs space to think. The question of Will can be sorted when she feels more sorted in herself.

She throws her phone onto the bed next to her mother's papers. There seem to be a lot of them. She doesn't know if she can really be bothered. Mamma had never wanted to talk much about her Italian life when she was alive. It seems a bit late to be doing so now from beyond the grave.

Settling down under her warm duvet, she falls asleep.

Chapter 2

It is dark when Anna is woken by the long bellow of a car horn. She glances blearily at her bedside clock and realise she's slept through most of the day - it's now five o'clock in the afternoon.

This morning's package has fallen onto the floor from her bed. An assortment of papers, note-books and envelopes have spilled out – some of them numbered with red crayon. Number one is a large brown envelope. Number two is a scuffed school exercise book. Instead of lines, the pages are segmented into little squares, like graph paper. She remembers Mamma explaining how different types of copy books were used by different school-years in Italy, laughing when Mamma described the overalls and huge bows they wore to primary school – even the boys. She had taught her a few simple words in Italian when she was little but never when father was around. He went berserk if he heard her speaking Italian, 'You'll confuse them. How many times do I have to spell it out, woman?' he'd shout, his face turning purple.

Then there would be a row. There was always a lot of shouting. Anna would retreat to the bottom of the garden and climb the copper beech or hide under the stairs clutching Edward Bear to her chest, whispering into his furry ears, 'There now Eddy Teddy, soon be over, they'll stop soon, you'll see!'

She plumps up her pillows and opens envelope number one. Inside is a hard-backed, vellum ledger. As she opens it, a slip of paper falls from between the covers. The hand-writing is again her mother's.

Anna,

Here is part of your father's story. I found this book in his shed when I was sorting out his effects. Do you remember how it was a "no-go" area for us all? Your father's sacred den!

I never knew he spent his time writing in there. I thought he was simply escaping from us, with the excuse of mending something or other.

I have read it through but it is only part of his story. I think he must have written it after the war. It doesn't seem like a journal to me. He was on the move a lot – as you will see if you read on – and he wouldn't have had time to keep a record.

I decided to add this to my own record of what happened, to try to fill in the missing bits of our story. They say everybody has a book inside them but what I have written isn't fiction, it's the truth. And I believe our story deserves to be told. The war still casts its long shadow over our lives even though more than fifty years have gone by.

It made me sad to read your father's words. For a while he transported me back to the time when we

fell in love. How things change. What a lot of rubbish life throws our way.
Mamma.

Anna has a vivid childhood memory that haunted her as a little girl - another type of 'occupation' in Dadda's shed, besides writing and mending second-hand furniture. She was about nine years old. Unusually, he had left the shed door unlocked that afternoon and she'd slipped in to have a nose. A magazine lay open on his work-bench, revealing a photo of a woman's legs spread wide, her breasts naked. She didn't understand the 'rude pictures' and it didn't feel right to gawp. Backing out of the shed, she fell over a bucket, sending it clattering onto the path. Her father, hoeing in the vegetable garden, looked up and rushed over, shouting, twisting her ear, 'I thought I told you never to go in there.' He'd slapped her hard on the back of her leg and she'd run up the path and into the kitchen, sobbing. Mamma was ironing while she listened to music on the radio.

'Darling, whatever is the matter?' She unplugged the iron, resting it on the side of the kitchen table. 'Did you fall? Show me.'

'I hate him, I hate him.'

Her mother pulled her onto her lap, wiping her tears with the corner of her pinafore. 'Now tell me what happened, *tesoro*. Stop crying, I can't understand anything if you keep making that noise.'

Her father stormed in, reached for the tin on the dresser where the change was kept. 'You spoil that brat. Next time I find her in my shed, she'll get such a hiding, she won't be able to sit down for a week.' He pulled on his jacket. 'And you needn't wait for me for supper. I'm going out and I'll be back late.' The door slammed.

Her mother sighed, pulled her closer. 'Never mind – we'll have a special supper - just you and me on our own - with spaghetti, then gelato for afters.' She held her daughter close and safe and Anna listened to the kitchen clock ticking as her mother rocked her.

'I meant it', she'd sobbed. 'I *hate* him. He's always so *cross.* I think he hates me too.'

'Shh – don't talk about hate.' She undid Anna's plaits, re-plaiting them as she searched for words. 'Your Dadda doesn't hate you. Not one little bit. Sometimes he just hates life…how can I explain? Now you must be a big girl and listen to what I'm going to tell you and try to understand.' She lifted Anna from her lap and fetched onions, celery and carrots to chop up for the meat sauce. 'Come and help me with supper. We'll have a little talk.'

Together they prepared the sauce and now, whenever Anna eats pasta and ragù, she always associates this meal with the strange conversation of that evening. Afterwards, she felt less of a child, as if her mother had been trying to give her a glimpse into what it was like to be a grown-up.

'Dadda wasn't always such a cross-patch. But the war changed him, you see. Lots of horrible things happen in wars and Dadda had a difficult time. It was difficult for everybody - but the young men, they saw cruel things that people do in times of war. We must make allowances for his tempers. Now, lay the table and we'll eat'.

And as far as mention of her father in the war was concerned, that had been that. Her mother never spoke about it to her ever again. Anna's childhood was filled with shouting, slamming of doors, stormy arguments, her parents' constant bickering, moody silences at meal times and then snatched moments when her mother would scoop her up in her arms, cuddle her, pour out Italian to her as if she could no longer keep the words inside. But that happened only when her father wasn't around. Once, she'd picked a bunch of pretty red flowers off his runner beans for Mamma and arranged them in a vase on the kitchen table. Dadda was furious, 'Stupid, stupid child,' he'd shouted, smacking her and sending her to bed early, 'now they won't fruit.' He was never there to play with like other children's Dads, there were never games of cricket on the back-lawn or rough and tumble on the lounge carpet. When he was home, after long spells away from the house, he would complain about the noise, 'Can't hear myself think in this place! What about a bit of hush?' was his constant refrain.

Her father died suddenly of a heart attack when she was ten and she wasn't allowed to attend his funeral. He just seemed to disappear from their lives. Not long afterwards they'd moved to Willow's End. 'We'll start afresh,' Mamma had said, packing away his photo from where it stood on the piano. It was as if she had wiped him from her mind.

The writing in the mildewed book is clear, precise, with tiny script and very upright letters, unlike her mother's artistic scrawl. Her father was a meticulous man, rebuking his family whenever they left possessions around the house. 'You're not in the army now,' her mother would snap at him as he squared up the cutlery and glasses on the supper table or passed a finger over the top of the door to inspect for dust.

Campo Fontanellato, somewhere near Parma.

2nd September 1943
My leg is still playing up but Bob says the climb up to the top bunk is good physiotherapy for me, so he is below. I need to get some strength back into the bloody thing for when we leave this place. It's siesta time and there's quiet for a couple of hours. Although it's early September, it's still hot and the cicadas are making us very aware of their presence. Laying up here on the scratchy blanket, I am staring at the frescos on the ceiling of the villa where we are 'confined'.

There are naked cherubs and bare-breasted virgins with harps, garlands of fresh fruit, puffy white clouds and trails of ribbons. What wouldn't I give for a handful of bare breast right now!

Bob's trying to read, but I'm restless. Eight months of being cooped up with a gang of smelly men is getting to me.

This place is better than the last dump however. Here, the Italian Comandante speaks some English. He studied at Cambridge before the war and he actually lets us have our Red Cross parcels. Decent of him!

There are bars at the windows and I want freedom again. My last escape was short-lived. I'd faked sickness for three weeks with delirium and headaches and was escorted to the local hospital. As one of my 'imaginary' symptoms was diarrhoea, I made several trips to the toilet each night, much to the amusement of the guards, who eventually grew used to me staggering back and forth from the ward. One night, I managed to climb out of the toilet window but I hadn't banked on the crumbling masonry on the ledge and I fell awkwardly into the street below. I gained one night's freedom out of the bloody venture though. One glorious night in a drain culvert dreaming of re-joining my platoon! A painful, uncomfortable night but proving to me that escape is possible. And the sounds of the night were infinitely better than the sound of a room full of snoring, farting men. My souvenir is this gammy right leg. Understandably the Comandante hadn't wanted to send me back to the hospital and I reckon the bugger's set wrong now.

'What's the first thing you'll do once you're free?' I ask Bob. He grunts at me from below. His nose is stuck in a book, as usual. Bob's the academic type: round, glinting specs, a complete duffer at anything athletic; a daydreamer with an educated brain. I bet he was nicknamed Four-Eyes at school. He's been planning our next escape and teaching us all some German phrases. Once we leave this place we reckon we could pass as Germans as we've mostly got the blond hair and fair skin of the Teds. (That's Fritz to you and me – the Eyeties call them Tedeschi). No point in trying to pass off as Eyeties. We're mostly too tall.

No answer from Bob, so I stick my head below the parapet, so to speak. He looks up at me. 'I say, this book is fascinating...did you know Leonardo da Vinci invented the concept of the helicopter and the tank? Take a decko at these illustrations. These Eyeties are not as daft as they seem, you know.'

There are a few dog-eared books in the camp that are passed around in some kind of fair system. Bob has probably read them all three times over. He needs books like I need women.

'Bob!' I go again. 'What will be the first thing you do once you get back to Blighty?'

He puts down his volume. We often have these daft, meaningless conflabs. Lately we have more of them - probably because of the rumours. A couple of months ago we hear a rumpus coming from the guards' quarters: whooping and cheering. Then one of them – we call him Joey, though Giuseppe's his real name, he comes and explains, 'Old Mussolini's been deposed. He's no longer our great leader.' He makes an obscene gesture with his arm. 'The *fascisti* are finished.'

That was around 21st July and ever since we've not heard another dickie bird. Our escape plan's been put on hold.

The SBO calls us to meetings regularly to plan our course of action. He tells us we can't just disperse. He says we have to stick together. 'In an orderly fashion' is how he put it. 'We don't want escaped POW's all over the shop, struggling around the Italian countryside. It would be one almighty mess for our men to try and recover us all.'

There's a different atmosphere in the camp. The Italians have painted over the Fascist slogans. They're friendlier with us and the SBO has warned us that, to all intents and purposes, we should soon be free. We're just waiting for them to sign the Armistice but until then, we're still prisoners-of-war. Barmy if you ask me. It's frustrating, this waiting game.

I ask old Bob again, 'Go on, what are you going to do when you get back home?'

He says, 'I'll have a clean set of clothes, a plate of bangers and mash and onion gravy. And a deep, hot bath - plimsoll line or not...'

I agree with him, 'A clean set of clothes with no more lice, no body odours...'

I've grown expert at de-lousing (another pastime to while away the siesta hours). The first time I discovered the little buggers in the seams of my trousers, my skin was covered in welts. The irritation was enough to drive a man round the bend. When we complained to the Comandante, he shrugged his shoulders, in the way the Eyeties do. His hands went palm-up and he told us all his men suffered from the same trouble and to stop complaining. It was '*normale*'. 'There is nothing I can do about it, *signori*. My men too have to bear this discomfort.'

You can squeeze the blighters between your finger tips but it's a lengthy occupation. A set of clean clothes would be the bees' knees. I agreed with Bob.

'Clean clothes and a big, curvy woman.' I begin to drool at the thought of it.

Bob throws down a dirty sock at me. 'Don't start, Norman!'

Then we are interrupted by a stampede of feet up the stairs to our dormitory and in burst the

Eyeties, brandishing rifles, *'Fuori, fuori, fuori tutti...'* (Everybody out!)

Mutters and groans all around from the men resting on their bunks.

'What the bloody hell?'

'What do they want now?'

'Pipe down, chaps!'

'Can't a man get a decent kip round here?'

Bob's talking to the guards. He speaks passable Italian as well as German. He's softened down many a sticky situation by acting as our interpreter

The Eyeties are even more excitable than usual. There's lots of gesticulating and shouting.

'What's up, Bob?'

'It seems they've signed up to us lot at last. The armistice has been signed at long, bloody last. We're no longer prisoners. They're opening the doors and cutting the wire at the back of the exercise ground. We'll be free to go...'

Then there's shaking of hands all round from our guards and they're off, clattering down the stairs with much excited yelling.

At first there's euphoria, then stunned silence and then somebody tries the door. It isn't a trick. It is open. Somebody else finds the keys to the kitchen and we have an impromptu feast of fresh bread and cheese washed down with vinegary wine. It's like Christmas in September, even if the wine is foul. Still, it's alcohol!

Our SBO thumps on the table, stands up. He's a good sort, although he likes to use big words to show off his education, but he's kept us all in some kind of order all this time.

'Gentlemen! Before we get carried away, I think now is the time to put our plans into action. You are all perfectly aware of a risk of a German attack on the camp. None of us, I am sure, wants to be transported back to Germany. Although the Italians will now ostensibly be in a position to defend us, I can envisage a stronger German counter-attack. I therefore propose to delegate guard duty from the roof terrace. At the first sight of a German approach, the bugler will sound the alarm and we shall march out in good order to a point just south of the village.

The Comandante has provided me with a sketch and this afternoon I need six volunteers to do a reconnaissance with me.
In the meantime, gentlemen, I recommend we have our wits about us. We should tap these bottles of disgusting wine and prepare for imminent departure, packing just one small bag of essentials to take with us. We must travel light and fast. Our route is north along the Apennines and onwards to Switzerland. The going will not be easy.'

I hobble up the stairs, with Bob taking the steps three at a time. I've never seen him so nimble. We waste no time in gathering together our most essential possessions. Our food parcels from the Red Cross are received sporadically but the Eyeties always pierce the lids of canned goods understanding our need for escape and knowing that preserved food is useful. Nevertheless, Bob and I have devised a recipe for providing ourselves with essential protein and vitamins. It tastes foul but it will supply us with nourishment when needs be. We've mixed bacon fat with raisins, cocoa, marg and condensed milk and melted the mixture into bars. Inside tins of 'Germolene', we've hidden money wrapped in cellophane. We 'acquired' the money from the guards, who are always keen on buying our ciggies. A few of these bars go into my knapsack as well as knitted socks. Some of the chaps who have been holed up here for a while have warned us of the freezing nights in winter. Folk back home would be surprised to know that the temperature drops below zero in the hills. Who knows how many nights we will have to spend up there? I shove in my regulation jumper. At the last minute, I decide to pack a note-book and I slip in my photo of Phyllis. It's a bit creased but she's still a cracker! Absence makes the heart go fonder and I could do with her company right now. It's a pity Ma and Pa don't approve... Bob's made a compass from an old button and a magnetised safety pin. We're probably going to need it.

At the end of her father's account, stapled onto the next page of the book, is a letter typed on official notepaper from Free time Press, a publishing house.

APRIL 16TH 1956

DEAR MR SWILLAND,

THANK YOU FOR YOUR MANUSCRIPT OF WHAT IS, I REGRET TO SAY, YET ANOTHER WARTIME STORY TO ADD TO THE MANY OTHERS PILED ON THE FLOOR BY MY DESK.

I SHOULD POINT OUT THAT ALTHOUGH YOU HAVE RECOUNTED SOME INTERESTING ESCAPADES, WE HAVE BEEN INUNDATED OVER THE LAST FEW YEARS WITH THESE PERSONAL ADVENTURE STORIES.

I REGRET TO HAVE TO INFORM YOU THAT OUR READERS ARE LOOKING FOR LESS CLICHÉD SUBJECT MATTERS AND LIGHTER SUBJECT MATTER.

THANK YOU FOR SENDING US YOUR NOTES, BUT I AM RETURNING THEM TO YOU AS WE ARE UNABLE TO USE THEM AT THIS TIME.

YOURS CEDRIC BROWNING-ROBINSON.

Anna feels her anger rising at the curt and dismissive tone of patronising Browning-Robinson. Damn you, Cedric, she thinks, I hope you were run over not long afterwards by a bus.

Chapter 3

Anna knew her father was an escaped POW when he met Mamma but that part of her parents' lives was never discussed. They used to describe the shortages of the war to their children, made them finish everything on their plates, telling them how lucky they were.

'You couldn't afford to be fussy when I was a girl,' Mamma had said after Anna turned her nose up again at odious liver and bacon. 'If you didn't eat what was on your plate, somebody else would and there would be nothing else to eat until the next meal.'

They described coupons and rations and how they registered Harry as vegetarian when he was a toddler so they could receive bigger cheese portions, but she never heard any talk of fighting. So although her father's account reads like an adventure comic, her heart is pounding because she knows they are real events. The troubled, reclusive father she recalls, in his baggy cardigan smelling of cigarettes, is totally opposite to the picture of the cheeky young POW in his notes. She considers how the young believe they will be forever young and the old have always been old. She knows this is ridiculous but she has never imagined her parents as young people.

His next entry is dated September 1944, leaving nearly a whole year to be accounted. Her mother had commented about him being on the move. This might explain the gap.

September 1944 – The camp in the Apennines

Last night I dreamt of my room at home.
I was in my own bed with crisp white sheets next to clean skin, an eiderdown warming me, a fresh spring breeze blowing the curtains at my window. The smell of bacon and eggs was drifting up from the kitchen downstairs. I could hear singing.

But my mother never sings and though I try to open my eyes, it's hard. Yet I can definitely hear a woman's voice, soft and soothing as a song. *'Signore, Lei deve mangiare...si svegli....*[sir, you must eat...wake up]'

My dreams deceived me. I am still in Italy. A young girl is trying to spoon soup into my mouth. She could be quite pretty with those long curls of hers escaping from her scarf, her skin soft, olive-brown.

In the prison camp at night, I'd often dreamt of holding a woman, making love to her slowly and now the opportunity is here, within my grasp. She leans over me, an arm supporting me, feeding me like a baby. I could sink my face between her breasts she's so close. I sit up and immediately the world spins again. When will this bloody fever go down? I wince as a shooting pain goes up my right leg. The girl rolls up my trouser leg, grimacing. She calls a man over. He crouches down and they talk. I understand a few words in Italian now after weeks of being sheltered by peasants. Bob's Italian lessons at the camp have helped too. I wonder where the poor bugger is now and if he's still alive.

Some of the words I recognise: *'medico, ospedale.'*

'Infezione', she says.

'I grab her arm, 'No hospital…too many Germans.'

I have been down that route before. I don't want to go through any more bloody escapes from hospital. It would be pushing my luck.

The girl scrabbles in her pockets and speaks to the man again, 'Mamma gave me this. I could try. I've watched her often enough.'

The man shrugs and I try to catch what he says to the girl.

'It will be better for us too. We can't risk another trip down the valley to the hospital. There are too many Fascisti in the area as well as the bastard Tedeschi. I'll send Tonino over to help. He speaks English.'

The girl drips an infusion into my wound made from a concoction of herbs or leaves which she produces from a cloth pouch. The pain is bad. I think I yelp before passing out again and dreaming. But this time the dreams are crazy.

Visions of buxom, flaxen-haired angels clasping harps like the painted virgins on the prison camp ceiling, transmuting to SS guards brandishing blood-tipped bayonets; sounds of blood-curdling screams interspersed with arias from Puccini; feeling cold, plunging into freezing river water then burning on an open fire like a chicken on a spit, flames licking open sores on my leg.

The next thing I know, an ugly, pock-marked face looms over me and someone is shaking me. 'Wakey, wakey, mate! So you've decided to come back into the land of the living. Welcome back, comrade, we thought we'd lost you. How about I make you a nice cuppa? Always what an Englishman wants - only it will have to be a brew of acorns.' He laughs, revealing gaps in his front teeth. 'Tonino's the name -Tony to you, me old mucker.'
'Norman Swilland. Can't say how pleased I am to meet you.'
And we shake hands.
'You look as if you could do with a wash and shave, Norman,' he stands up, 'I'll go and rustle up room service.'
And he disappears.
I feel as if I am surrounded by Alice in Wonderland characters. In my fevered state, I half expect the Mad Hatter to turn up but instead the girl appears again from the shadows. She kneels down beside me and smiles, wiping

my forehead with a cloth impregnated with sweet-smelling ointment.

I have obviously done something to deserve this up-turn in fortunes. Or have I died and gone to Heaven? I turn my head cautiously. No more thumping pain but when I try to get up, I have no strength.

'No signore, stay there,' the girl says, 'you must get strong first.'

I am inside a kind of wig-wam constructed from coppiced branches. In the top of the roof there is an opening and in the centre of the wooded 'tent' a small fire has been lit and the smoke spirals out of the hole. I am stretched on a mattress made from sacking and stuffed with what seem like the dried, outer leaves of corn husks. As I move, it rustles and crackles but is surprisingly comfortable.

Tony returns with a receptacle made from an old food can containing a warm, sweet drink. Tea it definitely is not but it is very welcome all the same. And he has a bowl of warm water, a razor and some soap for a wet shave.

'Where did you learn your perfect English?' I ask him.

He hunkers down next to my make-shift bed. 'My people came over to London before I was born. Reckoned they could make a better life for the family. And they've not done too badly, I have to say. My Dad has a barber's shop in Soho. Quite a little Italian community there is round there. They never needed to learn English but I'm more English than Italian now, went to school in London, got an English girl back there an' all.'

'Why are you here then?'

'Got rounded up in London at the beginning of the war and shipped back to Italy. They didn't want us in England and they bloody didn't want us back here either. Thought we were spies, banged us up but I escaped. Campo P.G. 82 it was. They got us working in a brick factory near Arezzo. Made a run for it one day...been here ever since.. Always wanted to get in touch with my roots - never thought it would be like this though. What about you?'

'I've ended up in a few places too,' I told him, 'Fontanellato was the last camp. When they opened the doors, most set off north for

Switzerland but I'm heading south - though I've been holed up in so many barns in so many places I think I'm going to write a bloody guide-book about Italy if I ever get back.'

'I'd say you're going nowhere fast with that leg, mate. You won't make it on your own either. The hills are crawling with Jerry and you'd stick out like a sore thumb. You're best letting this lot take care of you for the time being. They're a good band - not like some of the trigger-happy robbers passing for partisans... this leader knows what he's doing. Been responsible for quite a bit of sabotage round here.'

I feel woozy again. Tony can see I'm done in and gets up off his haunches. He speaks to the girl and then to me. 'Get all the rest you can, Norman. I'll see if I can rustle up some more food for you. Take it easy for the time being. I'm sure you'll be needed in some way or other as soon as you're strong again.'

For a few days I take him at his word. Tony tells me the girl is called Ines. I don't see her for a while. A pity! In the daylight hours, Tony ties open the flap to my 'wigwam' and I watch proceedings from my makeshift mattress. As far as I can make out, there are roughly twenty or so men of all ages milling around the camp, which is really just a clearing in the woods. We are in a hollow with natural battlements formed from boulders fallen from the peaks above. It seems to me, from the snatches of conversations I hear, that the men and boys here are not all Italians, although I've been told there are many different dialects throughout Italy.

Tony puts me right.

'In this band there are the usual anti-Fascist Italians. They stick together. One of them, Alfonso, he's an excellent cook. I keep in with him! He makes miracle stews. God knows what he throws in. He told me he'd caught a porcupine the other day and in it went into the pot - I don't ask too many questions! Then there are a couple of Russians and Slovenians who escaped from the concentration camp down in the valley at Anghiari. You have to watch them if they get hold of the 'grappa'. Fiery lot they are - even more so after the alcohol. And then there are the deserters from the Alpini regiment. Great men! Have all the time in the world for them, would trust them with my mother's life.'

The girl called Ines appears again three days later. Once more she's dressed in a heavy, tattered overcoat, her face smeared with dirt. If you didn't know she was female, you would take her for a young lad. That is, until she draws closer. As she changes the dressing on my wound I can see her fine features and, beneath the patches of dirt, her delicious nose. Her hands are gentle and she smells like a woman too. I wink at her. She blushes.

'Your name is Ines,' I say in halting Italian. She smiles and answers shyly, her eyes cast down. 'Your name is Norman.'

I like the way she pronounces my name.

I look forward to her visits and discover she is eighteen and her brother, Davide, is one of the young Italians in the camp up here in the woods.

'Where do you sleep?' I ask her one day.

She giggles. 'Not here, for sure. It wouldn't be allowed. I stay down at our Mulino[1] with my parents. I have to help them with a lot more work now that Davide is busy with the partigiani. Can't you remember *anything* about your stay with us or how I brought you up the mountain?'

In fact I can't. I must have been in a worse state than I thought.

'I'm sorry,' I say, 'is the mill far away?'

She points down to the valley. 'Five kilometres if you come up the road but I always keep to the animal tracks. It's too dangerous to use the road with the German soldiers and the Fascisti. Following the animal tracks, though, it's easy to pick up ticks.' She grimaces. I don't understand the word 'zecca' and she mimes a wriggling insect with her fingers and then a pulling action from the skin on the inside of her wrist.

---

[1] Mill

Eventually I cotton on and laugh at her acting skills.

'Do you come all by yourself? Aren't you scared?'

'Why do you think I dress like this?' She tugs at the patched coat and the cap pulled down over her hair.

I want to pull it off her and see her curls tumble down her back, but of course I don't. It's too soon. I know enough to understand the rules. A young, single girl like her is normally chaperoned. It's only due to the war she's been allowed to come up the mountain to tend to me. She is very brave.

'You must get up and move more, Norman. Your *muscoli*, they will not be strong again otherwise.'

When she says my name, she rolls the "r". My ordinary English name has never sounded so exotic.

Each time we meet she encourages me to exercise my weakened leg muscles and we walk a little further along the track when she comes up to the camp. It's an old mule track and in the winter months, she tells me, it will be impassable when the rains turn it into a stream.

  My Italian vocabulary is expanding all the time. In exchange, I teach her some words in English. I have to admit I select a few words beginning with "th"...I love to see her dissolve into giggles as she tries to get her tongue against her top teeth.

'It is too difficult, your language,' she says, 'why are there so many words with these stupid sounds? Italian is more...like music.'

We don't stray too far from the camp on our walks. I would love to be alone with her but if we left the shelter of the canopy of pine-trees, any sniper on any one of the ridges in the surrounding hills could pick us off. And she is shy, a good girl, innocent. A completely different kettle of fish from Phyllis and anyway, there is always somebody about – Tony or Davide or one of the Slovenians. We have plenty of watchers, so it's pointless to try anything on. There will be no hanky-panky - not yet, unfortunately.

My ulcerated leg takes nearly a month to improve. It still aches a little when I'm tired but I no longer need a stick to help myself around. Ines hasn't put in an appearance for several days and I almost wish my wound hadn't healed so quickly so she could return to the mountain camp to dress it.

Tony and I sit by the fire one evening. He has drunk quite a lot more of the red wine than usual. He stares into the flames, smoking a Malboro.

'A penny for them,' I say.

'You wouldn't want to know.'

He takes another swig from the bottle and then offers it to me. I wipe the top with a corner of my shirt and gulp some down. God it's bad. But it warms the belly. I like Tony. He is good company. He makes me laugh and God knows the laughs have been few and far between lately. But there is a serious side to him too.

'When I escaped from the camp at Arezzo,' he begins, 'I couldn't believe my luck.' He kicks a log further into the embers and sparks fly up into the night sky.

'Originally my people are from these parts, you see - from a village near Casteldelci, about seventeen kilometres away, so the idea of looking up my relatives came to me. Easter is a big feast here and on Good Friday I decided to go and find my Pa's sister. I'd get a decent meal from her, she'd look after me. Family is everything for Italians. Anyway, it took me over a week to make my way through the hills; I had to skirt around fucking Ted's machine-gun posts and sleep in barns and ditches. The weather wasn't too bad. Spring was in the air. It was wonderful to be free, to listen to owls, the rustlings at night in the open after months of being locked up in a dormitory full of men, with bars at the window. You know what I'm talking about.'

I do. I don't interrupt. I feel his need to talk.

'As I drew nearer the village of Fragheto I started to recognise landmarks. My parents had talked about the place often enough so I recognised the narrow wooded valley, the stream tumbling at the bottom. The track snaked up the hill and the view of the mountains stretching down to the plains of Rimini was magnificent. I forgot about the war for a while. What a view! It was like gazing on a painting. I passed through the hamlet of Ville Fragheto and guessed I had another half hour's walk in front of me, so I rested for a bit. Suddenly there were gun-shots and I dived for cover in a ditch. The shooting went on and on. When I was sure it was over I crawled from my hiding-place and continued up the hill. As far as possible I kept to the fields - I was wary of using the road. But at a certain point it became impossible not to and then I heard footsteps. Nearby was a thicket of trees and I hid in there.

A family was hurrying down the road away from the village. One of them, a lad in his late teens, was carrying an old woman on his back. Another woman had a toddler by the hand. The kid was sobbing and the woman was dragging him along behind her. As she hurried past me I could see the little boy's knees scraping on the road. The woman didn't stop to soothe him, she just continued in her hurry. They were just ordinary country people, they weren't going to hurt me, so I came out from my hiding place in the trees and I asked if I could help. But they were terrified and hurried past. A bit further up the hill I came across a shrine by the side of the road. An old man was sitting underneath, wrapped in a blanket, his eyes closed, muttering to himself. I crouched down near him. He opened his eyes and started babbling even louder, 'Shoot *me* instead, shoot me,' he gabbled half crazed 'don't touch the babies.'

I didn't know what the Hell had happened in this place but I soon found out.

I approached the hamlet with caution. Something was burning, thick smoke filled the air. A dog scampered out of a building and scared the shit out of me. I went down an alleyway leading to the little main piazza and then I came across a scene I never, ever want to witness again.' Tony pauses and rubs his eyes with the back of his hand. 'Heaped up against the side of the church was a pile of bodies. Blood ran down over the cobbles. It was sticky under my feet. The smell of burning was awful, I gagged and tied my handkerchief round my mouth and went nearer. A child of about two or three, I don't know how old exactly, lay there with his back on the ground. He looked asleep but the top of his head had been blown off. His mother lay near him and under her, a baby still clasped in her arms.' He breaks off.

I don't know what to say and when he is ready, he continues his grim story.

'I found out much later that my aunt and her two babies were amongst the dead. Maybe she was the woman I saw in the pile of mangled bodies, I'll never know. I was too young when we left Italy to remember what she looked like. The bastard Germans and Fascisti shot *thirty-three* civilians. There had been a skirmish with the partigiani the day before, further down in the valley. A couple of Teds were shot and they found *one* wounded partisan in the village so they decided to make a reprisal, didn't they, the fucking bastards. Most of the dead were women and children. There was even an old man of seventy-four. What had they ever done to anybody? They weren't armed. They were just simple peasants, going about their business, working on the land.'

The fire crackled and sent sparks like ammunition into the black night.

'You asked me what I am doing here. Well that's my real fucking reason for coming back here. Revenge! I want to do as much as I can, with my last dying breath if necessary, to avenge the death of my family. Talking is not enough.'

He spits into the fire.

I still don't know what to say, so I don't say anything. I offer him the bottle and in my head I promise to help in whatever way I can. It's the least I can bloody do to repay the kindness and courage shown by these people sheltering me.

Chapter 4
Ines explains her side of the story.

Flicking through the pages, Anna finds another couple of pages in her father's hand-writing but several pages have been stapled in between. The paper is faded and the handwriting smudged in places making it difficult to read. Her mother has pencilled a note at the top:

Anna, I too kept a diary for a short while during the war. It was something I shouldn't have done because if it had been discovered by the wrong people, there would have been reprisals. I've kept these few pages ever since but not looked at them for years. Reading them again, I can hardly believe I was the young author. I hope you will be able to understand it because some of the Italian is old fashioned now. You have to remember that it all happened half a century ago. How times have changed!

Skimming through the first lines, Anna knows she will struggle. Mamma had taught her a smattering of simple words in Italian but all three children were brought up with English as their main language. She makes a start but is soon certain she will need to buy a good dictionary.

Rofelle, September 8th 1944

He's still in the stable. Mamma made up an extra plate of pasta with zucchini we'd bottled last spring and when it was dark, she told me to put on my scarf and take some chicken feed with me, in case anybody should be watching and ask what I was doing out at that time of night. I know she's terrified somebody will find out we're hiding an 'inglese' but Capriolo said we must, for he will die otherwise. But we are all terrified. Last week we heard they shot the Benuccis because they wouldn't vacate their house. The Germans only gave them a day's notice. Poor old souls, they refused to go; they had nowhere to go to anyway and the old signora was riddled with rheumatism and couldn't walk far. They are cruel these Germans. We're scared but Capriolo says they won't break our spirits. We use this name for him because we have been told again and again by the *resistenza* not to call him by his real name. His family would be executed if they discovered his identity. He's named himself after the mountain deer, nimble and fast as they scamper on the mountains. 'Capriolo' comes automatically to my tongue now, but he would skin me if he knew I was writing this. If I don't tell someone I shall burst – so I'm telling my diary which I hide behind the loose stone in the niche in my room. Nobody will ever find it. And if they do, they will think it's just my old school-book.

It takes Anna over an hour to translate one paragraph. And she is not sure if she's really grasped the full meaning. There are still plenty of pages left to tackle. Flicking through, she finds her mother's handwriting in English on some pages written post-war but she wants to read everything in the correct order. If she is going to find out more about her parents, it will be important not to tangle up events. Eventually she comes to the conclusion that the Italian will have to be translated by somebody more proficient than herself.

She wonders if her brother and sister might know more about her parents' time in the war - they are a lot older and are bound to remember something. She dials Jane's number, letting it ring to give time for her sister to come to the phone in her vast house.

'Anna, how are you? This *is* a surprise. To what do I owe this honour? Twice in the same month - what with the funeral and that ghastly solicitor's meeting. So depressing!'

She ignores her sister's typical sarcasm. She can hear the clattering of dishes as she moves about in her kitchen, picturing her emptying her dishwasher with pink 'Marigold' encased hands, phone lodged under her chin, shoulders hunched up to support it. She is irritated Jane cannot be bothered to concentrate properly on their conversation but there is no point in starting an argument, she will never win. Instead, she explains about the papers. 'I've started dipping into

Mamma's diaries. The first part is in Italian and it's beyond me I'm afraid but…'

Jane interrupts. 'But I thought she was *always* rattling on at you in Italian – you should be almost fluent, I would have thought. It was quite rude once you two got going - I used to feel quite left out.'

'I can only speak a few phrases of basic Italian so her diaries are beyond me. I'm going to have them translated.'

'Can you be bothered? They're probably just mad ramblings. You know what Mamma was like at the end. Whenever I went to visit her in that ghastly, smelly old people's home, I could never get any sense at all out of her and Harry told me it was a *complete* waste of time his going. She never recognised him and it used to take him a whole day with that awful traffic on the M25. He was always fed up about the faff of it all and it makes my blood boil the more I think about it. So unfair! That he should inherit Willow's End and you and I just get a pile of old papers and tatty, worthless jewellery…'

Anna holds the phone away from her ear as her sister's sentences grow longer and louder and decides not to retaliate. Jane hardly ever visited Mamma in the home, but there is no point in arguing.

'Anna! Are you still there?'

'Yes, Jane. I was only calling to find out if they ever talked to you about the war? I've been reading Dad's accounts too about his time as a POW – they're amazing, like a Boy's Own Adventure… And if I've translated correctly, I think Mamma may have been involved with the partisans.'

Jane's laugh is more a snort of derision. Anna realises the conversation is not going anywhere and wonders if she might get more sense out of her older brother, Harry. But he is always hard to track down, always busy with some property investment deal or other, often abroad. From the way his girth is spreading, she reckons he probably dines out frequently on company expenses. In the background Jane's door-bell rings and her sister brings their frustrating conversation to an end. 'I've got to go. Look - come for dinner this Saturday - stay the night. Harry and Cynthia are coming too. You can talk to your darling brother about Italy and I won't have to talk so much to ghastly Cynthia… Got to dash, people have just arrived for bridge.' She thumps down the phone and Anna listens to the empty whir at the other end for a while, before clicking shut her mobile.

Later that afternoon she is sitting in front of a mirror at the salon explaining to André that she is sick of her hair. 'Just do something with it please. Anything!' He runs his fingers through her dark brown tangles and she watches him pulling faces in the mirror, doing nothing for her morale. 'I've been trying to get you to chop this off for yonks, Anna. It's pulling your features down, hiding those gorgeous sparkling eyes.

You need to accentuate those cheekbones too. How about I put a few lowlights in? A hint of copper and auburn, shape it here at the back. You'll love it.'

'Go for it!' she says.

He starts up his usual patter. 'Got anything planned for the weekend? Got your hols booked yet?'

Instead of hiding her nose in a magazine stuffed with articles about the latest celebrity wedding in the latest 'in' castle with the latest footballer and his latest trophy woman, she talks to him. 'My mother died a few weeks ago and I've now lost my job.'

'Oh, sweetie! No wonder your hair's looking so dull and lifeless.' He looks at her with genuine concern. 'When my darling Mum died, I didn't know what to do with myself. If it hadn't been for Marcus, I would have thrown myself off a cliff, I kid you not.'

As she tells him about the diaries, he stops snipping and shaping and with hands on hips, gazes at her in the mirror. 'Wow. That's absolutely *brill*, darling. How *exciting*!' He stands back surveying his handiwork, frowning slightly at some straggly hairs at the back of her neck, then starts crimping again. 'And are you going to go out to Italy to see where all this happened? How fascinating – a mother in the partisan movement – it's just like one of those old movies on telly they dig out for winter afternoons. Love it!'

'To be honest, I hadn't thought about going to Italy.'

'But why on earth not? What are you waiting for? You've got no job. You're not married, are you? No kids, no ties…go for it, woman. You'd be mad not to. You wouldn't see me for dust if it happened to me, I'd be *aching* to find out more about it all. Ooh, lucky you! All those handsome men and scrummy clothes. Gucci, Versace…And the food…just to *die* for.'

All the while, he continues to shape and snip away faster than ever, her dark brown hair falling onto the salon floor and she hopes he is concentrating.

'You could go there for a kind of…what do they call them…sabbatical or something? Nice little pad in the Tuscan countryside. All that wine and those gorgeous colours…burnt umber, Tuscan terracotta…'

He holds up the mirror to reveal her new look, angles the mirror so she can see from all sides. 'There we are, Madam! What do we think?'

He was right. The haircut has taken years off her and she looks more twenty than thirty three. Before, her hair had hung below her shoulders and she stuck it up in a chignon for work. Now it is shaped in a bob, shorter at the back. She loves it and nearly kisses him.

But not just because of the new hair style. He has also planted the germ of an idea in her head. There really is no reason why she can't go and spend time in Italy. She rents the flat where she lives at the moment, so she only has to hand in her notice and ask Jane very nicely if she will store her few possessions in one of her spare rooms. She has £50,000 from Mamma's inheritance and can live off that for a while until she finds a job. But first she has to speak to Will. She has promised to meet him later on today.

When Anna started work at "Move It", it was only going to be temporary. Then she would sort out her career once and for all, maybe apply again for the PGCE she'd started years ago and abandoned. Since then she had flitted from job to job in an effort to find what she really wanted. But then she met Will, and before she knew it one month at "Move It" had extended to two years because the job made it easy to stay in London to be near him.

They'd met within three weeks of her starting. He'd walked into the Estate Agent's and although she thought she might have seen him somewhere before – there was something familiar about his craggy looks, pepper and salt hair, mesmerising blue, blue eyes - she couldn't quite place him. She never watched Channel Four News, otherwise it would have clicked. That was one of the first things that had appealed to him, he'd told her later, the fact she hadn't realised he was famous; it was refreshing to be liked for *who* he was and not *what* he was. She'd shown him round a top floor flat in an Edwardian villa on the edge of Clapham Common and she'd liked him straightaway, their age difference somehow making him even more appealing. 'Let's talk this sale through at dinner tonight,' he'd said. But they hadn't talked about the house. Instead he'd told her about his tired marriage, how their three children had flown the nest and he and his wife were now trying to get to know each other again; how they might use the London flat so she could come up to town, see a show together, visit an exhibition. They were preparing for retirement, he'd said, for the next stage, and he was nervous about growing old. In turn, she'd found herself telling him about her near escape in her early twenties, how she almost made it to the altar, the church and reception organised, only a few details of flowers and seating arrangements to be finalised. Her fiancé had let her know, in a letter stuffed under her door, how he had changed his mind, how he wasn't ready for marriage, might never be ready. She'd had boyfriends since then, of course, but as soon as any relationship threatened to turn serious, she would end it. 'Once bitten, twice shy,' she would explain, 'I don't do promises'. Months would pass by without a man on the scene and she was happy enough with her own space.

Anna had known Will was married from the outset. He had never pretended otherwise and it was an uncomplicated partnership. Every now and again she would experience a niggle that it wasn't an ideal situation, but she was good at pushing any concerns she might have to the back of her mind. One day she'd seen a photo of him and his wife Tricia in a magazine. They were guests at a charity function at Claridge's. She'd been surprised at how elegant his beautiful, silver haired wife was. He'd dropped into conversation more than once that she was letting herself go, had taken to gardening and slopping round their house in the country in her baggy tracksuits but Anna couldn't match his description with the sophisticated, well groomed woman in the photo.

Will has booked their usual table at "Chez Nous", tucked discreetly away in an alcove. She is slightly early and orders a glass of chilled Pouilly Fumé. The owner, Jean-Luc, is very complimentary of her new hair style. He jokes and flirts with her, despite his partner cooking in the kitchen. He brings her a red rose from a vase on a vacant table, bends low over her hand, bestowing a kiss on it, saying 'Mademoiselle, pour vous.' She sits waiting, nibbling on a roll, wondering how late Will be tonight. The restaurant is quite full for a Tuesday. She wonders, had she ever kept a record, how many times his keeping her waiting would have amounted to.

'Sorry, Sooty.' He stoops to plant a kiss on her lips. 'Had a report to finish. Big news story about to break about Blair.'

She also wonders how many different excuses she could add to his 'lateness record' she'd been mentally compiling. It has never mattered to her before but tonight she finds it irritating.

'You look different,' he says as he takes off his coat, arranging himself opposite her. 'It's your hair. Yum, yum! It's much shorter isn't it?'

She pats the back of her head. 'I like it,' she says, 'it's sort of ...liberating. I felt in need of a change.'

'Oh dear, that sounds rather ominous.' He laughs and picks up the menu. 'Have you ordered yet?'

She says pointedly. 'No! I was waiting for you.'

He sweeps a cursory glance over the menu and then calls Jean-Luc over.

'What's the special today?'

'We have some very nice veal. Or the mussels are very good...and boeuf bourgignon.'

'Veal, we'll have the veal.' Will snaps shut the menu. 'And bring us the usual bottle of Chateau Neuf.'

Normally she is happy for Will to take control and place the order but tonight she turns to Jean-Luc, 'No veal for me. Just poussin and a salad,' she says.

If Will is surprised, he doesn't comment.

They sit in silence, sipping the excellent wine, dipping into the bowl of black olives Jean-Luc has brought while they wait for their meal. A sudden roar of laughter from the busy table in the main part of the restaurant causes Will to turn round and investigate.

'Oh, Jesus!' He puts down his glass, 'I don't believe it. There's a whole bunch from the newsroom over there. Not good. Anna, I'll see you back at yours, we can't be seen together by that lot. I'll just slip away now.'

He throws his credit card on the table, scoops up his jacket from the back of the chair and leaves.

She explains to Jean-Luc that Will is feeling unwell. He looks at her, shrugging his shoulders. She leaves him a generous tip on Will's card.

Will has let himself into her flat. He's sitting in the small living-room, his long legs taking up most of the space. When she closes the door behind her he looks up, smiles his lazy smile, offering no apology.

'Shall I order us a take-away?' he asks, 'I'm starving. Been working all day on a report about the new cabinet reshuffle. Blair's bringing in a load of women, kicking out the old guard. There'll be a right rumpus.'

She kicks off her shoes and sits opposite him in a rocking chair she rescued from her mother's room at Claremont. He pats the settee but she doesn't move.

'You go ahead and order for yourself,' she tells him, 'but I'm not that hungry.'

'What's up? Are you cross with me?'

'I told you, I'm just a bit out of sorts at the moment. I've got lots on my mind.'

'Is it the time of the month or something? Tricia always used to get very niggly when she was on.'

His casual comparison of her with his wife's personal details annoys her tonight and she snaps.

'I am **not** pre-menstrual… and I wish you wouldn't bring Tricia into it.'

He flinches, frowns, puzzled at her reaction.

'It's losing your mother, isn't it? You should give yourself time to grieve. Poor Sooty!'

Anna wonders how it can be possible for the same person to be so sensitive and yet so thoughtless, but she knows his concern for her is genuine. She makes an effort to be more civil.

'Mamma left me some diaries. They arrived the other day and I started reading them and my mind's on all that, I suppose.'

'I could have a look at them if you like, cast my journalist's eye over them? You might be able to publish them, you never know.'

'Thank you but no. It's not publishable stuff – it's just that the papers all need sorting and they don't seem to be in any particular order. There's even an old bit of cloth she's written something on. And it's mostly written in Italian...'

'Are you sure it's not just your Mum when she went a bit potty? I mean, she was banged up in that old home for a while, wasn't she? Old people do these daft things. I'll be like that soon.' He laughs and she wonders if she is supposed to contradict him.

'Anyway come here, you ravishing young thing with your new sexy hairstyle. I feel I've got to get to know you all over again from top to toe.'

He gets up, pulling her close to him, nuzzling her neck with soft kisses and moving his hand to the buttons on her blouse but she pushes him away.

'Anna?'

'I'm sorry. I'm not in the mood.'

She sits down and he joins her but doesn't try to touch her.

'Will - I'm thinking of going to Italy for a while.'

'What a good idea. You need a break. Perhaps I could pop out for a couple of days and join you. I could do with a spot of sunshine myself.'

'I don't mean for a holiday. I'm thinking of going for longer. To see where my mother came from. I've never been. And...' she pauses, not knowing what to say to him.

Before she has to explain, he takes her hand, finishing her sentence for her.

'You need some time on your own?'

She looks at him, wishing he wasn't being so understanding. It would be far easier if they were shouting at each other.

'I suppose I've been expecting this for some time really,' he continues, stroking her fingers. 'I've often wondered what a beautiful girl like you sees in an old codger like me. An old married codger, to boot.'

She doesn't comment on this last remark and he lets go of her hand, moves over to the drinks cupboard and pours himself a glass of Glenfiddich from the bottle she keeps for him. 'When were you thinking of going? Not too soon, I hope?'

'Quite soon. There's only a month left on the contract for this place and I've got no job at the moment.'

'Bit of a shock, I have to say.' He slumps down again, slopping a little of the whiskey onto a cushion. She watches the stain spread but doesn't bother to rush to the kitchen for a cloth.

'We can keep in touch, Will, but I need to do this.'

'Well, a girl's gotta do what a girl's gotta do, as they say, but I don't want you to disappear completely out of my life.'

The silence between them is awkward now and, knocking back the rest of his whiskey, he unwinds himself from the saggy sofa. She follows him to the door and he stops to wrap her in an avuncular hug. They stay like that for a few moments and then he drops a kiss onto the top of her head. 'Keep in touch, dear girl,' he says as he leaves.

She remains seated for a long time after the door shuts behind him, thinking that explaining to Will was far easier than it probably should have been.

Chapter 5
England, 1999. Jane's house.

Jane lives alone in a five-bedroom mock Tudor house in a part of Surrey that estate agent's parlance would describe as 'Purley, a most desirable location'. When her husband, Charlie, left Jane nearly ten years previously for another man, Anna hadn't been surprised. She'd often wondered about their marriage, what gentle Charlie had seen in her domineering sister. Jane had returned alone from their family holiday in Madeira, announcing that Charlie was 'researching a new enterprise abroad'. Charlie, however, had no qualms about being open and coming out. He sent all his relatives a cheerful 'round robin' at Christmas, explaining how he had met the love of his life and had decided to stay on in Madeira to help Santos run a fabulous boutique hotel in Funchal. He was ecstatically happy,(if they would pardon the phrase). As their sons, Stephen and Julian, were almost through university and practically independent, he felt it time to start living his own life now and separate from Jane. Everybody was very welcome to come and visit whenever they wanted. Anna had taken up his offer and had one of the best holidays of her life, but Jane and Harry had erased him from their radars.

She hires a taxi to take her from the station to Jane's house. Two stone lions guard the porch, together with a matching pair of clipped laurel obelisks and not a weed dares to lift its head in any flowerbed. The family house is large for one person but Jane is reluctant to move. Her bridge-playing friends live nearby and there is a parade of rather exclusive shops that she can walk to. She can easily afford help in the house and garden on the generous allowance that Charlie has provided.

'Come in, come in, you're letting in the cold. We're having drinks in the sitting-room,' her sister pulls her in to the hall, whispering, 'Thank God you're here! It's so difficult to make conversation with that woman. And Harry's obviously had a dram or two before arriving.'

Harry and his third wife, Cynthia, sit at opposite ends of the chintzy sitting-room. She has her legs crossed and is turning the pages of a glossy house and country magazine she's found on the coffee table. She is a good twenty five years younger than Harry's fifty two but her make-up is so heavy it disguises her age. Anna wonders if there is anything real about her at all. Even her breasts seem disproportionately large for her small frame. She glances at Anna entering the room, barely raising her manicured hand in acknowledgment. Harry heaves himself up from an uncomfortable armchair covered in Colefax and Fowler, his glass splashing gin and tonic onto the pale carpet. He seems relieved to see Anna. There is a frosty atmosphere and Anna wonders what their argument is about this time.

'Let me take that from you, Harry.' Jane swoops on him, taking his glass, depositing it on a mat on a side-table beyond his reach.

Jane has inherited their father's lanky, Anglo-Saxon looks, although her waistline is not as slim as it used to be, but Harry and Anna are more like Mamma. Harry could have been very good-looking with his dark, Latin features but he has put on weight in the last few years and is a little too fond of his wines.

'Come here, little sister. Give your old brother a hug.'
He isn't much taller than Anna. As he crushes her to his beer belly, the smell of wine on his breath is overpowering. 'We've just been talking about Willow's End, having a little discussion…'
He indicates Cynthia and pronounces his words slowly and carefully in the way someone who has been drinking too much tries hard not to show he has downed one too many. 'She doesn't like the place, doesn't like it at all…what's to do? I see battles looming.'

Cynthia uncrosses her legs, pulls her tiny skirt down as far as she can and crosses her legs again. 'It's pokey and draughty,' she says, 'more of a liability than an asset. It needs so much work doing to it, a total revamp, in my opinion. I think Harry should just knock it down and start again but he's got some hare-brained idea about living in it!'

Anna could never see Cynthia living in the draughty, rambling Thirties house and she is surprised that Harry wants to. She has already imagined him bulldozing the place and squeezing in half a dozen executive-style houses onto the back lawn.

'Well I'm getting tired of the flat up in town. All that glass and open-plan living. A man's got no privacy at all, it's like being in a ruddy great goldfish bowl.' He looks around for his drink and makes his way to the nest of tables. 'I just thought it would be nice to do the old ancestral home up and try living in a proper house again… with rooms how they should be. A snug and a breakfast room - even a nursery, maybe.' He beams at Cynthia, swaying a little. 'How about it, Cyn? Pattering of tiny feet appeal to you?'

'Dream on, Harry!' Cynthia throws the magazine onto the coffee table, 'I need the loo', she announces and leaves the room, making it clear that any discussion about children is over. Harry watches her totter out in her high heels, attempts to lighten the atmosphere with a joke. 'Mind you, the only pattering of tiny feet at Willows at the moment, are the mice, ha ha! More's the pity!'

Anna feels momentarily sorry for her brother. She knows he misses his daughters. His second wife, Melissa, has custody of their twin girls but they are away at boarding school and he rarely sees them. In their school holidays they are always booked in for tennis lessons or adventure holidays to keep them from under Melissa's feet.

Jane returns to the lounge with a platter of meat just in time to prevent Anna from having to comment. She does not feel qualified to offer advice on Harry's marriage, thinking wryly that none of them have been particularly successful in that department.

'Where's Cynthia gone?' Jane looks at the armchair where Cynthia had been sitting. 'Lunch is ready. It's nothing much but it will go cold if we don't eat now.'

Anna knows about Jane's "nothing much meals". She is a Cordon Bleu cook and likes to show off her efforts. They are treated to a home-made terrine of paté, followed by stuffed loin of pork and roasted vegetables. Cynthia picks at her food, pushing a slice of aubergine round her plate and Anna wonders what new diet she is on. The meal helps Harry sober up and while Jane is in the kitchen, Anna picks his brains.

'Do you know anything about where Mamma came from in Italy? I've started reading those papers she left me and I realise I know absolutely nothing about her background – or Dad's for that matter.'

'Rofelle, you mean?' he asks, leaning back in his chair, wiping his mouth clean with a damask serviette. 'Haven't been back since before you were born. I must have been a teenager – let's think, over thirty years ago. God! Where does the time go?'

Cynthia sighs, raises her eyebrows and excuses herself from the table. 'I'm going outside for a smoke. Tell Jane not to serve me any pud.'

Anna watches her open the French window and sit on a wrought iron bench on the patio. She rummages in her Mulberry handbag and produces a mobile phone, nails flashing Smartie red as she begins to text, cigarette smoke spiralling into the winter sunshine. Harry stares wistfully through the dining room window. 'She's always on some diet or other. She'll waste away one of these days.' He reaches for the bottle of wine, pours himself another glass, offering some to Anna who covers her glass with her hand, 'None for me thanks, Harry. Tell me about Rofelle.'

'Absolute dump of a place. Primitive! I don't think Dad liked it very much either – I remember some God-awful rows about spending time there. I think that was the last time we ever went there on holiday actually. It was about the time he had his breakdown.'

'I never knew about that,' Anna looks up.

'Oh yes, it was a *ghastly* time. He spent time in hospital but Mamma never wanted anybody to know. That was the way they were, their generation. They didn't talk about things, open up like nowadays. Mind you, it's gone too far the other way today – everybody talking about piles and hysterectomies in the media. Too much information, I say.'

Jane places a crystal bowl containing tiramisù on a serving mat, glances through the window, tutting as she sees Cynthia. 'What *is* she doing out there? She'll catch her death in that skimpy outfit.' She knocks on the window, beckoning Cynthia to come in, who holds up her hand indicating she will be five minutes longer. As she serves dessert, Jane asks, 'Did I hear you talking about Rofelle? Do you remember, Harry, there was only *one* single bed in that hole of a room we had to share?'

'Yes - and *you* made me sleep on the floor. How could I forget?'

'Quite disgusting that they expected us to share. I mean you must have been nineteen because I was definitely sixteen. I know that for certain because I distinctly remember feeling quite left out when I went back to school that September. All the girls were going on and on about the fab times they'd had in their summer hols and all I could think was 'sweet sixteen and never been kissed'. There was nobody in Rofelle I would have let come near me with a barge pole. I was so glad we didn't go back again.'

Anna listens to her brother and sister talking about a time when they were young, before she was born, as if listening to the history of another family, one she doesn't belong to.

'But don't you find it at all strange they didn't go back? Didn't Mamma ever return on her own?' she asks.

Jane starts clearing away the dishes. 'Not that I'm aware of. I don't even know if there is any family left out there. To be quite honest I'm not that bothered. It was dreadfully boring for us teenagers, not the sort of place I would ever have chosen for a holiday for children of that age.'

Harry reaches for the bottle of wine again.

'There's water on the table too,' admonishes Jane. He ignores her and pours a full glass of Merlot, emptying the bottle.

'To go with the cheese, old thing. That is, if the cheese-board is ever going to put in an appearance.' He winks at Anna while Jane moves Stilton and mature Cheddar from the sideboard, placing it just within reach of her brother.

'No wonder you've got gout. I don't know how Cynthia puts up with you, really I don't.'
Anna thinks that maybe Cynthia might not be putting up with him for much longer. She is still outside, texting. She decides to tell her brother and sister about her plans. 'I've decided to go out to Italy for a couple of months or so, as soon as I've packed up the flat. I was going to ask you, Jane, if you could hang on to my stuff for a while. I want to spend some time looking up the location in Mamma's diaries.'
Both Jane and Harry look at their younger sister as if she is mad. Harry is the first to speak. 'What on earth will you do out there? How will you manage?'

'I haven't totally finalised that part yet but I've got some redundancy pay from the agency… and then there's the £50,000 Mamma left us each.'

'That won't last forever. I would have thought you'd have been better off putting a deposit down on some property instead of swanning off to Italy. I could help you if you like.' Harry helps himself to a generous chunk of ripe Stilton.

'No thanks. I've made up my mind to go.'

'Come on, Anna! What's the real reason? Things not working out between you and lover boy?'

Anna thinks Harry is the last person to be commenting on the state of relationships. She bites back a sarcastic comment but she's still indignant. 'It's got nothing at all to do with Will...or *you* for that matter.'

Jane intervenes, 'If I were you, I wouldn't set too much store by those diaries. I mean Mamma wasn't exactly all there at the end. I think it will be a complete waste of your time.'

'Quite apart from the diaries, I mean, even if they had never existed,' Anna tries to explain, 'aren't you at all curious about their past in Italy? When all's said and done, we're half Italian after all.'

'No!' Harry's reply is immediate, 'Absolutely not. I feel British through and through. We've been brought up here, schooled here, spoken English in the home.'

Now it is Jane's turn to try to persuade her sister against her Italian project. 'I really can't see the point. All I remember is the almighty rows when Father was alive whenever the subject of Italy was brought up. Maybe it's slightly different for you - at least Mother taught you some Italian, but we couldn't speak any and all the relatives used to natter away, nineteen to the dozen. We couldn't understand a damn word. There was nothing to do in Rofelle except eat vast quantities of fattening pasta and cool down in the river full of tadpoles, snakes and God knows what else.' She pulls a face at the memory. 'Rather you than me. I don't feel Italian at all. I'm not interested.'

It is fruitless trying to explain her need to go to Italy and she realises there is not much more she can find out about Rofelle from her brother and sister. She will have to find out for herself.

Chapter 6
April 1999 – Anna arrives in Italy

The plane touches down in early morning sunshine at Perugia. The tiny airport is surrounded by fields with a forlorn scattering of last year's drooping sunflowers. On the tarmac by the modest arrivals hangar, two men in bright orange overalls wave their hands about as they discuss something which might be vitally important but could equally be a discussion of what they had for dinner last night. They break off to watch a pretty Italian girl who descends the steps of the plane in front of Anna. As they look her up and down, Anna imagines she wiggles her bottom just a little more as she struts over the tarmac in her skin-tight jeans and leather jacket. It is as though Anna has been thrown onto a stage-set with mountains in the distance forming a scenic backdrop. The contrast between busy Stansted airport and this sleepy place is stark. She left England wearing an overcoat but the sun here is warmer and she takes it off and carries it over her arm.

She has booked a hire car to drive to San Patrignano, the village near to where her mother was born and where she has found, via the internet, a room in a little *agriturismo*. After completing the paper-work for Avis, she practises manoeuvres in the car park. It's a while since she's driven a car in England, let alone abroad, but after ten minutes on the main road leading to Sansepolcro, she begins to relax. It feels good to be behind the wheel of an Italian car pretending to be Italian; a start towards merging into the local culture. Fiddling with the radio dial, she finds a station playing Italian ballads but there are so many interruptions for adverts, she switches off the radio and lets the scenery provide the entertainment instead.

Just over one hour later, she leaves the busy dual carriageway that cuts its way through tobacco fields sprouting green shoots and takes a mountain road joining Sansepolcro to Rimini. On the lower slopes, farmers have been pruning olive trees. Piles of silver-grey foliage have been left round the knotty trunks like discarded petticoats. The road climbs steadily and at the Viamaggio pass, she parks the hire car in a lay-by and takes photos of the valley with a large lake glistening below in the sunshine. These might well be the mountains where her father had hidden and fought during the war, where each fold or clump of forest held danger and death. She feels a tingle of excitement as she stands there, the wind whispering through flattened grass on the slopes dropping down from where she stands. In the deep ditch next to the car, there are patches of lingering snow and daisies open their faces to the sunshine trying its best to warm up the banks.

She sets off again and not long after, she uses Italian for the first time, stopping to ask the way of an old man sorting logs onto piles by the side of the road. He peers at her suspiciously, looks at the number plate and then gives directions to the *agriturismo*. She is delighted to have managed to communicate in her mother's language! Her father had forbidden Italian to be spoken in the home because he had a theory, one quite prevalent in the Fifties and Sixties, that it was confusing for his children to learn two languages; that they would end up speaking neither language well. It strikes Anna now how hard it must have been for her mother not to be allowed to sing her babies Italian lullabies or tell them stories in her own language and she resolves to learn as much Italian as possible during her stay. In a way, she feels she owes it to her mother.

The owner of the *Agriturismo Casalone* is Teresa Starnucci, about Anna's age, with elfin features and cropped black hair. She ushers Anna in. 'Welcome to our family guest house,' she says in halting English. Anna replies in Italian, 'Please speak in Italian. I'm trying to learn.' Teresa looks relieved, a smile lighting up her striking face. She shakes hands and switches to Italian. 'Phew. I'm pleased about that. We studied English at school but it wasn't my best subject. When Francesco comes later, you'll see he speaks excellent English. So if we have problems communicating, he can help interpret. Let me show you around. Tell me if I'm speaking too fast.'

Anna is pleased she understands most of Teresa's tour round the beautiful old farm building. She learns that Teresa's father had been born in the house and that it has been in the family for over a hundred years. Two years ago, they had decided to restore the place before it fell down. Nobody had lived in it for over thirty years as Teresa's mother had preferred to live up in the village in a modern apartment when she married. Many families from this hamlet did the same and until recently there has been only one elderly couple living here permanently.

'But our generation feels it's important to rescue a part of our history before it's too late,' continues Teresa. 'Our parents thought we were mad at first, to want to live in an old building, but when they saw the way we were modernising with central heating and bathrooms, they could appreciate what we were doing. We hope that more young people will follow our example and then the village will come to life once again.'

The farmhouse has thick stone walls to keep the cold out in the winter and the cool in during July and August, when the sun bakes the countryside. A main feature of the dining room is the huge fireplace large enough to stand in, where all the cooking was done in the past by Teresa's grandmother. On the walls hang old metal cooking pots and utensils.

She follows her guide through the dining-room, up some stairs to a landing, everywhere gleaming and decorated in spotless white-wash. Teresa stops at the first door, 'And this is your bedroom, with its own bathroom.'

On the door is a wooden plaque bearing the name *Ortica*. 'It's a plant grown everywhere,' she explains. 'We even use it in some of our recipes.' She points to a picture of a stinging nettle, telling Anna how they have themed the bedrooms according to plants growing round and about in the woods.

'I'll leave you to unpack and make yourself at home. If you need anything at all, just come and find me. I won't be far away.'

Anna is more than delighted with her internet find. The whole place has been restored with great taste and attention to detail. At the little windows of her room are simple linen curtains, decorated by hand with lace worked locally, Teresa had explained. A wrought iron double bed, made at the forge in the little town of Badia Tedalda, further up the hill, is positioned on a compact mezzanine level. The view from the tiny window of the soaring mountains surrounding the hamlet is breathtaking. The lower slopes are thickly forested, with intermittent lighter green strips of meadow. Higher up she can make out the outline of a village perched precariously on a peak, its roofs poking above the mist like funnels of a liner at sea. Throwing open the shutters she takes in deep breaths of clean air and looks forward to waking up and starting her day with this view of lush countryside.

The dinner table in front of the fire is laid for five, with a white cloth, gleaming cutlery and simple posies of primroses next to each place.

'Do you mind if we sit with you tonight, Anna?' Teresa comes through from the kitchen carrying a basket of bread. 'You are our only guest and we hoped you wouldn't mind.'

She is tired, would really have preferred a quick supper and an early night but she likes the informality of the little guest house and doesn't want to offend her host. 'That's fine. But don't expect me to keep up with you. My Italian is *very* poor.'

'Two weeks here with us and you will be practically bi-lingual. Your accent is already quite good.'

'My mother was Italian.'

'Ah, that explains your dark hair. You could almost pass for an Italian woman.'

'Until I open my mouth…'

'Oh, I would never dare say anything like that.' Teresa laughs.

A man enters the dining room, carrying a couple of bottles of wine. He is wiry, a little taller than Anna with a shock of black hair, peppered with grey. A little girl trails after him.

'Teresa, I brought up these bottles of Sangiovese. I think they will go with tonight's menu.' He greets Anna with a slight, formal bow before placing the bottles on a side table.

'Anna, this is Francesco,' says Teresa.

He grasps her hand firmly and then gently pulls the little girl from her hiding place behind him. 'And this little monkey is my daughter, Alba.' Francesco's English is good. He has a slight American twang. Anna wonders at the use of 'my daughter', thinking he might be a bit of a chauvinist, the way he has left Teresa out of his introduction. The little girl slips back behind her father again, her eyes cast down. She is thin and her complexion is very pale, maybe eight or nine years old but it is hard to tell her exact age. Her thumb goes straight into her mouth and she remains behind Francesco, clutching hold of his shirt.

'Ciao, Alba,' says Anna, bending down to her height, but the child remains hidden behind her father's back without responding. Anna decides not to pay her too much attention, thinking she will come out of her shell when she wants, but Alba continues to remain silent throughout the whole of the meal, taking tiny bites of her food, only nodding or shaking her head when Francesco and Teresa speak to her.

A plate of starters could have come straight from a Still Life: stuffed zucchini flowers, little squares of *crostini* topped with spicy tomatoes, liver paté, a creamy relish made from dandelions flowers, roasted bay leaves topped with ovals of melted cheese. It has all been delicately and painstakingly prepared, using ingredients locally sourced. The main course is a luscious pink, blackcurrant risotto. Anna has never tasted anything quite like it.

'It's like a meal from a fairy tale' she says. 'Thank you! *Grazie!*'

'What made you decide to spend a holiday in this area? Francesco asks as they finish off supper with a dish of pannacotta drizzled with fruits of the forest. 'We don't usually have foreign tourists here, we're off the beaten track somewhat.' He speaks English with confidence, his expressions sometimes rather old fashioned, as if he has studied them from an old text book.

Anna explains a little bit about her parents and the diaries and her determination to find out more about her mother's past. He listens intently as he pours Limoncello into three liqueur glasses.

'What was her name before she married? Everybody knows everybody in a place like this.'

'Ines. Ines Santini.'

Teresa gasps, 'but that is *such* a common name round here. There are lots of Santinis in our neighbourhood.' She leaves the dining room momentarily and returns with a telephone directory, thumbing through the pages until she finds a long list of Santinis.

'If you go to the *Comune* you should be able to find out more about your mother's family. Maybe Francesco can take you tomorrow morning. I've asked him to collect some guest-forms for me.'

'Oh, I forgot to tell you, Teresa.' Francesco interrupts. 'I can't tomorrow. They've asked me to pop in to work and I have to give a lecture for Tosti.'

'*Again?* Teresa thumps the table. 'You're *always* being asked to step in for him. I hope you're being paid this time?'

'Teresa!' There is warning in his tone. 'Don't start up again. I haven't the energy right now. You don't understand anyway. The man's ill.'

'The man's incompetent and should have been given the push ages ago.'

He stands up, his chair scraping across the cotto floor. Anna feels embarrassed listening to the pair of them having what is obviously a familiar squabble and gets up to make her leave. 'I'll say goodnight. I'm very tired and it's been a long day.'

Francesco makes a move as well. 'It's time for Alba to go to bed too. School tomorrow, young lady!' He scoops her up and leaves without saying anything to Teresa: no thank you for the meal, no see you later or good night. A typical spoilt Italian male, Anna thinks, as she undresses for bed back in her room. It was obvious he didn't want her tagging along with him to the Comune either. She doesn't believe his work excuse.

But she doesn't dwell on the evening for long. There is no London traffic noise to disturb her, no music thumping from the flat below. All she can hear as her head touches the crisp linen pillow-case is the gentle sound of the wind playing round the old stone building. She falls asleep immediately.

Chapter 7
Tuscany. April 1999

Anna had forgotten to close the bedroom shutters the night before so the sun streaming through the window wakes her early. The view of the hills, zigzagging against the sky like the spiny ridge of a sleeping dinosaur, is too inviting for dawdling in bed. She pulls on jeans and a fleece, runs her fingers through her newly cropped hairstyle and lets herself out quietly so as not to wake anyone.

She follows a narrow, well-trodden path dropping down in front of the guest-house. Later on there will be blackberries to pick from the thorny bushes but for now cyclamens peep between rocks studding the path edges, their leaves patterned in marbled white. The morning air is fresh and she is pleased she put on her warm fleece. The mountain ridges above her are sprinkled with a dusting of snow, reminding her it is still early in the season. There is the sound of running water and as she turns the bend, a river comes into view, splashing noisily over a weir under the bridge. She isn't the only early riser after all for Francesco is fishing from the weir. Not far away, Alba is crouched down by a rock pool, stirring the water with a stick. *So much for the feeble excuse of an early lecture,* Anna thinks to herself, *he could have just said he had no time to come with me.* Raising his hand in greeting, he calls her over. Alba ignores her and continues with her game. She wonders what explanation Francesco will have up his sleeve this morning. She would actually prefer to continue her walk but doesn't want to appear rude.

'Didn't you sleep well?' he asks as Anna approaches.

'Like a log,' she replies in Italian.

'We say 'like a dormouse' in Italian,' he laughs at her and translates the expression into English. She is peeved he doesn't seem to want to make an effort to listen to her attempts at Italian and watches as he expertly reels in his fishing line and casts it out again into a deeper part of the pool. 'It's a beautiful morning,' he says, 'I thought I would help Teresa's menu along. These little fish are delicious deep-fried, served with garlic and chopped parsley. If I'm lucky I'll catch her some trout too.'

She gives up speaking in Italian and comments on Alba, playing at the water's edge. 'Obviously she doesn't like staying in bed either in the mornings.'

The little girl is building a tower of stones, carefully balancing one on top of the other in decreasing sizes.

Francesco glances at his daughter. 'It's become a bit of a habit. She likes to be with me for half an hour before breakfast. If it's not raining, we go for a walk or come down here to the river and then the school-bus arrives to fetch her.'

'She's a very quiet child.' Anna thinks back to last night's meal.

He gives a wry laugh. 'Yes, very quiet. What I would give to hear some noise from her.'
Anna looks at him questioningly.

'She has decided not to talk,' he tells her. 'She has kept it up for nearly half a year now. She has such a strong will. She's as stubborn as a mule.'

Once again she is impressed at his command of English.

The noise of the water rushing over the weir prevents their voices from carrying over to the child, so she asks why Alba has decided not to talk, trying to imagine how difficult it must be to keep quiet for so long. Years ago, when she was still at convent school, the nuns had made all the girls go on a silent retreat, but she hadn't managed even one afternoon of not speaking. Six months of silence is quite another thing.

'We don't understand why for certain she does it,' he replies, 'but what we do know is that she hasn't uttered a word since her mother died.'

'But I thought Teresa was her mother,' she says in surprise.

'Teresa is my sister. I'm staying with her here in the family home in the hope that the peace and quiet of the place will help Alba. Maybe by being away from Bologna, where we usually live, she can begin to forget. I've taken time away from my work at the University.'

Anna feels awkward. She's jumped to the wrong conclusion, assuming Francesco and Teresa to be a couple and Alba their moody, spoilt child.

'I'm sorry. I feel so clumsy...'

'Why? You English are always saying sorry!' He bends down to open a tin of worms, selects one and attaches it to the hook on another rod. 'Actually it's good to be able to talk. Everybody tiptoes round me as if I'm some kind of precious piece of porcelain about to break into fragments if they mention anything about the past.'

He casts his second rod, the line cutting the water, the float settling as ripples extend across the surface. Anna waits, feeling there is something else he wants to tell her.

'Silvana, my wife, was killed in a car accident. Alba was in the car too but she escaped without a scratch. Or at least she escaped without any visible scratches, I should say.'

'Poor kid. Who knows what must be going on in her little head?'

'Exactly! Who knows? It doesn't take much to understand *why* she's retreated the way she has. What I need is something magic to unlock her silence, to break her suffering. I thought coming here would help but we've been here since Christmas and nothing has changed. The irony is that Silvana would have known exactly what to do. She was a wonderful mother.'

He starts packing away his rods and fetches a basket resting in the shallows. There are half a dozen fish trapped in it but he throws them gently into the current. 'Better to let them go. They won't make any type of feast.' He calls over to the little girl, switching into Italian. 'Come, Alba. Time to get ready for school.'

She stands up and with a piece of driftwood knocks over the tower of stones she has been carefully constructing. Hopping from stepping-stone to stepping-stone, she comes over to join them by the weir, her curls bouncing as she moves.

'We'll have to get you out of those wet tights in time for the bus. I hope Teresa has some clean ones ready.' She puts her hand into her father's. She still hasn't acknowledged Anna in any way, not even with a smile. It's as if her father is the only other person present.

'Let me take the rods,' Anna says, 'then you can concentrate on Alba.'

He smiles at her as he passes up the fishing paraphernalia. A smile which completely alters his face that, up until now, seemed to Anna permanently fixed in a scowl. Then he hoists his little daughter up onto his shoulders and they return up the path to the *agriturismo*. Early sunshine has now been replaced by a mist that suddenly swirls down from the mountains without warning. It sticks half way down, tangling in the branches of the firs, in cotton-wool wisps. The temperature drops too. Yesterday had been above fifteen degrees but it feels about four degrees today with the sun gone in.

'It's freezing today,' Anna says as they walk up the footpath, 'I may need to buy some warmer clothes.'

'We're in the mountains, don't forget. The weather can change quite suddenly.'

'My father mentions that in something he wrote. I think it had an impact on the fighting round here too.'

'For sure it did. And I think that was another reason why our *partigiani* were so useful – they knew this area and the weather conditions. When we go to the tourist office, maybe you will find out more. They're trying to record as much detail as they can for an exhibition.'

'But I thought you had to give a lecture this morning.'

'It's been cancelled. I'm free now.'

Anna wonders if the lecture has really been cancelled or if he has simply changed his mind.

'If you *really* don't mind,' she continues, 'it would be a great help. My Italian is still not up to much beyond the basics of shopping and asking the way.'

'I said I am free.'

She cannot make him out, so prickly one moment and charming the next. They are silent on the way back and Anna drinks in the scenery. She cannot imagine such a beautiful spot brutalised by war. She wonders if soldiers had ever come down to the river and walked along the same path they are following. The place is already having an effect on her. She feels a deep sense of history and for the first time in her life, a kind of belonging.

Egidio, the manager of the Tourist Office, has twinkling brown eyes and a weathered face that could have told a story or two. He is delighted to have a visitor showing interest in the collection of records written by old people from the town. He explains to Anna that they are being gathered by children at middle school to mark the Millennium. At first he speaks slowly and then gradually gathers speed until she has to ask him to repeat. Francesco fills in the details she has missed.

'Are you sure he doesn't mind copying them for me?' she asks, as Egidio sorts photocopies of some of the records into a folder. 'I don't want to be seen as an intruder, but I am really interested in finding out more about what happened here in the war.'

Francesco explains her fears and the old man takes hold of her hand, turning to include both of them in what he has to say, 'From what you have told us about your mother and father, I would not say you were an intruder. You are practically one of us. Wouldn't you say, Francesco?'

Francesco nods agreement and explains to Anna why Egidio is pleased to let her have the documents. 'He's collated all these accounts because he firmly believes the stories should never be taken for granted and I agree with him totally. And you have a right to know about your own family. Take the papers. Now come and see Egidio's exhibits. He's very proud of this tourist office and it is completely run by him and other volunteers.'

They wander into a side-room. There is a glass case containing a stuffed wild boar and a wolf's head is mounted on the wall. Shelves display snakes pickled in large jars that once contained olives and in smaller glass cases there are intricate fossils discovered in rocks in the hills or along the river. Francesco points out a board mounted with sepia photos of the town as it was just after the war. She peers into the grainy faces, wondering if she could possibly be related to any of the figures in the square: women with long woollen skirts, scarves on their heads, men with bandy legs and long whiskers, some with hunting guns slung over their shoulders, all looking very stern for the photographer. Egidio follows them into the room and shows them other photos of local people who went to the area known as the *Maremma*, guiding sheep out of the hills, with the help of big, white dogs, to better pastures nearer the coast. It was an annual event, he explained, taking place from October to June and many peasants saw it as the highlight of their year – a chance for a type of hard-working holiday. Some of them never returned, finding these living conditions better than the hard graft of a mountain existence.

'Have you time to grab some lunch and come on a mystery tour with me?' Francesco asks, 'there's a place I want to show you. We could first go to the drugstore before it shuts and buy picnic ingredients.'
'What about the weather? It was very misty before.'
He points out of the museum window. 'Look now.'
The sun has come out again and the sky is cloudless, blue and inviting.
'But won't it change again?'
'We'll be fine,' he reassures her.
She bows to his local knowledge and they say goodbye to Egidio, Anna thanking him again for her precious papers. They cross the square to a tiny supermarket where one forlorn trolley is parked outside. The shop isn't big enough to fit any trolleys in or even more than four customers at a time and she wonders about the purpose of the lone trolley outside. Francesco explains that it is for delivering purchases to old people who can't manage to do shopping for themselves. She smiles at the thought of the contrast with the supermarket vans back in England. When she enters the shop, her nose is assaulted by a mixture of smells: ham, salame, soap powder, cheese. Francesco introduces her to the shop keeper perched on a high stool behind the counter. When she moves to fetch a large cheese from the shelf behind her, Anna sees she is quite crippled and needs the stool for support. The trolley outside is probably used also as a walking aid, Anna thinks. Fresh ciabatta, a paper twist of black

olives, a couple of slices of pecorino cheese, two apples and a bottle of wine make up her first picnic lunch in Italy.

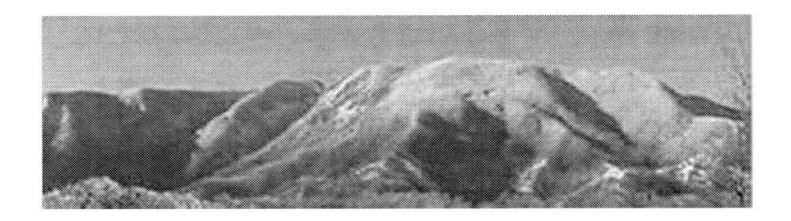

Francesco's Fiat Panda bounces over the dirt track higher and higher into the mountains facing Badia Tedalda.

'We call these *Le Alpe della Luna* – the Mountains of the Moon. Few people live here anymore and there are many fables and ghost stories about the place. For me it has a special atmosphere.' He tells the story he learnt at elementary school. In the Middle Ages, young Count Manfredi of Montedoglio and a beautiful peasant girl, Rosalia, had fallen madly in love, much to the disapproval of the Count's family. One evening when they were alone together, whispering words of love to each other on a balcony facing the Mountains of the Moon, Rosalia told him that if they were to climb the mountains opposite and touch the moon, all their wishes would be granted. They set off towards the Mountains of the Moon never to be seen again. And now, at full moon, it is sometimes possible to hear the galloping of two horses on the peaks and to see two shadows with hands extended towards the moon.

She laughs. 'Well, you never know. These stories often have a grain of truth behind them – otherwise why did people start telling them?'

'Indeed!' He smiles at her, stops the car and points at the view and she appreciates the derivation of the name. Tracts of impenetrable woodland are interrupted by friable masses of grey-brown rock, rising like craters. He points out two peaks that are over 1,400 metres high, covered with fresh snow. The scene is dramatically beautiful yet sinister. She takes a photograph and then peers at the image in her new digital camera. 'I can see why you think it's a special place but it's hard to capture the atmosphere in a picture.'

' It's a place to store in the memory. Now hop back in the car and I'll take you to a restaurant, the like of which you've probably never visited.'

'Where did you learn all these English expressions? Not all from a text book, I'm sure.'

'I'll tell you over lunch.'

Putting the car back into gear they climb higher still up the mountain. Anna is mesmerised by the views. Throughout the trip they haven't seen another soul and she feels they are the only people in the world but when he parks the car in a clearing, a fenced-off picnic area proves they have not been the only visitors. Leading her towards some rocks opposite the picnic site, he pulls aside slender branches to reveal a narrow opening to a cave. They slip through, entering a chamber wide and high enough for standing. Her eyes adjust to the gloom; only a thin finger of day light penetrates an opening in the cave roof, circled in black. Francesco explains it was caused by smoke from a fire made by people seeking shelter. Built into the side of the cave is a man-made trough collecting a trickle of water seeping through the rocky surfaces. She gasps when he shines torchlight on fantastic stalactites twisted into elaborate patterns, hanging down like glass chandeliers.

'This place has been used by woodcutters and peasants working on the land but during the war partisans sheltered here too. I remember my father telling me he had to sleep here once.' Francesco says. 'Last year, when *il corpo forestale,* the forestry workers, were coppicing in this area, they discovered a stash of ammunition hidden further down the chamber. Then they decided to tidy up the place and make it into a tourist venue, but it's too far off the road for most people to venture. I thought it would be of interest to you. Who knows? Maybe your father may even have sheltered here as well?'

'That's exactly what I was thinking. It's given me goose pimples. I can't explain properly but I feel this place is alive. Full of ghosts from the past.' She shivers.

'Let's have our picnic at the tables outside,' he suggests, guiding her out of the gloom. 'I think we need sun-shine.'

They unpack their simple feast at a table with the best view and Francesco uncorks the wine then raises his plastic beaker to the hills. 'I propose a toast to the mountains and the secrets they hold and a toast to you too, Anna. Welcome to your mother's land!'

They touch beakers and while he cuts slices of *ciabatta,* Anna asks him again where he learned to speak such good English.

'In Africa. After I finished university I travelled to Tanzania to help on a programme documenting wild dogs in the Serengeti. It was run by a young American couple.'

'I'm confused. An Italian in Africa working for Americans!'

He laughs. 'You will come across the system of *raccomandazione* sooner or later.'

She looks puzzled.

'It's a matter of survival, Anna. Often in this country it's *who* you know, not *what* you know! One of the Americans is a cousin and he more or less created some work experience for me. We Italians end up everywhere, you know. After the war there was mass emigration to find work and that is how my uncle landed up in Boston.' He cuts more Pecorino, handing her a generous wedge and continues, 'Africa was an unforgettable experience. Such an amazing country! I would love to go back one day and show Alba.'

'I've never been out of Europe. I used to have so many dreams about travelling. You know that feeling when you're young? When you believe the world belongs to you? That you can put your arms around it and embrace all the opportunities?'

The wine is loosening her tongue. He laughs.

'But you're still young. There's a world out there waiting for you, Anna.' He points to her head. 'It's up there that matters.'

She helps him pack up the remnants of the picnic and then walks to the edge of the picnic area, absorbing the view of the mountains. 'You toasted the secrets of the mountains, Francesco. I was wondering - could you help me with my mother's diaries?' She turns to look at him as she says this, needing to gauge his reaction. It is important that any involvement he has with her mother's story is done in the right spirit.

'I wanted to do it by myself,' she says, 'but it would take me ages and I'm frightened of missing something.'

'Of course! I would be very interested in helping you when I have time - between looking after Alba and the occasional lecture.'

'Thank you. I would pay you.'

He looks at her, the scowl returning to his features.

'I don't want paying. It will be a challenging project.'

She is not sure about his use of the word 'project', but she is keener than ever to understand what her mother has written. There is no going back now.

'I'll give the papers to you when I've got them into some kind of order.'

'Whenever you're ready.'

The return journey down the dusty tracks is spent in silence but Anna is tired and enjoys not having to talk. All in all, it has been a good afternoon.

Chapter 8
One week later

The monthly market in the piazza is only a small affair, a chance for villagers to meet up with friends and family living in hamlets scattered through the mountains. Teresa had asked Anna at breakfast to join her in shopping and they immediately make for the busiest stall. A round-faced, story book figure, surrounded by squawking caged hens and baskets of eggs is keeping up a good-natured banter with a queue of customers.

Teresa introduces Anna, 'Evalina, this is my English friend.'
The diminutive old lady holds out a work-weathered hand, thrusting a twist of newspaper containing half a dozen brown eggs at Anna. 'Taste these, Signorina and then tell me next week how good Italian eggs are.' She refuses payment and Teresa laughs at Anna's unsuccessful protests.

'She's a clever business woman. It's her way of luring you to return. They are fresh eggs and free range from *polli ruspanti*.'
Anna has seen plenty of these 'scratching about' hens in villagers' backyards - happy hens scavenging in the grass and dust. They move on to a colourful stall selling materials and Teresa haggles for a length of linen, edged with fine lace. 'I need to replace the curtains in one of the guest-rooms,' she tells Anna,

who listens to her arguing good naturedly with the stall holder, laughing when he tries to sell her some towels as well. She follows the gist but wonders if she will ever be able to rattle off her Italian at even half the speed. A bright table cloth with a colourful pattern of olives and grapes catches her eye and she buys it to remind herself of the friendly market.

Next they browse at a stall selling knick-knacks and old furniture. Teresa holds up a wooden-frame contraption. 'We call these priests. And we put them in our beds in winter.'

Anna laughs at the irreverence. 'A priest in the bed! I can't imagine anything less cuddly!'

Teresa explains that the frame holds up the bed-covers and then a pot of hot ashes from the fire is placed underneath to heat up the bed. She asks the price and then bargains hard again, finishing up with a handshake and a smile. 'Another antique for my city guests to admire.'

Anna enjoys the way local people shop and decides to try and drive a bargain too. In the corner, under the shade of the lime trees, she spies an old man wearing a wide brimmed hat sitting behind piled pyramids of golden jars of honey. When tries her Italian out on him he stares at her for a few seconds, scratching his head, shrugging his shoulders, making no effort, it seems to her, to understand. And when he mutters something about *americani*, she retorts in her best Italian, '*Sono inglese, non americana.*'

At this he pulls a face and sits down to read his newspaper, even though Anna can see it is upside down. Teresa comes to her rescue, pouring on his head what Anna hopes is a stream of Italian curses. He scowls and holds up five fingers, '*cinque mila*', he pronounces slowly and deliberately, making Anna feel like the idiot he obviously thinks she is. Retaliating and, equally as slowly, she replies, '*Non grazie, troppo caro.*' (No thanks, too expensive), wishing she knew the expression for 'up yours!' in Italian.

Teresa laughs and putting her arm through Anna's, they wander over to the bar behind the honey stall. 'Don't take any notice of Danilo, Anna. He lives way up in that hamlet you can see from my house. Deep down, he's a good man.'

'Well I think he's totally objectionable. My Italian's surely not that bad.'

She sips her cappuccino. Teresa knocks back her tiny cup of espresso, after commenting that she's noticed *stranieri* always seem to prefer cappuccino – even after a big meal. Italians cannot understand it. Anna leans back in her chair to enjoy the theatre of market day. It is like having a seat at the opera, only a whole lot cheaper. She glances over at the old honey-seller, who is staring at her but when he realises she is watching him, he hides behind his newspaper again. The cantankerous old devil is soon forgotten as they look at each other's purchases and Teresa chatters away, slowing down every now and again when she realises Anna has been left behind in her stories about various village personalities. When Anna comments that she seems to know everybody, Teresa shrugs and says it is not surprising, as she has lived here all her life.

It is all so different from Anna's life back in London where she does not even know the name of her neighbour in the flat across her landing.

Before lunch she spreads her mother's papers over the bed to sort into some kind of order for Francesco…and herself. The earliest, written in Italian in old exercise-books, date from summer 1944 and she slips these into one of the large envelopes donated by Teresa. There are far more post-1945 and these go in another. The remainder, mostly written in English, have been scribbled in a variety of journals, on backs of shopping lists, scraps of paper and – bizarrely – on an old pillow-case.

It is strange to be filing a life into envelopes and she suffers a moment of doubt that a stranger should read her mother's words before her. But before she can change her mind, she bundles the Italian papers together for Francesco to translate.

In the afternoon she collects Alba for her first English lesson and hands the envelope to Francesco. He senses her reluctance. 'Don't worry, Anna. I shall treat your

mother's words with respect.' And she is grateful for his sensitivity, watching him place the envelope into a folder on the desk in the reception area and telling herself to let go.
'Rather than stay indoors I'd like to take Alba down to the river in the sunshine. Do you think she will come?' He talks to Alba. It is obvious she is not keen. Eventually she shrugs her shoulders and pulls a face. 'I've bribed her with the promise of her favourite cartoon programmes,' Francesco explains, 'but I think we should just make it a short session. I'll come and meet you down by the weir in about half an hour.'

Anna has suggested the river thinking it will be easier for Alba in the fresh air… her silence will be less obvious with the sound of birdsong and water splashing over the rocks in the river. Lately Alba is more accepting of her, smiling more and not averting her eyes so readily. Maybe because being early in the season there have been few guests in Teresa's *agriturismo* and they have fallen into the habit of sharing a table together in the evenings, like a family.

Anna had watched Alba sketching in her note-books and wondered if drawing might be a good start to the lesson. 'Can you draw me a cat like this, Alba?' she asks in English, trying to engage the little girl by showing her a picture of a cat from a magazine.

It had worked well when they'd been sitting together at the table in the dining-room. Today it isn't clicking at all. Alba pushes the sketch pad away and instead picks up a stick to stir water in a pool. Then she is distracted by tiny darting fish and after that she finds a stone encrusted with quartz and starts to extract the white crystals by beating it against a rock. Anna gives up. There is no point in insisting and in any case she doesn't have the patience today. So she sits on a boulder watching her play, immersed in her mystery world.

She reminds Anna of herself as a little girl. So often she'd been left to her own devices for long stretches of time. Harry and Jane would be busy with their studies or out with friends and sometimes Mamma would leave her at home, asking her father to keep an eye on her. He would promptly disappear to his shed. As children they were not allowed to sit in front of the television for hours and Anna's imagination became her entertainment.

At the bottom of their garden was a huge beech tree. Its branches drooped down like the walls of a tent and the trunk was knotted with gargoyle joints and holes where she imagined a gang of miniature-sized friends lived. They all had names: Scar-Face was the leader - a pirate who had been washed up on a Sussex beach and jumped onto the tow-bar of a caravan to hitch a ride and ended up in their tidy Surrey garden. He had a girlfriend called Molly who could do the can-can and had once been on stage in Paris. There was a kind witch called Spellerina who reversed unkind spells and a twin sister for herself, called Emma. She would tell Emma everything, but only when she could find her because she wasn't always in the tree, being very popular and always invited round to friends' homes for tea.

One afternoon, when Jane came home earlier than expected from a cancelled piano lesson, she caught Anna talking aloud to Emma, 'Don't you know that mad people talk to themselves?' she teased her little sister, 'that's the first sign of madness… and the second is hairs growing in the palms of your hand.' And she fell about laughing when her little sister anxiously inspected her palms. Her brother and sister also delighted in telling her she must have been adopted because she was 'so much younger and uglier than them.' Small wonder she felt like an outsider in her own family and that she had created a fantasy family for herself. She could understand that Alba maybe felt more secure within her silence.

As soon as the sun falls behind the ridge, the air turns chilly and Anna calls to her little pupil that the lesson is over for today. 'We'll try again another time and anyway, here comes your Daddy.'
She hopes that by talking to her in English most of the time she will learn something and, by attuning her ears to different sounds, she might pick up a word or two. As Francesco approaches down the footpath, Alba runs to him and he swings her round and round.

'Babbo has come, not Daddy,' he shouts, using the Italian translation 'Who is this Daddy, Daddy, Daddy?'

She squeals with laughter. It's the only sound Anna ever hears her make. She wishes she could find a way to break her silence.

'How did it go?' he asks, setting Alba down as they begin the walk back together.

'*Cosi cosi*...so-so!' Anna replies, twisting her outstretched hand up and down, palm facing downwards, the way Teresa has taught her. 'I'm not giving up though! Did you enjoy a peaceful half hour?'

'A *fascinating* half hour. I started to read your mother's diary and if I have time, I'll write the translation out for you.'

Alba has stopped walking. She is standing still, blocking the path, her arms crossed, an obstinate look on her face. Francesco speaks firmly to her, telling her she is too big to be carried and that they will be late for Teresa's supper. When Anna tries to help by suggesting they have a race back to the *agriturismo*, the child puts out her tongue at her and runs off in the opposite direction, back to the river.

'You go back by yourself, Anna,' Francesco calls as he goes in pursuit of Alba. 'Tell Teresa we won't be long.'

She continues up the mule-track to the guest house. As she passes their vegetable plot with the neat rows of seedlings pushing up through the soil, she glances up to the village of Montebotolino silhouetted on the peaks. She remembers Teresa telling her that the village is almost deserted, being full of holiday homes for people from Rimini and as far away as Rome. Its only permanent resident is the irascible old honey-maker from the market. Teresa had thought he might be persuaded to talk about his memories of the war, but in the meantime Anna cannot wait to hear what Francesco has found in the diaries.

Chapter 9
The next morning

At breakfast next morning Alba is even more subdued and hardly touches anything, even though Teresa produces her favourite chocolate drink and biscuits for dunking. After Francesco has seen her on to the *scuolabus,* he comes into the kitchen where Anna is helping tidy up. He pours himself another espresso and Teresa warns him it will make him *nervoso,* tetchy, that he has already had too much caffeine this morning.

'Don't you think I am already *nervoso*?' He yawns and turns to Anna, 'I'm sorry but I didn't find any time last night to work on your diary. It took me ages to put Alba to bed. I couldn't seem to do anything right. First she wanted to wear a different pair of pyjamas but they were in the wash, then she insisted on me telling her another two stories. It was almost midnight when I turned off her light. If anything she's growing even more demanding.'

Anna is beginning to think the child might be ruling the roost and could do with firmer handling. But she doesn't comment, reminding herself she has never been a parent and that it is none of her business. 'Don't worry. I can wait,' she says. Secretly she is disappointed. Teresa and Francesco talk away in Italian but she can't follow, their words spilling from their mouths faster and faster. Finally Francesco raises his voice, leaving the kitchen abruptly and slamming the door behind him.

Teresa throws her dishcloth into the sink, turns round to lean against it and folds her arms. 'He is so tired and worried about Alba. I'm sorry about the shouting.'

'I couldn't understand anyway. My Italian still has a long way to go. Can I help at all?'

'Actually it was about you.' She hesitates, obviously embarrassed.

'Go on, Teresa! *Dai! Forza!* Remember you taught me that expression the other day?' Anna tries to make light of the situation.

'Right then! It's about your room. I have a long standing booking at the weekend and I need all my rooms for five nights and I didn't know how long you might be staying? Or if you would mind me moving you into a different room, that still needs a bit of work doing on it? I'm sorry!'

'Why are you sorry? You're running a business after all. In fact I was going to chat to you soon anyway. I love my room but I can't afford to stay in a hotel all the time I'm here and I was going to ask you for advice about finding somewhere else anyway. Please don't worry, Teresa. You've been so good to me.'

'It's just that you are becoming such a friend. Francesco is angry with me as he says I should let you stay where you are but he's not the one running the business and …'

She takes Teresa's hands in hers. 'I'm *honestly* not offended and I *really* don't mind – what is the expression? *Non faccio complimenti.* And thank you for considering me a friend…because I feel the same way.' Teresa smiles in relief. 'Thank you. Then, I have a suggestion. Come!' She leads Anna round the corner from the front door of the *agriturismo* into a small square and up a flight of steps into a narrow house. They step over a couple of cement bags and Teresa moves aside a tin of paint standing at the entrance to what will eventually be a small kitchen. 'I was going to advertise this for a long let but it's not quite finished, as you can see.'

It is already delightful, bearing the hall marks of Teresa's tasteful restoration in the *agriturismo*. An original stone sink, far too low for modern use, is fixed below the window overlooking the square. Anna imagines a trough spilling with red geraniums or basil on its ledge. There is a fireplace which Teresa assures her is functional and a log burner waiting to be installed in the far corner of the room, where a dining table and four chairs have been placed.

'It used to be my aunt's house and she left it to me when she died. And some of the furniture was hers too. I'd much prefer to have somebody I know living here. And if you like it, we can go on seeing each other and I can make sure you are practising your Italian.' She waggles her finger in pretend strictness. 'But it's not quite finished.'

'I don't care. I absolutely love it. Show me the rest.'

There are three storeys, each containing one room. The middle floor has been refurbished as a bathroom, with a shower, toilet, bidet and tiny bath fixed cleverly into a corner, the walls lined with hand-painted tiles. The top floor in the eaves is the bedroom, open-plan, with another small fire-place and a wall to ceiling window that frames a view of the spectacular mountain tops.

'When can I move in? And how much is the rent?' She cannot believe her luck, especially when Teresa tells her she only wants 400,000 Lire a month, explaining that, in return for the low rent, she could help her out occasionally in the *agriturismo,* especially when the summer season starts.

'Another thing that worries me,' Teresa continues, 'is that I haven't finished furnishing the place. It might be a bit sparse for you.'

'I prefer it this way. I was brought up in a home where we were always tripping over furniture. Our parents' generation were making up for a lack of possessions during the war. But there I go again, always talking about the war!'

Two days later and Anna moves in. Teresa has left a basket of vegetables on the stone work-top, with a note:
A house-warming gift for you, fresh from the vegetable garden this morning. The first salad of the

season and spinach beet from autumn. Wait until the tomatoes start coming and I can teach you some delicious recipes.

Everybody is so kind and Anna doesn't know how she can ever repay them.

It doesn't take her too long to unpack her few possessions. However she decides she needs to buy some more cooking utensils from the market and a warmer counterpane for the brass bed in the eaves. The bed takes up most of the room and she sits on it for a while taking in the view. The bell-tower of the chapel in Montebotolino sits atop the mountains, splashed yellow with *ginestra* that she's noticed sprouting everywhere along the road sides and steep, stony banks. She decides to walk up to the village in the afternoon. The weather is dry and she is eager to talk to Danilo, the old honey seller who lives up there. Teresa had said he might have some interesting stories for her about the war, so while she is waiting for Francesco to find time to translate her diaries, she may as well do some research of her own.

Teresa tells her to follow the path which is marked by red and white way marks on the sides of houses, tree trunks and rocks. 'It will take you a good half an hour to climb up there. Take your mobile phone with you, Anna. You never know what may happen with the weather at this time of year. There've been landslides this winter and the path may have changed and it's easy to get lost if you don't know the mountains. Are you sure you want to go alone?'

'I'm a big girl now! Don't worry.'

She leaves straight after a lunch of bread and pecorino cheese. The path starts after the cemetery at Rofelle and after crossing a weir, climbs steadily. At first she walks under a canopy of pines, the wind moving gently through the branches, trunks swaying in the light breeze, her feet crunching over last year's fallen pine cones. After twenty minutes she stops in a clearing and gazes at the valley below. In the distance she can hear the tinny music of bells from a flock of sheep, toy models in a meadow sliced out of the forest. The houses of Montebotolino are above her, looming over the edge of the path. She thinks how difficult it must have been to construct villages like these, in a time before machines and vehicles. Some of the houses are complete ruins; some are shells, with just the sky for a roof. One is obviously under reconstruction: a cement-mixer and roof tiles waiting to be used lay piled beside the track.

Danilo's house is just off the village square. She works this out for herself as it is the only building showing any real signs of life: a patch of earth in front has been planted with a few courgettes and tomatoes. There is a dish of pasta and milk by his front door, food for an animal perhaps. A couple of strings of last year's onions and chilli peppers hang from rusty nails in the stone-work and a shirt flaps on a make-shift washing line slung between plum trees. The door is open.

'*Permesso?*' she calls, asking if it is all right to come in, waiting for the usual response of '*Avanti!* But nobody answers.

She pokes her head round the open door and peers into the gloom, her eyes not immediately focussing after the bright light outside, nearly jumping out of her skin when she is grabbed roughly from behind. She screams and tries to back out of the door to escape. A voice growls at her, 'What the devil do you think you are doing in my house? Get out, thief!'

She cannot think of any Italian words for a moment, shouts in English, 'let me go!' and scrabbles for her mobile phone in her pocket. Realising she would not know which number to punch in for the police, she shouts again as loud as she can, 'Take your filthy hands off me!'

The old honey seller scowls. He releases her and she steps outside but he follows and grabs her again, 'Who are you?' he shouts, peering at her more closely, 'I've seen you somewhere before, haven't I?'

She tries to calm herself down and to think of the words she needs in Italian, 'The market, at the market. With Teresa. From the *agriturismo* at San Patrignano,' she stutters.

He nods recognition, gesturing to her to sit down on the wooden bench outside his door. He talks quickly – she doesn't recognise many the words, thinking maybe he is speaking in dialect, so she asks him to slow down, '*piano, piano, per favore.*' He starts again, explaining that he is suspicious of strangers, that here has been a burglary up here. When she says she doesn't understand, he throws up his hands in exasperation and then mimes until she begins to understand. Four houses were broken into - he holds up four fingers. '*Bastardi,*' he says, spitting onto the dirt. 'I have nothing valuable in my house', he tells her and then raises his voice again, 'I have no antiques to sell you, signorina.'

'I'm not interested in antiques, signor…'

She realises the only name she has for the old man is Danilo. It feels offensive to only use his Christian name.

'Just call me Danilo,' he says, as if reading her thoughts, 'that's what everybody calls me,' and he pushes his cap back off his head and scratches, 'so, you are an 'inglesina?'

Feeling she might be gaining his trust, she broaches the subject of the war. 'Would you tell me something about the occupation? Teresa told me that you were a partisan.'

He stands up, the smile wiped from his face. 'That's all over and done with. Long gone. I never talk to anybody about that time. It's best forgotten. Now, signorina, I have to go and feed my hens and lock them up. Because of the wolves.'

'Wolves!' Anna wonders if he is joking. 'Did you say wolves?'
'Some idiot in the bar told me it's just a stray dog abandoned by a city family but I know better,' he says, throwing up his hands, 'I found its spoor. It is definitely a wolf. Nobody can teach me anything about these mountains, what goes on and what doesn't go on up here.' He taps the side of his nose and winks at her and continues to chat, but she doesn't understand the rest of his diatribe and she is ready to leave anyway. He all but pushes her away from his patch of garden, directing her towards the track, his hand guiding her brusquely in the small of her back. 'Inglese, are you?' he concludes his rant, 'I don't like the inglesi, signorina…'
Anna decides she doesn't much like him either. The ruined houses with their windows like empty sockets in dead faces stare at her as she hurries past down the track. She cannot wait to be away from the place.

Chapter 10

Anna has the dream that night she's had on and off for years: a soundless scream that goes on and on, issuing from an open mouth, wide enough to swallow her whole. All the while, she tries to escape, her feet sticking fast in treacle mud, her arms held by something she cannot see. The dream is not in black and white but shades of red and purple. And when at last she hears the scream, it is coming from her own mouth.

It wakes Anna, her heart hammering, eyes focussing on beams above her. She wonders for a moment where she is and then remembers she has spent her first night in Teresa's little house. Tangled in bed sheets and wet with perspiration she hears knocking on her door. Opening the window wide, she leans out to see Francesco at the door peering up anxiously. 'Are you all right?' he calls, 'I heard a scream.'

'It was me… just a silly dream.'

'Teresa sent me round with this.' He holds up a breakfast tray. 'Coffee, fresh bread and home-made jam. Aren't you going to let me in?'

Dragging on her dressing gown she hurries down the stairs and unbolts the heavy oak door. 'How wonderful! Thank you so much. But tell Teresa this has got to be the first and only time. I'm an independent woman now.'

'I was hoping you might invite me to join you. I've been busy with the diaries.' He pulls the brown envelope from under the basket of bread rolls, waves it enticingly in front of her.

Over breakfast he tells her there was nothing much wrong with her translation; that he has left that alone and managed to work on almost everything she had given him.

'I found it fascinating. I won't give anything away, Anna but after you've read it through, I would like to take you to some of the places mentioned. That is, if you don't mind.'

'Of course not. Why would I? I just hope it didn't take up too much of your time.'

'Once I started, I couldn't stop! When Alba went to sleep I burnt the midnight oil, as you say.'

'How is she?'

'Difficult! But I have to keep reminding myself she's had a difficult time. Changing the subject and before I forget, there's a music festival at the weekend in a town not far from here and I wondered if you would like to come along with Alba and me.'

When she hesitates, he adds, 'there's music from all over the world performed in the street. It's a great event.'

'I'm sure it is but I was thinking that maybe Alba might want to go just with you.'

'She has to learn that grown-ups need to do what they want sometimes too!' Anna agrees but says nothing and Francesco gets up from the table, 'have a think about it and in the meantime, enjoy your mother's diaries. I'll leave you in peace and go and see if Teresa needs any help. Ciao!'

'Ciao, Francesco! And thank Teresa again for the wonderful breakfast.'

Without clearing away the dishes, she takes the envelope and runs up to her top-floor bedroom. There are no chairs in the house yet, so arranging the pillows on the bed, she pulls out Francesco's typed translation and starts to read.

Rofelle, September 8th 1944

He's still in the stable. Mamma made up an extra plate of pasta with zucchini we'd bottled last Spring and when it was dark, she told me to put on my scarf and take some chicken feed with me, in case anybody should be watching and ask what I was doing out at that time of night. I know she's terrified somebody will find out we're hiding an 'inglese' but Capriolo said we must, for he will die otherwise. But we are all terrified. Last week we heard they shot the Benuccis because they wouldn't vacate their house. The Germans only gave them a day's notice. Poor old souls, they refused to go; they had nowhere to go to anyway and the old signora was riddled with rheumatism and couldn't walk far. They are cruel these Germans. We're scared but Capriolo says they won't break our spirits. We use this name for him because we have been told again and again by the *Resistenza* not to call him by his real name. His family would be executed if they discovered who he really was. He's named himself after the mountain deer, nimble and fast as they scamper about on the mountains. It comes automatically to my tongue to call him that now, but he would skin me if he knew I was writing this. If I don't tell someone, I shall burst – so I'm telling my diary which I hide behind the loose stone in a niche in my room. Nobody will ever find it. And if they do, they will think it's just my old school-book.

The *inglese* was still asleep on the planks above the cows. The nights were chilly and the animal warmth and dry hay made a comfortable bed-room, much better than mine. I have to share with *nonna* and she kicks and tosses at night. She snores like the pig we used to fatten for Christmas. There have been no pigs this year. The Germans have 'requisitioned' ours and everybody else's in the area. 'Pigs eating pigs,' we muttered amongst ourselves.

'*Signore*,' I whispered.
There was no response. His face was long and pale, blond curls fell over his forehead which was bound with a dirty cloth. Blood had oozed and crusted onto the material. He was like a big baby.

'Signore!' I said it louder this time. There was still no response. I put the bowl of pasta down and gently shook him.
He opened his eyes, shouted and grabbed me round the neck. I pummelled him with my fists, I could hardly breathe, 'let me go, leave me alone!' I shouted. And then he recognised where he was and dropped his hands from round my neck, '*Scusi, scusi*. Sorry, sorry, signorina.'

'You nearly knocked over the food.' I was shaking and I rubbed my neck. His grip had hurt me. The cows below seemed to sense something was wrong and they mooed and stamped their hooves.

I pushed the dish nearer to him and he struggled into a sitting position. He looked very young to me, not much older than Capriolo, maybe in his early twenties. We had lent him some of our clothes and burnt his uniform but he still didn't look like one of us. His hair was too blond. We'd talked about shaving it off or dying it with plants. *Nonna* had told me about a woman in the next village who used walnut shells and spindle berries to keep the grey from her hair. Her husband was younger than her and so she was frightened he would run off with a younger woman. One day she was caught in the rain without her scarf and the dye ran down her face, the colour of dried blood. I thought I would bring the *inglese* one of Papà's cloth caps next time I came to the stable. He could pull it down to cover his hair.

'Eat, eat!' I mimed, my hand going to my mouth. 'You must get strong again.'

He repeated the words: '*mangia, mangia*'. I giggled. It would be best if he pretended to be a mute. If he opened his mouth to pronounce words in such a ridiculous accent, then that, together with his blond curls, would give him away immediately.

The door of the mill opened, casting a triangle of light onto the path leading to the stable, 'Ines, Ines,' mother called. I had been gone too long so I left the dish with the *inglese* and hurried back to the fire-side.

They were sitting round the hearth in a semi-circle – Mamma, Papa, Davide and *nonna*. Their faces were sombre, the fire-light enlarging their features, creating a grotesque group.

Mamma was the first to speak. 'We can't do this. It's too dangerous. There are too many Germans around.' Davide piped in, 'It's not just the Germans – we can't trust anybody. Carlo told me at the bar there were ten women, children and old men butchered in Gattara in retaliation for the *partigiani* killing one German soldier. There's no telling who is spying on us at any moment.'

'Carlo is always in the bar,' said my father, "the only truth he knows is the bottom of a glass. How can *he* be the judge between what is true and what is tittle-tattle?'

'No, Papà, honestly – it's not just him who knows about it,' my brother explained, 'the Germans put up a poster in the square yesterday offering a twelve hundred lire reward for information about prisoners-of-war on the run. You and I know only too well that many people would give their right arm for such a sum.'

The ashes hissed and spluttered sending sparks up the tarry chimney. Davide continued, 'Didn't you hear about Pippo who was out herding the cattle? The Germans shot him, no questioning, nothing… they told his parents he was a partisan, that he would have no proper burial. They were to leave his body up on the mountain for the wolves.'

'Stop your scaremongering or I'll give you such a beating, you young rascal,' my father shouted, rising from his chair, his arm raised. 'Stop frightening your mother.'

'I know about it already,' our mother said quietly, putting down her mending and staring into the fire. 'When I was at the fountain two days ago, all the women were talking about it. When the Germans warned the priest not to conduct his funeral, the whole of Montefaggio turned out to attend. Padre Luca carried Pippo's body down from the ridge himself. One by one the people opened their doors and came out onto the track following him down to the Church. Everybody! The old, the sick, the young...everybody crowded into the church to give that poor boy a proper send-off. And the German soldiers stood there with their rifles aimed, shouting at them to go back to their houses. Nobody obeyed and there was not a thing they could do - save shooting the whole village. The people were so brave. But I *am* scared. I don't want the risk of that Englishman laying up there in the stable. I don't mind the cooking, sending up medical supplies and clothing up to the boys but - this is too close for comfort.' She lowered her voice as if the walls had ears.

'Capriolo will know what to do,' I said. 'He's coming later to see us.'

Davide teased me, 'See *you*, more like, everybody knows he just comes down here for you.'
In return for that comment, he received another cuff round the ear from our father. I rounded on my

brother, 'Capriolo and I are like brother and sister. We've known each other all our lives. Don't be so stupid. Your brain is being stewed by this stupid war.'

Capriolo was two years older than me. We both learnt our lessons in the same classroom in the village school. We were considered star pupils by the old headmaster who had a soft spot for us because we were eager to learn. He said we would go a long way, that we understood there was a world beyond the mountain walls of our village and gave us extra lessons in mathematics and history when the other children straggled home down the hill from our tiny elementary school.

Three months ago he had come up to find me in the meadow where I was tending our Chianina cattle. I was sitting on a boulder, dressed in one of Davide's old coats, belted with a length of rope, one of Papà's hats pulled down over my dark curls and *nonno's* boots on my feet. Mamma had warned me to keep away from the German soldiers and had dressed me up in shapeless rags to make me look as ugly as possible. I was half asleep. The spring sunshine was pleasantly warm and the tinkling of the bells round the necks of the cattle was like a lullaby I had undone the coat to feel the rays on my winter skin. A wolf whistle startled me from my snooze. Wrapping the scratchy coat tighter round my body, I jumped up, terrified. I couldn't see anybody and I called the dog to my side. He was wagging his tail, not in the least alarmed. Then Capriolo jumped out of the tree above me, knocking me to the ground. I screamed and hammered at him with my fists and he laughed.

'Whoa Ines…quite the she-wolf …but not in sheep's clothing…in scarecrow's clothing…*Not* a sight for sore eyes.'

I pulled off my cap and my hair tumbled down below my shoulders. I don't know why I did that. I didn't really care what he thought of me.

'Don't ever do that to me again. I nearly wet myself.'

'We couldn't have that, could we?' He laughed at me again. 'It would take you three hours to take all those garments off. No, seriously, you should be more vigilant, there are all sorts of people wandering round in these hills at the moment.' He looked me up and down and then sat down with me on the boulder. 'It's good you look as ugly as a tramp though. Remember Ines – you are not just a woman, you are a communist too.'

I laughed and he caught hold of my sleeve. 'Ines – it's no laughing matter - we need your help. I'm being serious.'

And so began my initiation into the *Resistenza*. I became a '*staffetta*', running errands for them. More times than I can remember from that day onwards I had hidden medicines, food from my mother's kitchen, spare clothes beneath my bulky overcoat and left them in the ditch that ran alongside the track where I led the cattle up to the summer pastures. Sometimes I passed on messages that Davide asked me to relay. I didn't understand them and I never asked where Capriolo took all these things. It was best not to know too much, he'd told me.

But to return to our problem of looking after the *inglese*… Capriolo turned up one hour later. Four knocks on the door and a cough. His password. He came near the fire, rubbing his hands. 'Warm during the day but the nights are beginning to grow colder.' My mother rose to pour him a cup of coffee. Made from ground acorns these days but it was the best we could manage.

'Capriolo,' my mother said as the hot liquid poured into the little cup, 'we can't keep the *inglese* here. It's too dangerous. Not only for us, but for all of you up there too.'

He touched her arm. 'I know, Signora Assunta. That's why I have come to talk to you. Can he be moved, do you think? Are his leg and head wounds healing?'

She shrugged. 'In normal times, I would make him sleep and rest for a couple more weeks, but these are not normal times.'

'Maybe I could take him up on the mule,' I suggested. 'If we planned the route along the edge of the forest, there would always be somewhere to hide, if necessary.'

He shook his head. 'The Germans have a machine-gun station dug in just along that path where it forks. No good.'

Papà was sitting by the fire, making a new wooden sole for his work-boots. He said quietly, 'Sometimes the obvious is not what it always seems. Maybe we should try some kind of disguise.'

Chapter 11
Ines continues her story.
September 9th 1944

In the morning, a storm had turned the river outside the mill to the colour of milk and coffee. Huge branches were being swept down with the current, turning the river into a vicious, foaming flow and we had to shout above the roar of the water.
Papà held our mule as the *inglese* was helped onto the cart and into his make-shift bed. Mamma had killed a precious chicken and used its blood to soak rags to daub on our faces, to resemble sores. Charcoal from the fire was rubbed into our skin to complete our appearance, for we were to pretend we were *carbonari*. These were the charcoal burners who were a race unto themselves. They worked for weeks in the clearings in the forest, slowly burning their wood within mounds of heaped up branches covered in dirt. They camped out whilst they were working and fed on potatoes and whatever they could store for their time in the mountains. Nobody mixed with them but we knew of their presence because of the wisps of smoke that spiralled up through the trees. Occasionally one of them would break into song and a chorus of voices would rise into the mountain air: ghostly voices, like long-lost souls lamenting.

'Keep still, Ines. Stop your wriggling.' My mother smeared my face with a piece of blackened wood from the hearth. 'Open wide and I'll find you an evil-looking husband to match your ugliness.' She was trying to smile but she didn't want me to go. She blacked out my two front teeth and gave me her mirror to look at my reflection. 'If you are going to carry out this madness, I shall at least try my very best to make you look as ugly as old Befana on her broomstick in the sky.'

The *inglese* and I were dressed in vile-smelling clothes trampled on overnight by the cattle in the stable.

Capriolo was hovering about, watching my mother complete my disguise. 'Don't forget, Ines,' he said, 'if the German soldiers stop you, act stupid. Pretend you are a half-wit. If they ask you something, just act dumb. I have instructed the *inglese* to lie completely still and not to talk to you at all during the journey. There are tedeschi all over the mountains and he **must** stay down. Let's hope this foul weather keeps the bastards in their rat holes.'

When we were ready, Mamma and Papà embraced me. My mother started her wailing again. 'I don't want you to go, Ines,' she cried. 'It's too dangerous. I'll be praying for you every minute until you come back.'

Capriolo caught hold of my mother's arm, 'Assunta, I have told you we shall never be far away from them, we'll be shadowing from the woods. If it looks as if Ines is in any danger, then we will be there. And I shall use this.' He brought his rifle round from where it was slung over his back and at that my mother started to wail again. She drew out her rosary beads from her pocket. 'Take these, Ines and God and the angels protect you. I shall pray to the Madonna for your safe keeping.'

I pushed the rosary into the pocket of my tattered coat. Earlier Mamma had given me a cloth bag holding herbs for the inglese's wounds: dried elderberries for the inflammation round his leg wound, calendula for his fever. My mother's distress was infectious, making me want to stay at home round the mill hearth, safe with my family. But at the same time, I wanted to go. I wanted to be of use in the fight that was destroying so many lives. My heart was beating so loudly, I was sure everybody could hear. Capriolo sensed my hesitation. He pinched my cheek between his fingers, 'Don't worry, little Ines, it will go well. You are doing what you have to, like a brave communist. This is the best way to get the *inglese* away from here.' He slapped the mule's rump and we were away up the track.

The rain had stopped by the time we reached the ridge where the pines grew. Fat drops still splashed off the branches, trickling down my neck and onto the path. Here and there large snails emerged from their hiding-places, leaving silver trails. Capriolo had suggested that if I began to panic, I should distract my fear and think of ordinary things.

I couldn't talk to the inglese, so I talked to myself, inside my head: *Look at you, you wonderful snails. Nonna would love you for her sauces. Should I take some of you back for her? No. No point. Who knows how long it will be before I come back down the mountain. They wouldn't last, they would go bad. Ugh, great, big slimy things. Nonna loves you for the sauce she makes from you. She would drop you in a bucket of water, clean out your insides overnight and pop you in a pan of boiling water.*
Don't worry, snails. You are safe from me, I could never eat you. Ugh!

Further on I spied some porcini mushrooms growing in a coppice of holm oak and I started off another silly conversation in my head. *Mmm! I'll have you instead. Pull you up, shake off your spores so I can come back again and pick some more. Clean you with a cloth, slice you thin as thin can be and fry you in butter. Eat you with a plate of mamma's tagliatelle. Sell the rest at market in the town, buy a scarf for Sunday Mass to tie around my head.*

If I had been wiser, I would have talked these fantasies aloud to make my act as the village idiot even more convincing. Who knew what the *inglese* would think of me then? As it was, it helped calm me a little as we continued on our way; I urged the mule on with a thwack of my stick whenever he wanted to stop.

We approached the fork in the path. One route descended towards the river Marecchia. There was a small bridge here and it led back into the town of Badia Tedalda. Our route met up with yet another track that led down into the valley and the city of Sansepolcro. Many villagers had used this route to escape from the Germans when they carried out their *rastrellamenti*, clearing the hamlets for fighting. The Germans could only have found out about this route from Fascist informers, for it was not on any map. In the evenings, round the fire at the mill, I had listened to Capriolo and the others talking and my narrow world had stretched as I followed their discussions. He had mentioned the fortifications that the Germans were building from one coast to the other, turning our beautiful mountains into a big trap, with machine-gun pillboxes and camouflaged pits. And they were everywhere. Our country was like a huge cauldron of minestrone with many different flavours. Each mouthful was different: some you wanted to spit out, some you could swallow and some you were not sure about. That is what Capriolo had said as he explained the situation to us. We had Germans, Fascists, Communists, Muslims, Christians, Slavs, Croats and Slovenes all dotted about the place in our mountains.

And it was hard to know who we could trust.

The sun came out and the path steamed as it warmed up. I was perspiring and trickles of sweat ran down my face. I hoped it wouldn't wash away the sores and charcoal that Mamma had drawn on my face.

'Halt!' A young German soldier jumped onto the track. Another was crouched behind the rocks by a machine-gun. I hadn't noticed them as I day dreamed. 'Documenti!' he shouted.

My heart was pounding so much I thought it would burst through my rib-cage. I stared at him blankly as Capriolo had instructed and then I gave an idiotic, toothless smile, showing off my blackened teeth to their best advantage. He shouted again, waving his gun at me. 'Documenti, documenti!'

I reached in my pocket, wafting a wave of cow-shit stench towards him in the process. He covered his face and stepped back, glancing at my papers. I still had my Fascist Party documents that we had all been issued with. He spat on the ground and made some comment to the other soldier that met with laughter and walked round behind the mule to the cart. My knees were trembling. It was just as well my coat was long and covered my lower limbs.

The *inglese* groaned and I stepped towards the soldier, saying: *malato*[2], followed by, '*colera*'.

---

[2] Sick

That was what Capriolo had told me to say. I mimed vomiting and squatting down as if I were defecating. The German started to prod the sacking covering the *inglese* and I chose that moment to feign a violent coughing attack, making sure I spluttered over the soldier. He shoved me away and waved me on. The two young Germans roared with laughter, their words sounded hard and guttural.

It took all my self-control not to make the mule break into a trot to get as far away as quickly as we could.

'Above all, remain calm. Act stupid…think of other things than the situation you are in,' Capriolo's words of advice echoed in my head.

I tried to imagine a better time. A time without war and hunger and fear. A time when I could once again dress up on a Sunday and dance in the village square. But I couldn't. I was terrified.

We continued up the path for almost another hour. I was exhausted. My heart had stopped its furious beating but my head was aching by this time as I forced my feet to take one step after another. Just when I felt I would faint, there was a low whistle from within the trees and Capriolo suddenly appeared on the track in front of us, together with Paolo and Stefano. I hadn't seen these two for some time. I had thought they were dead. We'd lost so many of our friends. They looked like men now, not the young boys I remembered from our school-room.

Capriolo swept me into his arms and then just as quickly, dropped me. '*Porca miseria*[3], but you stink. Let's get you out of those rags and washed as soon as possible.' He laughed. 'No wonder they wouldn't touch you. You've done well, Ines. Congratulations! You are one of us now.'

The *'inglese'* climbed slowly off the cart. He limped over to me, looked into my eyes, kissed my hand, '*Grazie, signorina*!' he said. Then he collapsed.

---

[3] Italian swear word

Chapter 12
The last weeks of September 1944

I hadn't been able to go up to the camp for over two weeks. I couldn't sleep at night for thinking about the *inglese*. I whispered his name as I lay on my bed, with *nonna* snoring next to me. '*Norman*'. His name was hard to say. He'd told me it meant man from the north and really he was so different from the young men I knew round here, with his long legs and blond hair. His skin was brown from the mountain sun by now but it was milky white like a baby before and when we were looking after him in the first days, in the Mill, he had a moustache but Mamma shaved it off. She said his fair hairs would show anybody straightaway that he was not Italian. He looked younger without it. He'd told me he was nearly thirty. Our lessons in the camp were fun. His accent made me laugh but he was a quick learner – although sometimes he came out with blasphemous words that the men should not have taught him. Life down here was dull, so tedious in comparison with up at the camp.

How could I find an excuse to go up the mountain again? Mamma kept giving me jobs in the mill and they filled my days. I spent whole afternoon sweeping dust from the machinery, cleaning out hoppers for the grinding, setting traps for mice. We were extra busy because we had to prepare for harvest-time, at least for those few people who had any wheat to bring down to us for grinding. Papà said it would be a very lean harvest and that only a few old men had been able to work in the meadows. He kept moaning on and on about the crops left to rot last year when so many of the young men had fled to hide in the hills, to escape from being sent to work in Germany. And this year the Germans had taken much of the grain to feed their horses.

'Bloody war, bloody Germans, bloody Fascists', he swore as he chopped up the wood for our fire.

Mamma came rushing to find me as I was sweeping round the mill stones. 'Quick, the finance guards are coming down the road Ines. Go and tidy yourself, put on your new head scarf. Keep them busy.'

I hated oily sergeant Ezio, the worst of all the guards. I hated the way his eyes slid up and down my body, undressing me. It made me feel like one of the women who stood on the corners down in San Sepolcro, keeping themselves warm by their fires. Davide had told me they called them *'lucciole'* – what a pity to call them fireflies. These little insects suddenly arrived in June, sprinkling our hayfield at night with stars, but one I caught in a jam jar looked so ordinary in daylight - just a dirty little grub after all. Mamma warned me about Anna Maria up in Badia and called her a *lucciola*. She said she'd 'been' - (whatever that meant) - with a German soldier and that the women in the village were bound to punish her one day. They'd pin her down at the fountain where they did their washing and shave off her hair and then she would have to wear a headscarf for months until it grew again. I didn't want Ezio thinking I was like Anna Maria. I shuddered at the thought.

'Don't worry, Ines, I won't leave you alone with him for long, I'll come and help you out,' Mamma continued, 'Papà caught a trout in the river yesterday.

That will keep him happy and stop him poking his nose about.'

Mamma was worried too about the guards finding her hiding place in the woods. Strict rationing had been introduced, with severe penalties adding to all our other burdens. At the mill, we were meant to distribute 250 grams of grain per month per person. But Mamma knew many families and especially widows couldn't manage on this ration. Many households had extra mouths to feed with evacuees from the cities or young men avoiding conscription.

'Aldo', she'd said to my father one evening, as we sat eating our polenta supper, 'I can't sit by and see our friends starve because of these stupid rations.' He looked up, a mushroom from the woods speared through his fork. 'And what do you suppose we can do about it? The police are always hanging around when we distribute the stuff.'

'We'll hide it for them.'

'Hah!' he grunted scornfully. 'And where do you plan to do that? Up a tree?'

'No, **under** the trees.'

'Now I know the war has really got to you, woman. You're even crazier than your mother.'

Nonna was deaf, so she couldn't hear my father's insult.

'You could dig a hole in the woods over there for me.' Mamma gestured to the window overlooking the trees on the other side of the river.

'And fill it with flour!' Papà finished off her sentence. At that my mother flew into a temper and stood up at the table. I was waiting for the argument to follow. My mother is a fiery woman. When she has an idea in her head, nobody can shift her.

'Aldo – if **you** don't dig it, **I** will. And then you can sleep in the stable with the cows. Where are all your principles now? You're good at spouting them when you've got your drinking friends around you in the *osteria*, but here at home, you sound like a defeated coward.'

She reached angrily for the bottle of red wine to stop my father drinking any more.

'I will not be spoken to like this in my own home,' Papà shouted, "Stop your nonsense talk, woman.'

I tried to intervene.

'I'll help dig it, Papà. It's not such a bad idea.'

'Don't you start too. I'm surrounded by women here. Even the damn dog is a bitch.'

I ignored him and went over to stroke Mimi and cover her ears in case she was upset by Papà.

'We could line the hole with wood, so the flour doesn't spoil,' I suggested from where I was crouching, stroking Mimi.

'And leave it in sacks there at night,' my mother continued, 'and the people could collect it under cover of darkness, away from the mill.'

My father eventually grudgingly agreed to the plan. 'We must all be careful, for if we are caught…' He dragged his hand in a cutting gesture across his throat.

And so for two months we had been leaving flour in the woods and Papà had begun to think Ezio was growing suspicious. He had seen him loitering on the other side of the river too often. Maybe somebody up in the village had opened his mouth in the *osteria*. We had to be so careful. Dreadful things were happening all the time to people we knew. Papà had told us of the latest victims of the Germans – Gino and Tommasina, an elderly couple in their seventies who were shot because they hid a wounded partisan in their pig sty. The partisan was their nephew.

'You're looking very pretty today, Ines.' Ezio leant against the side of the stone wall of the mill pond, twiddling his moustaches, his uniform too tight on his fat body. He smelt strongly of olive oil. He'd smeared it on his head in an attempt to smooth his few thin hairs over his bald patch. I wanted to giggle for he looked like a pig ready for the spit. I cast down my eyes demurely, hoping the laughter in my eyes wouldn't betray me.

'Are you coming to the dance on Sunday afternoon? The Party is putting on a special celebration. There will be music and the Germans are providing food. A pretty girl like you shouldn't be hiding herself away from the world down here. The Germans want a bit of company and so do I.'

If only he knew, I thought to myself. If only he knew about my escapes up the mountain, about the company I kept with his enemy. Little did this fat, oily pig know!

'You know my parents wouldn't let me,' I mumbled, 'it wouldn't be right. Davide is away and I wouldn't be allowed to come alone.'

'Leave it with me. I shall talk to your parents.' He pushed himself away from the wall towards me and I stepped back, increasing the distance between us. I couldn't step back any further – I would have fallen in the river. His unwashed greasy smell was strong in my nostrils as Mamma timed her appearance perfectly at the top of the steps. A second later and I would have slapped him but it did not do to anger the police and especially vile Ezio.

'I have something for you, Ezio.' Mamma handed him a trout wrapped in wet sacking. 'Give it to your mother to cook for you tonight. It's freshly caught today.'

He had the grace at least to bow slightly to my mother. 'I want your permission to dance with Ines at the festa on Sunday.' he said. 'There will be a celebration for the arrival of the new German platoon in Badia. We are expecting as many people to turn out as possible.'

I was standing behind Ezio and I gave my mother a pleading look.

'I'm not sure we can spare her,' she said, 'there are so many jobs to be completed and with so few hands to help...' She shrugged, a defeated look on her face.

'We have already noted your husband's absence from the Party meetings lately, Signora,' he said menacingly. 'You would all be wise to show your faces more often. A good start would be to come to the festa.'

'I will speak to my husband,' my mother replied, 'but if Ines goes, we will of course go with her.'

Over our supper of bread and beans we talked and talked about what we should do for the best.

'Please don't make me go,' I pleaded. 'If Ezio so much as lays a finger on me, I swear I shall scream and make a spectacle.'

Mamma backed me up. 'If Ines kicks up a fuss and refuses to dance with him, then it will make life even more difficult for us. At the moment we can give the guards fish and distract them but it wouldn't take much to make them turn nasty.'

Papà agreed. 'I will not let any Fascist walk out with any daughter of mine.'

There was silence in the kitchen, save for the occasional crackle from a burning twig and *nonna's* sighs as she sat crocheting near the hearth. At length Papà sighed too, 'there's nothing for it. Ines will have to go up to the mountain again for a while. We'll explain to Ezio that she has gone to stay with your sister in Pennabilli. We'll say she's ill and that Ines has to go and look after her zia Elda.'

'What a good idea, Aldo. Bravo!' My mother rose from the table. 'Ines, help me get together some things for your stay. Davide will take care of you up there. You can take up some more herb and medicines for the men as well. And we have one spare Pecorino cheese left that you can give them too.'

'Give them the rest of the ham too, Assunta. We can manage without it. And you can take the dog to help guard you and send her back down after you arrive. She knows the way back and we need her down here to guard the animals.'

My parents wanted to avoid my having anything to do with Ezio and so did I. My honour was at stake but they didn't know of my growing feelings for Norman, although, in truth, even Norman didn't know. They were feelings that I kept inside my head and yearned about when I was in my bed at night. Of course I wasn't going to tell anybody about it, especially not my parents, otherwise I would have been forbidden to go up to the camp ever again. I was to leave at dawn the following morning and we worked into the night preparing a bundle of clothes for myself, medicines for the men and food. I was excited and anxious at the same time.

I had a feeling my life was never going to be the same again and as I embraced Mamma and Papà in the fresh September morning, I clung to them and covered their faces with kisses. My mother was crying again as she tied the belt round my filthy coat and checked no curls were escaping from my brother's cap which I'd pulled firmly down over my brow. My faithful disguise.

I avoided the route taken with Norman in the cart earlier in the month. Capriolo had once told me of an alternative route but warned me I still had to be very careful as the Germans were always changing their guard posts. They continued to dig new trenches all over the mountain, to house their machine guns.
The moon hung in the sky like a cold river pearl and leaves on the oak trees rustled like long skirts. The scent of dew-soaked pine needles was strong. A twig snapped somewhere in the woods and my heart hammered. Then the sound of galloping through the undergrowth nearly had me screaming with terror. I'd thought it was soldiers on horseback but I saw a dozen deer scamper deeper into the trees and my heartbeat slowed down. I was still an hour's trek away from the camp, feeling very alone, very afraid and I didn't honestly know what I would have done if even oily Ezio had appeared in front of me and offered to accompany me for the rest of the journey. To my shame, I would probably have said yes. Once again I used Capriolo's strategy, diverting myself from

descending into sheer panic by making pictures in my mind.

What if I made a life with Ezio - cooked for him, produces his children? I would probably live in the village, step across the square every morning to the grocer's store knowing I was being stared at by old crones behind shuttered windows. At the fountain where the women washed clothes, nobody would talk to me and all my school friends would despise me for having succumbed to his persuasions. But at least I would still be alive.

Then I pictured myself in the arms of Norman, living in a house far away over the mountains and sea. In a house like the ones I had seen in the couple of American movies flickered onto the screen erected in the piazza at festa time before the war. It would be a square house, with flowers at the windows and a veranda at the front with a swinging seat. I knew Norman wasn't American, he was English. But he spoke the same language and to my way of thinking, the houses were bound to be the same. I wondered if we would have children with blond curls. Or if they would have my dark looks? Would they be tall? What would it be like to sleep in Norman's arms night after night? What would it be like to lie with a man? Norman hadn't kissed me. No man had ever kissed me properly; Capriolo's childish, after school kisses didn't count. But I wanted to kiss Norman.

Then I wondered how I could ever have even thought of comparing Norman with loathsome Ezio.

At the base of the rock where I knew one of Capriolo's band would be on guard, I threw up a handful of stones. And I whistled the first line of the mountain song "Ciao, bella, ciao…" as he had instructed me. It was light now, the birds had started their morning greetings. I needn't have gone through the cloak and dagger sequence because Mimi started to bark excitedly. She must have sensed Davide was around and as luck had it, he had been on guard that night. His sleepy face appeared from above the rock, breaking into a grin when he recognised Mimi.

'Ines, what in the devil's name are the pair of you doing up here?' Then a worried look came over his face, 'What is it? Not Papà? Mamma?'

'No, don't worry. Just come down and get me, I'll explain later. And bring something to shut Mimi up. She'll be waking up the whole of Tuscany before too long.'

Davide was joined by Capriolo and another two men I'd never seen before. They led us through a passage concealed by creepers into the heart of the camp and tied Mimi to a tree, throwing her a bone and placing a bowl of water nearby. Davide helped me with my heavy bundles.

'Careful with that sack,' I said, 'there are some jars in there with Mamma's medicines and Papà sent you up the last of the prosciutto.'

Davide fetched me coffee and a hunk of bread and I told them about Ezio. 'He's getting worse. He hangs around too much and is always bothering us about not attending the Fascist meetings. And yesterday he asked me to the dance and I thought he was going to grab me but Mamma arrived just in time.'

Capriolo spat into the dust. 'He always was a little shit. Even at school he used to lift the girls' skirts in the playground. Well Ines, you will have to make yourself useful if you stay up here. We have a big project planned in the next few days. Davide is leaving tomorrow for Rimini with information needed for the next big assault.'

'Papà told us that Firenze was taken back from the Germans last month. Is that true?'

'Yes. And the British are heading this way. It will be Rimini next that falls. The way we are going, the war will be over before too long and we can return to normal life. We can settle down, reclaim our country, plant our crops again.'

'You're beginning to sound quite old and settled!' I teased him. I looked at my class mate, the boy who'd shared my childhood games. I pinched his cheek between my fingers and he grasped hold of my hand. 'Don't laugh at me, Ines. If you had seen even half of what we've seen, you would understand how sick we are of all this. We don't enjoy fighting, you know. It's not a game.' He looked into my eyes and I turned away, pulling my hand from his, puzzled at this young man I thought I knew so well.

'Where shall I sleep? I'll go and sort out my things.' I felt awkward in his company.

Something of his old sense of humour returned. 'Well, there is the double room with the view over the Apennines or the single with its own terrace and view of the German trenches but no bathroom I'm afraid.' He gestured to a sheltered part under the rocks, a small hollow in the stone face where the rain and sun wouldn't reach. I dumped my bundles and went to see if I could help in the kitchen area.

I didn't see Norman until later that evening. He, Tony and a couple of others had been away all that day and returned to the camp tired and hot. A month of mountain air had built him up. He looked stronger, more handsome and taller than I remembered, maybe because he wasn't limping like before. His hair had grown longer too and he had caught the sun, losing the sick, sallow look of weeks ago but there was still no way he could ever pass for an Italian. He smiled at me and I smiled back, my heart turning crazy somersaults.
'Have you learned that English tongue-twister yet, Ines?'
I made him laugh with my attempt at 'sixty six thick thistle sticks' and asked him to repeat an Italian one.

We all ate by the fire. It could only be lit at night, when darkness hid the smoke from anybody searching for signs of partisan presence in the mountains. We were camped too far away from any '*carbonari*', so couldn't use their fires as our cover. No flames or sparks would be seen in the night sky by anybody outside this camp as we were in a deep hollow. It was a kind of natural fortress.

Norman and I talked softly. My brother and Capriolo were further away, deep in discussion about the mission tomorrow.

'I've missed you, Ines. It's so good to see you again.' His Italian was much improved.

I explained why my parents had sent me up. 'I just hope Ezio believes them and doesn't take it into his head to check my whereabouts in Pennabilli. It's not that far away from Badia.'

'Maybe I should go looking for *him*.'

I put my hand on his arm. 'Don't be so foolish! You would be recognised straightaway as an Englishman. There is a high price offered for prisoners-of-war and there are enough starving people round here who would be pleased to claim the money.'

He caught hold of my hand, his fingers big and strong on mine. I felt myself blushing.

'Anyway,' I continued, reluctantly pulling my hand away, 'you will be gone soon. The English have won back Firenze, then it will be Rimini and then you will disappear back to Inghilterra. You will forget all about Ezio, all about me.'

I wanted to provoke him into denying this. I thought I knew what he felt about me but I wanted to hear it from his own lips and wished we were alone.

Capriolo's voice startled me. I jumped away from Norman, feeling guilty. 'Norman, I need to talk to you about what you found out today. Davide leaves camp early tomorrow. Come.' And to me, 'I think you should go and talk to your brother, wish him luck. He will be away for a while. And then, I think you should sleep. We need you up sharp tomorrow. This is not a holiday camp.'

I felt like answering 'Yes, Papà!' and then sticking out my tongue at him. But I didn't.

Davide was sitting by the fire and I sank down beside him. He was staring into the flames and hardly looked up at me. We sat for a while in silence. He looked so much younger than Norman and so Italian with his dark hair and skin burnt by a summer of living outside on the mountains. Eventually he turned to me and I thought I saw fear in his eyes.

'Ines, tomorrow I'm starting out for Rimini with Tony and the others. There's lots of fighting down there. We have information they need for the counter attack. If anything happens, I want you to take this to our parents.' He gave me a folded piece of paper.

'Don't give it to them unless anything happens to me. And Ines, promise me you'll look after them.'

I put my arms round him and held him tight. 'Don't talk soft, little brother. Everything will be fine.' But I dug deep into my overcoat pocket and pulled out Mamma's rosary beads she had given me when I brought Norman up the mountain. I wound them round my brother's hands. 'Take these. They've kept me safe and they'll keep you safe too.'

The next day was hot and sultry, the type of heavy weather that comes before a storm. The air had no breath, the mountains seemed to close in and suffocate the land. The camp was nearly empty. Capriolo and Davide had taken most of the men with them and we didn't know when they would be back. The journey usually took two hours by road but of course they would not be in a vehicle. They would be criss-crossing the hills on foot, making their way stealthily down into the valley, no doubt coming across Germans dug in their bunkers as they made their way down. I didn't want to think about it. The only people left in the camp were me, the old cook and a couple of lads recovering from wounds. They were pleased to have me there with Mamma's salves. One had been bitten by a viper and I used sunflower seeds to paste onto his swollen ankle and gave him wormwood for his fever. I did what I could for the other young lad, the butcher's son. I was more used to seeing him chop up meat, wrapping up parcels, whistling as he went about his work. But he lay there on his makeshift mattress of sacking, ashen-faced, with violent stomach cramps. I brewed him a drink from basil and boiled water and sat holding his hand until he dropped back to sleep. He was far too young to be fighting in a war and I didn't imagine he would see the war end.

    The other person in the camp that day was Norman.

Chapter 13
Ines continues her story. The last days of September, 1944

It was still hot. Even up here at over one thousand metres, where the snow fell deep in the winter months. The cicadas kept up their noise, their monotonous, insistent song, intensifying the heavy atmosphere. There was no breeze and the trees stood perfectly still, like sentinels guarding the cloggy air. The whole world dozed but my senses were wide awake. My eyes traced the bark along the tree-trunks – the crevasses, knots, ants marching in file through dried leaves and pine needles, wind purring through the feathers of a honey buzzard coiling in thermals high above me.

But most of all I was aware of Norman sitting opposite me, leaning against a boulder. My eyes followed the contours of his mouth, the cleft in his chin, his Adam's apple, hairs in the hollow at the base of his neck; the rising and falling of his chest as he breathed. I thought how fragile we were; how a sniper's bullet could still our breathing in the blinking of an eye; how fragile our time was together.

It didn't surprise me when he looked up and our eyes locked, my stare was so intent.

'Come for a walk, Ines.' He pulled me to my feet and we started down the mule track. It was cooler here under shadows cast by beech trees. The track was so narrow we bumped against one another. Each time my body brushed his was like a shock. I was a moth attracted to a candle flame, burning but compelled to return to the heat. We came to the pool where water for the camp was fetched and where we washed. There was nobody else about. We waded into the water together, my dress clinging to my thighs. Norman pulled me closer, looking into my eyes, his hand caressing my breasts through the thin material. 'You are so lovely,' he said. I pressed against him and then I kissed him. His lips were gentle at first and then I was surprised to feel his tongue inside my mouth. He groaned and his hands reached inside my dress, touching my breasts with the tips of his finger, tracing circles round my nipples which aroused wonderful, sinful sensations. He kissed my throat, pulling my dress buttons apart and sucked at my breast. Sliding my wet dress up my thighs, his fingers felt for the button on my knickers.

And then a pheasant calling in the wood cut the air with its raucous cry, brought me back to where we were and what we were doing. What if somebody was to walk round the path to fetch water and find us, half undressed, doing such things? I pushed him away: 'No Norman...not like this. I'm sorry, I shouldn't have let you.'

He seemed not to hear. He tried to kiss me again. I pushed at him harder, shouting, 'no!' He covered my mouth with his hand to stop my cries. Then he muttered under his breath and stepped away. 'I'm sorry. You're so lovely. You're driving me mad. I've spent too much time in the company of ugly men.'

I was embarrassed now and went behind a tree to tidy myself. The buttons on my dress had been pulled off their threads. I didn't have any spare in camp and wondered how I was going to mend it. Norman saw me fumbling and he took a safety pin from the waistband of his trousers. 'Here, use this,' he said.

'But how will you keep your trousers from falling down?'

He laughed. 'As long as you keep your distance, I shouldn't have any more trouble with my trousers.'

'Don't make fun of me, Norman.'

I felt confused, dirty, like Anna Maria who had gone with the German soldier. My mother had talked about her often enough, warning me not to be alone with a man but I wanted to be with Norman. I didn't want Norman to think I was easy but I'd liked him kissing and fondling me and now I wondered if that meant I was a *puttana*. Even though I had been brought up in the countryside and seen couplings between bulls and cows, rams and ewes, I was still innocent about what went on between a man and a woman. And I dare not ask anybody, not even my own mother. I would have died of shame.

Norman pulled me to him again and this time I held myself away. 'I've fallen in love with you,' he said, 'but I can wait until we are married if that is what you want.'

I couldn't believe he was talking of marriage.

'But we don't truly know each other,' I said, 'normally two people grow to know one another over many months, years even. They visit each other's families; the man has to ask permission from the father; they are never allowed to be alone like we have just been. I can't believe what you have just said to me, you are crazy.' I looked up at him in puzzlement but he was smiling down at me. He kissed the tip of my nose. 'You said normally, Ines. These are not normal times. But I will do what you want and ask your father.'

'And we mustn't be together like this up here. If Davide were to have caught us, he would have killed me and probably you as well.'

I had given Mamma's rosary beads to my brother but I wanted them back now. I wanted to find myself a quiet corner in the camp and pray to Our Lady for forgiveness, ask her to calm my wild, sinful feelings by reciting the Ave Marias I had been praying with Mamma since I was little. The way Norman had made me feel in the pool had frightened me and now I wished he was somewhere far away. But when I looked at him, the lovely, shameful feelings returned all over again and I wanted him to kiss me again. I was so muddled. Norman took my hands in his. 'So, will you marry me?' he asked, 'I haven't heard your answer. And you don't seem very happy about my proposal.'

That was how I became unofficially engaged. He found a piece of creeper tangled in the briars and wound it round my betrothal finger, promising me he would buy me a beautiful ring when the war was over, when we returned to England.

When I think back upon it now, I realise how naïve I was. Life changes forever when a girl marries but the changes that were to overtake my life were greater than I could ever have imagined.

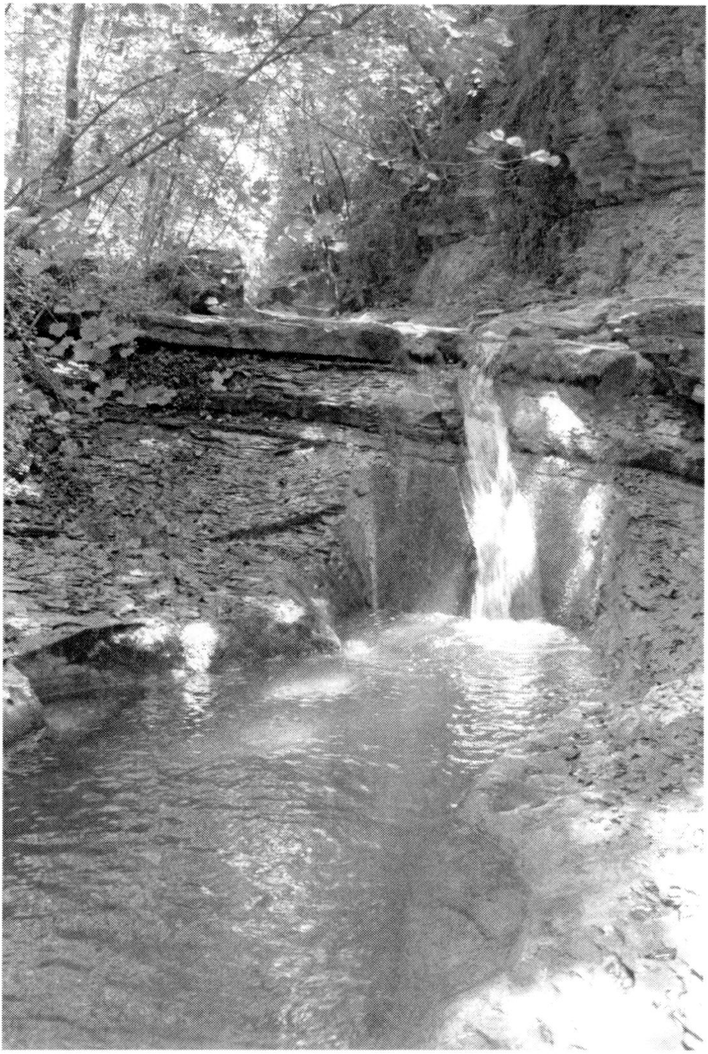

Chapter 14

Anna can't help thinking that her parents' love story is the stuff of old black and white movies shown on wet, winter afternoons on Channel 5. And yet she knows she is reading truth, not fiction. She has never been one to believe in falling in love at first sight. Cynical it might be, but she believes her mother was swept up in the excitement of a first crush, literally carried away by a romantic notion. But she was only eighteen; a country girl who had never travelled further than the town in the valley. The war and its hardships had been grinding along for four long years and Norman must have been a wonderful distraction for a girl of her age. At the same time, Anna can imagine her father being delighted and flattered by the attentions of this innocent, beautiful young girl.

And she had been *very* beautiful. When Anna visited her in the Care Home, she sometimes helped sort through a box of her old photographs. Her mother would peer at them and once again her Italian would take over as she described who was who. She would start in Italian and then the words would melt into dialect and Anna was lost. When she cleared out her mother's room, she had kept the box and brought the photos with her to Italy. Now, she roots through them until she finds what she is looking for. A photo of her parents as a young couple, her mother's flashing, mischievous eyes, her hair arranged round her face in shining sausage curls, as was the fashion in those days. Pencilled on the back is June 1945, just after the end of the war, but Norman is still wearing uniform. The pair of them are standing, arms linked, in front of the Town Hall and Anna now realises it is outside the old *Comune* in Badia Tedalda. A group of villagers are clustered round them. She wonders if any are still alive; there are a few scrawny children in the group, looking as if they need a good meal – which was most likely the case.

Francesco has inserted the remaining pages in her father's handwriting between her mother's notes. She is supposed to meet him later that afternoon but is so hooked by the latest twist in her parents' story that she calls to postpone their meeting.

'That's a pity,' Francesco says. 'Alba was really looking forward to being with you again. She's drawn you a picture.'

'Once I started reading your translation, I couldn't put it down. I promise I'll make up for it tomorrow. Tell Alba I'll take her for a long walk by the river after school to look for fossils and special stones. I'm sorry, Francesco. Catch up with you in the morning.'

'Tomorrow I have to be in Bologna for a faculty meeting but Alba will be waiting for you.' He hangs up on her abruptly before she has the chance to thank him for all the work he has done. Once again she is puzzled by his mood swings but she puts it down to him being the stereotypical Italian male who likes to have his own way and settles down to continue with her father's account.

September 6th 1944
Capriolo (C) asked me to go down to Rimini with him and Tony. He wants me to help with translating if we come across any other British POWs. I must say it will be jolly good to meet up with some Brits and have a chin wag. I've learnt a lot of the native lingo but it's tiring having to speak it all the time. Maybe it will be good to spend some time away from Ines too. She is one hell of a girl but I have to tread carefully from now on. Obvious as it sounds, she is not like the typical English girl, either stuck up, prim and proper or like Phyllis, a real goer.

I am going to get Ines into bed but all in good time. *Slowly slowly, catchy monkey.* At any rate I cannot afford to upset anybody in the camp. My life depends on them and they have been good to me, I have to admit.

Everything I ever heard about the Eyeties back in Blighty is tommyrot. They are generous people. All the chaps I have spoken to haven't a good word to say about Mussolini, saying he was the blighter who got them into this mess although some of them praise the pension scheme he devised for them, the draining of the Pontine marshes and other projects.

My leg is giving me less gyp and it's good to see some action again – albeit without uniform and proper equipment. Still, we did as well as we could. We dug in just outside Pontemessa that first night with a good view of the road snaking down to Rimini. There was a German position on the hillside just below us. With the bins, we made out the thin, snout-ended 88 mm gun of a tank sunk into a camouflaged pit. When the wind died down, we crept closer and could make out men's voices. There were women beating their washing against rocks in the river down in the valley. I think Jerry must have been distracted by the sight of the females for even when a partridge flew up from the spinney where we lay watching, the soldiers in the dug-out didn't turn. It was too easy, like a walk in the park. With a nod from C we broke cover and rushed forward as one, crouched low over the hillside, dry from the scorching sun, our feet sliding on chalky stones. We had been ordered not to open fire if at all possible and it wasn't necessary. There were only two of them, just boys with startled faces. I hadn't forgotten my training: a quick movement of the knife across their throats, a gurgle and then they were slumped forward. Gone! Jerry is capable of heavy reprisals: one German soldier killed means ten civilians killed in return. Bastards! But we couldn't dwell on that. Instead, I grabbed any weapon of use, rifled through their pockets for any possible information and then we were off.

C was pleased with the haul. In the past his men have captured guns or ammunition of no use whatsoever: He swore at Davide when he brought back small arms ammunition of the wrong calibre. On the same mission, Davide and the others returned with a new-fangled anti-tank weapon which nobody knew how to use. But that is the way of war: you win some, you lose some. This time we were successful.

September 10th

Davide is missing. I fear for the reckless boy at times. Last month he shot a German major on a motor-bike on the Rimini road and found important documents. Success went to his head. Admittedly, it was a brilliant "scoop" - the documents in the side-car contained plans for the eastern half of the Gothic Line defences. My school-boy German came into use because I realised their importance and C said immediately that the information should be taken to either Siena or over to Arezzo to the "Pro Borri" Garibaldi division of partisans. Davide was the first to volunteer. I think he felt the documents were his baby, so he wanted to deliver them. I hope pride doesn't come before a fall.

Apparently C knows a chap in Siena who is in contact with OSS and General Clark. I had not realised how influential our leader is. Nobody would ever suspect. He seems so ordinary, scrawny and young but looks deceive because he is also extremely agile and intelligent.

Davide has been away for over a week now and no word yet. Ines asked me if I knew his whereabouts. I fear the worst. It is one thing to know your own mountain area but, once out of one's patch, the terrain can be completely different and above all, it isn't easy to know whom to trust. There are still plenty of Fascist sympathisers around.

I hope I am proved wrong.

September 12th

We have had word about fighting round Rimini. There was a hard battle between the rivers Metauro and Foglia on around the 25th August at Coriano, not far from Rimini. There are many casualties. I grow increasingly frustrated knowing my fellow troops are so near and yet so bloody, tantalisingly far away. C says he wants me here but I must get back to my regiment. I feel I'm letting the side down staying here.

As we sat by the camp-fire last night, Tony told me the King had come to Arezzo in July – just two months ago for Pete's sake - offering support to the King's Dragoon Guards pitched up there. And all the while I was holed up a stone's throw away with my gammy leg. The old cook in camp who conjures up soups we have to swallow, also told him there were *'Inglesi'* up on the Viamaggio pass. I can't stay here knowing my own countrymen are only ten miles away. I leave tomorrow night. C did not kick up too much of a bally hoo when I told him I was leaving, after all. He said there were plenty of other escaped POWs knocking about the mountains and if he needed help with interpreting, he would call on them.

  The rain continues to fall in sheets. It's like standing under a waterfall. The ground turns quickly to sticky clay and clings to the soles of our shoes. I know the going will be difficult, it will take me longer than usual, but I am determined. I can't spend the rest of my war like this.

  C advised me not to say I am English if I should come across anybody on my walk up to the Viamaggio pass and to trust nobody. There are many Fascist sympathisers hiding in the hills in remote houses and barns, escaping from the bedlam of the towns. He told me to say I am a soldier from the Italian 4th Army trying to return to Trieste after having been disbanded in Toulon. I told him it would be a problem trying to explain how the devil I ended up so far south, if I had been travelling from France! But he shrugged his shoulders, in that typical Italian way, a long, drawn out gesture, accompanied by a throwing of the hands in the air, as if to say, 'You are mad not to heed my advice! Take it or leave it!' He said with my fair hair and complexion I could easily pass for a northern Italian and that the soldiers of the 4th Army have a reputation for being crazy anyway. (I took that as a compliment). There are several of them in the hills helping the Partisans already.

I have decided to take my chances and use his knowledge and travel by night. In this way I should not have to do any explaining to anybody. My Italian is still poor - Ines always laughs at the way I sound so I prefer the idea of not having to talk at all.

I'm not sure how she will react to me leaving. I'm torn between a quick marriage or whether to cut my losses and say farewell. There are plenty more fish…but she is a sweet girl and it might be interesting to make a life with her back in Blighty. I would love to see the old folks' faces if I were to turn up with her on my arm. That would put a stop to their whingeing about the unsuitability of Phyllis.

Chapter 15

Anna is appalled.

How did Mamma react when she came across these cold, calculating words written all those years ago?

Even as a little girl, she knew her parents weren't happy together - that much was obvious from their noisy arguments and frosty silences. The nightmares she suffers even to this day started from then, when she would wake up to her father's temper as he shouted at Ines in the kitchen beneath Anna's bedroom. She would try to block out the sound by hiding her head under the covers, only to wake up later, hot and sticky in the night, her pillow suffocating her. She sits for a while, staring through the window at the darkening mountains, listening to the twilight bird song. It is peaceful, sweet and she wishes she could pick up the phone and talk to her mother.

She should be hungry - it is nearly dinner time - but she isn't. Instead she slips downstairs to fetch a glass of chilled Grechetto from the fridge to take back upstairs. Francesco has managed to translate another two sections of her mother's "scribblings". For that is how Mamma has described the story of her life.

Early October 1944

Mamma and Papà sent word for me to come back down from the camp. Davide was missing and they wanted me near them while we waited for news. And I was pleased to be back in my own home. The last few weeks on the mountain had been intense. I wanted to be near Norman and at the same time I was scared to be near him. Surely my mother had an inkling that something had happened to me for I felt as though she could see into my mind, could picture me with Norman at the pool. She was constantly short-tempered, 'I knew we shouldn't have sent you up there. Just look at the state of you – all thin and wasted. You can't do anything properly at the minute either, Ines! What have you done to this polenta? I shall have to throw it to the hens! What a wicked waste.'

If Mamma had slapped me at that moment I would not have been surprised, even though I had never seen her raise a hand to anybody. My father used to, but never my mother. She was right to chide me. Sitting by the hearth, I'd been stirring and stirring, not noticing the polenta in the cauldron hanging over the flames had caught. My mother smelled the scorched odour but I'd been daydreaming - wondering what Norman was doing up in camp, wondering when Davide would return; wondering what would happen between Norman and me in the future. He hadn't yet talked to Papà and I wondered if he ever would. At night I cried myself to sleep, wishing I had given myself to him. Maybe by now we would have been officially betrothed and I wouldn't feel so unsettled. This business of love was so mysterious.

Those were days of watery sunshine. On the following morning the sky was leaden and the trees drooped with rain sodden foliage. I needed to be outside and I called to Mamma that I was going to look for mushrooms in the meadow and wouldn't be long. The ground was muddy and my boots were soon clogged underfoot with sticky clumps of clay. Early morning mist was pinned in the fir trees on the lower slopes of the mountain, like a shawl round a woman's shoulders. I made my way up the path, never intending to go as far as the camp but I felt a need to be nearer Norman. Half way up, I stopped to sit on a rock. The valley below was still shrouded in mist. Nothing in my life seemed clear anymore and there was so much unhappiness around.

Tears trickled down my cheeks as I thought of what my father had told us last night at our fireside. Another school companion of mine, Silvestro, had simply been minding the pigs but the Germans were convinced he was a partisan and that he was pretending to be a swineherd. He was only a boy, fifteen years old. He knew even less about life than I did. The soldiers beat him up. They beat him with their rifle butts until his face was unrecognisable - the sweet face of a boy who hadn't even started to shave. There had been blood everywhere and they had thrown him to the pigs to finish him off. But next morning when the cowards returned, he was still alive. The pigs hadn't touched him. Papà said that spoke volumes - that animals were less savage than men. Then the *tedeschi* made the poor boy crawl on his hands and knees while they kicked and spat on him forcing him to dig his own grave. And then they shot him.

I wanted this craziness to end. In the past, Papà had rebuked Davide for talking about these acts of slaughter, but now even he dropped these brutal stories into conversation, as if they were routine. I wanted to run far away and start my life afresh.

Suddenly the mist lifted, as if a giant had puffed up his cheeks and given an almighty blow and then I realised I had to hurry home. It wasn't safe to perch on a rock, thinking. The *tedeschi* might spy me through their binoculars and wonder what a girl on her own was doing on the mountainside without cattle or sheep to tend. I ran home down the path and only when I reached the steps to the Mill did I remember I hadn't searched for a single mushroom. Now there would be even more reason for my mother to nag me. From the kitchen, I could hear people talking and I wondered who could be calling at such an early hour.

Norman and Capriolo were sitting at the kitchen table with my father. My heart missed a beat and I felt a deep blush starting in my cheeks. Turning round to cover my confusion I knocked a glass over with the corner of my shawl. As I stooped to pick up the pieces, my mother, busy at the hearth making *piadine,* shouted at me to be careful not to cut myself. An open bottle of Vinsanto sat on the table. 'Have you found Davide?' I blurted, thinking this the cause of their celebration.

Norman rose from the table, offering me his chair. 'That's not why we are here, Ines. I promised you I would talk to your father and here I am.'

Mamma came over to stand behind Papà, who looked at me very seriously and asked, 'is it true you love the Englishman?'

I nodded shyly and Norman smiled encouragement, 'I have asked your father's permission for your hand.'

Then Capriolo interrupted, 'But Norman is leaving today. You must think very carefully. Now is not the time to be making plans like this.'

I was angry with him for interfering. 'What has it to do with you? What do you mean by "plans like this"? We love each other. That's all that matters.'

Norman took my hand. 'He is right to make you think, Ines. I *am* leaving today and whilst I'm away, you will have time to think again about us.'

'But where are you going? Why didn't you tell me before? I don't understand why you are leaving now. It's far too dangerous.'

My father interrupted my outburst, 'Capriolo is right. It is wiser to wait. If signor Norman returns and you both still feel the same way, then I shall give my blessing. I've seen he is a brave man. It would be an honour to have an *inglese* as a son-in-law. But you are very young, Ines, and time will tell you what to do for the best.'

'May I take Ines for a walk?' Norman asked my father.

Papà made Capriolo chaperone us. That was the way it always was in those days. Once we were outside, Capriolo told us he would give us some time alone. He spoke to me in dialect so Norman wouldn't understand and I thought him very discourteous, but I was too excited to say anything. 'Be sure you know what you are doing, girl,' he muttered and then he added something which I did not understand at the time, 'the grass is not always greener, you know.' He sat down on the stone bench near my parents' vegetable garden and waved us away, telling us to be five minutes at the very most.

I can't remember everything Norman said to me that morning. I just remember feeling overwhelmed. On the one hand I was happy he wanted to marry me, on the other I was distraught that he was leaving. I was angry too with Capriolo for not seeming to approve of our engagement and I could not understand why, if Norman loved me so much, he could think of going away. He explained he was going to try and join up with British soldiers on the Viamaggio Pass and he said he would come back when he could and in the meantime he asked me to wait for him. 'If it weren't for the war, Ines, I could buy you a proper ring. I could put it on your finger and you would be my '*fidanzata*'.'

'If it weren't for the war, we wouldn't have met,' I replied.

'I'll come back and if you still want me, we'll marry.'

'Do you think I am so fickle that I would change my mind? Let me come with you? I could show you the way - you have no idea of the correct paths over the pass. I'm frightened I'll never see you again.'

He kissed away my tears and gave me a rag he'd been using as a handkerchief. I kept it inside my blouse from that moment on; never washing it, keeping it near me at night and sobbing into it when I thought of how I might never see him again. That was the kind of childish notion I had. I was as green as unripe barley.

After a while, Capriolo coughed and I untangled myself from Norman's arms. We returned to the kitchen and Papà handed us all a glass of Vinsanto, toasting us and wishing Norman a safe return. Then Capriolo and Norman left and I did not to see my English *fidanzato* again for more than seven months - until the end of the war, in May 1945.

Chapter 16
Late November 1944

It rained and rained and rained that autumn. It was as if the Gods were crying their despair over man's stupidity. Capriolo told us the war would have been over long before the end of 1944 if it had not been for the rain. Soldiers of both sides were holed up in the mountains, like rats in drains and even the tanks could not operate properly, slithering and sliding down the mountain. No progress was made by either side. Mud and cold added to everybody's misery. Crops were ruined and work at the mill stopped. The river was fuller than we had ever remembered and rushed past the mill like an angry beast. We had to shout to make ourselves heard above the roar of the water.

Then one day in late November, the land warmed up in unexpected sunshine, causing fantastical mists. Montebotolino floated on clouds, its roofs ghostly cut-outs against the sky.

'It will hold tomorrow,' said Papà, who could read the weather perfectly. 'We will start grinding at dawn.'

In the early morning, he lifted the planks to the mill-race and I watched the water gurgle and rush with a whoosh down the channel at the side of the meadow. I ran inside to the room next to the chamber where the mill-stones were already turning.

'Help me load the meal into the hoppers.' My mother was forced to shout to be heard above the storm of water below us and the grating of huge stones grinding on stone. Beneath us water funnelled through two narrow channels, revolving the paddles which turned the stones. 'These sacks over here are full of maize. We'll do these first and then the corn.'

There was much less work for us at this stage of the war. The *tedeschi* had been quick to take hay for their horses and much of the grain had been left to rot in the fields.

'Mamma,' I yelled above the clatter, 'one of the stones isn't grinding properly. I'll go and tell Papà.'

It was a nuisance when this happened. Sometimes a block of wood or a tussle of brambles would clog the paddles.

'Let's hope it's another baby boar like last time,' my mother shouted. 'We could do with some meat in the larder.'

I ran to tell Papà who was unloading sacks from a customer's donkey. He shouted at me over the noise of the water. 'Go below and see what is happening.' I sped down the slope at the side of the mill to the archway where the water should have been gushing out, turning the paddles on the shaft which drove the mill stones. It reminded me of games I used to play with Davide when he used to snatch my headscarf from my head and toss it into the mill-race. 'Run, run Ines - before it's too late,' he'd shout, laughing at my dismay. Off I scampered, as fast as my little legs could carry me, trying to retrieve my scarf before it was swallowed up by the paddles under the mill. Once, I'd tripped before I could catch it and Mamma had scolded me for being careless and losing my only scarf. She made me wear a rag on my head until she had time to sew me another one.

'The water's not flowing properly from the funnel on the left, Papà,' I shouted. He fetched his long pole from the store-room and stood on the wall of the mill-pond, prodding the mud. 'There's something stuck fast in one of the funnels,' he shouted, 'I can't move it. There's nothing for it - we'll have to drain the pond.' He swore. This extra work meant losing a whole day's grinding. I hated it too when we had to drain the pond because of the stinking, rancid water and the way the smell lingered in the mill for days afterwards.

Slowly the water drained away through the funnel on the right and we stood together on the mill steps, waiting to see the cause of the blockage.
Even before Papà jumped down into the sticky mud and turned the body over, I knew it was him. Davide's poor face was unrecognisable. Fish had nibbled away at his eyes and the hollows stared blindly up at us. Mamma screamed and howled like a dog in agony - a sound I shall never forget. Papà had to pull her away from Davide's body as she keened over and over again, 'My son, my only son! What have they done to you?'

News spreads fast among us mountain people and friends and neighbours started to appear down the mill track offering condolences. There was help too. Davide's body was lifted gently out of the mud and kind souls washed his body, arranging him on our kitchen table, as was the custom. The men helped fill the mill pond again and finished the jobs that we had set out to do that day. I cannot recall exactly who came that afternoon. Those hours were a blur of misery, with my poor parents inconsolable. I felt numb, unable to cry. Later on, when our little family was alone again, I helped my mother lay his body out. We covered the bullet hole which had taken away half of the back of his head with one of Papà's caps and we dressed him for burial in his Sunday suit. 'I shan't need it anymore,' Papà said, 'I shan't be going to Mass again.' We removed his river-soiled trousers and in the pocket I found the rosary beads I'd pressed into his hands to keep him safe. I flung them on the fire. Then I fetched the letter he had given me before he left from the trunk at the foot of my bed.

'Read it to me, Ines.' Mamma whispered.

We sat in the dark and I leant into the dying glow of the fire to read his words. His letter had been written in neat script on a page torn from his old school book.

My dear parents,

I am sorry I will not see you again.

I am sorry I will not be there to help you with the grinding.

I am sorry I will not bring grandchildren to your fireside.

But I am not sorry that I die for the freedom of Italy.

Your loving son, Davide.

Chapter 17
November 1944

Capriolo found me in the cemetery. I had picked a
bunch of white Vitalba seed-heads for Davide's grave.
It was all I could find in the November landscape.
With my brother's old jacket round my shoulders, I sat

listening to the wind moaning through the coppice of firs planted along the cemetery walls. I stared at the photo of him we had found to place on his stone, wanting to talk to him, but I couldn't equate the handsome, cheeky young face beaming at me from his picture, with the rotting corpse half buried in mud at the bottom of our mill pond.

The cemetery gate was rusty and it creaked as Capriolo let himself in. He sat beside me on the ground. Neither of us said anything for a while and I was pleased he didn't try to fill the silence with empty words. Eventually he took my hand and then, the tears that I had held back in front of my parents spilled down.

'He was a brave young man, Ines.' He spoke softly. 'You must remember him with pride. Before he died, he saved many lives by carrying important information to Siena.

Wiping the tears angrily from my cheeks, I withdrew my hand from his. 'Does it really matter?' I said dully, 'Does any of this stupid, stupid war matter? I can't bear it. I can't bear all this pain and hatred. And I can't bear to be here anymore.'

'Yes, there's hatred and there's certainly pain. But there's good too. You have to remember why we're fighting.'

'I've forgotten why. It all seems pointless.'

'Then Davide's death will have been pointless too.'

'He was too young to die.'

'Then we will remember him always young.' He put his finger under my chin, lifted my face, wiping a tear away. 'Come on, Ines. *Su*! Talk about him. Talk to me about your brother. Don Luca performed his funeral Mass, but we shall perform our own service for him up here where he loved to be.' He gestured to the mountains behind us. 'You start. Tell me the first thing that comes into your mind.'

I looked at him, frowning, thinking his idea was a little crazy but then the pictures came to me. I started, hesitant at first. 'I remember when the three of us were in trouble with Don Luca.'

Capriolo took up the story, 'We were conducting our own flying experiment after school.'

'We'd been learning about Leonardo da Vinci and his marvellous inventions and Professor Gerico had shown us a huge book with pictures of his flying machines, wheels and other contraptions. The three of us spent ages trying to design our own aeroplane.'

'Dio mio! I remember tying home-made wings round your arms and making you stand on the edge of the ridge behind the church in Rofelle.'

'We'd collected feathers for weeks from Carlo's chicken run to make them and we'd made Davide sneak in under the wire because he was the smallest. I was so scared, you know. As I stood there on the edge of the meadow, staring down at the river and rocks below, with those ridiculous wings on me which I knew would never work, I thought I would wet my drawers.'

'Thank God Don Luca turned up when he did. He was furious! I can remember his words like yesterday - *What in the name of Jesus, Mary, Joseph and all the holy saints are you three doing out here?*

'Davide ran off and hid behind the church but you and I had to spend the rest of the afternoon polishing candle sticks in the sacristy.'

Then we were laughing. In between our laughter, Capriolo said, 'he had an appalling sense of humour too, your brother. He always laughed at his own jokes and they were crap.'

'And when he laughed,' I continued, 'he would throw back his head and open wide his mouth, roll about the floor sometimes. It was infectious. *Nonna* actually did wet herself once. She laughed so much watching *him* laugh, she couldn't help herself.' We smiled at each other and then I said, 'Now you tell me something else about him.'

His head down, he thought for a moment, then he began, his voice barely audible. 'He was the younger brother I never had. I used to think he was a pain, always tagging along, asking annoying questions about how to shave, how to make smoke rings. And then later…' he looked at me when he said this, pausing – 'questions about what women liked…but after a while, age didn't matter. War is a leveller, if nothing else.'

There was silence for a few seconds. Maybe Capriolo was considering whether to share a detail with me. We had spent so many hours of childhood together, he and I – sometimes I felt I knew what he was thinking. He had taken his cap off and his hair flopped down over his face as his fingers plucked at tufts of grass at the edge of the grave. Eventually he looked up, pushed his hair back from his face. I saw the sadness in his eyes 'He was very brave. Back in August, we were fighting side by side. It was blazing hot. We were down near Coriano, on the road to Bologna, sheltering in a bombed out farm. Davide needed a smoke. I remember him saying he'd give anything right then to jump in the sea, that he'd never been down to the coast and he'd made himself a promise to go down to Rimini when the war was over. He'd take the mill-cart, he said, and spend a day down there with you and your folks. We talked about all kinds of things that afternoon - our plans, our dreams. My guard was down, I suppose. We left the farm house and the next thing I knew I was in the dirt, Davide on top of me, the rat-a-tat-tat of tracer bullets from a *tedeschi* machine-gun bouncing dust up all around us. Then, in the split seconds while the machine gun crew were blinded by their own fire, he hauled me to my feet and we were up, stumbling away and into another doorway. He saved my life that day, covering me with his own body without thinking of his own safety.'

Both of us fell quiet then and I saw the tears on his face. 'His death wasn't pointless, Ines. You must never think that.'

The November air was chilly. I shivered and he started to take off his scarf. He would have wound it round my neck but I stopped him. 'I have to get back,'

I said, 'Mamma is in a state at the moment so I have to cook supper and take care of all the household chores. All she does is sit in her chair by the fire. She doesn't even light it. That's my job now too.'

'Before you go…' He took hold of my arm. I wondered what he was going to do. He moved closer, Davide asked me to look out for you, to check on you and the *inglese*.'

'You mean Norman? He *does* have a name you know.' I moved away from him so we were no longer touching.

'It was something you said earlier,' he persisted, 'you said you couldn't bear to be here anymore. Is that why you are marrying him? So you can escape all this? Your memories will chase you wherever you go, you know.' He had raised his voice when he said this, but I was angry too and I shouted back. 'What are you talking about? I am marrying him because I **love** him.'

'And how will your parents manage now that Davide lies here?' He pointed at the freshly dug grave. 'Don't you think you should be staying with them? I didn't expect you to go to Inghilterra with him after this. I thought I knew you better.'

'You don't know me at all. Just because we've lived near each other all our lives and gone to school together, it doesn't mean to say you know me and what goes on inside my head, inside my heart. And anyway what do you know about love?' I was in full flow by then, anger and guilt making potent ammunition. 'You're just in love with the war and your beloved Communist ideals. That's all you know about. You don't know the first thing about love.' I was crying noisily; great sobs welling up from deep within me.

He didn't attempt to console me. He pulled his cap firmly down upon his head and left the cemetery.

I listened to the gate clang against its metal post, the harsh sound echoing into the soughing of the pines and the sound of his feet trudging down the path back to the village.

Chapter 18
Early June 1999

The ringing of Anna's mobile drags her back to the present. '*Pronto!* Francesco here. How are you?'

'Fine.'

'You don't sound too sure.'

'I've been immersed in 1944. I feel I've been reading a novel and I need the next instalment'. She adds a 'please' and Francesco laughs. 'I'll see what I can do. I may be able to translate more later on today. But back to 1999 - are you free tomorrow afternoon to come out with us? Remember I told you about Pennabilli and The Festa of the Street Musicians?'

'That place rings a bell – wasn't it where Mamma was supposed to be staying, looking after her sick aunty instead of being in the camp! I'd love to come along and see what it's like.'

'It will be an introduction to the locations you're reading about.'

'Great! And what about the mill where my mother lived?'

'From what I've heard, it's a ruin. But I'll see what I can find out. Oh, and bring something warm for when it's dark and the temperature falls.'

They take the road down towards Rimini, Alba sitting in the back, hunched in the corner, staring out of the window, ignoring Anna, who gives up trying to include her in the conversation. And anyway, turning to speak to her is making Anna car-sick on the hairpin bends. Francesco knows the road well and she feels safe, despite the steep drops. The road winds down one side of the mountain range with the river Marecchia below. Rocky, impenetrable, forested slopes snake up from the river valley. Every now and again they pass a cluster of ruined houses perched impossibly on crags high above.

'Do you realise how beautiful all this is?' Anna says, 'and how lucky you are to live here? Or do you take it all for granted?' She compares it with the view from her train window on her commute in London; how she used to gaze into gardens backing the tracks. A few neat, with vegetable patches or patios; most unkempt, dumping grounds. She'd count the many abandoned supermarket trolleys in the back yards and try to imagine what kind of people lived in each house.

Francesco shrugs his shoulders, 'I suppose we are used to it. Most of these hamlets in the mountains are uninhabited now, with maybe a few houses used by weekenders.' He points to a building on a ridge above the valley, towering above the countryside like a lone guard. 'See the crane up there? That farm house is being restored for an English family.'

'I can't begin to imagine how they built those houses in the past or how they worked such steep land.'

'They didn't have any choice. If you could have seen this countryside thirty, forty years ago, there were far fewer trees everywhere. People needed every bit of land they could use for cultivation to grow food for their families. It was a hand-to-mouth existence. Many found it too hard and after the war there was no work round here. Italy was on her knees. Some peasants went north to work in factories in Torino. Others went abroad, many to France. But their houses remained in the family…like that house with the steep outside staircase in our village. That belongs to another aunt of ours who speaks French just as well as she speaks Italian. She returns every August to live in it just for a month. That same story is repeated all over Italy. Roots are very important to us, we need to return to them and we tend to say 'I am Florentine' or 'I am Roman'. We rarely say 'I'm Italian'.

'I've noticed that. But it makes it all the more strange to me that I know so little about my mother's roots.'

'Maybe you will find out why, Anna.'

They continue their journey in silence and as she enjoys the spectacular mountain scenery, she thinks about her parents, imagining they too might have used this same road in the past, wondering where they might have been going and why. She thinks about the passage of time – how short a lifetime is in the scheme of things. As they pass another rocky outcrop, she cranes her neck to look up at it, picturing a soldier dug in, waiting to take a shot at the enemy and she murmurs, 'What a terrain to have to contend with!'

'What did you say?' Francesco asks, changing down gear to negotiate a sharp bend.

'I was thinking about what my father had written about fighting in the hills and I was trying to imagine having to do battle on these slopes.'

'The Germans used these mountains to form a line of defence. It was known as the Gothic Line.'

'My mother wrote about that too!'

I'll give you a potted history now, Anna! The Apennines form a spine along our peninsula and they used the mountains as one part of a barrier. Then, in the plains on the East and West coasts, near Rimini and Pisa they added their man-made barriers.'

'You know a lot about it!'

'But of course! It's Italian history and, don't forget, my father was a partisan too.

'What was his name?'

'Dario.'

'Were you close?'

'Very. But he didn't talk about the war very often, just one or two stories. For example, how they sabotaged the concrete the Germans ordered for their pill boxes. They made it so it wouldn't set. But there were repercussions. There were some who thought the partisans caused more harm than good when the Germans went on to punish ordinary citizens - but we won't go into that now.' He gestures discreetly to the back seat where Alba is staring out of the window.

'It's so sad to be discovering about my mother's past life now she's no longer alive. There are hundreds of questions I would have liked to ask her. In England we know a lot about the French Resistance but you don't hear much about what went on in Italy.' She sighs, deciding she is in danger of becoming obsessed. 'Let's change the subject and have a break from the war.'

'Okay! *Va bene!* We're nearly there anyway.'

They turn right off the Rimini road and after a short drive up a narrow lane they enter a town after a sign announcing: *Pennabilli – Città amica degli artisti* [A city that welcomes artists]. As soon as the car stops, Alba clambers out, jumping up and down in excitement. 'This is one of her favourite places.' Francesco explains. 'You'll see why.'

After paying 5,000 lire entrance fee to a barefoot youth with dreadlocks, sitting cross-legged on a table blocking the alleyway, they stroll up a cobbled street closed to traffic. To Anna the place seems at first another typical picturesque mediaeval town, one of so many to be found in Italy. Alba pulls her father up a narrow lane and they climb to an area at the top. In the walled gardens of a ruined house, unusual carved stone statues bearing inscriptions have been arranged to form 'a sanctuary of thoughts'. Francesco helps Anna decipher messages written for travellers bound for eastern shores. As they make their way back to the main square, he points out colourful sun dials painted on the facades of certain buildings.

'This is Alba's favourite,' he says, resting his hand on his daughter's head. She has stopped beneath a bright blue and yellow image of a duck floating on choppy waters and she leans up to trace the outlines with her finger.

'She used to call this her picture story place. When Silvana was alive, we often came here as a family. I thought she would find it upsetting to return, but she never does.'

Anna watches Alba skip towards the next sun dial. Onlookers would never detect her problems; she seems like any ordinary little girl of her age. 'I think she's a very artistic child, Anna says. 'I love her paintings. She has talent and probably feels at home here amongst the art. Perhaps you shouldn't analyse so much. Maybe it's simply a place she loves, a place of happy memories.'

'You're probably right. But if she would only talk, then maybe I'd stop trying to analyse. It's so hard.'

He looks sad, she feels like squeezing his hand, hugging him. But she knows Alba would be jealous, so she says and does nothing. They walk back down to the square, packed now. He explains how two years previously a young man started up a festival for buskers and invited performers from as far away as South America to attend. As word spreads, it is growing in popularity. They stop to listen to a group of Mongolian throat singers and their melancholy tunes. Alba crouches down near the only woman in the group. Her fingers coax plaintive chords from a zither and she's dressed in an elaborate beaded costume, long, black plaits hanging below her bonnet. It is a completely un-Italian music but the sound drifts round the square and lingers perfectly with the atmosphere. After a while they move on to the source of jazzier music coming from a turret on the old walls. A group of English musicians, led by a diminutive girl-saxophonist, has everybody tapping their feet and a few couples jigging to the cheeky lyrics. Alba persuades Francesco to dance and Anna watches him bend his dark head down to hers and scoop her into his arms, whirling her round and round until she squeals.

'After all that, I need to sit for a while,' he laughs as he sets her down, watching her regaining her balance from their dizzy dance. 'Let's go and sit quietly in the amphitheatre. I'll fetch us all a drink and we'll watch the mime artists.'

They find front row seats. It's beginning to grow dark and the town is filling up with people coming from work, looking forward to an evening of unusual entertainment. The two young mime artists on stage are talented. They juggle with coloured balls, pretending to be inept at first, dropping them into the audience which serves to highlight their true skills when they transform themselves ingeniously into different characters and objects merely with a roll of masking tape. Alba claps her hands when they create dancing partners from the tape and perform an extravagant tango. Next they don long black cloaks and become spooky giants, swooping down suddenly onto the audience of children in the front row, who shriek in terror and delight. As they wave goodbye at the end of their act, Francesco grabs Anna's arm, 'Where's Alba? Is she next to you?'

The little girl is nowhere to be seen and Anna tries to reassure him, 'I don't think she liked it when they were in those cloaks. Maybe she moved further to the back?'

They can't find her in the amphitheatre. In the main square, Anna pounces on a little girl with the same bouncy curls but when she turns round, it isn't Alba. '*Mi scusi!*' she says to the anxious mother, who pulls her child closer. Francesco is growing more and more worried. 'I think we should go and look in the stone sanctuary and if she isn't there, I'm going to the *carabinieri.*'

They hurry up the narrow street to the old town again, pushing people out of the way in their need to reach the top. Every band or performer they rush past on each corner plays a different kind of music and now the sounds jar and jangle their nerves, like a sound-track to a thriller movie. When they reach the sanctuary, they search frantically behind the strange stones, calling Alba's name but she isn't there either. Francesco pulls Anna by the hand, 'This way - there's a short-cut back to the square.' They run up crooked steps to a grassy slope above the rooftops, where a

Buddhist prayer wheel sits incongruously opposite a rusting metal cross, and they make for a narrow path leading down the opposite side. Right at the top of the climb is a ruined house fronted by a patch of overgrown garden. Anna almost trips over a shape in the gloom and stops still. 'Look, Francesco!'

At the edge of the garden, Alba is crouching by the railings.

Francesco grabs her, 'Are you hurt, *tesoro*?' he asks, covering her face with kisses, following this up with a severe scolding, 'Why did you run off like that? We've been so worried.'

She struggles in his arms, pointing at something below. They follow the line of her outstretched finger and approach the railings. On a ledge in the rocks is a tiny kitten in danger any minute of falling to its death. Without thinking, Anna pulls off her jacket, lays flat on the ground and pushes her arm through the rusting rails, grabbing the terrified, scratching little bundle of fur and pulling it to safety. Alba kneels next to her, stroking the trembling animal.

'Gently', Anna says, 'you mustn't frighten it. Keep very, very still and quiet.'

After a while, she wraps the kitten in her jacket and places it in Alba's arms and she stares up at her father with imploring eyes, not needing words to convey what she is asking.

'I personally think it would be a good idea,' Anna intercedes before Francesco can refuse. 'I'm sure

Teresa would be pleased to have a mouser round the *agriturismo.*'

But he disagrees, 'Teresa would not be at all pleased to have a dirty animal around her paying guests.'

Alba squeezes the kitten tighter to her chest, looking up at Anna, who suggests, without having thought it through, 'Why don't I keep it? Then Alba can come and visit and help look after it. What about that for an idea, Francesco?' She looks meaningfully at him, willing him to agree, but she doesn't have to plead for long.

He leans over his daughter's head and strokes the tiny animal with gentle fingers. 'The first thing we shall do is call in at the vet's tomorrow morning.' Turning to Alba, he says, 'And you must say a big thank you to Anna.'

They find a box beside an overflowing bin outside a bar and the kitten, newly christened "Billi" after the hill-top where he was found, scratches and mews in its cardboard prison all the way home. Anna wonders what on earth she has let herself in for, but one look in the mirror and the sight of Alba's happy little face, reminds her why she offered. Alba beams her a huge thank you smile and Anna wishes the little girl could allow herself to say it in words.

'I have a suggestion,' Francesco says, 'your hands will be full this evening with your new house-mate, so how about I sort supper and bring it round to your place?'

Back in her house in the square, Anna decides to temporarily confine the kitten to the bathroom until after the visit to the vet. In that way, it will be easier to clean up any messes. She takes a quick shower. Billi cowers in the corner, looking up at her with big, startled eyes after the watery christening he receives after his first, and probably last, exploration under the spray. After changing into clean jeans and a red silk blouse she lays the table for three in the corner of the living-room, using the bright tablecloth bought in the market at Badia. It is perfect, adding a touch of homeliness to the minimalist room. It will not look half as good back in England.

Francesco arrives as she searches for paper napkins, wearing a tailored white shirt and black jeans and looking stylish, in the way only Italian men can. He greets her with a kiss on each cheek. She likes the musky scented aftershave he's splashed on his face and nearly asks him what it is. 'Where's Alba?'

'She is – how do you say it - zonked out! Teresa's put her to bed with the promise of missing school so she can come to the vet's in the morning. I think she thought if she went to bed early, then the morning would come sooner.' He chuckles.

She isn't disappointed. It will be good to have a chance to talk to him without feeling she almost has to ask Alba's permission first. With a flourish, he pulls a cloth from the tray he's carried in. 'We need to eat this while it's still warm. Teresa gave me some extra restaurant food and I'm not going to tell you what anything is. You'll enjoy guessing. But first, try this.'

She picks up the glass of red wine he's poured, in the way she always does, cupping the bowl in her palm. He puts his hand over hers, and lifts the stem between her thumb and forefinger. His fingers feel warm and she's surprised when she realises she doesn't want him to let go. 'Otherwise you will heat the wine,' he explains, removing his hands from hers. 'Now hold it up to the light, swirl it round and look at the sides of the glass. Look for the arcs the wine leaves – they are far apart – that shows the strength of the wine. Next savour it in your mouth before swallowing it. Wait for the after-taste.'

'History and wine-tasting lessons all in the same day! Is there no end to the man's talents?' she says jokingly. But she does as he instructs and the wine tastes good.

'Do you remember we were talking about how the peasants scraped a living from the land?' he asks as he holds up a plate of starters. 'Before the *agriturismo* opened, Teresa and I researched recipes by talking to older women round here and looking at documents at the *Comune*. These are some of the results!'

The dish contains a variety of starters. She can identify the tomato *bruschetta* easily enough, with its added kick of chilli pepper. But she would never have guessed the identity of deep-fried borage leaves or bladderwort if Francesco hadn't told her what they were. They have to look up the words in her dictionary, they are too specialised for his vocabulary. With these unusual dishes, Teresa has made a reputation for the *agriturismo,* popular with people living down on the coast who don't have access to these plants. He slices portions from a cheese pie with added ingredients of Vitalba tips and wild asparagus. Afterwards there is a salad made from poppy and dandelion leaves, nasturtium and borage flowers, that Teresa harvested earlier that afternoon.

Anna holds up her glass between thumb and forefinger in a toast: 'This is the best last-minute supper I've ever tasted. Thank you, Francesco.'

'*Prego*! I told you the peasants had to be resourceful. You wait until I introduce you to edible *funghi*. I'm quite a dab hand when it comes to preparing wild mushrooms.'

'You'd make somebody a very good wife.' She realises what she's said and stammers, 'I'm sorry…'

'There you go again with your English "sorry"! I enjoy cooking. Silvana didn't, so that was fine by both of us. What about you, Anna? Have you ever been a wife?'

She picks up a piece of bread from the basket and breaks off a piece to mop the tomato spilled from her *bruschetta.* 'No, I've never been married.'

'But there must be somebody in your life – someone important?' His tone seems merely interested, but his eyes gaze into hers with a quiet intensity. She wonders whether all Italian males are taught the art of seduction by their mothers at the knee and then silently rebukes herself for being cynical. She is really enjoying his company. When she hesitates with her answer, it is his turn to apologise. 'Forgive my nosiness, Anna…'

She throws a piece of bread at him. 'How come I'm not allowed to say sorry and you are?'

He ducks, laughing. Then, feeling she has embarrassed him somehow, she says hastily, 'Sorry Francesco, you've every right to ask. There is somebody in London but it's a bit complicated.'

'A woman!' he interrupts, his brown eyes laughing at her now.

She carries on the joke. 'How did you guess? No …' she suddenly feels the need to put his mind at rest, 'not a woman, although I sometimes think it would be a lot easier if it were. But he's married to somebody else.'

'Ah, I see.' He picks up his wine glass and takes another sip. 'And will he leave this 'somebody else' to be with you always?'

'It's not like that.'

He looks at her, frowning slightly. 'And do you love him?'

'I suppose so. I mean we get on very well. But lately…' She pauses, trying to put into words an explanation she hasn't quite fathomed herself. Then looking at him she says, 'Lately, I've felt it wasn't enough or that I needed to re-think my life. Something like that…'

'Is that why you came here, Anna?'

She is uncomfortable with his questions for she has no real answers. She snaps her reply, 'I came here to research my parents' story.' And she swallows another gulp of wine, forgetting his advice about how to hold her glass, cradling it once again in her palm.

'Anyway, this is boring. Let's change the subject. What about you? Were you married for long?'

'No. But we'd known each other since we were at school together.' He stacks their plates, pushing them to the edge of the table, then leans back in his chair, folding his arms and watching Anna as he continues. 'We were what people call a "modern couple"…not believing in marriage. And then, two years ago we decided it was the best thing to do for Alba. Silvana felt strongly about her being labelled 'illegitimate' and she thought it might cause problems for her in the future. So we had a big, fancy wedding, inviting all our family and friends, booking an expensive restaurant in the centre of Bologna for the wedding breakfast. We even took Alba on honeymoon with us afterwards to Zanzibar.'

'I don't think I believe in marriage. I seem to come from a family with an allergy to marital bliss.'

He raises an eyebrow and she explains, 'My sister is divorced, my brother's been married three times and it looks like he's heading for a third divorce and let's just say my parents' marriage made in heaven turned out to not be quite so fantastic . I've always said though, if I ever did marry, I'd like a quiet affair. No extended family, nothing fancy.'

'Very wise! Thinking back, I suppose Silvana and I were just papering over cracks in our relationship. It was bizarre, but once we married everything went downhill. We both felt... stifled, I suppose. It was only Alba that kept us together.'

She is surprised to learn of his unhappy marriage. For some reason she had imagined it to be good; had him summed up as the grieving widower. Finishing the last of the wine in her glass, she shrugs her shoulders, saying, 'Life is complicated.'

'I think it's people who are complicated.'

The wine has gone to her head. He reaches across the table and takes her hand. Turning it over, he kisses her palm. 'Your married man is a fool.'

She pulls her hand away.

'What are you so afraid of, Anna?' They sit for a moment, watching each other. Anna doesn't know what to say and he is the first to break the silence. He is gentle, calm. 'I know we've not known each other for very long but I'm growing very fond of you. I think you like me too?' He gets up from his side of the table, comes over to her, pulls her to her feet and they kiss tentatively. Then he pulls her closer and when she doesn't resist, their kisses grow more passionate.

A knock at the door makes them spring apart. Teresa calls urgently from outside. 'Francesco, I'm sorry but Alba's been very sick. She's calling for you.'
He smiles ruefully. 'Now I really *can* say sorry with good reason. I'd better go. Thank you for sharing supper with me, Anna. I'll see you tomorrow.'
He lets himself out - but not before blowing her a kiss. She is disappointed but also faintly relieved that he has left. It is simpler this way. She hadn't planned on falling in love when she left for Italy.

 Next morning, waking early, she stretches luxuriously, reaching over to the other side of her lovely old bed. She wonders for an instant what it might have been like to have turned to see Francesco laying next to her on the linen sheets and then dismisses the idea quickly. She gets up, wraps her dressing gown round her and goes downstairs to make a cup of tea. Francesco almost certainly would be a 'black coffee person' first thing, she thinks. Would he be a morning person or a night owl, like her? They know so little about each other, but she feels comfortable in his company. Alba provided her with a lucky escape last night, because she knows they might well have ended up in bed. It would have been too soon. Not her style. Her mobile rings and she grabs it eagerly.

'Anna, darling. At last! I tried to call you yesterday but your number was always unavailable.'

It takes her a moment to register the very English public school voice. 'Oh Will, it's you.' Disappointment flattens her tone. 'Reception's not very good here up in the mountains. Er – how are you?'

'Well, you're about to find out, Sooty. How's this for a stroke of luck? They've put on a team-building exercise for us in San Marino of all places. I've had a look on the map and it's a stone's throw from where you are. So tomorrow evening, I plan to whisk you away for a romantic Tuscan dinner with all the works and then you can fill me in on what you've been getting up to.'

Chapter 19
June 1999.

Supper with Francesco last night has stirred up new feelings and she's not sure about seeing Will again. In the shower she tells herself not to be stupid: he is just another aspect to the romance of the place and it's simply a case of Italy's magic sweeping her off her feet. She chooses her outfit carefully: a coffee coloured linen trouser suit and a cream blouse which look much better on her now she has some colour to her face. The mountain air is doing her good and, remarkably, despite the wonderful food she's been eating over the last few weeks, she's lost a couple of pounds. Her diet is more balanced with no takeaways or calorie-laden croissants which she used to snatch on her morning dash to work. The reflection in the mirror tells her she's looking good.

But she doesn't feel good inside. Will's phone call has sent her into a spin again. A knock at the door and Francesco's face is almost hidden by a huge bunch of sweet smelling, yellow *ginestra*. Beaming, he hands the flowers to her, but Anna is immediately tongue-tied. 'I just stopped off at the most expensive florist in the area to pick these off the mountains myself,' he says, 'And may I say how smart and beautiful you are looking this morning, signorina.' He bends to kiss her and Anna flinches.

'Anna? Are you unwell? I hope I didn't poison you with my culinary delights last night?' he laughs, nervously. She avoids his gaze, and shrugging her shoulders says, 'No, of course not. How's Alba this morning?'

'Oh she's fine now. That kind of sickness thing has happened before when I've been out in the evening. I have my suspicions... She's already gone with Teresa to the vet with Billi, so we have a couple of hours to ourselves.'

She puts the flowers on the table and he comes over to her, smoothing her hair back from her face, 'You don't feel the same way this morning, do you?' he asks, ' What's up?' And tilting her face so he can see her better, adds. 'Something's happened to make you change your mind. Tell me.'

'The man I was telling you about last night…'

'The *fool* you were telling me about last night...'

'Don't say that, what you really mean is - *I* am the fool.'

She pulls away. She is angry with herself but she knows it comes over as anger against him. 'I'm in a hurry so maybe you could drop by later?' she says, reaching up to the kitchen cupboard to find a vase. 'He's arriving early this afternoon and I've got a million and one things to do before I see him.'

He raises both his hands as if in surrender and turns for the door, his jacket catching the *ginestra* on the table, sending them hurtling to the floor where they remain scattered on the cotto tiles. 'Don't worry,' he says, 'I know when I'm not wanted. I wouldn't want to get in the way of your *million* things to do.'

In dismay, she watches him stride across the piazza, regretting her bluntness but at the same time reminding herself she needs fewer complications in her life right now.

Will sticks out amongst the tables of smartly dressed Italians, his panama hat and cream linen suit screaming "Englishman abroad". They have arranged to meet in a bar near his hotel in San Marino. The sophisticated atmosphere is completely different from the sleepy corner of Tuscany she is growing to love. She feels ill at ease and realises how much she has changed in a few weeks.

'Darling, you look divine. Italy obviously suits.' He shouts across the occupied tables as she enters the smart bar with its trendy chrome fittings and expensive orchid arrangements. People look up as he welcomes her and she wishes he were more discreet. Bending to kiss him on both cheeks in the Italian way, she thinks how much older he looks. His face is flushed and there is an unattractive sweat stain on his pink shirt, one side of his collar is sticking up and she has to stop herself from adjusting it.

'My, my… how very formal! I was looking forward to a bit more than that, Sooty,' he says, pulling her closer and planting a wet kiss on her lips. The nickname jars on her today. He'd named her Sooty after one of their first dinner dates together. Her mascara had run when they were dashing from the restaurant in the pouring rain to a waiting taxi, leaving dark smudges round her eyes. She pulls away from his grasp and sits down. 'Will,' she hisses, 'you've obviously already had a drink or two. Everybody's looking. Keep your voice down, *please*.'

'So bloody what if I have? Nobody knows me here. The Prosecco's damn good, damn cheap too.'

People at the table next to them are exchanging knowing looks and, beckoning to the waiter, she suggests he has a strong espresso instead.

'Don't start bossing me about!' Will waves a finger at her, his voice booming out above other people's conversations. 'God, I've had enough of being told what to do at home. No, I'll have another glass of this excellent vino.' He half rises from his seat and shouts to a waitress: 'Vino blanco over here and bloody pronto!'

'Will! Let's go for a walk.'

'Oh, I see, darling. Can't wait to get me back into the bedroom! How long has it been? I'd say it's about two bloody months since we hit the sack. Old Will's willy's getting very rusty, ha ha!'

She cringes, getting up to leave at the same time as Will, who knocks his glass off the table in the process. A waiter approaches and bends to mop up the mess. Anna thrusts some lire notes into the young man's hands and guides Will to a bench outside under the shade of an umbrella, calling for a taxi to take him back to his hotel.

It is dusk when she lets herself back into her house in the square. The lights are on in Teresa's guest house and through the windows she can see Francesco waiting in the full dining room. She closes her shutters and sits in the dark thinking about the events of the past few hours, wondering why, where men are concerned, she always seems to make such a muddle.

When Will phones much later she is still awake, her mind too tangled for sleep.

'Sorry, Anna… empty stomach and too much wine. Unforgivable! Please can we meet again tomorrow? My flight's not until the evening and I can skip the stupid sessions they've arranged. We could spend the day together. Let me make it up to you. Please!'

She hesitates. She should say no but he sounds so contrite. 'You *were* rather awful tonight, Will. I've never seen you like that before.'

'Just give me a chance to explain. Please? For old time's sake?'

'Oh, you're impossible. Listen, I can manage one hour tomorrow morning, but you'd have to come away from San Marino and meet me down in Sansepolcro. I've promised to collect something there for my landlady. I'll meet you in the little bar in the corner of Piazza Torre di Berta at 10 o'clock.'

Sansepolcro is bustling. It's Tuesday - when inhabitants reconnoitre in cafés, exchanging news and gossip; when old men stand in huddles on corners, deeply involved in conversation, gesticulating and arguing about the latest political cock-ups. People are down from towns and villages in the mountains, searching for bargains on market stalls that village stores cannot afford to stock. Anna sips a cappuccino in the bar in the main square, watching and listening to the spectacle of market day. Will is only five minutes late. He looks tired, preoccupied. He stoops down to kiss her on the cheek and orders a double espresso from the pretty girl who comes to take his order. 'You're looking so beautiful, Anna, so well.' He takes her hand and kisses it. 'I've missed you.'

She withdraws her hand and settles back into the easy chair, while the waitress sets down their order. He seems like a stranger to her, this man who occasionally shared her bed over the last two years.

He watches her nervously, knocks back his espresso in one gulp, 'You're cross about yesterday, aren't you?' he mutters. The coffee leaves a dark stain on his upper lip, like a badly drawn moustache. Shrugging her shoulders she replies, 'It wasn't like you. I was embarrassed.'

'I've left Tricia.' He blurts it out, without preamble.

'I beg your pardon?'

'I've left her.' He leans forward, looking at her again, trying to gauge her reaction. But she is so taken aback she says nothing and so he continues. 'I've missed you more than I can say. As soon as it registered you were really gone, I realised what a fool I'd been.'

She tries to interrupt, to prevent him from saying any more but he is in full flow now. 'I know we both said there were to be no strings… that we were both happy for it to stay that way but - it's over with Tricia. It's been over for years, really. The children have gone, they're independent, we've done our best for them. There's really no reason to stay together anymore. Anna…' He leans further forward. 'I've come to Italy to ask you to marry me. Naturally I'll have to sort out the divorce first and that will take a while but we can marry as soon as that's over. I don't want to lose you.'

She is still reeling with surprise at his proposal, the last thing she expected to hear. Finding her voice at last she shakes her head in disbelief. 'I can't marry you, Will.'

'But why not?'

'Because I don't love you.'

He slumps back in his chair, winded, as if it has taken all of his strength to come out with his proposal. She thinks again how much older he looks, how he could almost be her father.

'I often wondered what you saw in me,' he says, echoing her thoughts, 'silly old sod like me...'

'You're not silly. We were good together and it worked while it lasted, but things change.' She is amazed at how rational she is, how clear everything suddenly appears to her. 'Maybe you're in a bit of a panic, kind of scared of what's coming your way, leaving television, going into retirement? They say it's one of the most traumatic of times. Have you tried to talk properly to Tricia?'

'There's no point.' He sits for a few seconds, silent, picking up his panama hat, fidgeting at it. Life continues round them, coffees are ordered at the bar, teaspoons clatter onto saucers, stall-holders exchange banter with housewives over prices, a scooter whines in a side street, its tinny echo bouncing off high palazzo walls and she knows with absolute certainty that she could never share her life with Will.

'You loved me once, didn't you?' he continues, 'if I had asked you to marry me earlier on, do you think you would have said yes?'

She pauses, searching for words that will not hurt this man she once adored. 'You made it plain you were married already and that was fine by me. I wasn't looking for marriage, Will.'

'That evening in your flat – you told me you needed space. I misunderstood... I thought you were really sending me a message that you were fed up waiting for me to commit.'

'You thought wrong then. I'm sorry.'
There really is nothing much else to say.

When Will returns from paying for their coffees inside the bar, he pulls her into a bear- hug, 'Oh well!' he says, 'Nothing ventured and all that. We're still friends, aren't we?'
She kisses him soundly on the cheek, 'Of course, you idiot. But I still think you should go home and talk, you and Tricia. *Really* talk.'

On the opposite side of the square, Francesco emerges from the stationer's to see Anna locked in an embrace with a man who could only be the English lover she had talked about the previous evening. He stares at them for a while, angry at himself for feeling jealous, thinking it is probably the right time to return to Bologna.

Chapter 20

There is a package waiting on Anna's doorstep when she returns from Sansepolcro. A note is attached:

This is the last translation I can manage.
I'm returning the papers to you before we leave for Bologna.
F.

She isn't surprised – she messed up last time they met but she hopes he will return soon and they can talk.

After quickly preparing a salad lunch for herself, she settles down to read Francesco's latest translation.

The end of the war. May 1945

Farmers had started to bring grain to the mill again, gleaned too late from the meadows. Some of it was bad, the result of last year's meagre harvest, and had to be discarded. Despite the end of the war having come and gone, nothing much had changed in the way of food supply. We were still short of too many things.

'Ines, spread all this grain onto sacking and pick out the bad. Everything you can possibly save, then save it. Nothing can be wasted.' My father shouted above the noise of rushing water. I was in the room leading to the machinery, collecting sacks of grain from our customers. He had made sure the mill pond was filled and we were starting grinding that afternoon. I welcomed the hard work for it served to pass time, which lay heavily.

There had been no word from Norman since I kissed him goodbye seven long months earlier. Capriolo had visited a few times to keep us company. He understood the hole Davide's death had left in our lives. Over the hard winter of 1944 he had knocked on our door as often as he could in the evenings and tried to fill Davide's space round the hearth. But he had become more and more involved in the fight with the Allies and towards spring he had kept vigil by the hearth with us less and less. 'He won't come back, Ines, your fine Englishman,' he'd said to me, 'you'd best forget about him. He's gone back to his English women with their blond hair and blue eyes. Not to mention their long legs.'

I wasn't sure if he was teasing. But lately I'd started to think there might be truth in his words. That winter was long, wet and miserable and there was too much time spent cooped up indoors, too much time to think. When I tried to visualise Norman's face or the way he pronounced his Italian words in that funny way that made me smile, I couldn't even remember what he looked or sounded like.

The May sunshine was more like August and I took our couple of remaining sheep up to the pastures above the river. I rolled up my sleeves and undid the top buttons of my blouse, feeling like a lizard savouring the first sun after months of hiding away in the boulders. The grass was perfumed, the rock behind my back comfortingly warm and the first spring flowers nodded their heads in the breeze. Life would have been almost perfect if Norman had been sitting beside me.

I jumped as a stone slithered down the bank beside me. Maybe it was a viper also coming out of hibernation. They were at their most poisonous at this time of year. But it was only Capriolo. He jumped down and came to sit near me. 'You need to stock up now with more sheep,' he said, 'tell your father I could take him down to market at Pieve next Monday and help him load a decent number onto the cart. Business is slowly starting again.'

'I thought you are needed again down in the city? What about your office job?'

He picked a stalk of grass and chewed on it, 'They gave it to somebody else. But I don't mind. How could I stay cooped up in an office after these years on the mountains?'

'But those were years of fighting. There's no fighting anymore, no battles to be won.'

'You're wrong there. There are plenty of battles to be fought. If we want the Italy we fought for, we have to keep up the political fight. I've been asked to stand as the local party representative. I can't do that from the city.'

'Won't you miss it? There's not much to do here.'

'I could never go back to the city. You'll miss this place too if you go to England, believe me. I've been to more places than you and there's nowhere that compares. The war has taught me a lot, not just about fighting. It's taught me more about life than I would have learnt in a normal life time.'

'I can't wait for Norman to come back and take me away.'

'Do you really think he is going to come back?'

'Of course! Why do you say such stupid things to me?'

'Because I am a man and I know what men are like.'

'He's different.'

'Yes, he's different. That's what worries me.' He got up and walked to the edge of the hillside. 'You think you want to escape from all this,' he gestured to the horizon edged with the Apennines, blue in the afternoon sun. 'You don't realise how much a part of this place you are until you are in danger of losing it. When you go away you will have to start again. You will be nothing when you leave here.'

'You talk such rubbish. I shall be Norman's wife. I shan't just be the miller's daughter who sometimes takes the sheep and cows up onto the hillside.'

'You are so young. You don't understand what I'm trying to tell you.'

'And you sound like a boring old man. You can stay here and fester but I won't. You are welcome to this place.' I got up and smacked the sheep into moving down the path, leaving him to think his lofty thoughts on the hillside.

Approaching the mill, I noticed someone waiting on the bridge. A tall stranger with short, blond hair, dressed in a British soldier's uniform. It looked like Norman and when he shouted my name, I dropped my stick and ran as fast as I could and he swept me up into his arms. I could feel his bones through his shirt, he was gaunter than when he had left us in October - paler, smoother shaven. He looked very English in his neatly pressed uniform and suddenly I felt shy.

'You're back' I said, for loss of anything better to say.

'Did you ever doubt me, Ines?'

'It's been such a long time. I began to think it was a dream, that I had imagined you.'

Then a crowd started to gather. My parents, people from the village who had seen the British jeep arrive in the piazza and drive down to the river. Everybody wanted to shake his hand. 'We always thought you were an *'inglese'*, one of them said. 'But it seemed too improbable. Bravo, bravo.'

His hand was pumped up and down in grateful thanks so much that he told me later on he thought it was going to be pulled off. Everybody wanted to touch him, to thank the '*inglese*' for helping bring about the end of the dreadful war - as if he had been the sole soldier in the whole of the British army. But he was the only one to make it back to our village so soon after the end of the war.

'Keep still, Ines...if you wriggle I shall be sticking the pins in you instead of in the material.'

'Nobody will realise it was a nightdress, Mamma, it's just perfect. The material is so fine.' I ran my fingers along the lace-edged hem, the silk soft and cool against my skin. I had never worn anything made of such fine material. I was used to wartime 'make and mend' working clothes, hand-me-downs from my brother. I felt beautiful. I turned to look at myself in my mother's cracked mirror.

'If you bend like that again, the hem will be up in front and down at the back. You're worse than a child today.' My mother had pins in her mouth, making it difficult for her to talk. 'I can't spend too long on this, so hold still. We still have so much to do before tomorrow.'

The next day was to be my wedding day. There had been very few occasions in the last years for celebration and what with the relief of the war coming to an end and the announcement of our marriage, everybody had rallied to help us prepare a special feast. Neighbours had been leaving baskets of vegetables, jars of jam, bottles of wine – anything they could spare – on the steps to the mill for days since Norman's return.

'I can help you make the *cappelletti* afterwards, Mamma.' We had been given a basket of fresh eggs the night before to prepare the traditional hat-shaped ravioli for our wedding breakfast.

'Why do you think I got up this morning at five o'clock? While you were sleeping, I was busy rolling the pasta. But we still have to decorate the stable for the party afterwards. I cannot believe it is twenty years since Papa and I danced in there for our own wedding.' She had removed the pins from her mouth and was rummaging in the trunk at the end of the cherry-wood double bed where she and Papà had slept since grandfather passed away. 'Come here, child. Let me fix this on you.' She held up the veil she had worn on her own wedding day. It was yellowed with age, hand-embroidered by my great grandmother who had been the first woman in our family to wear it on her special day. 'I'll wash it carefully and soak it in lavender water and it will come up fine. Today is sunny and it will dry on the bushes in no time'.

My father shouted up the stairs, 'Assunta, there's nothing here! Somebody has stolen our things!' Mamma went to the top of the ladder leading to the floor below and shouted down. 'You're searching by the wrong tree, Aldo. Look for the oak tree with the arrow.'

A few months after the start of the war, when the Germans had rolled into our town with their half-tracks to occupy Badia, we, like many other villagers, had buried possessions in boxes in the woods to stop them from being looted by the soldiers. As it was, many houses were ransacked and our hay had been stolen for the troops' horses. Now it was time to retrieve the bottled vegetables, wine, linen and whatever else had gone into the secret stores. I think Mamma had even forgotten what she had placed there over two years ago.

'Come and help me yourself if you're so sure,' my father shouted again, 'but I think some bloody thief has taken our stuff.'

My mother hurried outside, muttering as she went, 'I really don't know how you would survive without me, Aldo. I have to do everything round here and more besides.' She took the spade roughly from his hands and started to dig a few metres away from where Papa was standing. The sound of metal striking metal proved she was correct. It was often the way with my parents. My mother had a great deal of common sense. Some of the linen had turned mildewed and a jar of zucchini had spilled and we hoped for the best that the wine hadn't turned sour.

I shall always treasure the last afternoon that I spent with my parents as a *signorina*. We walked up the meadows together, gathering wild flowers that had grown where crops would in normal times have been sown - vetch, harebells, purple orchids, dog daisies, sweet-scented ginestra and garlands of vitalba to wind around the beams on the stable rafters. We swept the floor clean and arranged wide planks on blocks of wood. My mother, hands on hips, looked satisfied as she inspected our afternoon's work. 'Tomorrow morning we'll arrange *nonna's* sheets over the planks and scatter petals of briar-roses round the plates and our celebration will be one never to be forgotten. Aldo, go and chop the wood for the oven. Ines and I must talk.'

We walked together in awkward silence along the mule track by the river. I had an inkling of what was coming. 'Tomorrow,' my mother began,' you might not like what will happen to you when you and Norman are alone. When you are in bed together, tomorrow night after the festa, do not be frightened at what he will do to you...it may be painful for you down below at first but you will get used to it...it is what a wife has to do for her husband and if you are lucky it will make a baby for you and your family will start.' All this she said in a rush, never once looking at me, staring straight ahead of her, her face very pink.

I picked up a pebble from the shore and skimmed it across the water as I had often done in childish games with Davide. I didn't know what to say to her. Presumably what was going to happen tomorrow wouldn't be too bad because she and Papà still slept together in the same high bed. Tomorrow Norman and I would sleep there and a few days previously my mother had washed and pressed the linen sheets for us.

'I have had to patch them,' she had said, 'but they are still fine quality and they will have to do.' I helped her fold them from the line. 'They belonged to *nonna*, God bless her. She would have loved to have been at your wedding feast, Ines. You look a lot like her. Think of her on your wedding day. She made the lace on all these pillow-cases. Look at the beautiful work she did. If the war hadn't come along I could have taught you how to sew like this too. But how could we get hold of the cotton? Thank God the war is over.' Mamma paused in our walk along the river bank. 'Norman seems a kind man, but he's not one of us. My heart is breaking at the thought of losing another child.' She cupped my face with her hands, a rare gesture of affection, and her tears began to fall. 'First I lose Davide and now you. England is too far away. How can I help you be a wife? Who will you talk to when you need advice? Are you sure you know what you are doing, child? The thought of you having to travel all that way by yourself to England fills me with worry. How will you manage?'

'Mamma, we have talked and talked about this.' I tried not to show the impatience I was feeling. 'Norman has to finish serving his time with the British Army. I've explained this so many times. He will join me after three weeks, it won't be too long. He's managed to get me a special train ticket and his parents will fetch me from the station. They will look after me as if I were their own daughter and Norman has told you he will bring me back often - every summer. Don't you believe him?'

'Saying and doing are two different things altogether. What if he cannot find work? Or if the fare is more expensive than he thinks? I know I'm being a selfish mother...I should be pleased you are so happy but...I only have you now.'

I folded my mother in my arms. Up until now it had always been the other way round. She had been the one to comfort and guide me. 'Mamma, I'll write to you often and tell you all about my new life in England.'

'What good are letters to me?' she whispered.

'You can ask Father Luca or Capriolo to read your letters. Please don't tell me not to go, Mamma. I love Norman and I can't stay here without him.'

On the eve of my wedding, my mother held back her tears. I was still none the wiser about the 'dreadful things' which might take place in bed with Norman but I wasn't worried. Every time he took me in his arms, kissed me, fondled me, I didn't want him to stop. I kept those thoughts to myself.

'Remember Ines, you can always come back to us.' Mamma said as she straightened the ribbons on my wedding dress hanging from the wardrobe in her bedroom. 'You will always have a home here.'

I couldn't imagine why she needed to say such things. I was as happy as I had ever been and couldn't wait for my new life to begin.

The rain poured down on us on our wedding day. Father Luca arrived late because the track was a quagmire and he had to rush through our Mass because he was needed elsewhere to administer the Last Rites to an old woman who had died in Fresciano. We had planned to walk from the church to the stable in a procession, carrying candles in our jam jars to guide the way but the rain put paid to that too. My silk dress was spattered with mud and the flowers drooped in my hair but I hung onto my handsome English husband's arm and felt I was the most beautiful bride that had ever existed.

Everybody came to the stable not only to celebrate our marriage, but the end of the terrible years of war we had all suffered. In my excitement I wasn't hungry enough to do the meal justice but my eyes feasted on the spread. I couldn't remember when I had last seen such an amount of dishes: plates of ham, preserves of walnuts, zucchini, aubergines and mushrooms, wild salad leaves from the meadows sprinkled with grated truffles, roasted pigeons, pork, chickens and a whole boar. The wine flowed, faces grew redder, jokes became bawdier and then the music started. My father lifted his accordion onto his shoulder and after a rusty start, the music sang into the air. The planks that had served as tables were cleared from their supports, the leftovers tidied away into baskets to be carried home by our guests and the dancing started.

'You'll have to show me the steps,' my husband whispered to me as we moved into the empty circle of smiling faces, 'The dances are different from the ones I know.'

'Just listen to the music, we'll be fine.'

He clutched onto me as if he was about to fall and our first waltz wasn't as smooth as it could have been but it didn't matter as the floor soon filled up with other dancers and we were swept round in the throng.

'Thirsty work this dancing!' Norman stopped and a couple bumped into us. 'And my leg is hurting.' He led me off the dance floor to the corner of the stable where most of the men were congregated round the barrels of wine. Some of them were already unsteady on their feet and they clapped him on the shoulders, congratulating him and pumping his hand up and down again. I watched him knock back a couple of beakers of wine and then I joined Mamma. For this day only she had changed out of her black mourning clothes, worn since Davide's death, but her best Sunday frock of polka dot blue hung off her and her face was sad. As I went over, she patted the empty chair beside her and I took her hand in mine. The music was too loud for talk but we both understood what was in our hearts.

Norman and I were escorted to our bedroom with songs and laughter. The bed was strewn with flowers and my mother had laid out her best nightdress for me on the pillow.

'Carry her in, Norman, carry her in,' our guests shouted.

Norman was embarrassed too and whispered that he couldn't wait for them to leave, to be alone with me. But when we were alone, I was suddenly afraid, remembering my mother's words by the river.

'I'll leave you for a few minutes, Ines.' He closed the door and I undressed, shivering a little in the cooler night air. I lowered the flame on the lamp and caught a glimpse of myself in the mirror. There had been no mirror in the bedroom I had shared with *nonna* and I had never seen my naked reflection. My breasts were full and the triangle of hair between my legs was obvious in the gloomy light.

  Norman came back in before I had time to put on my nightdress and I hurried over to the bed where it lay folded. He looked at me and after a sharp intake of breath, he whispered, 'Don't put it on. Stay how you are.'

  I covered myself with my hands but he pulled them away and bent to kiss my breasts and then he knelt, his tongue licking my belly, his fingers feeling inside me, making me tremble. He moaned and stood up, pulling off his clothes, swearing as he fumbled with the buttons on his trousers and sat on the edge of the bed to remove them. I couldn't take my eyes off his nakedness. He picked me up and carried me to the bed. It creaked as he climbed on top of me and then creaked some more as he thrust himself inside me, a strange look on his face as he moved up and down and then he cried out and lay heavy on me. Grunting, he rolled away, blew out the light and within seconds he was asleep. I lay motionless in the dark, remembering what my mother had told me about the duties of a wife. I throbbed. I was sticky and sore. I wanted Norman to talk to me and tell me everything was all right; that what I'd had to do had been done well. Turning towards him, I gently prodded his side. 'Go to sleep,' he mumbled.

But I didn't feel sleepy. In the darkness, I listened to the water rushing past the mill, wondering if the same thing would happen again the following night.

Chapter 21
June 1999

Anna spends the rest of the day pottering: planting up an animal feed trough outside her front door with basil and parsley, hand-washing a silk blouse, but all the time her mind is on the diary. She goes to bed early, thinking about her mother, before falling into a fitful sleep in the early hours.

She sleeps in late. Papers are strewn about on the floor beside her bed and as she makes herself a pot of strong coffee instead of her usual tea, her first thoughts are again about her mother's wedding. How many daughters get to read detailed descriptions of their own mother's first night? How many women of that generation were as innocent and ignorant as her mother about what went on between the sheets? She feels uncomfortable reading about these private moments and yet, she reminds herself, her mother intended her to read her diaries. Presumably, married life had improved as time went on; Ines gave birth to three babies after all.

She ponders about her own generation and the freedom she is able to enjoy. Maybe life, in some senses, had been less complicated fifty years ago. Women shouldered their lot, accepting what came along, especially in country areas where the rhythm of life only altered with the seasons and news from the outside world was slow to trickle through. But how many unhappy lives had resulted from this ignorance? And what would they have made of Anna's own muddled love life? Surely not everybody would have stayed on the straight and narrow? The war must have turned lives upside down in so many ways.

In the early days of her stay, Francesco had shown her round a folk museum in the little village of Casteldelci, in the next valley. She was fascinated to read descriptions of how people lived from day to day; how they used ashes from the fire to wash their clothes; slept on the first floor of their houses with animals on the ground floor providing heat rising through wide gaps in the floor-boards. And, as she is finding out, the war impacted heavily on these people's lives. The museum had displayed gruesome photos of dead partisans arranged on the bridge beneath the village, a warning by the Germans not to support them.

A simple banner with the words, **'Our past is the counterweight to our future',** hanging in the centre of the exhibition had touched a chord and given relevance to reading her parents' story. It is dawning on her that if she can learn more about her mother and father, she might know herself a little better.

Her thoughts are interrupted by the arrival of a worried Alba at the door, with Billi clasped in her arms. As far as Alba is concerned, Anna has become an unofficial vet and cat counsellor and she holds up

Billi for inspection. The cat's tail is wrapped in a blood-stained handkerchief.

'Oh, poor little thing!' Anna says, bending down to stroke the cat. 'Is he in the wars again? Come in, Alba and we'll bathe his tail. Has he been in the wood pile again looking for mice?'

She has grown expert at this one-way conversation with Alba, feeling instinctively that she shouldn't be forced into talking. One day, when she is ready, she will rediscover her words. ' It's not a deep cut,' she tells the little girl, ' maybe his tail got pecked by the hens - the silly things thought it was a fat juicy worm.'

Alba giggles and helps bathe Billi's tail in boiled, salted water, holding fast to the wriggling bundle of fur.

'How about another English lesson later on today, before you leave for Bologna?' she suggests, when they have finished with Billi, 'We'll learn some more words along the river. It's a sunny day and I want to be outside too.'

Alba nods and Anna tells her in English what time they should meet, asking her if she has understood. Alba holds up three fingers and Anna smiles her approval. 'Well done. See you later, alligator!'

Francesco drops her at Anna's front door just before three, hovering on the threshold. They haven't spoken since the morning after their supper together. She wonders if she will ever have the chance to tell him what went on with Will. She misses Francesco's company, regrets the frosty atmosphere between them now, but doesn't know how to break it.

'I've got to go to Bologna to finalise plans for our move back,' Francesco says, handing over Alba's rucksack. He looks tired and refuses Anna's offer of coffee. 'No thanks, I'm late enough already and I heard on the radio that traffic is bad. There's been a nasty accident on the main road and I don't know what time I'll be back. Teresa says she will look after Alba this evening and she's expecting her about five.'

'We'll be finished well before then.' She wants to tell him to drive safely and come back in one piece, but he's already climbing into his car. They wave him goodbye as his old Fiat Panda disappears down the dirt track.

'Come on then, Alba. I've packed us a picnic. We're going further down the river today. New words need new places and we're going to find a little chapel downstream that your daddy told me about. Then we'll find a comfy rock to sit on and have our English afternoon tea. I've even baked you some special English buns which we call rock cakes!'

Alba laughs and carefully pulls her rucksack onto her back. The bag wriggles.

'Oh no, Alba, Billi can't come, he'll be a distraction and he won't want to get wet. Cats don't like water either.' She wonders if the little girl has taken on board she will be returning to Bologna soon and if

Francesco will let her keep Billi when they are back in their town apartment.

Each day now the weather is improving and the June sunshine is warm enough for dips in the river. The little girl squeals when Anna points out long necklaces of toad spawn tangled in the pools. Disturbed by their approach, a pair of egrets further downstream rise from the shallows where they have been fishing, their wing spans casting graceful shadows over the stones.
'Let's see how many heart shaped stones we can find and some flat ones to paint and write words on in English.'
A pleasant half hour later they reach the path leading to an abandoned chapel, a humble stone building with a corrugated metal roof. Inside is an altar and a gaudy image of the Madonna. Artificial flowers are arranged in jars on a darned altar cloth and outside, on an enamelled plaque, is a simple inscription:

In this little church where on Sundays Eliseio used to listen to the walnuts falling onto the roof, he kept his wife company as she came to clean and place plastic flowers in jam-jars on the altar. Now that he has passed away, the words he used to say to me about the existence of God, remain hanging in the air: "To say that God exists may be a lie but to say that He does not exist may be an even bigger lie."
Tonino Guerra.

Anna likes the sound of this poet who feels free to leave his thoughts for people to find, scattered about the countryside. She has been brought up to button her feelings and Jane and Harry were always ready to laugh at her if she confided in them. During these past weeks she has noticed how gregarious Italians are and once again marvels at the huge cultural changes and loneliness her mother had endured by leaving Italy.

A huge clap of thunder echoing from the next valley makes them both jump. They'd started their walk in brilliant sunshine but now the sky is overcast and the temperature has suddenly dropped several degrees.

'Quick, Alba. Run for shelter! We're going to get soaked in a minute.' Looking up at the menacing clouds, she grabs the little girl's hand and they make for a ruined barn. Half the roof has caved in, but there is a dry corner where the timbers above offer some shelter under the cracked tiles. Alba is shivering in her skimpy clothes and she pulls the trembling child into her arms. 'It's only thunder, nothing to be scared of. Soon be over and then we can go home. We'll have our picnic here and pretend it's our own house. I'll be the farmer's wife and you're my little girl and we're having a rest before we go to milk the goats.'

Alba smiles and runs into a corner where a woodwormed stool lies discarded on its side. She rights it, brushing off most of the dust off with her hands, arranging cakes and plastic beakers on her makeshift table. Rain is falling heavily now, curtains of water blocking the view of outside. Fat drops occasionally fall on them between the broken tiles as they eat their picnic. *Rock cakes in Tuscany, now there's a cultural exchange,* Anna thinks to herself.

Alba tugs at her arm, pointing at something on the wall beneath a half-rotten manger and smiles. Inside a heart, crudely scratched into the crumbling plaster, are four intertwined letters and a date:

DS & IS, agosto 1966

'One day', Anna tells her, 'somebody will write your name like that and you'll break somebody's heart too.'

The little girl covers her mouth with her hands and laughs out loud.

'Come on, Mrs Mummy Cat,' Anna continues, using the name that always makes Alba giggle, 'Let's clear up and get going. The rain's stopped and if we don't start back now we'll be very late and your Aunty Teresa will be wondering where we've disappeared to.'

They retrace their steps along the river, Alba hopping from stone to stone. The level has risen slightly and the water has turned murky after the recent deluge. They are almost at the bridge where they should clamber up from the river bed to join the road, when a sudden roar causes Anna to looks up. A wall of muddy water is gushing towards them as it funnels through the arches of the bridge.

She has to shout to make herself heard above the water's furious approach. 'Quick Alba, run to the bank as fast as you can. Get out of the river bed.' But the storm surge is upon them sooner than Anna anticipates.

The river boils, crashing over boulders, dragging tree trunks and branches in a crazy helter-skelter of water. At any minute the flood will catch them up and knock them over. Alba is already half way up the bank and Anna throws the rucksack up after her to lighten the load. She puts all her efforts into catching up with the little girl but loses her footing on an unsteady rock, tripping and sliding back down the bank into the foaming river. For what seems like minutes but is really only seconds, she is hemmed beneath the water, stones and debris crashing against her, knocking her breath away. Each time she thinks she will surface, passing logs catch her, bruising her and stopping her from regaining her balance. Then at last her hand makes contact with the branches of a willow growing out of the bank and she clings on, pulling herself up with both hands, bracing her body against the racing water. She is only yards away from the dam and if she doesn't hang onto the willow branch she will be tossed over the twenty foot high wall to the rocks below. And then she remembers Alba who was in front of her before she fell. 'Alba, Alba,' she shrieks, but the crazy river whips away her words. Clawing her way along the thicker branches of her perch, her heart in her mouth, for they could still snap under the pressure of the storm water, her left foot finally makes contact with the bank and she gains a foothold. But when she puts down her right foot she yelps with the pain, almost losing her grip on the tree. It takes her a few seconds to compose herself before climbing again but her right leg is useless.

Then she hears her name and looks up to see Alba, eyes huge in her ash-white face. 'Anna, Anna!' the little girl cries over and over. Never has her name sounded so sweet to Anna's ears. 'Alba – thank God you're safe.' Her arms are sore from hanging on against the fast flowing current and she doesn't know how much longer she can grip. She's cold, near to panic but she keeps her voice as calm as she can so as not to frighten the little girl. 'Alba, run back along the bank, look for my rucksack and mobile. Phone Teresa! Tell her what's happened. Tell her to be quick.'

Anna cannot remember much about her rescue. Later on, when she is sitting beside the stove, wrapped in Teresa's bath-robe with Alba snuggled next to her on the sofa, Teresa explains how she had grabbed the gardener working on her vegetable plot. Together they had jumped into his truck and sped down to the river. It had taken Arnaldo no time to attach a length of thick rope to the back of the vehicle, tie the other end round his waist and scramble down to Anna to rescue her from the freezing water. A few minutes later and they reckoned it would have been too late. Anna had fainted just as Arnaldo reached her and he had to jump into the water to carry her out.

'I was so frightened, I thought you were going to drown,' Alba is bubbling with words so long unspoken, 'I'm so glad now we didn't take Billi.' She starts to cry and Anna pulls her close, kissing the top of her head, wincing as she moves. Teresa gently pulls her niece away, 'Come and sit over here, Alba. Anna is very sore.'

'I am a little sore,' Anna says, 'but it's medicine for me just listening to Alba speaking again.'

'When I answered my phone, I didn't recognise you at first, Alba.' Teresa says as she pulls her onto her knee. 'You were fantastic. What a brave little girl you are.'

'I'm going to find Billi and tell him all about it.' Alba struggles from her aunt's arms, 'Can I go and find him upstairs, Anna?'

'Of course. He's probably under my bed.'

When they are alone, Anna tells Teresa how frightened she had been for Alba's safety. 'I never would have forgiven myself if anything had happened to her.'

'Don't worry – it wasn't your fault, you weren't to know. When it rains hard further up the valley, the river turns like that, almost without warning.'

'It's an awful thing to say, but it's almost been worth it to hear her talking again. I can't wait for Francesco to hear her.' She shuffles her bottom to find a more comfortable position and grimaces as pain shoots up her right side.

'I phoned him about the accident.' Teresa says. Two beams of light stroke the room from outside and there is the sound of a car pulling to a halt. Teresa gets up to look through the window. 'Speak of the devil, it's him. He must have driven really fast.' Turning back to Anna she says, 'I don't like the look of that leg and you're covered in bruises. I think we should call for the doctor tomorrow.'

'I'm sure it's nothing serious...' Anna says but before she can finish, the door is flung open and Francesco bursts in, shouting in Italian. Anna hears Alba's name mentioned but she can't understand what he is saying in their heated exchange, Francesco waving his hands as he shouts. Then he turns to Anna and says in English, 'What the hell were you thinking of, woman? Taking a child down to the river in a storm like that?' Hearing him, Alba comes rushing into the sitting room, flinging herself into his arms, 'Babbo, we've had an adventure - Anna fell in the river and I had to find her mobile and call Teresa and then Arnaldo came and rescued us and we've had hot chocolate and cake and I can't find Billi...and let go of me, Babbo, you're squeezing me too tight, it hurts.'

His voice is gentle now and he kisses his child over and over. 'Alba...you found your voice ...'

'Don't be silly, babbo, what do you mean? I never lost my voice - I just put it away for a little while.

Anyway, words are much easier than keeping quiet and I was getting bored with not talking. Can I have another piece of chocolate cake now, zia Teresa?'

Francesco and Teresa laugh. Anna watches the three of them, still upset by Francesco's outburst. Suddenly she feels she doesn't belong. If she could walk, she would quietly leave the room, make her way upstairs and let the family be on their own, but she is marooned on the sofa.

Without acknowledging Anna's presence any further, Francesco picks up Alba and nuzzles her, 'I think you have had quite enough chocolate cake and excitement for one day, young lady. Bed-time! Maybe you can miss school again tomorrow and Teresa will let you have a slice for breakfast.' He has another exchange in Italian with Teresa, too fast for Anna to follow, although she knows he is talking about her again and then he and Alba leave.

'He's really angry with me,' Anna says after they have left the room.

'Take no notice, he'll calm down. He doesn't know whether to be angry or happy that Alba's speaking again.'

'He blames the accident on me. She could have died.'

'But she didn't.' Teresa sits on the arm of the sofa, next to Anna. 'He's had a lot of worrying and thinking to do since Silvana's death and I think he's quite exhausted. Sometimes he over reacts. I was trying to point out to him that nothing happened to Alba and that he should simply be pleased she's speaking again. And I also lost my temper with him for not caring about what happened to you.'

'I think it would be better for everyone if I left.'

'Anna – don't be so ridiculous. Look, it's been a long day. Get some sleep and everything will seem better in the morning.' She laughs. 'I sound just like my own mother! Will you be all right sleeping where you are on the sofa? Can I get you another pillow or a glass of water?'

'No thanks, Teresa. You've been an angel. Just put the light out for me when you leave.'

Teresa bends to kiss her friend. '*Sogni d'oro*, sweet dreams. See you in the morning but call me if you need anything. Anything at all.' She closes the door gently behind her. A tear rolls down Anna's cheek. She tells herself it is shock after the day's dramatic events.

Chapter 22

She is sore and stiff next morning. Trying to walk upstairs to the bathroom, she can't put any weight on her leg and resorts to calling for Teresa on her mobile.

'You poor thing,' she says when she comes over. 'Look, I'm definitely calling the doctor to check you over and, in the meantime, you can't possibly stay by yourself in this house with the bathroom upstairs.'

She tries to protest but Teresa is adamant and Anna knows it makes sense. Teresa describes the little apartment opposite the *agriturismo* that she's modified for disabled guests, where Anna will be much more comfortable. 'Stop protesting, Anna! I've made up my mind. Tell me what I can pack for you and we'll get you sorted in no time.' She bustles round collecting toiletries, clean underwear and a comfortable track suit. 'Shall I pack these too?' she asks, holding up the diaries.

'Please! Then I can translate them while I'm immobile.'

'I thought Francesco was doing it for you.'

'He can't if he's returning to Bologna. Anyway, I don't want to bother him.'

Teresa frowns. 'That's news to me about Bologna.' She shrugs her shoulders. 'I'll ask Arnaldo to come and carry you over to the apartment.'

'I'm being such a nuisance. You've all got better things to do than run around after me.'

Hands on hips, Teresa retorts, 'Wouldn't you do the same for us?'

'Of course, but...'

'No buts. End of discussion. See you in a while – I'm off to make a phone call to the clinic.' Scooping up Anna's bundle of possessions, she hurries out. She slumps back against the sofa cushions letting out a huge sigh of frustration as she looks round the little house where she has started to enjoy her independence. Italians would say *Pazienza!,* she thinks, wondering how long she will have to be patient.

It is Francesco who comes to fetch her. 'Arnaldo's busy ploughing a neighbour's field, so Teresa sent me instead. Are you ready?' he asks.

'I think so. Thank you.'

He bends down to pick her up, neither of them looking at each other. 'Put your hands round my neck,' he says, 'otherwise I can't lift you properly.' She leans away from him as he carries her but he increases his grip. 'Relax Anna, then it will be easier for me.' He's strong, despite his lean build. She smells his familiar aftershave, sees a mole beneath his right ear she hadn't noticed before, wonders if he thinks she's heavy. She might have made a joke about it if she weren't feeling so awkward.

'Here we are,' he says, nudging the apartment door open as they arrive. 'I'll put you down here for the time being. Teresa is coming over to make up the bed for you.' He helps her onto a leather armchair in the lounge area. Stepping back, he leans against the kitchen counter that divides the two living spaces and folds his arms. They both start to speak at the same time.

'I'm sorry I'm being such a nuisance,' she says.

'I'm sorry I lost it last night,' he says.

She laughs nervously and he continues, 'I was out of my mind with worry. Alba is my world but I shouldn't have shouted at you like that.'

'Please don't apologise. I understand.'

'She hasn't stopped talking about yesterday.' He smiles, 'in fact she hasn't stopped talking, full-stop. It's amazing listening to her. Teresa has told me off because I keep asking her questions so I can hear her answers.' He pauses, 'To be honest, Teresa also told me off for being objectionable to you last night.' Anna doesn't comment and he continues, "She's also persuaded me not to leave quite yet for Bologna. I think the saying is "don't upset the apple cart"?'

'In what sense?'

'She thinks it's best to stay here for a while, for Alba's sake. Now that she is talking again, Teresa reckons we should stay put. Another change might upset her again.'

'She has a point, I suppose, but what do *you* think? She's your daughter after all, you know best.'

He shakes his head, 'If only that were true. Anyway, the faculty are being good to me and letting me do my research from here. I think we'll be staying for another month or so.'

'I'm pleased.' She smiles at him but he doesn't reciprocate. Instead he asks her rather abruptly what her plans are. She is about to answer when Teresa knocks on the open door, *Permesso,* Anna? The doctor's here.'

Behind her is a handsome, silver-haired man of about sixty, sporting an oiled, combed moustache that Anna cannot take her eyes off. He is wearing an expensively cut suit and carrying a battered leather doctor's bag. Shaking Anna's hand, he bows so low she thinks he might kiss it. 'Delighted to make your acquaintance,' he says, in old-fashioned English, 'and so enchanté to have the opportunity to use my English.' She has to stop herself from giggling - she can imagine him on stage, in an Edwardian play. 'My name is Edoardo. My wife and I, we go to Cornwall every other year. We like England very much but not so much the food. You eat too many boiled potatoes.' He removes his jacket, arranging it carefully on the back of a chair, rolls up the sleeves of his crisp cotton shirt and waves Francesco out of the apartment, asking Teresa to stay while he gives Anna a thorough examination.

'Nothing broken, just big contusions,' he pronounces finally, replacing his stethoscope in his bag and snapping it shut. 'You need to rest your leg as much as you can but I think after three or four days you will be beginning to feel much better. I am suggesting Arnica and lots of repose and a glass or two of our excellent Tuscan wine in the evenings. Good day, Miss Anna! I shall be seeing you at my clinic next week to do some more controls. Maybe Miss Teresa will be so kind as to make an appointment.' He bows low again as he leaves.

As soon as he is out of earshot, Anna can't hold back her laughter any longer. 'Goodness me! Is he real or am I suddenly watching a scene from a Pirandello play?'

'No, he's real. Very real indeed!' Teresa replies. 'Wait until you meet his wife. She's a big woman with huge bosoms and she wears designer clothes but very *old-fashioned* designer clothes with padded shoulders, very 1980, and she has no colour sense at all. I don't go, but they say she's always late for Sunday Mass. She makes her entrance during the priest's sermon so everybody can admire her and she wears dozens of gold bracelets which make such a racket, you can hear her approach up the path to the church. Father Giovanni is too scared to tell her off. He's a little Sicilian priest about half her size and anyway she would eat him for supper if he tried.'

'I'm afraid I won't be making Mass any time soon,' Anna wipes away her tears of laughter, 'what a shame I won't get to meet the signora.'

'Oh but you will. You'll bump into her one day. Literally!' Teresa laughs too as she makes up the bed for Anna with linen sheets and a soft, woollen blanket. 'I'll leave these towels for you in the bathroom.'
When she returns, Anna tells her, 'I meant what I said last night, Teresa, Maybe it's best if I found somewhere else once I'm on my feet again.'
Teresa sits down in the leather armchair opposite Anna. 'Why are you continuing to talk such rubbish? I thought we were supposed to be friends?'

'But I'm beginning to feel I've outstayed my welcome.' When Teresa begins to protest, she quickly adds, 'It's not you. It's Francesco. I think he would be glad to see the back of me, quite frankly.'
Teresa tuts, 'You're too sensitive. You shouldn't take things to heart so. And anyway, what about your project? What will happen to that if you leave?'

'My Italian needs to improve before I can finish the translation. Actually, I could do with a good dictionary. Do you have one I could borrow until I can buy one?'

'Well there you are, that proves it - you can't leave – you need Francesco to help you.'

'I don't think he will.'

'He's not going back to Bologna yet so he has plenty of time now and no excuses.'

'Please Teresa, just leave it.'
Teresa looks at her for a long moment, 'I thought you two were getting on so well.'

'I thought so too but...' Anna explains briefly about Will and how Francesco had thought she was stupid to meet up again with him, how he's stormed out on her. It's a relief to talk about it, a lot easier than she had thought, and Anna can't help wishing Teresa could have been her sister rather than Jane.

'Do you want *me* to talk to Francesco and tell him your friend has gone back to England?' Teresa asks when Anna has finished telling her about Will's proposal.

'No. I want to find the right moment myself.'
Teresa looks at her, pausing before asking, 'do you like my brother?'
Anna looks up, 'A lot.'

'I thought so. Well then', Teresa gets out of her chair and comes over to hug Anna, 'You must make sure you find the right moment before it's too late,' she says, as if it were the easiest thing in the world. 'Now I'm going to go and make some lunch and you must have a rest, like the doctor ordered. But ten o'clock in the morning is a bit too early for good Tuscan wine,' she says, checking her watch and grinning.
'Afterwards I'll go and hunt for my school dictionary.'

Anna sleeps for the rest of the day and it's almost dark when she wakes to Alba's chatter. She switches on the bed-side light and the little girl runs over to her bed carrying a picture of the stormy river and chatting nineteen to the dozen in a stream of Italian. Although Anna's Italian is improving, she can only catch a few words, "Billi" and "Teresa" and "*fiume*"(the river), being just some. She is followed by Teresa and Francesco, who is carrying a huge wicker basket covered in a white cloth. Anna feels dopy after her long sleep, she rubs her eyes saying, 'Whoa, Alba – if I'd known you could chat for Italy, I'd have preferred you not to find your tongue again!' Francesco rebukes Anna, in English, 'I know you don't mean that', he says, and then in much slower, clearer Italian, so she can understand, says, 'Alba, slow down a little so Anna can follow what you are saying.'

He helps Teresa carry a table into the bedroom and she spreads the cloth, laying four places, asking Francesco to fetch another basket they've left outside the door, containing more food and wine.

'Hey, are we having a party?" Anna says, pulling herself up in the bed. Teresa plumps up her pillows for her and Anna catches hold of her wrist. 'You're spoiling me,' she says, 'I'm sorry I can't get up to help.'

Alba climbs up next to her. 'That's exactly what this is: it's a party for you and me, to celebrate. I love parties, don't you? But usually we buy a new dress for a party but this is a different kind of party. Babbo said it was to be spon…spon…'

'Spontaneous!' Francesco helps his daughter.

'That's right,' she continues with her chatter, 'a party that you don't have to plan too much, a party without balloons or presents.'

Anna understands the drift and replies in halting Italian, 'The best present for this party is your voice, Alba.'

The timely sound of a bottle of Prosecco being uncorked and Alba's begging for a glass, 'Me too, me too. It's my party too,' makes them all laugh.

'You can have just a drop, as long as it doesn't make you bubbly too,' her father says, pouring her a thimbleful measure.

Teresa has thrown together a wonderful feast with what she already had in her larder: free-range eggs made into a huge *frittata* containing zucchini flowers and red Tropea onions, sprinkled with shavings of *parmigiano* and browned under the grill until bubbling and golden; stuffed tomatoes and aubergines roasted in the oven and portions of rabbit and chicken roasted in garlic and rosemary with tiny crisp potatoes. They finish off with bowls of *ricotta* topped with the first wild strawberries of the season, picked on the slopes above the *agriturismo*.

'I shall be getting so fat if my leg doesn't heal quickly,' Anna says, leaning back against the pillows, feeling full and relaxed.

'Don't worry,' Alba pipes up, 'Babbo has found you a job. So, when you are better there will be no time for getting fat.'

'What job?' Anna looks at him.

'I was going to talk to you about it. Maybe later, when I've put this chatterbox monkey to bed?' He picks up his daughter and holds her upside down, much to Alba's delight, who squeals and shouts, '*ancora, ancora!*'

Teresa, who is clearing away the dishes into the big basket to carry back to the *agriturismo,* tells him off for making her over-excited.

Anna suggests a story to calm her down. 'Come and sit next to me and I'll tell you about my friends who used to live at the bottom of my garden in England, when I was a little girl.' Francesco plonks her down onto the bed next to Anna who proceeds to tell her about Scarface, Spellerina and the other invented characters from her lonely English childhood. She has never told anybody their stories before.

Just after eleven Francesco returns from putting Alba to bed. 'I hope it's not too late. Teresa was right, it took me longer to settle Alba tonight.'

'Don't worry, I'm not tired at all – I've been asleep most of today.' She watches as he pulls up one of the leather armchairs and then says, 'you must be so happy to have her back to normal.'

'I can't describe it.' He stops, the joy shining in his eyes speaking more than words.

'Tell me about this work idea,' she says, to break the silence.

'It was really Teresa's idea, not mine. But of course it depends on your plans. I've told her it won't work.'

'Why?'

'Well, you won't be staying, will you? Not after meeting up with your partner again.' he says, tapping his foot on the tiled floor.

'You mean Will?' She feels the need to name him, to stop skirting around the issue and remembers Teresa's advice. It is now or never. 'Will and I have no future,' she tells him.

'It didn't look like that to me,' he looks at her, daring her to contradict.

'What are you talking about?'

'Don't lie to me, Anna. I saw you in the piazza down in Sansepolcro. You looked very much together to me.' He rises from the arm chair, 'I knew it was a mistake to come round to talk to you.'

'Have you been spying on me?' It's her turn now to raise her voice. 'That's unforgivable. I didn't have you down as a typical jealous Latin lover.'

'And I didn't think you were like all the other English women who come over here to have a romantic fling – to see if we Italian men are as good as they say.' He is about to leave when she bursts out laughing. 'Just listen to us, Francesco. We are being ridiculous.'

He looks at her, then raising both hands in exasperation, sits down again.

'Can we start again, do you think?' she says. When he doesn't object, she tells him everything about her meeting with Will. 'But we parted friends,' she ends her explanation, 'even if we never see each other again, we will always be friends. That's just the way it is.'

'I got the wrong end of the stick – another expression I learnt in Africa. I do have a tendency to speak sometimes before I think.'

'Well, now you know. And for the record, I'm *not* doing a piece of research into the romantic habits of the Italian male species!'

He looks sheepish, 'we've both come out with some huge generalisations this evening! I don't know why I said that.'

'Because those sort of things have always been said about our two cultures.'

'It seems to be a big thing with you, Anna - this two cultures argument. We have a saying *'tutto il mondo è paese'* – you should think more along those lines.' She doesn't understand and he tries to explain. 'I think there is a saying in English, 'it's a small world', but that doesn't quite express the same notion…' He searches for the words, 'or…observation of life.' He pauses before continuing, 'In the end, people are not so very different from each other, you know.'

She is quick to disagree. 'But there are *huge* differences. You Italians are more gregarious. We English will go to great lengths to find places where we can be on our own.'

'I have a few Italian friends who like peace and quiet too. What else can you come up with?'

'La bella figura?'

'Oh, that old cliché.'

'Is it? The *passeggiata* in the evening, showing off the fashions, worrying what people will say about you…'

'I think you've been watching too many old black and white films, like '*La Dolce Vita*'. And what's so wrong with fashion anyway? It's one of our main exports. Go on, you'll have to do better than that. Admit it, you English care about what people think too. What about keeping up with the Jones's?'

'I once read Italians live to eat, not eat to live.'

'Well thank God for that. I have to say the food my American friends ate was quite disgusting. Fries and burgers with ketchup and hot-dogs… I think I prefer Italian food any day, thank you.'

'I have to agree with you on that one.'

'In any case, Anna,' he waves his hands about as he enthusiastically comes up with another point, 'What is so wrong with differences? What is wrong with the idea of mixing up the differences that you seem to worry about and creating a wonderful new recipe?' She laughs. "Actually, I've just thought of another 'difference'. I remember when I sat in a café and did my first serious bit of 'people-watching' in Italy…'

'People-watching?'

'Oh yes, people watching – it's a very serious pastime, you know.' She laughs and then continues, 'I thought everybody was arguing. People all around me were talking with raised voices, waving their arms about, prodding each other when they wanted to reinforce a point. I thought a riot was going to break out at any minute, I was quite worried. But I know now it's just your way of having a conversation!'

He laughs at her description. 'But it's *good* to talk!' She smiles at him, 'yes, it is! It's *really* good to talk.' They sit for a while and then she asks him to tell her about his work idea.

'Teresa and I think you could develop your teaching. We've seen how good you are with Alba. The long summer school break is nearly here and there must be many more parents who would welcome a chance for their children to learn English.'

'But I'm not qualified.'

'Who cares? You are wonderful with Alba! A natural teacher.'

'You're very kind but I'm not the best person for your idea. I didn't even finish my studies.'

'And so? What does that matter? What did you study anyway?'

'Don't laugh but…' Anna trails off, wondering if she dare admit what she was going to say.

'You need to have more confidence in yourself,' he chides, 'I think you have very low self-esteem and you don't deserve to think that way.'

His encouragement spurs her on to explain, 'I started a degree in Italian when I was eighteen. I suppose I've always wanted to find out more about my Italian side. But the course wasn't right. There was too much

Renaissance literature and not enough everyday stuff. It didn't seem relevant to me at the time and so I dropped out. Then I tried a teaching course, dropped out of that too and finally I did a secretarial course – a means to an end really. I drifted from job to job and ended up working for an estate agency. Then I met Will when he came in to look for a house. End of story.'

'Why do you say 'end of story'? It makes you sound old and defeated. *Su – coraggio,* Anna! You're not that old. Actually – how old are you?"
She laughs. 'That's not the sort of question a gentleman asks a lady!'

'*Coglioni* – there you are – a new word for your vocabulary list.'
She laughs, 'I already knew the word for bollocks! It's one of the first I learned. And I'm thirty three – but don't tell everybody!'

'Wonderful! Three is a special number. Your life is just beginning. I'm forty soon, so I know what I'm talking about. And late development runs in my family. My father was in his late forties when Teresa and I were born. Have a good think about the teaching idea. Sleep on it!' He gets up to leave, but stops just before he reaches the door, 'Before I forget – where are the rest of the diaries? I may as well continue with them while I'm here.'

She grins at him, 'Has Teresa been talking to you?' She picks them up from the bedside table and hands them over.

'*Buona notte,* Anna!' he says as he shuts the door behind him.

Before putting out the light, she lays in bed thinking over the idea of teaching English to local children. She needs a job. Expanding the *Scuolaclub* won't bring in bundles of lire but it will be a start. If she is careful, these earnings can top up the money Mamma left her and buy her extra time to stay and complete her mother's story. She decides also to ask Teresa if she can take over Francesco's jobs round the *agriturismo* once he returns to Bologna at the end of the summer. If she agrees, it will make her feel better about staying on.

PART II

Chapter 23

A couple of weeks later and Anna is hobbling around unaided. Teresa allows her back to her little house, helping her pack up the belongings she'd brought with her to the apartment. 'Don't forget I'm only round the corner. If you need anything, just call.' Handing her a folder she tells her that Francesco had asked her to pass the diaries on. 'He's managed to do some more translating. He would have dropped by himself but he's busy with research down in Romagna today.'

Home, sweet home, Anna thinks to herself after Teresa has left her alone in her little house in the *piazza*. The sky is sullen, threatening more rain and storms, so she is quite happy to light the stove, 'batten down the hatches' and read her mother's next instalment.

Francesco has scribbled a note on the envelope:

I reckon this was written a few years later than 1946. My guess is she wrote it retrospectively. See what you think.

SEPTEMBER 1946
The train seemed to chant "arrivederci, arrivederci" as it chugged its load of war victims across Europe. I

stared out of the window at the scarred landscape: stumps of houses like necks with heads blown off. I shuddered at the devastation and forced my gaze back inside the carriage. Opposite me a pair of weary soldiers slept, their heads thrown back against the seat – the young blond's mouth wide open, dribbling like a baby. His older companion had looked me up and down earlier and I'd cast down my eyes modestly and thrusting my left hand further forward on my lap, making the shining gold band on my finger more obvious. An old lady was huddled in the corner seat, a basket of vegetables held fast to her. My belongings were on the shelf above me in a battered suitcase which Mamma had insisted on tying up with thick rope before I left. 'You can never be too sure,' she'd said, as if she were a seasoned traveller, 'in case anybody thinks they can put their thieving hands into your bag.' The woman opposite seemed to me a country person too and I kept glancing at her to reassure myself. She made me feel less shabby, less strange. She'd only left her seat once in the whole twenty four hours, asking me to keep an eye on her belongings while she excused herself. The rest of the time she'd spent crying quietly into a large handkerchief, her age-blotched hands twisting and kneading the cloth. I watched her bony fingers in fascination. They reminded me of *Nonna's*. Before she died she used to sit all day in the kitchen, rocking back and forth, lost somewhere in the past. If my own heart had not been so full, I would have offered comfort to the old lady but I too was on a difficult journey.

'So near, so far, so near, so far…' The train continued to taunt me with its rhythm, until we suddenly screeched to a halt somewhere on the edge of a town in the middle of France. Such vast stretches of countryside we'd crossed, broken now and again by hamlets, bullet holes polka-dotting the abandoned houses. Hands reached up to our open windows, hands offering bread and produce, voices beseeching, 'S'il vous plait, s'il vous plait, Mesdames, messieurs.'

At home, Mamma always cut the bread in the same way for every meal. She cradled the big, round 'pagnotta' in her left arm; she cradled the staple food next to her heart while with her right hand she held the knife and cut towards her body. 'I won't harm myself,' she would say to Davide and me when we warned her to be careful. 'This bread is a gift from God, it's precious. The good Lord won't let me come to harm.'

This French bread being waved to us through the train window was long and thin. How could a French mother hold that to her heart?

As the train carried me further and further away from my Italy, this was one of the first differences I encountered between our countries. When we crossed the soupy-grey stretch of water between France and England, I could no longer hold back my tears. On that crossing, the umbilical cord connecting me to my home-land was well and truly severed and I began to understand a little of what Capriolo and Mamma had been warning me about. This was the hardest thing I had done in all of my nineteen years so far. I was terrified and excited at the same time.

Later on, from another train window, I stared out at my first glimpse of the green, English countryside. I looked but I didn't really see it. I was listening to the train as it rocked me to its clattering rhythm, *please be kind, please be kind, please be kind.*

We pulled into the station with a screech and a jolt. Norman had taught me a few basic phrases: 'Good morning', 'How are you?', 'My name is Ines Swilland.' Try as I could, my tongue just couldn't manage my new surname and I was really anxious that I might not be able to tell anybody who I was. Norman had written a letter to his parents with the time of the arrival of the Dover train to Victoria. He had managed to buy me a second class ticket on 'The Golden Arrow', a very smart train that had been put into storage during the war. He described me to his parents in a letter he had sent earlier: I would be wearing a grey skirt and jacket with a white blouse, I was just over five foot and my hair was dark, dark brown and curly. He told them I would probably be wearing it up, but a few of my hairpins had fallen out during the journey and now it was half up, half down. I hoped they wouldn't think I was too untidy. The chill air made me shiver. In my geography text-book at school, England was described as a country of pea-souper fogs and rain but this afternoon the sky was crisp and clear. The sun shone but it was biting cold and I was afraid my light clothing was not going to be adequate for this climate. Back home the September sunshine could sometimes be as warm as during August. But I had to stop thinking of Rofelle as "home" now. England was my new home. Taking a deep breath to calm my nerves, I gathered my belongings. Doors slammed, a whistle blew, on the platform people scurried past me purposefully, greeting each other with words I didn't understand. Suddenly I wanted to turn round, stay on the train and go back to my family in Italy.

And then an elderly couple approached me.

'Ines?' the woman asked, inclining her head towards me, wispy grey hair escaping from an untidy bun. When I nodded she stepped forward to kiss my cheek. Her skin was dry and smelt of soap. I recognised Norman in his mother: he had her blue eyes and long nose. And when she smiled at me, I saw she had the same gap between her front teeth. She spoke slowly at first and I could follow most of her words. 'Welcome to England, my dear new daughter. Let me take a good look at you!' She stepped back an arm's length and peered into my face. We were about the same height and I was surprised, thinking all English women were tall and slender but she was short like me – and quite plump.

'You are *much* prettier than Norman described,' she said and held out her hand for me to shake.

'My name is Freda and this is John but you can call us Mum and Dad. It will be much easier for you and you are part of the family now. Do you understand me when I talk, Ines?'

I nodded again although I couldn't understand everything she had said and I didn't feel ready to reply or utter any words in English myself and then 'Dad' kissed me too, his whiskery sideboards brushing my cheek. He smiled shyly. 'Yes, welcome Ines. Let's be getting you back home. We have to catch another train. It will take an hour.'

I only caught a few words of what he was saying because he spoke much faster than my mother in law and I realised how much I would have to improve on my very basic grasp of English if I was going to manage. I was beginning to have more sympathy with the struggle Norman had in trying to learn basic Italian and I wished now I hadn't teased him so much.

Norman's parents could see how exhausted I was and I was relieved I didn't have to keep up polite conversation with them on the final train journey. Before dusk fell, I looked out of the window at the neat rectangles of gardens lined up alongside the track. Most of them were laid to vegetable beds; some had swings; I saw cats sitting on window-ledges, washing flapping on lines. There were gaps where houses should have been. The bombs must have fallen in England too, I realised. Looking at these everyday scenes unfolding outside the train gave me some comfort. I dozed off with the thought that although I'd travelled hundreds of miles, people here had ordinary lives like ours back in Italy; they grew vegetables, hung out their washing and kept animals. Everything was going to be fine.

Mum and Dad lived in West Croydon, in a street full of houses that looked identical. Number 20 East Park Road was just the same as numbers 22 and 24 and I made a mental note to memorise their house number. I didn't want to get lost if I ever went out on my own.

'Well, here we are dear. This is our palace.' Freda guided me down the short front path to a door painted bottle green. John carried my old suit-case while Freda stopped to search for the key. She looked in her handbag, then in her pockets and eventually found it in her handbag where she had looked first of all. She chattered all the while but most of it washed over me. A couple of words like garden and Mussolini, I understood. John stood patiently behind us, waiting for Freda to find the key and I couldn't help thinking how much more shouting and waving of hands would have gone on back home, if Mamma had lost the key to our front door.

'Freda', said John, 'shhh! No talk of the war.' The last words he said in a whisper, as if he was ashamed.

Freda covered her mouth with her hand and I think she must have been trying to say sorry but I didn't really understand. A loud cough from Dad stopped her in mid flow and she caught hold of my hand, looking very embarrassed and asking me if I wanted a cup of tea. Norman had talked to me, before I left, about the difficulty some English people would have with me being Italian. First of all we had been enemies and then we had seemed to switch sides. It would be hard at times, he'd warned me, and maybe this was what he had meant. I wished I knew enough words to tell them none of it mattered, that the war was over and this was the start of new beginnings. I wished Norman was standing next to me, but it would be another two months before he could join me. He'd explained how he had to be de-commissioned from the British army and that there was nowhere for me to live with him during that time. I'd been anxious to escape from Rofelle and start on my new life, so I didn't mind, but I was already beginning to regret my adventurous spirit. It was too late now. I had to get on with it.

My in-laws' house was like a doll's house, with two rooms and a small kitchen and bathroom downstairs and two bed rooms upstairs. The ceilings were higher than in our mill and the walls were covered in coloured paper, unlike our white-washed walls. There were carpets on the floor and the little house was bursting at the seams with ornaments and plants.

Freda took me upstairs to the back of the house. She drew the curtains. 'This is your room until Norman gets home,' she said, 'It's his room, where he's slept since he was a little boy. But you shall have our room with the big bed once he comes back and until you can get sorted and find a house of your own, although that might be difficult with the shortage of housing.' It took her a while to explain all this to me. She was very patient and at one stage she found a note-book and pencil in Norman's desk and drew a picture of houses and bombs to help me understand. She showed me where to hang my clothes in the narrow wardrobe in the alcove next to the fire-place, gave me a clean towel and then left me alone while she prepared a meal.

I sat on Norman's narrow bed looking at the relics of his boyhood. A teddy bear perched lopsidedly on a shelf next to a row of well-thumbed books. A rusting model of a steam train and a box of metal soldiers completed the shelf's contents. Davide and I had no toys like this when we were children. My father had once carved me a tiny wooden doll for Epiphany, the feast of La Befana, when I was about six years old and Davide had managed to get hold of a pig's bladder before the war, when the January slaughter of the pig used to take place. He and his friends kicked it around the yard below the mill, laughing and jostling each other for their makeshift ball until it eventually burst. There had never been spare money for toys or spare time for playing either because we were always too busy with chores.

It felt uncomfortable to be sitting in Norman's room, spying on a part of his life that I knew nothing about. I suddenly felt he was a stranger too, despite the new gold band on my finger and I rubbed it to prove to myself that what was happening was real. A wave of homesickness came over me as I imagined Mamma and Papà sitting on their stone bench outside the mill, watching the sun go down behind the mountains. We had no toys but we had each other. I wondered if they were thinking about me and felt tears prickle my eyes. Then I shook myself and decided in the morning I would write them a letter for Capriolo to read to them, if Freda could show me where to post it and buy a stamp.

'Tea's ready, Ines.' Mum called up to me from the kitchen, just in time to stop my tears. 'Just you wait and see what I've got ready for you, my dear,' she said as I came into the tiny kitchen. She was stirring something in a pan on a modern gas cooker. Mamma always cooked over the open fire in our huge fireplace. This looked easier. I hoped Norman would buy a cooker for me too and maybe, if I was lucky, a refrigerator like the ones I'd seen in American kitchens in the movies.

'There you are, dear. Something Italian!'

Norman's parents watched over me as I stared at the plate of bread and what looked like a heap of maggots in red sauce. I had no idea what Mum had prepared for me but I didn't want to seem ungrateful.

'Go on then...don't hold back!' she urged me, 'we thought you'd feel more at home if we cooked you one of your dishes. We know you Italians eat it all the time.'

My special surprise was Heinz tinned spaghetti on toast, which I later realised had been acquired with coupons, saved carefully for my arrival to make me feel welcome. Each mouthful made me want to heave. It was sugary and like no pasta I had ever eaten in my life. But I recognised their kindness and ate as much as I could.

'Thank you.' I said, trying to hide half of the soggy mess beneath my knife and fork.

'Would you like anything else?' Freda went to her larder and returned to the table with an apple pie. The pie looked mouth-wateringly good but right from childhood we had been taught that it was impolite to accept any offering straight away. Only when the host or hostess insisted, were we to say 'yes, please'. So, being the polite girl I had been brought up to be, I said, 'No, thank you'. And I waited for my mother-in-law to offer again, only to see the pie whisked away and stored in the larder again at the side of the kitchen.

The same thing happened in the next few days with food, cups of tea, coffee. They would offer and I would decline, expecting them to insist and ask me again. But a second offer never came. After a week, I was very hungry. One night, when I was sure Mum and Dad were fast asleep – their snores coming loud and clear through the thin walls - I crept downstairs, avoiding the bottom creaky step and, opening the larder door, I gorged myself on bread, jam and a hunk of cheese. Only when Norman came home to England, after being de-commissioned, did I learn that it wasn't impolite to say yes the first time. He laughed at me and called me a silly goose.

Mum was kind. It must have been difficult for her as well with a stranger in her home. One Wednesday morning we went to market together and when we'd finished buying fish and a new saucepan, we went for a cup of coffee. (That was another thing I found strange at first. English coffee was too milky and weak but I found if I added three or four spoons of sugar, it was more drinkable. After a few occasions watching me do this, Freda had to gently explain that sugar was still rationed, showing me her ration book and telling me about the system of coupons everybody was expected to follow. John kept bees and she didn't mind how much honey I used in my drinks at home but sugar was another matter. There were so many new things to learn about). Anyway, two women sitting at the table next to ours in the tea-room overheard my stumbling efforts at conversation with Freda and must have made some comment about me that Freda took exception to. She got up, squared her shoulders, held her chin high and even though we hadn't finished drinking our coffees, she pulled me up with her, saying something to the women as we left. On the bus home she warned me this kind of thing would be likely to happen again, but that I shouldn't worry about it, 'Ignorant women like those. Got nothing better to do with themselves. War's over and it's not your fault you're Italian, after all.' And then she changed the subject, telling me how busy we were going to be that afternoon. As it was a sunny day we would clean the windows with vinegar and newspaper.

I hadn't thought that my being Italian could be a problem and it made me self-conscious whenever we went out. I never ventured out alone again until long after Norman returned.

Freda taught me English recipes so that I could impress Norman on his return. One morning she explained we were going to bake toad-in-the-hole. When I looked up the word 'toad' in my dictionary, I was horrified. I couldn't stomach the thought of even eating frogs and I wasn't looking forward to this new dish at all. 'But when do you add the toads?' I asked Freda, after she had put the dish of batter and sausages in the oven. She laughed so much and so did John that evening when she served it up. Freda had me stand next to her on other days when she cooked hot pot, Yorkshire pudding, Victoria sponge cakes and custard. I loved the puddings she made but I yearned to flavour the bland savoury dishes with herbs and full-bodied wine. But at the same time I wanted to learn to be a good English wife.

'Oh we don't drink wine very often in England.' Freda was shocked when I suggested adding wine to her gravy. 'Only on high days and holidays – you know, Christmas and New Year – special occasions. You are a funny little goose, Ines.' I wondered why the English found geese so amusing. Some of the expressions were so very hard to understand. Freda told me Norman said I was the apple of his eye, I warmed the cockles of his heart, the local butcher was as sly as a fox…there was a lot to learn, even though my English was slowly improving.

September turned to October and the weather grew colder. The house was freezing. The only warm place was in the kitchen by the boiler and at night I wore all my clothes in bed. I put my coat on top of the bed-clothes and still I shivered to sleep. Freda came to find me one morning when I had overslept and was late coming down for breakfast. 'Well, bless my soul. Look at you as snug as a bug in a rug.' She laughed at me hidden under my mound of bedding. 'Are you cold, my duck? You should have said. We can't have you freezing to death. We'll sort you out tonight.'

From then onwards, every night until Norman came back, she filled a stone bottle with boiling water from the kettle to warm up my bed. She knitted me a hideous pair of pink bed-socks with wool unravelled from an old cardigan and finally I felt warm. I wondered whether Norman would be able to find me in bed in my bundled up state. I missed him and couldn't wait for him to join me. I felt sure that once we were together again, I wouldn't feel as homesick and that he would make love to me the way he had done when we were in the mountains. I blushed when I thought about it. Freda and John were kind, but they weren't my mother and father and I hated the food and the dreary weather. I was much thinner too and I worried Norman would not find me attractive anymore.

November 6th 1946

It was a drizzly, Tuesday afternoon. The weather was very cold that winter and I was waiting at West Croydon railway station, dressed up in my best suit, my hair newly washed and curled, wearing a pair of gloves and scarf that my mother-in-law had knitted me, with scarlet wool she had put by for a special occasion. 'I reckon meeting your husband again after so many months counts as a special occasion. You want to look pretty for him, don't you? You need something to brighten up that grey suit of yours, it's well cut but it's a bit on the drab side. You could do with a bit of colour, you're looking a bit peaky lately. Don't want Norman to think we're not looking after you properly.' I was growing used to my mother-in-law's plain speaking. 'And he'll love that fruit cake. He always did love a fruit cake.' I was confused when

I'd helped her bake the cake. She told me we needed flour and I'd gone out to the garden, returning empty handed. 'No flower', I'd said, 'too cold, winter… no flower.' And then she'd got out the packet of self raising flour from the larder and pointed at the spelling. So many words sounded the same. Later on I understood she'd swapped cheese coupons with Mrs Hawthorne next door for half a pound of raisins. That was the way it was in the years after the war. People had to improvise. Freda had made a new set of curtains for the bedroom for Norman's return too. She'd dyed some plain cotton sheets a pretty apple green. As it turned out, I'm sure that Norman didn't notice. But it made Freda feel better.

My tummy was bubbly, full of butterflies. Norman was due back in England. I hopped from foot to foot. I didn't know what to do with myself. I couldn't settle to anything. Another of Freda's strange sayings described me as "a cat on a hot tin roof".

The train drew in and Freda and John waited discreetly in the waiting room to give us some private moments together. I saw him straightaway amongst all the other men. He was thinner and his hair was shorter but it was definitely my Norman. 'Tesoro, tesoro, my darling,' I shouted, as I raced up the platform, calling to him at the top of my voice, flinging myself into his arms.

He frowned down at me, unwrapped my arms from around his neck and told me everyone was looking and not to make a show of myself. As far as I could see, there were couples all around us, locked in embraces and I couldn't understand why he was so cold.

From that moment on my heart began to shrivel a little more each day, like the sweet grapes that turned into dried fruit on Papà's vines. That night when we went upstairs to Freda and John's bed, he undressed quickly, slung his trousers and shirt over the chair, switched off the light and turned over on his side. I moved closer to him, moulding my body into his, like in the nights after our wedding.

'Not tonight, Ines', he muttered, 'it's been a hell of a day. In fact these last months have been worse than hell. I'm tired. Go to sleep.' And he moved further away.

I wondered what I had done wrong.

I lay in the dark, feeling colder and lonelier than I had ever felt in my life and I turned away from my husband so he wouldn't hear me crying. Why didn't he want me anymore? What could I do? I needed my mother. I wanted her advice. And then it was as if she was beside me in my cold, English bedroom. The curtains stirred in the night breeze and it was if she was talking to me across the miles. I could hear my practical, wise mother telling me to snap out of it and get on with the new life I had wanted so much. I felt ashamed to be crying in bed and instead I lay still and planned what I could do.

Freda had said I looked thin. Then maybe Norman would love me more if I tried to put on weight. I didn't like most of the food but I liked Freda's homemade cakes and biscuits. I decided I would eat more and make my curves return. I'd buy some lipstick at Woolworth's to make myself look pretty and desirable. I would make Norman love me again.

Chapter 24.

Ines continues her account of her new life in England.

Your grandparents were illiterate, Anna. Their families needed them to work on the land and they were young when they stopped attending the little school at Rofelle.

When I wrote letters to Italy I knew they would be read aloud by Capriolo or Padre Luca. So, I never felt I was able to speak from my heart.

Your grandparents died and my letters were returned together with their wedding rings, the only jewellery my mother possessed.

I never wrote to them about my unhappy times for fear of upsetting them but sometimes I needed to express what I really felt, so sometimes I wrote letters to Mamma and Papà that never made it to the post box. I found all of them when I was clearing the house before we moved. I had forgotten so many details of my early married life and reading them was like watching an old film about myself.

Keep a diary so your memories can help you grow wiser...I call them 'memory pearls'.

This was one of the letters that Capriolo returned.

> 62 Sanderstead Rise,
> West Croydon,
> Surrey.
> January 6th 1947

Dearest Mamma and Papa,

Today is not a feast day in England but I have a picture of you in my mind, preparing chicken and polenta in the hearth for this special day and maybe Papà, you going to the Osteria, to drink a glass or two of wine with Giacomo and Giorgio. I went to Mass today because it is the Feast of the Epiphany and it is only Catholics who do that here. But children don't celebrate like they do in Italy. Here, they receive gifts on Christmas Day instead. There are very few Catholics in England. Freda calls me a Papist but says she doesn't really mind one way or the other. She is a kind woman and has taught me how to make English cakes and I am getting fatter with every week that passes. She asked me if I was expecting, because she noticed my skirt was tighter. But, although I would love a baby, nothing has happened yet. Sorry, Papà, if I embarrass you with woman talk but how else can I speak to Mamma about these things? It would be wonderful to talk by telephone. Norman thinks we may be getting one soon for his work and maybe we could telephone you at Piero's bar at an arranged time? He has been promoted in the sales department at the airport and it may mean we can manage in the future to get airline tickets at a special price. I am frightened at the thought of being in a plane so high in the sky, but if it means we can see each other without a long journey by train, then that will be wonderful, don't you think?

When I was at Mass this morning, there was a woman two rows in front of me and I was absolutely sure she was not English. There was something about her. She had dark hair like mine and she wasn't very tall. (English women generally tend to be quite tall.) Anyway, I plucked up courage at the end of the service and tapped her on the shoulder and simply said, 'Are you perhaps Italian?' Well, it was as if we had known each other all our lives. She shouted 'si' at the top of her voice and we both wrapped our arms around each other although we had never met before. Although Tiziana is from Rome and nowhere near our Tuscany, we had so much to talk about and we have arranged to meet next week for a cup of tea. Not for a coffee, because English coffee is disgusting - watery, bitter and quite awful. I have taken to drinking tea instead. You see, I am becoming an English 'milady'.

Norman and I are very lucky that we can move into our very own first house. There are long waiting lists as so many people lost their homes to the German bombs. It is not just in Italy that people suffered in the war. Norman had enough cash to buy our new house, otherwise we would have been in a queue for months, maybe years. The English queue for everything. Even if there are only two people waiting for something, they queue one behind the other. It makes me want to laugh sometimes but I suppose people laugh at our ways too. Norman is always scoffing at me when I worry about being in a draught. He always tells me that nobody ever died from fresh air and he opens the window even wider just to tease me.

We have a coal fire in our living room and I light it as soon as I get up in the morning. It feels strange not to have to collect wood from the river bank or from Papà's neat log pile. Coal is delivered by a man with a horse and cart and I rush out into the street to collect the droppings before anybody else to put them on our vegetable garden. When the fire burns, it smells different from wood smoke but it stays alight much longer. I don't like the smell and when you walk in the street on some days, you can't see your way easily because of the fog and Norman says it is because of the coal smoke.

Last week I had a cold and have been off my food ever since but don't worry, I'm sure it won't last long. And anyway, as I said, I have begun to put on weight and Norman says I look much better than when he first came back from Italy. I've learnt to make rock cakes and sponge cakes. Freda gave me a recipe for a fruit cake, rich and heavy, but Norman loves it. I bet you can hardly believe it is me talking, Mamma. You used to say I was capable of burning water. I've changed.

It would be wonderful if one day you could come and see our house. We have a small garden at the front, full of roses smelling of soap and perfume. At the back, there is a line for me to hang clothes to dry (that is, when the weather is good enough.) Some days I long for the breeze to dance up from the river, like it used to do at the Mill to dry the clothes on the bushes. Norman has his vegetable garden at the far end, just in front of the railway line. The trains disturbed me at first with their clattering but now I like them. Sometimes children wave at me if I am in the garden and I wave back. I wonder where the passengers are going and Norman says, mostly up to London to work. The train brought me here to England and I wonder if there are any other women like me on the trains, arriving to start new lives. After Norman has left for work and I have finished my household chores, I write in my journal and sometimes I jot down a few lines of poetry.

Next weekend we are buying two arm chairs for the living room, as at the moment we are using oak dining chairs that Freda has lent us. They are hard and old fashioned and full of wood worm. But they've helped us out. I have chosen green upholstery for the settee and arm chairs and Freda is going to help me make curtains with material patterned with green roses to pick up the colour. The houses need curtains here to keep in the warmth - there are no shutters like in Italy. Norman is borrowing a camera from a friend at work and will take some pictures for me to send to you in my next letter so you can see where we are living.

Please can you send me your delicious recipe for your bean soup, Mamma? I dream about it and it would be an excellent recipe for this cold winter.

Your loving daughter,
Ines.

And this is one of the letters I never sent.

Friday night.

Dearest, darling parents,

I hate it here.

I hate the cold, the food, the unsmiling, sunless people with their pale white faces.

I hate my cruel husband who is so different from my Norman, whom I loved to distraction in beautiful Tuscany.

I miss our *mulino*, hidden in the folds of the Alps of the Moon where the sun sets from jewel red skies behind misted blue peaks.

Mamma, when you tried to talk to me on the eve of my wedding, why didn't you prepare me better? I try to please my husband. But I hate going to bed with him. I hate him when he forces himself on me with his heavy, beer-smelling body, even when I have my monthly bleeds. And if I tell him I am tired, he shouts at me. Sometimes he lashes out and hits me. I never know when it will happen.

He never strikes me where it will show. There are bruises on my ribs and thighs that some days are so sore I cannot bear to feel the weight of clothes against my skin.

Please Mamma, let me come home. I tried to put some house-keeping by for a train ticket. I hid it on a shelf in a cocoa tin at the back of the larder. But he found it. And that gave him another excuse to give me a beating, accusing me of stealing money instead of buying food. He yanked me by the hair and I saw a fistful of my curls clasped tight through his knuckles. Next morning I combed my hair in a different style to cover the bald patch.

And when the beatings are over, he cries. He holds me tight and his tears soak into my nightdress. He promises he never meant it, that he loves me, that he will never lay a finger on me ever again. He begs me not to leave him and then I know I can't. It is my duty now in life, to honour and obey him like Padre Luca told me on our wedding day. But I can't love him. I feel so ashamed, Mamma, at how my life has turned out. I long to be back with you and Papà again, back in the mill where the hearth is warm with real love.

Each morning when he leaves for work I say '*coraggio!*' Things will improve, I tell myself. If I become more English, then he will love me once again.

But I shall never love him back – not in the way I once hoped.

Here is another letter posted and later returned..
62 Sanderstead Rise, February 10th 1947

Dearest Mamma and Papà,

I'm sorry I haven't written for ages. You know my cold that was taking so long to get better and making me feel ill? Well, I started to be sick in the mornings too. I thought I had an awful disease because it went on for days and days and, eventually, I went to the doctor. Well, Mamma and Papà – your daughter is going to have a baby! The baby is due at the end of August and, God willing, you are to become grandparents. I would so love you to be able to be here with me, Mamma, but I know how difficult that might be. We won't be able to come and visit you this summer, as we had hoped, as Norman doesn't want me to travel in my condition. I still feel really sick and have lost a lot of weight but Freda is taking great care of me. She makes me chicken soup and toast. I haven't the heart to tell her that I can't abide her chicken soup. It is not at all like your wonderful broth and home-made cappelletti, Mamma.

I have tried to knit a cardigan for the baby but there are so many holes in it where I have dropped the stitches that it looks more like a shopping string bag. Freda laughed when I showed her but she loves knitting and has said she will make the baby's wardrobe. I pity the baby when he or she arrives, as Freda's wool is mostly from clothes that she unpicks and some of the colours are not really baby colours. Maybe our child will be the first baby to be dressed in mourning! She presented me with a pair of black bootees last week made out of an old shawl. The wool is lovely and soft. I don't know if I shall ever use them but I don't want to hurt her feelings. I have been in tears a lot recently and she managed to find out where Tiziana lived, by going to speak to the 'Papist' priest, as she calls him, and I had a wonderful surprise when Tiziana knocked on my door last Monday morning.

Write soon and tell me you are proud of your daughter (and maybe you can send me some <u>white</u> bootees, Mamma!)

   With love and a thousand kisses,
     Ines.

***

When Tiziana knocked at the door that Monday morning, I wasn't going to open it. It was ten o'clock, the grate needed emptying, last night's supper dishes were in the sink and I was still in bed. Norman was away for a couple of days for work and I couldn't see the point of getting up. I felt sick and unhappy. I ignored the knocking at the door and turned over again under the snug blankets and eiderdown.

Knock, knock, knock.

Whoever it was, they were insistent. And then I heard the flap on the letter-box clatter open and Tiziana's voice calling to me. '*Puttana Eva*! Ines, you lazybones – open up! It's only me. I know you're in there! Come and open the bloody door.'

It was good to hear Italian spoken – even if it was ripe with swear words. Tiziana stood on the door step, wearing her new mink coat, stamping her fashionably clad feet in the cold. She had once confided in me how she'd met her husband in a brothel along the banks of the river Tiber in Rome. 'It was only temporary,' she'd told me when she saw my mouth drop open in shock, 'You'd have done the same, *cara mia*, if you'd been stuck in Rome with nothing to eat and brothers and sisters starving at home. It was alright for you jammy lot in the country with your nice fat pigs and hens.' It was pointless arguing with her once she got going. She was quite unashamed of the way she'd 'snared', (as she put it), her husband Denis. 'He has something missing up there', she'd said, drumming the side of her head with her finger, adding with a cackle, 'but not down there'. As far as she was concerned, her slow English husband had been her passport out of poverty. We were very different types of girl but I was fond of her nevertheless – because she was Italian.

'Brrr! It's freezing out there,' she said as she swept into the hallway, 'I wouldn't let a dog go out in this shitty weather. Make me a coffee, there's a darling.' She enveloped me in a hug and my tears flooded up and they wouldn't stop.

'Hey, Ines. Come on, my love. *I'll* make us a coffee. Look what my folks managed to send me.' And she pulled out a brown package and dangled it under my nose.

I gagged. Coffee was one of the many things I couldn't stomach at the moment and the rich aroma made me heave.

'Whoops, sorry, I forgot about your condition. Well, tea it will have to be then. I'll keep the coffee for when your taste buds start behaving again - 'cos they will Ines, I promise you. You won't go on feeling like shit forever. And just for you, I won't light up. How's that for friendship? I remember when my sis' was in the family way...she couldn't stand the smell of fags. You're probably the same.'

She bustled about, making tea, finding the cups. 'You go and get yourself dressed, there's a good girl, and I'll see to the fire and then we'll have a jolly good chin-wag when you've decided to turn off those waterworks. You're only pregnant, *cara*; you're not going to pass away just yet. Come on, hurry up! I've got to be back to cook Denis's dinner for one o'clock. I can't stay long.'

Half an hour later, sitting next to a glowing fire, I began to feel better. 'I don't know what I'd do without you, Tiziana,' I said.

'Don't talk rubbish. The feeling's mutual, *carissima*. England's all very well but an Italian girl needs a pinch of Italy now and again and that's what we can do for each other. By the way, my folks are coming over for Easter. They're driving. My uncle's bringing them in his taxi. Don't ask me how he's managing with the petrol – I never ask him any questions - he's got his connections and he gets us loads of stuff. So, if you want anything, then have a think and let me know. Pasta, olive oil, parmigiano ... anything, within reason of course. It's better than over here but they're not finding it easy to get hold of stuff even though the bloody war's well and truly over. They have to keep going into the countryside to see what they can find. Speak to people they know. You know what I mean.' She touched the side of her nose and winked at me.

I began to cry again.

'God, you're all over the place today, aren't you?' She crouched down in front of me, taking hold of one of my hands, a frown on her powdered forehead.

'What's really the matter, Ines? It's not just the pregnancy, is it? Tell Aunty Tiziana.'

I didn't know how far I wanted to confide in her but I needed somebody to talk to. I blew my nose on the handkerchief she thrust at me, tried a smile and said quietly. 'I feel too embarrassed to talk about it.'

'There's nothing will embarrass *me*. You know that. Good God, Ines...when you've been brought up in a family like mine, all squashed into the tiniest of flats in Trastevere, then you'll know nothing could embarrass me. My parents slept in the same room, just a curtain hanging between our beds to give them a bit of privacy. Well, I learnt all about the facts of life from a very early age, I can tell you.'

'I don't think Norman loves me anymore.' And I dissolved again.

Tiziana laughed. 'You great lump...you're pregnant, aren't you? Your hormones are making you feel all mixed up and peculiar. My mamma even took to eating bits of furniture whenever she was expecting. We had teeth marks in the kitchen chairs.' She fetched a comb from her handbag. 'Just look at the state of this haystack, *caruccia*, when was the last time you looked at yourself in the mirror?' And she started to gently comb out my tangles. It was soothing, relaxing. After a little while she started to talk to me again. 'Look, Ines, of course Norman loves you. If he didn't touch you, neglected you, never came home to you at night, then maybe I'd start believing he didn't love you. But you're pregnant, girl. That didn't happen by immaculate conception like the Madonna, I'm sure.'

'Don't laugh at me, Tizi.'

'*Porca Miseria*. You've got it bad.'

'I'm pregnant, yes, but I didn't enjoy getting pregnant. I don't like it when we're in bed. It hurts and I just always want it to be over and finished.' I said all this in a rush, my cheeks turning redder than sun-blushed Marzano tomatoes.

Tiziana sat down on one of Freda's hard chairs and crossed her legs, pulling her skirt down over her stocky legs encased in silk stockings. It was hard to gauge her age under her heavy coat of make-up but she was definitely older than me by at least ten years. She had let that drop into conversation by mistake. I felt she was very worldly wise compared to me.

'Well darling, all men are a bit rough at times. Take it from me, it's quite normal when they get a bit excited. But if you're not enjoying sex at all, then that's not your fault. As far as I'm concerned, if he can't make you feel good, then it's his fault.'

Maybe I should have opened up completely to her at that point, showed her my bruises, asked her if *they* were normal. But I was ashamed and somehow felt it was something I had brought upon myself. Nevertheless, I needed her reassurance, 'But at home...' I quickly corrected myself... 'In Italy, before we married, it always felt so good when we were together. I mean, we didn't go all the way or anything - I made him wait until we were married. But then, when he came back, at the end of the war, he'd changed. He was colder, as if he didn't care anymore.

Or maybe I've changed.' I wiped my eyes with her sodden handkerchief and looked at her.

She sighed and raised her hands, as if to say: what do you expect? 'It's never going to be like it was at the beginning, Ines. Marriage isn't a fairy story. And you have to understand about men. Once they've got what they want, they get lazy. Believe you me. You have to be a bit more cunning, *bella*, tease them a little.'

I looked at her, with her pretty face and matronly figure. Her tight mohair jumper looked as if it had been painted on her bosom, leaving little to the imagination. We weren't the same type of girl but she was my only friend in England and I'd never talked to anybody as openly in my life about these things. If we had met in Italy, I doubt we would even have said "*buongiorno*" to each other. And yet, alone as I felt in Croydon that morning, I trusted her advice.

'Thank you, Tizi. I've got so much to learn, I can see that. I sometimes wonder if I made a mistake marrying Norman and coming here. I should have stayed to look after my parents and...'

'...and lived a life of misery in a dead end village in the mountains, having to piss in a hole in the ground and working from morning to night to die an early death. No thank you very much. I'm much happier here in Inghilterra and you will be soon, Ines. You're just feeling like this because you're pregnant. It affects women in different ways, believe me... My *nonna* talked to me a lot and so I know - she was an expert on all things to do with babies. She used to deliver all the babies in our block of flats and if she'd known how to write, then she would have been able to produce a manual with all a woman needs to know about pregnancy. Now wash your face and take this lipstick.' She rummaged in her crocodile effect handbag and produced a stick of Woolworth's Ruby Lustre. 'It's nearly finished but put some on tonight when Norman gets home. Undo some of those buttons on your starchy old blouse and cook him a delicious meal. The way to a man's heart is through his stomach. And his cock! Let me know how you get on darling, I have to dash now but I'll come and see you again next week.'

And bestowing a hearty kiss on each of my cheeks, she let herself out into the cold morning air, tottering down the front path on her high heels.

Chapter 25
February 1947

When Norman's key turned in the latch at 6 o'clock that evening, I quickly took up position in the kitchen. With Tizi's lipstick applied as thickly as I thought acceptable, without ending up looking like a clown, I'd been practising pouting at myself in the mirror. She'd suggested leaving a few buttons open on my blouse but I'd decided to go further. It was a huge extravagance but I'd lit the boiler in the afternoon and dragged the tin bath into the kitchen for a long, bubbly soak. A generous splash of 'Gala Affair', that Norman had bought me for Christmas and, dressed in my flimsiest nightdress, I was ready for him. It was freezing, but I'd been warned about working hard to "keep my man", so feeling cold was something to put up with.

'What's burning?' Norman rushed into the kitchen. The gas was too high and the soup had boiled over. I still hadn't got the hang of my modern cooker. 'Are you feeling sick again?' Norman threw down his newspaper on the table I had carefully laid, squashing a serviette that had taken ages to fold into a lily shape, like in the *trattoria* in Badia. 'Why aren't you dressed, Ines? Have you been like this all day?'

My seduction plan didn't seem to be working. I wasn't going to give up though. Letting my dressing gown drop to the floor, I revealed myself in my see-through, nylon nightdress.

'Ines. You'll catch your death like that.' He picked up my dressing-gown and held it up for me to feed into my arms.

'Why don't you love me anymore?' I flung myself at him, pummelling his chest in despair. 'What have I done wrong?'

He looked totally perplexed, his mouth half open as he stepped back from me.'Ines, what on earth's got into you?'

'*Sono stufa*...I'm fed up, that's what ... fed up, fed up, fed up and I want to go back to Italy.'

He came over to me and started to rub my back. 'It's your condition, that's what it is,' he said, in a calm voice that did nothing whatsoever to soothe me, 'it's making you talk nonsense. Come and sit down and I'll serve up the soup.'

'It's burnt. I don't want any *stupida* soup. Let go of me, *cretino*.' I pushed him away. The tears I had promised myself were all finished and dried up, started to flow again. I was embarrassed at my attempt to seduce him and frustrated. I didn't know what to do anymore. I never knew what sort of mood he would be in from one day to the next. Wiping my tears away angrily with the backs of my hands, I tried another tack. I would be firm and reasonable with him. Taking a deep breath I looked at him in the face and asked, 'Do you still love me? You *must* be honest with me.'

He was embarrassed. He sat down at the table avoiding my gaze. I repeated my question, louder this time.

'Keep your voice down' he hissed at me, 'You're giving the neighbours a real treat tonight and you're talking daft nonsense.'

'I don't care about the bloody neighbours. Answer me!' I shouted.

'Don't swear! You've been with that Italian girl again, haven't you? She's got a mouth like a sewer. I can always tell when you two have been keeping company. She's a common...'

'She's my friend and stop changing the subject. I asked you a question. Do you still love me? Like you did in Italy?'

He fiddled with the knife and fork on the table I had laid so carefully for my special supper. His hands were shaking, he was likely to lash out at me at any moment. But my conversation with Tiziana, when she'd told me Norman was at fault, had given me strength to face up to him. There were to be no beatings that evening, just a sad, thin smile when he eventually returned my gaze, mumbling, 'It was never going to be the same as it was in Italy. We're here now and life is different.'

'But you're still Norman and I'm still Ines. That shouldn't be any different. If you tell me you don't love me anymore, then I think I shall kill myself.'

'Now you're being over-dramatic like a typical Eyetie. Calm down. Think of the baby.'

'*Uffa!* I can think of nothing else! And you married an Eyetie - as you so kindly call me - so what did you expect? *Madonna buona*! I don't want this baby to be born in a family where there is no love.'

'I've never said I don't love you, Ines,' he said, sounding tired, defeated. He came over to the chair where I had slumped, pulled me up and put his arms round me. 'I can't always show you in the way you want. Now dry those eyes and let's eat.'

I wanted him to undress me, tear off my nightie and make love; cover my body with tender but passionate kisses, make me feel how I'd felt on that afternoon in the river. I had begun to wonder if I'd imagined the whole scene and turned it into a romantic fantasy.

Instead of making wild, urgent love, we finished our burnt soup and the stodgy apple pie and lumpy custard he had insisted Freda taught me how to make. Afterwards, he switched on the wireless, listened to the evening news and after giving me a goodnight peck on the top of my head, went upstairs. When I came up ten minutes later, he was fast asleep, on his back, snoring. I pulled off my nightdress, rummaged in the drawer for a pair of his warm flannelette pyjamas and slid into the icy bed.

Chapter 26
July 1999.

Anna sits on her step outside her front door with her mug of tea, brooding over the events in her mother's account of early married life in England. Billi seems to sense her mood, tries to coax her into playing, biting her bare toes with his sharp little teeth. She tickles his tummy and says aloud, 'it's all right for you little fellow, with nothing to worry about except when your next meal will be.' Deciding she needs human company she wanders round to Teresa's after clearing away her breakfast dishes.

'*Permesso?*' she calls, pushing open the door to the *agriturismo*. Francesco is reading a newspaper in the dining room. He looks up as she comes in.
'Buongiorno! *Che muso lungo stamattina.*' When she looks puzzled, he translates. 'You have a very long face this morning. What's up?'

She sits down opposite him, leans her elbows on the table, her head in her hands. 'I finished reading what you translated for me,' she sighs.

'Your mother didn't have an easy time, did she?'

'No. If it had been me, I wouldn't have put up with him. If a man ever so much as laid one finger on me, he would be out immediately.'

'Times were different.'

'It's still no excuse. Poor woman!'

Folding up his paper, he suggests another excursion. 'It's a lovely day, Alba's playing with friends, there are no jobs to be done for Teresa as she has no guests staying at the moment. You look as if you need a good dose of distraction.'

'That would be lovely.'

'Why don't I take you to see the watermill where your mother lived? '

'But I thought you said it was a pile of stones?'

'... ruins. It's covered in brambles and uninhabitable but most of it is still there.'

Down at the river near the start of the path leading to the mill, there are a few sunbathers; families up from the sweltering, congested coast enjoying picnics in the mountain air. Francesco and Anna soon lose them as they walk downstream to where the river forks.

'The river has changed over the years,' he explains, 'it used to run in one continuous flow at this point but nature does what it wants. We'll take the right fork. I hope it's not too overgrown, I haven't been down here for a while.'

She follows him as they step over large boulders and wade through the water in river-shoes. Willow branches, olive-green and silver in the breeze, stroke the surface of the stream and cicadas keep up their noisy sawing racket. Suddenly Francesco stops, turning slowly to her, finger to his lips. Upstream a mother deer is drinking at the water's edge, her fawn close behind. Then she catches their scent, lifting her head to watch them and then she is off, scrambling up the bank into the dense oak woods, her fawn not far behind.

'How sweet they were!' says Anna, 'It's the closest I've been to deer so far. My next ambition is to see a porcupine.'

'They're nocturnal, so we won't see one today. But we can keep a look out for their quills. Alba collects those. Look down there!' He points to a hollow in the mud, bending down to examine marks left at the river's edge. 'What do you think these are?'

'Maybe holes from somebody removing stones?' she suggests. 'They're so beautiful. In England they sell them for vast prices in garden centres. Somebody with the right machinery could make a fortune here.'

'Fortunately it's forbidden to take stones from the river without special permits. No, this hole has been made by a wild boar, cooling down in the mud.'

His company is always interesting. 'You know so much about the wild life. You'd make a great guide,' she tells him, hunkering down to examine the muddy hole. It smells strongly of animal and she wonders if a boar might be watching them within the bushes lining the river bank.

'My father often took me on walks right from when I was very little. That is, when he was feeling well enough. He was injured in the war and suffered poor health afterwards. He knew this place inside out. As a boy he climbed every nook and cranny, gathered chestnuts, hunted boar, played and hid in the caves.' He picks up a stone, throwing it into a deep pool. 'I miss him, he was very special.'

'You're lucky to have a father you loved. I never felt close to my father and, from what I'm reading now, I'm not surprised. He was a difficult man.'

They continue their walk, the vegetation thick in places so Francesco cuts away brambles and branches with his knife to clear a route. Round the next bend of the river, where the current is stronger, they come upon the ruined mill. It is little more in parts than a pile of stones tumbling into the water. She follows

Francesco to a flight of stone steps, each tread almost concealed by ferns and moss.

'Be very careful,' he turns to warn her, 'this staircase is leaning away from the side of the mill.'

She has no wish to injure her ankle again but at the same time she wants to explore where her mother spent the first eighteen years of her life. The paint on the front door has almost peeled away and the knocker, in the form of a lion's head, is rusting and about to fall off. She prises it away and puts it in her pocket. 'I don't care if it's stealing,' she says, rubbing the lion's head and knowing her mother has also once touched it.

'Do you know who owns the mill now? So far Mamma makes no mention of any other relatives in her diary, other than my grandparents and of course poor Davide. And they're all gone now.'

'No, but it's bound to belong to somebody, even if it's been divided up and different people own different rooms in the place. That's often the way with property here. We could find out for you at the *Comune*.'

Next to the door, tangled in ivy, are traces of an old bread-oven, its door rusting and full of holes. A long handled shovel propped against the wall is riddled with wood worm. She wonders who the last person was to use it for pushing in *foccaccia* beside the hot ashes.

'When they lit the oven,' Francesco tells her, 'they would use up all the embers and bake anything they could so as not to waste the opportunity of having the oven alight. And people nearby who didn't have ovens would bring along their bread or vegetables for roasting on allotted days.' He picks up the shovel, examining it carefully. 'I think you should take this back and clean it up. I'm surprised it hasn't already been stolen. You see these old tools for sale in antiques' markets nowadays. I saw some at the Sunday market in Arezzo and they weren't cheap.'

She fingers the hand-beaten, metal rings fixed into the cracked mill wall and he tells her how mules were once the main means of transport and would be tied up to the rings whilst their owners waited for grain to be milled. He bends down, worrying at a piece of iron in the earth near the door and pulls up an old mule's shoe.

'We hang those up in England and they are supposed to bring good luck,' she tells him.

'Take this as a souvenir too… We say go 'in the mouth of the wolf' when we wish somebody good luck and then you have to reply 'may the wolf die first'.

'We say break a leg!' she laughs. 'But I definitely don't want to do that…a twisted ankle is bad enough.'

'Even our proverbs and sayings are slightly different. We return once more to your point about differences in our cultures. I read somewhere that you say a person born rich is born with a silver spoon in his mouth. In Italian we say somebody born rich is born with a shirt on his back. I think that says something about different aspirations.'

'You see – I told you! Reading my mother's story, I realise more and more the differences she came across and how much she had to learn and adapt. It was hard for her.'

'It's easier now. We know more about each other from the internet and television.'

Anna wonders if a mobile phone or computer would have made much difference to her mother's life.

She rummages for her camera in her back-pack to photograph the mill and thinks about sending some pictures to Jane and Harry, wondering if they will be interested. Climbing down to the river to the arched space under the mill, she finds the remnants of the huge shaft that once turned the mill-stones. Francesco ventures further into the hollow and shouts above the noise of the river from within the dark space, '*Accidenti!* Somebody has sawn the paddles off and stolen them. *Peccato!* A pity!' He jumps down to where she stands and brushes the dust from his knees where he had knelt down to inspect the mill workings. Anna is angry at the thought of strangers plundering souvenirs from her ancestors. She knows it is irrational - until this morning she hadn't even realised there was anything left of her grandparents' mill. But her past is already so fragile.

'I'd like to go inside, to see where my mother lived. You've no idea how churned up I am.'

She lets him take her hand as he pushes open the door, telling her to tread carefully on the rotten floorboards. When her eyes adapt to the gloom inside, she makes out a cracked stone sink against the window. Walking over to it, she tries to imagine her grandmother washing pots while looking out at the forest opposite. It is very low - on a level with her thighs - making her think *nonna* must have been very small. A hole beneath the window shows how the sink drained primitively into the river below. Discarded on the floor are a broken colander, one leg missing, and a ladle without a handle. On a shelf in a built-in corner cupboard with one door missing, is a rusting tin of Lavazza coffee.

'I want to go upstairs to see where they slept – nonna, nonno, mamma and Davide'. The names trip off her tongue as if she has been saying them every day of her life.

Gingerly, she climbs the ladder which serves as stairs to the bed-rooms. It leans precariously against an opening to the upper storey. Plaster crumbles from the walls, there is a hole in the roof where she can see picture-white clouds drift across an azure sky. A crucifix hangs aslant above an old metal-bed holding a mouse-nibbled mattress. She pictures her grandparents falling into bed soon after dark and rising as soon as the sun climbed again, anxious to be at their tasks before the heat of the day. Stepping over to the shutter-less window she gazes at the indigo-blue mountains. Wisps of sugar-spun cloud are caught in the trees and placing her hands on the stone sill, she leans out to stare at the silver ribbon of water below as it dances its way down to the sea at Rimini. Sadness fills her and she shake her head. Francesco comes over and takes her in his arms, not saying anything, just holding her. After a while he releases her, suggesting they go out into the sunshine.

They find a large, flat rock to sit on. She doesn't feel like talking and he seems to understand her need to be quiet. She watches him unpack their picnic, carefully placing a bottle of wine in the shallows, wedging it firm with a stone. He spreads a cloth on the grass and lays out a half loaf of *Toscano*, a hunk of pecorino cheese, a jar of peppers in oil and a bunch of grapes. They eat in silence. The only sounds are the river and distant sheep bells. Slowly she calms, restored by the delicious lunch and grateful for his tactful presence.

'Grazie,' she says, draining the last drops of wine in her beaker. ' Having just read about my mother trying to be brave in her new life, coping with the way my father treated her…it suddenly overwhelmed me. The poor woman had gone through the war here and then she had another type of war to deal with in England. It's just so, so sad ...this old building in ruins, crumbling into nothing. It seems to mirror what I'm learning of Mamma's past.'

'There isn't 'nothing', as you put it .There is you and your brother and sister. She lives on through you all.'

'I wish she had been able to talk to me properly about her life.'

'She is doing it now, Anna, through her story. Listen to her. If you need more help, I'm here too. Maybe we could find other people who might have known your family. In those times, people used to come and sit in each other's houses in the evening, to keep company. It was called '*la veglia*'.

'I'd like that. You're a kind man ...'

'You're a kind woman, who's been very good with my daughter...so we're all square! Come on, let's go now. The clouds are telling me there's another storm brewing. Best to get back before the river plays its tricks on you again.'

She helps him pack up the remains of their lunch, being careful not to leave any rubbish behind. They set off for the village without dawdling on their return journey.

'Thanks for a really special afternoon.' She kisses him on the cheek when they arrive back at her house in the piazza.

'You're welcome. We must do it again. Good night, Anna.' He cups her cheek briefly in his hand and leaves her standing at the door, watching him walk over to the *agriturismo*.

Lessons at her *Scuolaclub Inglese* continue the following afternoon in the fresh air.

'Eugenio, come and sit over here and leave that lizard alone. Can you remember the word for lizard in English?'

Five hands go up, including Alba's but Anna resists letting her answer. Her English has come on in leaps and bounds but she wants to give other children a chance.

'Yes, Pina...'

Shy Pina takes her thumb out of her mouth to answer and Anna adds a sticker of a lizard to her name on the chart of local animals and plants they are learning.

'*Bravissima,* Pina. Very well done! Now, I'll give you each two minutes to think of as many words in English as you can for what you can see round and about you and then we'll go for a walk along the river.' Anna's Italian is improving too through contact with her little pupils who seem to enjoy helping her as much as she does them.

'Mees Anna. Can we go in ze water too? Not just for a walking?'

'Go for a walk, Piero,' she corrects the little boy. 'Yes, we'll swim in the river. It's a lovely sunny day.' Piero, ten years old and already a heart throb, is a 'water baby' and turns up at her class-room in the converted pig-sty next to the *agriturismo* with his swimming shorts, come rain or shine.

Half an hour later they are all down at the rock pool under the bridge. Alba holds Pina's hand and encourages her little friend into the water, where they crouch in the shallows catching tadpoles in their nets. Piero, Eugenio and Gianni add more flat stones to the dam they have started the previous week.

'We'll stay here for an hour, children. For the first half I don't want to hear any Italian...no Eugenio, that doesn't mean you can whisper in Italian! That's cheating. And after that, you can sing me a song. An Italian song, because as you all know, I want to learn your language too. And tomorrow we'll sing an English song.'

She watches them play in the water. Teresa has told her the locals call the pool "*la spiaggia*", the beach. During the war German soldiers used to come down here too under the baking August sun and strip off their uniforms to cool down in the mountain water. She is sure this river could tell a tale or two. In the evenings she has taken to walking along the banks before sun set, relishing the cooler air, looking for fossils, watching dragon flies skim across the dancing water. At times she fancies she can hear voices murmuring but when she turns to look, there is nobody, just the gurgle of water as it trips over the stones.

When the children have been collected from the "*Scuolaclub Inglese*" by their parents, she helps Teresa in the kitchen for an hour or so, preparing vegetables for the evening meal. A party of twenty for supper is in that evening and she is pleased to be able to offer an extra pair of hands.

'Can you slice the courgettes very finely for me, Anna? To make a Carpaccio of zucchini… Then pick some borage flowers to sprinkle on top.'

The vegetable garden is on a slope with a view of Montebotolino. As she fills a basket with purple borage flowers and gathers some cherry tomatoes that have fallen onto the soil, she glances up at the lonely village on the crags and decides she must brave another visit to the old honey-seller. She will not let him get the better of her. It is frustrating knowing that he was alive when her mother lived here and that she has not yet managed to talk to him. She wonders if there is a saying in Italian for taking a horse to water but not being able to make it drink. She will ask Francesco next time they talk.

Chapter 27
August 1999

The best kind of early alarm in the world, an August sun streaming through the window, wakes Anna. It is seven o'clock and still cool enough to pull on a light fleece on top of her summer 'uniform' of shorts and t-shirt. Breakfast on her front door step is becoming a routine and she decides to look out for a little garden table and chair when she is next down in at the market in Sansepolcro. She sets about boiling water for her cup of tea. Some habits die hard.

Sitting on the step, mug in one hand and bread liberally smeared with home-made plum jam in the other, she observes a lizard peeping out from behind a pot of white geraniums, waiting for a stray crumb or insect. Teresa is already up: a counterpane and pillow are airing on the window sill of her bedroom and the flick of a duster from another window gives away her morning cleaning.

Francesco is up too. Coming round the corner into the square with a basket of salad from the vegetable garden, he waves and she invites him over for a cup of tea.

'I'll bring my coffee instead, if you don't mind!'

She'd tried a mug of tea on him once before and he'd hated it, preferring it weak, with lemon.

A little while later they clink cups: one enormous, one tiny.

'Cheers!'

'Cin-cin! What have you planned for today?'

'I want to go up to Montebotolino again to speak to Danilo.'

'You won't find him there today. He has a market stall down in Pieve on a Thursday.'

'*Accidenti!*' she says, using another expression she has picked up recently. 'Well, I'll have to think again. Really, I need to clean my little house.'

'On a beautiful day like this? *No…*' He pronounces it in the Italian way, the 'o' drawn out, making it sound even more negative. 'I think you should come on another trip into our beautiful countryside with me.'

'What about your university work, your research?' she asks, trying to sound as if she is scolding.

'It's August. I'm allowed a holiday too, you know! How about this afternoon? I promised Alba I'd play with her this morning but I could come and fetch you later and we could go out for dinner afterwards.'

'Sounds good to me. But you do realise I'll now have to do my cleaning this morning!'

He turns to her in his car before they set off. 'Right! Yesterday you were upset when we were at *Il Mulino* and so I'm in two minds about our itinerary this afternoon. I'll let you decide, Anna. We could go to Caprese Michelangelo, the supposed birth place of Michelangelo or we could follow up another village described in your father's account. Fragheto? It's a sad place but the countryside round there is quite stunning and not touristy at all.'

'Remind me why that name is familiar.'

'It was the site of a massacre.'

She pauses. 'I might sound obsessive but, after all, this is why I came to Italy – to follow up my parents' early years. Andiamo a Fragheto.'

'*Va bene. Andiamo a Fragheto.*'

They drive for a good ten minutes, neither of them speaking, comfortable in each other's company, enjoying the scenery along the way. The sun burns down but the countryside is still green and lush. They pass through hamlets with old houses brightened by geraniums and other summer flowers planted in all kinds of containers. There are neat vegetable plots wherever there are gaps – even in the tiniest of spaces at the foot of steep crags along the road. It is too high for vines and olive trees and the scenery is different from typical Tuscan postcard views displaying cypress trees and elaborate villas but this landscape feels more 'lived in' to Anna, a place where people have had to respect nature in order to graft a living. Francesco pulls out to overtake a tractor laden with hay. The road is narrow but she feels safe; he doesn't take risks, which is understandable in view of how his wife had died.

'I should think you must be nearly half way through your mother's diaries by now,' he says as he pulls back onto the right hand side of the road.

'I was flicking through what's left. I'm more than three-quarters of the way. Mamma writes less and less as the years go by... the last pages are in English.'

'Well, if you think about it, she lived more years in England than Italy – so English had become her day to day language.'

'You're right. More than fifty years in England compared with eighteen here. She never lost her lovely Italian accent though. God knows why they chose a name such as Harry for their first born...she never could pronounce 'h' properly.'

'Maybe it was your father's choice? 'Arry,' Francesco tries to pronounce Harry but only manages 'Arry' and she laughs.

'We have 'h' in our alphabet but we don't ever pronounce it, so what do you expect?' he retaliates, 'have a go at saying Roma the way I do!' He rolls his 'r' and Anna fails to copy him, coming out with a sound that is more 'Roema' than his perfect pronunciation.

'*Ecco*! Same difficulty for you!' he chuckles.

After another couple of bends, he stops the car before a bridge spanning the River Marecchia. 'I think we should get out here so you can introduce yourself to the history of this particular area, Anna.'

Taking her arm they walk across a narrow stone bridge. The valley is wide at this point and a fresh breeze funnels through, even though it is the height of summer. San Marino is perched on her steep crag in the distance, the Apennines falling away on all sides. Anna remembers her father's description of the fighting, thinking it would have made yet another perfect vantage point for soldiers on the look-out for enemy. Young cyclists in bright yellow sportswear race past them in a group, their strong legs pumping fast, cheery voices urging each other on. A tourist notice displaying a map and a grainy photo of eight dead men is posted by the bridge. She reads that some of them were aged only nineteen and twenty, probably the same age as the youngsters who had just sped by.

'This is called *Il Ponte dei 8 martiri* - The Bridge of the 8 martyrs,' Francesco explains. 'Eight young partisans were shot by the Italian militia here. The Germans ordered the shooting – look at this,' he points to one of the names, 'this boy was even dragged from his hospital bed.' She looks down the list of names. Standing in the crisp sunshine, mountains soaring into a perfect sky it is impossible to imagine such an appalling event.

Francesco runs his fingers over the letters on the board and reads out – *'Il viaggio della memoria. Imparino i vivi dal destino dei morti.'*

She translates slowly - 'The journey of memory. May the living learn from the fate of those who have died.'

'It could have been written just for you - for the journey you're making with your mother's diaries. I've no doubt your father and uncle would have been involved in some way or other in the attacks leading to this reprisal. I know it is an event that my father talked to me about.'

'My mother often writes about a young man who calls himself Capriolo, quite an important partisan, but she never writes his real name.'

'She was correct not to identify him. It wasn't just the Germans they were up against. On this notice we've just read that it was the Italian militia who shot those boys. The local Italian fascists were much more dangerous in many ways, because they knew the routines of everybody; they knew the tracks criss-crossing the mountains and they spied on their compatriots. It was best he remained a mystery.'

She shivers and he again asks her if she is sure she wants to continue.

'I think so.'

The road to Fragheto is narrow and eroded by landslides. They pass through a pretty, wooded approach of mushroom and truffle reserves. Two kilometres after a tiny hamlet called Ville Fragheto they reach Fragheto itself. The place is deserted. Several of the houses look as if they haven't been lived in for a long time and the ones that are inhabited do not look welcoming, unlike the homes they passed earlier.

Outside a locked church, wind-chimes welcome them with hollow notes and another notice-board bears the simple message:

This place has been dedicated as a place of peace.

On the wall of a dilapidated house hangs a rusting blue sign barely showing the letter 'T', indicating it had once been the tobacconist's. Next to it is a plaque with fading writing and Francesco explains this is the actual spot where the dreadful massacre of innocent civilians had taken place, described to her father in the camp in the mountains. It is almost impossible to decipher the names engraved, but it seems to Anna that most of the surnames are the same: Gabrielli.

Francesco takes her arm again as they climb the short way to a gaudy shrine near the cemetery. A ripped Italian flag flutters in the breeze and plastic flowers have been haphazardly arranged in vases. Like a cliché, a buzzard chooses that moment to mew its plaintive call high up in the thermals. Her eyes scan the list of the massacred while, in a sombre voice, Francesco explains that on April 7th 1944 thirty civilians had been shot in reprisal by the Germans under the command of Herman Göering and members of the Italian Republican guard. There had been heavy partisan activity in the hills around but no partisans had been caught. The reprisal against innocent citizens had been carried out in anger, with the youngest victim a little girl of two called Giuditta and her mother, twenty six, Maria Gabrielli. The oldest to be massacred was a man of seventy three.

'No wonder we never heard all the stories…I am determined not to cry ...' He pulls her to him, rubbing her back with his hands as if to try and warm her. She would like him to kiss her too, to numb her from the horrors conjured by this place. Eventually he steps back but takes her hand firmly in his as if not wanting to break the closeness of their moment. 'Come on, let's go and find a bar.'

They stop at the first place they come to in Casteldelci and sitting at an outside table, order two large glasses of local red wine.

Taking one look at Anna's face, the bar-tender asks if they have visited the shrine. 'Do you know,' he continues, 'my mother was only seven at the time of the war but she tells me she could write a whole book about those terrible times and nothing about the present.' He wipes the bar top viciously with a damp cloth. 'They really suffered round here. I know the war is long since over, but we shouldn't forget.'

'This lady is here to see the places where her English father fought and where her Italian mother lived.' Francesco explains.

'You don't sound Italian, signorina, although you have dark hair… We are grateful to the Inglesi and all the others - Canadesi, Polacchi, Americani … At long last the authorities are putting up monuments… in preparation for the Millennium. Anyway, signori, the drinks are on me.' He pours two generous glasses of red wine. 'Try this... it's from my family's vineyard.'

The wine is good. Tipsy from strong wine in the afternoon, she leans over and kisses Francesco on the lips.

'What was that for?' He laughs, catching hold of her hands, not letting them go.

'Oh, just for being you. For today… I feel very relaxed whenever I'm with you. I never felt like that with anybody before.'

'With anybody?' He is teasing her, still clasping her hands.

'Well alright - I never felt like this with any other man before.'

'In vino veritas, we say. I'll take it as the truth, then. Let's go for a walk and then have something to eat back here. We need to soak up some of this alcohol before returning up the Rimini road.'

They wander arm in arm round the hill-top town, along alleys where shutters of tall narrow houses are half closed in the heat of the afternoon. Trailing geraniums splash primary colours against ancient stone and she keeps extricating her arm from Francesco's to use her camera.

'I'm collecting pictures of doors to make a collage, maybe frame it as a poster for the wall. You probably think I'm mad taking snaps of escutcheons and rusty door knockers but I find them quite beautiful.' She steps back to fit a particularly fine old door hinge into frame.

'And I take pictures of the water and stones in the river. There are blocks of river photos all around my living room walls which I'll show you when you come to Bologna.

'*When* I come?' She says, raising her eyebrows.

'You will come, Anna, won't you?'

'Yes. I'd love to.'

He turns to kiss her on the lips. She feels as giddy as a teenager as he tucks her hand in his and they continue their amble through the town. They stop at a fountain and sit on its steps. She leans against him. They are quiet for a few minutes and then he pulls her closer suggesting maybe Teresa might look after Alba the following weekend to give them more time together.

'*Buon'idea!*' She says, pulling him to his feet. They walk towards the centre, swinging hands like children. 'Do you know what I'd love to do, Francesco?'

'Surprise me!'

'I'd like to take Alba to the sea tomorrow and completely switch off from the diaries and the war. Just for a day. And I think Alba would love it.'

He groans. 'Alba would love it. I hate the seaside in summer. But if it's just for one day, then maybe I could put up with it. That is, if I'm invited too, of course.'

The town is coming to life now after the afternoon siesta: shutters are flung back to let in the cooler air; people dribble out into the streets to make purchases for supper; outside a bar, cards are slapped down on a table circled by old men, cursing good-naturedly, laughing at each other; mopeds rev up as youngsters set off down the hill to the sea; people are living their lives. Everything is more vivid to Anna as she shares this early evening with Francesco.

Back at the restaurant, a table had been laid for them in the corner. The proprietor comes over. 'If you trust me, I'll bring you the special dishes of the house, the best my wife can prepare. I can tell it is a special evening for you.' He winks and hurries back through the swing doors into the kitchen.

She bursts out laughing. 'He thinks we are having an affair.'

'That we're cheating on our partners' he takes her hand and kisses her palm. It tickles and she giggles. He continues to cover her wrist with tiny kisses and then pushes up her sleeve. 'And he thinks that I am going to take you back to a hotel room and have my evil way with you all night long, like a real Latin lover.' He finishes off in mock dramatic form, his lips kissing and kissing their way up her arm to her shoulder and then to her lips.

She pushes him away, laughing: 'Move over, idiot, there's a huge plate of crostini about to spill down you.'

The owner is back with two laden plates, smiling broadly.

She can't remember much about the meal. She only remembers thinking if this is what falling in love is, she has never been in love before.

They don't go to a hotel. They creep into her house on the piazza like two naughty adolescents and as soon as they are inside, he pushes the door shut with his back and drags her into his arms. They kiss passionately. She can feel him hard against her straightaway and they pull at each other's clothes. They don't make it to the bedroom. He pulls down her panties and lifts her, leaning against the door for support and enters her as she straddles him, her legs round his waist. They come together. Afterwards, he gently drops her back to the floor, tidying a strand of hair from her face and she whispers, 'let's go upstairs.'

A soft glow warms the whitewashed walls when she switches on the bedside light. They lay down on top of the covers, removing the rest of each other's clothes. She traces her fingers through the hair on his chest, greying like his salt and pepper sideburns. His body is trim and she kisses his flat stomach, butterfly kissing him on his groin, then licking him until he groans. She pulls away not wanting him to climax too soon and, turning on her side, he draws her close, cupping her breasts from behind, his fingers tracing circles round her erect nipples. Feeling him hard against her, she moves her pelvis to rub him. Then he turns her over, kissing her long and deep on her mouth, his tongue playing with her tongue, tracing a slow, wet line with his lips between her breasts, down her tummy and then, when she can't wait any longer, she parts her legs to receive him again.

In the morning she awakes alone and finds a note on the bed.

Anna, carissima. Thank you! You are beautiful. I hope I can stay all night with you soon but I had to be back for Alba. We'll pick you up at 10 for the seaside.

The next day is a blur of heat and confusion. She remembers people crammed on a beach, the golden sand raked and manicured to perfection by a toned, sun-bronzed *bagnino* who ensures the stretch near a group of topless young girls is cleaner than the rest. He moves his rake like a dancer, bending down to pick up a stray cigarette end, lingering to chat, chancing his luck with an invitation for a dance later on at the *discoteca* on the sea-front; and she remembers beautiful youths cavorting where waves lapped at the toes of girls, throwing themselves acrobatically at a beach ball, splashing them so they squeal and scream. And illegal African immigrants, *i clandestini*, touting armfuls of gaudy beads and slices of coconut; anxious mothers shouting at toddlers not to stray too near the water's edge; shamelessly fat ladies with red polished toe nails wearing leopard-skin thongs; the smell of fried fish and sun-tan oil and Italian ballads on a radio on the beach, crooned by Zucchero. They paddle with Alba and buy ice-creams from the bar; they even hire a *pedalo* to view the packed beach from a few metres off shore.

But all the time her mind is on Francesco and their lovemaking. Catching the longing gaze in his brown eyes, she knows he is thinking the same.

Chapter 28
August 1999

Francesco has to return to university for staff meetings the following day. He calls round early in the morning when Anna is still in bed. She comes, sleepy eyed, hair tousled, to open her front door and laughs when she sees him. 'I see you can't keep away,' she says, stepping into his arms, 'well, it's lovely to see you too.' She kisses him and if it had not been for Alba appearing to tell him Teresa has put his coffee and breakfast biscuits on the table, he would have stayed longer. 'I'll phone you,' he says as he leaves, Alba tugging on his hand to drag him away. 'It should only take a couple of days, but there are some problems with time-tables and all the usual stuff for a new academic year.' He kisses her again, lightly this time because Alba is standing there like a school monitor, hands on hips, glaring at the pair of them.

'I've left your papers with Teresa' he says, 'the rest are in English, so you won't need my help anymore. But I'd love to read properly to the end, if you'll let me. I feel involved myself.'

Blowing him a kiss as he leaves, which makes Alba giggle, she goes to run the shower warm before stepping in, soaping herself, stretching luxuriously under the steamy spray, remembering how Francesco touched her, loved her, wanting him to get back from Bologna soon.

She helps Teresa in the kitchen. Tomatoes in the *orto* are all ripening at once and she learns how to make *pomarola*, a tomato sauce. They bottle it in a variety of screw-top jars, sterilising them in a huge pan outside in the yard on top of a brazier lit by wood from a pile already well stocked for winter. 'This way,' Teresa explains, 'we save on gas and it makes less mess indoors.' After the jars have been simmering under boiling water for an hour, they are ready to store away.

'For a taste of summer sunshine in winter,' Teresa smiles, 'from our very own organic produce.'

Alba has stayed behind with Teresa and the three of them enjoy a picnic lunch outside, under the shade of a fig tree. They dip hunks of crusty *toscano* bread into a bowl of some of the left over *pomarola* and finish off with a slice of pecorino cheese and pears. Alba sits close to her aunt and at the end of the meal asks if she can go and play with Billi.

'Of course you can,' Anna tells her, 'he is really your cat after all. He only sleeps in my house – in his cat's *agriturismo*.' The little girl doesn't laugh. As she goes over to Anna's house, she shouts back over her shoulder, 'isn't it time for you to go back to England?'

The two women look at each other and Teresa tells the little girl off for being rude.

'Leave her be,' Anna says in a low voice, thinking Alba is probably jealous and that they will have to be more discreet. The sun is scorching, there is no breeze, even the cicadas seem to be complaining about the sweltering heat with their insistent screeching. There is nothing for it but a siesta and she retires to the cool of her bedroom with the papers she's collected from Teresa.

Her mother has attached another note to the next few pages.

In 1984, when you were eighteen, off you went to start at university and the house was empty and echoing. Harry and Jane were busy with their own young families and I had too much time in my own company, too much time to think.

One afternoon I saw a notice at the library which appealed to me – "Want to write a story"? I took courage in my hands and enrolled in the class. The teacher was very encouraging. For me it was a kind of therapy. She helped me gather the threads of my life together and one of the first tasks she set us was to write about the arrival of a stranger in our lives. I found myself writing about the birth of your brother. We had to start with the words – I remember. She asked me read it out to the class and because I didn't know anybody there, I didn't mind them guessing it was a story about me.

***

I remember the first words my husband uttered about our new baby who was born on August 10th 1947.

'He looks like a monkey on a barrel organ,' said Norman, holding our son gingerly in his arms. 'Here, you have him back, Ines. He might be sick and I've got my work suit on.'

Freda, my mother- in- law, took the baby instead, expertly wrapping the shawl tighter round her first grandson. 'Shame on you, Norman! Hand him to me,' she scolded, 'honestly, what a thing for a new father to say.'

I watched my mother-in-law, marvelling at her confidence, thinking that I would never get the hang of looking after this new baby. I was scared of dropping him and I couldn't seem to satisfy his hunger. Hardly had I fed and changed him, when his little mouth would open like a beak and he would cry for more. He cried all the time.

'He's going to be a big tall lad, that's for sure,' the midwife had said to me after the birth, 'you might have trouble feeding this one. A bottle for him before too long, I think.'

Freda was in her element. 'I've knitted something for baby,' she said, proudly presenting me with a heavy green and orange shawl with pink and turquoise tassels.

'It's wonderful. Thank you so much', I said, grateful that she could not hear my inner voice thinking what a fine dog blanket it would have made… if we'd had a dog.

I missed my mother in Italy. The birth had been long and painful; a pain I'd never imagined. I'd thought I was going to die and, apparently I had screamed for my mother over and over again. And when I looked down at my son for the first time, covered in mucus and blood, I felt such a wave of sadness at the understanding of the tie of a mother for her child; a tie which I had severed from my own mother by coming to live so far away. I wept for what I had denied her.

I was very sick afterwards. I feel so ashamed now as I write this but there were nights when Harry cried to be fed yet again and I wanted him to fall asleep forever, never to wake up. Freda was wonderful to me where Norman was bewildered and useless. I hardly ever saw him in those early days of our son's life. He stayed late at work and left the house just after dawn and he was often away overnight. Freda moved into our spare room and took over the cooking and cleaning whilst I recuperated from the birth. In the middle of September she brought me my usual cup of milky morning coffee for 'elevenses' and then, instead of hurrying back into the kitchen, she sat with me for a while. 'Now then, Ines my dear, it's nearly a month now and I think it's time I went back to my John. I can call in from time to time but you've got to make an effort now. The baby needs you and Norman needs you and so… here's a duster; you set to and I'll finish off washing his lordship's nappies while he has his morning nap and this afternoon I've arranged for you to meet your friend in the park. You can push your prams together and get some fresh air into those pale cheeks of yours.'

Tiziana, my Italian friend, had discovered she was pregnant not long after me and we spent as much time together as we could. I had felt very nauseous but she had sailed through eight months until she was confined to hospital with pre-eclampsia for the last weeks. She was lucky to survive. Our friendship became dearer to me when I realised I could have lost her.

Feeding the ducks on the pond in the park became an afternoon routine from then on. Tiziana had twin boys, born a few weeks after Harry and she too was finding motherhood difficult. We had made a pact that we would try and stick to talking English, but it was very tempting to resort to our native Italian.

'This bread is only fit for ducks anyway,' she grumbled, tossing half a loaf into the green water and setting off a squawking and fluttering of feathers from the geese and mallards as well as a stray sea-gull. 'What I wouldn't give for a *pagnotta* fresh from the *Panificio* back home. This stuff is like cotton wool and it's too salty. Yuck! *Schifo!*' She brushed the crumbs from her dress and rocked her pram to settle Luca and Giuseppe.

'Listen to you,' I said, 'who's longing for Italy now?' She had told me off in the past for always harking back to *il bel paese.*

'You try looking after these two on your own,' she retorted. 'If I were back home, there'd be Mamma to help, or Auntie, my sister, the woman in the flat next door, the road sweeper even. Here it's all down to me. *Dio buono,* I swear I'm going to tie a knot in Denis's willy. I'm not having any more babies and I've told him he's not coming anywhere near unless he dangles a condom in front of me. I've done my bit now. Jesus, two's more than enough.'

'Freda's really good and now I'm giving the bottle to Harry, he sleeps through the night.'

'Are you only just using the bottle now? *Madonna buona,* mine had to get stuck into bottles straightaway. No way was I going to let them chew on me. It's enough having my old man interfering with them.' She stuck out her breasts and patted them as if to reassure herself they were still there. 'I'm proud of these; they're two of my main assets.'

I laughed. 'What are you talking about, Tizi? You're a married woman.'

'And so? You never know what may happen, *amica mia.*' She wiggled her finger at me. 'He might leave me, I might leave him, you never know.' Tizi was a one-off and although she shocked me sometimes with her statements, I always felt better when I'd been in her company.

'Right then, Ines, seeing as the subject's been brought up, I've got to tell you. I wasn't going to, but maybe you ought to know.' She lowered her voice as if she was about to impart a piece of gossip that she didn't want anybody else to hear.

'Know what?' I was only half listening. Harry was crying so I'd lifted him out of his pram to wind him and was pacing around our park bench.

'Denis thinks your Norman is chasing skirt.'

'Chasing skirt? What do you mean?'

'Haven't you ever heard that expression? *Dio*, where were you born? Oh yes, in the country. I forgot. Cows and sheep don't wear skirts, do they?' She laughed and then, seeing the puzzled look on my face, she sighed and stood up, saying, 'Look, here is not the right place to have a serious talk. Let's go and have a coffee in the new Espresso Bar in the market square. Come on, we've got just about enough time before their next feed.' She kicked the brake free on the bottom of the pram and was off before I had a chance to tuck Harry in. 'Wait for me,' I shouted as she hurried up the path out of the park.

The Espresso Bar was half empty. It had been opened recently by an Italian who had been in a camp in England and married an English girl at the end of the war. Roberto – or Bobby as he liked to be known – was from Naples, and both of us found it hard to understand his dialect but he made a proper Italian coffee and we were pleased when he'd taken on the lease. He told us he was going to change the name to "*Piccola Italia*" and we liked to pretend it was our little corner of Italy. He had tried his best to create an atmosphere, with empty wine bottles with candles stuck in them on the tables and posters of Vesuvius and the Coliseum in Rome on the white washed walls. We chatted to him for a little until another customer came in.

'What were you saying about Norman and skirts?' I asked when Roberto had moved away. Tiziana took a deep breath and then, in her usual blunt way, hit me with her news. 'Denis says your Norman is having an affair with that Phyllis who works in Boots. That blonde girl, you must know the one I'm talking about. Tall…with a face like a horse but … enormous breasts.'

Harry was still grizzling and I picked him up and stood there, jiggling him up and down, trying to pacify him. My head was reeling at what I had just heard. He was crying properly now and I continued to rock him in my arms while Tiziana talked on, 'I really didn't know whether to tell you or not but we're friends, aren't we? And do you remember you talked to me before Harry was born and how you were so worried about Norman not paying you enough attention? Well, doesn't that explain it? He's got another woman. 'A fancy woman,' they call them over here. And by the sound of things, it's being going on for some time.'

I still hadn't said anything. I didn't know what to say. Eventually, despite Harry's loud complaining, I dumped him back in his pram parked outside and started back for home.

I strode through the park, the pram wheels stirring up the leaves that had begun to fall on the paths, ignoring the curious looks of other people strolling leisurely as I hurried past them like a mad woman ignoring my baby's hungry screams. I pushed the pram out of the park gates and bumped it down the narrow pavement, past the houses and front gardens that all looked the same. Leaving the pram on our path and hoisting my son on my hip, I flung open the front door so hard it chipped the green paint off the wall. Norman kept a bottle of brandy in the sideboard in the front room and, still carrying Harry, I poured myself a generous measure. I coughed and spluttered; it was strong and unpleasant but it helped calm me.

'Come on, Harry. It'll be alright, it'll be alright.' The baby could sense my anxiety and was still crying as I prepared him a bottle of milk, my fingers clumsy as I measured out the powdered milk but still doing what they were used to doing.

Half an hour later, with Harry asleep on the sofa beside me and the best part of half a bottle of brandy inside me, I hatched my plan. I was sick of tears. So far they had done me no good. Norman didn't want me but I wasn't ready to give him up yet and I wasn't going to let him get away with having dragged me all the way to England to then dump me. Deep down, and strange as it seemed, I still thought I loved him. What's more I had meant the marriage vows I had uttered in the little chapel in Rofelle – that we would love each other for better, for worse. I couldn't accept that the man I had fallen in love with in Italy had turned into a monster and I had to fight for him. I had Harry to think of as well.

My head was thumping in the morning but baby had miraculously slept through the night. I packed extra nappies and bottles of milk into his pram and hurried round to my parents-in-laws' house. Freda and John were in the middle of breakfast and surprised to see me so early.

'Please Freda, could you look after Harry for me today? I forgot I had a post natal check at the hospital and it would be so much easier for me to leave him with you, what with the bus journey and all.' All this was said without looking her in the face in case she could tell I was telling lies, while I busied myself with folding spare nappies into the tray below the pram.

Freda bent to pick Harry out of the pram, all fists and grumbling for his bottle. 'Of course we'll look after the little man. You won't mind being with Nanny and Grand-dad, will you? We'll put you out in the sunshine and you can watch us pick up the early windfalls. Remind me to give you a bagful for your pies, when you come back. Off you go...You don't want to miss the bus.'

I set off briskly down the road to the bus-stop, but my destination was not the hospital.

By the time I had made my way to the centre of West Croydon and found Boots, it was nearly midday. I wandered around the store, pretending to look at cosmetics, spraying samples of perfume on my wrists, looking at packets of nylon stockings until a sales-assistant talked to me from behind her counter.

'Can I help you, Madam?' She was in her fifties, grey haired, short and stout.

'I'm looking for a present… for my mother.'

'What about a lovely new lipstick? You're never too old for lipstick.' She rummaged in a drawer below the counter and then tried the colour on the back of my hand. 'If your mother looks anything like you, I think she could do with a much darker shade.' All the while she prattled on about make-up that my mother would never dream of applying, I kept looking round to see if I could recognise Phyllis.

'Are you French, my dear?' she asked, 'only you've got that continental look about you.'

'Italian,' I replied. I took the mirror she handed me so that I could smear on a sample of lipstick and observed my angry reflection. Behind me, in the mirror, was another woman in a Boots uniform. She wasn't a true blonde, her dark roots were beginning to show. She looked older than me and her blouse was straining at the seams, the buttons in danger of popping open at any minute. She wasn't pretty but definitely a 'man's type of girl'. She had to be Phyllis, the woman that Tizi had talked about. I dropped the mirror on the floor and it smashed. 'Oh dear,' the grey haired woman said to me, bending down to pick up the pieces, 'you haven't hurt yourself, have you? Are you all right, Madam? You look a little pale.'

'Sorry,' I said as I pushed past her, 'I've changed my mind'. I needed fresh air and time to think. It was drizzling. People scurried past, heads hunched in like tortoises to escape the rain drops. The downpour increased and I stood back in a doorway, watching people splash by in the puddles, trying to work out what I should do. In the shop it had taken me all my self control not to march up and slap Phyllis's stupid face. But that wouldn't solve anything and, anyway, I had to be sure she was the right woman. The door way where I was standing was a newsagent's. I stepped inside out of the deluge and leafed through a magazine without looking at its contents.

'No loitering in here, Madam,' said the old man behind the counter, 'and that'll be sixpence. I can't have people thumbing my magazines and not buying them.' I flung a shilling on the counter and hurried out of the shop because I had seen Norman appear on the other side of the high street, his trench coat collar turned up against the damp. I watched him turn into Boot's but even then I crossed my fingers inside my coat pocket, willing Tizi's bombshell not to be true. A few minutes later and my hopes were dashed when the pair came out of the shop arm in arm. I followed them to "The Wheatsheaf", a pub where Norman had taken me for dinner one Saturday evening before I was pregnant. I waited until I thought they would be settled and then I made my entrance. They were at a corner table and he was holding her hands. Outwardly I was calm but inwardly I was boiling like a huge pan of pasta. I made my way over to them and sat myself down. 'I'll have a double brandy and a nice roast beef sandwich please, Norman,' I said.

Norman's mouth fell open in astonishment.

'Are you going to introduce me to this - woman?' I looked her up and down, taking in her cheap clothes and her shoes with heels too high for her fat legs and I wrinkled up my nose as if I were breathing in the odour of sheep manure and I stared her out.

She eventually looked away in embarrassment, picked up her handbag from the floor and rose from her seat. 'I'll be off then, Norm...' she said, almost falling over in her haste to get away. She threw a worried look over her shoulder at us as she tottered out.

'Yes, I think you better had leave...I need to talk with **my husband**.' The last two words I yelled, so that the men on the table next to us looked at each other and grinned. I turned to them and said in the same loud voice, 'Yes, it's very funny, isn't it? Funny for you and funny for my husband! But not so funny for me and our son.'

'Ines, people are looking at us,' Norman muttered, looking round at the audience in the pub, who were interested in the free entertainment I was laying on for them.

The publican came over from behind the bar and bent down to Norman. 'Sir, I think it would be better if you took your troubles outside. You're disturbing my customers.'

As Norman and I went towards the door, he tried to take my arm and I shook him off. The men at the table cheered and I turned round, retraced my steps, picked up a glass of beer and threw it over both of them. 'If it's a circus you want to watch, then I can perform too.'

In the street I started walking away from the pub, Norman following behind as I shouted, 'I'm going home now and I'll expect to see you for tea. If you don't come home and explain who that woman was, then I am going to pack my bags and take Harry back to Italy.'

'Ines. Please let's talk...'

'Not here in the street.' I turned to some bystanders gawping at us and shouted at them too... 'Mind your own bloody business! Haven't you got anything better to do?'

Some of them had the grace to turn away. I heard a woman tut and mutter: 'Bloody foreigners.'

'It's up to you, Norman. That's all I've got to say to you now. I'll either see you later or I'll be at your parents, explaining to them why I'm leaving for Italy. I wonder what they will have to say about what their **darling** son has been up to.'

  I hailed a taxi, not caring tuppence about the expense. He had obviously been spending our money on his fancy woman, whilst I had been carefully saving for our trip to Italy next summer. I sat in the back of the taxi staring at the streets lined with monotone houses, at drab people walking along with solemn faces. I bit hard on my lip to stop myself from breaking down in front of the driver but once I was inside our house, the tears returned. I poured myself more brandy and was shocked to realise I had finished almost the whole bottle but it calmed me, dulled my anger and sadness, so that when I heard Norman's key in the latch, I was still sitting in the front room, nursing my empty glass. I felt exhausted.
  'Ines, I'm sorry.' He came to sit beside me and I didn't have the energy to push him away.
  'You are a bastard, Norman. You told me you were away on business but all the time you must have been with that...' I didn't know many bad words in English, despite Tiziana's introducing me to a few ripe expressions. I finished my sentence lamely: ...with that *puttana*.'
  'I really did have to go away on business for the airport. This was the first time I lied to you, Ines. I swear ...'

'So that makes it all right, does it? How can I believe a word you say? Why did you bring me to England? You promised to look after me - you promised to look after me in front of the priest. What have I ever done wrong?'

I stood up to leave the room and he caught hold of my arm. 'Ines, please let's talk about this calmly...'

'If you had wanted someone who was *calma e tranquilla* like your English women, you shouldn't have married *un'italiana*. Why didn't you just marry that '*puttana*' - because any woman who goes with a married man is a *puttana*, as far as I'm concerned.'

I slapped his hand from my arm and threw the empty glass into the fire, where it smashed, breaking a tile. 'You've not been the same since the day we married. Why did you bother to come back to Rofelle? Everybody was right… they warned me I didn't know you well enough, that none of us really knew you.' Then unable to stop myself, I screamed, 'GO TO HELL! I WISH I HAD NEVER SET EYES ON YOU.'

Freda rushed into the room. 'What on earth is going on? I've been knocking on your door these past five minutes…' and then, realising she had walked in on an argument she asked, 'Shall I make us all a nice cup of tea?'

'Oh tea, tea, tea,' I yelled, 'the answer to all English problems… No, I don't want a nice cup of tea, Freda.

I hate your tea. I hate England. And most of all, I hate your son!'

I pushed past her and in my haste to get away I collided with the pram Freda had left in the hall. Without thinking twice, I pushed the pram with our baby in it away from the house. Harry was still asleep. I could hear Norman shouting for me to come back but I ignored him. The park gates were still open; they were shut at dusk but the other mothers and children I usually saw in there would now be at home, busy with bath-time and peeling potatoes for supper. I made my way to the duck pond and sat down. In my rush to escape, I had forgotten my coat and so I draped a spare baby blanket round my shoulders. Sitting there on the bench, staring at the muddy green water I thought of the Marecchia flowing cold and clear beneath our water mill and tears flowed down my cheeks unchecked.

-0-0-0-

The people in my writing class applauded when I finished reading and asked me if I would write a sequel because they wanted to know what happened next.

I did continue to write from time to time but it was just for me. Writing helped me disengage from the pain.

Chapter 29
Autumn 1947

'Any room for another body on there?' The man's voice startled me and I made to get up from the park bench. He was scruffy, wearing a dirty grey raincoat and carrying two canvas bags, a mongrel at his side. 'Madam, don't be scared, I won't hurt you. You look hurt enough already, if you don't mind my saying.'

His voice was kind. When I looked up, I could see he was not as old as I had first thought. With a wash and a trim of his straggly beard, he would have been quite presentable. Back home we had worn whatever we could get hold of in the war, so I knew clothes never told the whole story. 'Sit down if you want,' I said ungraciously, wiping my tears with the back of my hand.

'Would I be right in thinking you're Italian?'

'How did you know?'

'From your accent, the way you stress your words.'

I thought it very clever of him to guess where I was from but I suppose I've never accepted that I have a strong accent when I speak English, despite family telling me so often. The man went on to explain he had spent time in France and then southern Italy during the war. 'Maybe one day I might go back and visit your beautiful country. I'm very interested in art.' He added, with a wry laugh, that the war hadn't given him much time for sight-seeing. He stopped talking and we sat for a while without speaking. I wasn't frightened of this stranger. Maybe I should have been, sitting all alone with him in the park, but he didn't make me feel uncomfortable. The dog had settled at his feet and he bent to stroke it. 'Do you want to talk about why you are so unhappy? It sometimes helps to talk to somebody impartial.'

I told him. It was like confessing to a priest. I told him how my husband was having an affair, how I didn't think he loved me anymore, how I missed Italy and my parents, how I wanted to leave England but I didn't know what I should do because of baby Harry and because I didn't want to break my marriage vows.

He listened without interrupting and it helped not to have to hold back, because I was talking to somebody I didn't know. Then he leant forward on the bench and staring into the distance he began to tell me a little of his own story. 'The war has a lot to answer for,' he said, 'not just for the deaths and destruction of so many beautiful places. It has churned up ordinary people's lives, ordinary people like you and me who will never be the same again. I don't have to tell you about the hardships of war but maybe you should get your husband to try and talk to you about his war. What it was like for him.'

'But we were together during the war. I know what it was like for him,' I replied, thinking the man was maybe a little slow in the head.

'Were you with him all the time?'

'No, ... not all the time. We met in 1944. He was an escaped prisoner of war and my family hid him when he was injured. He met up with the British army again a few months later, but he came back to my village at the end of the war and we married there.'

'So there were some months when you were apart. Where was he during that time?'

I shrugged my shoulders. 'I don't know.'

'Then you should ask him.'

'At the moment I don't care if I never talk to him again. Why should I, the way he's treated me?' I scuffed the path with my shoes, dug my hands in my pockets. I remember stumbling over words, I still had so much English to learn, but he understood what I was trying to say and spoke some Italian too. Languages had been his subject at university and after graduating, he had been head of modern languages in a college. Turning to look at me sitting there with my scowling face, he said 'I bet he doesn't love this other woman. In war, when men think each day is going to be their last, they do things they wouldn't normally do.'

'But the war is over. What do you mean?'

'Maybe the war is still going on in your husband's head. Maybe he is ill from the war.'

When I looked at him as if he was mad, he extended his hands towards me but didn't touch me. 'Let me explain,' he said. 'I was in France during the war. I was sent because I was useful with my languages - I won't go into the details of what I was doing - but during my time there I fell in love with a French girl.'

'And so?' I was growing impatient at this man's logic. 'It happened all the time. Norman fell in love with me. I'm sure thousands of young people all over Europe were falling in love all the time. It's normal.'

'But I was married already, you see. I had a wife and young children at home in England.'

'Are all you men the same?' I asked, getting up to leave, "that you have to go around committing adultery? I feel sorry for your wife.'

'Please don't go. Listen to me a little longer. Sit down again. Please!'

The dog had picked up on his owner's agitation and moved out from under the bench, starting to whine. The man bent to stroke it again and then continued. 'In a way, if that's your philosophy, you might say I was punished in the end… because I lost everybody. My family in England was killed when a bomb fell on our house and Josianne was gunned down on a mission we were both engaged in. I stayed on in France for a while at the end of the war. I suppose I felt nearer to Josie there, but in the end I had a breakdown. All I am trying to say to you is there are many reasons why people behave in the way they do. The explanations are not written on neat little notes and pinned to our clothes for all to see. You have to dig to find them. My advice is to talk to your husband. It's not easy, I know, but you should try'.

'I'm sorry for your loss,' I told him. But it still didn't take away my anger at Norman. Life had been hard for us too - women, children and old folk living in occupied land, afraid from one minute to the next at what might happen, but we had got on with it, quietly, with dignity for the most part. I was finding it hard to accept these excuses. For that is what I thought they were.

Harry was stirring. It would soon be time for his evening feed and I'd not brought a bottle for him. I had to go home. As I stood up to leave, the man spoke again, sensing my disapproval. 'I'm still finding life hard but I'm slowly learning that talking helps. They tell me that up at the hospital all the time. So Madam, talk to your husband before it's too late. He may have experienced situations he has never been able to talk about to anybody. Do it for yourself as well as for your son.'

He got up and so did his dog and together we walked along the path to the main entrance. After giving me a slight army salute and with a click of his heels, we set off in different directions. My route home took me past the church of Saint Mary Magdalene where I usually went to Sunday Mass. Leaving Harry in his pram in the porch, I slipped inside and pushed a penny coin into the box and lit a candle. The flickering lights cast a gentle glow and kneeling down in front of the statue of Our Lady, I bent my head to pray.

Ave Maria, please help me, I feel so lost. Guide me so I find the right way to go on. Bless my family back in Italy and bless my little family here. And bless the poor man in the park too, for he needs your help as well. Amen.

Harry started to whimper for his feed. I genuflected before the altar and after making the sign of the cross I left, pushing the pram as fast as I could through the twilight. I felt calmer and a little stronger.

I let myself into the house and Norman came hurrying into the hall. There was a smell of cooking and in our little kitchen, the table had been laid for two. A vase of russet chrysanthemums stood in the centre and a lighted candle in a bottle.

'We'll get Harry settled and then have supper,' he said before I could get a word in. 'Mum's popped round with one of her famous casseroles.' He looked at me anxiously and lifted Harry out of the pram.

Although I had told myself to try and stay calm and understanding, I couldn't stop myself from snapping at him, 'Don't think you are going to solve everything by a supper.' Kicking off my shoes, I bent down wearily to rub my sore toes. I could have said more. I felt like shouting at him but the words of the man in the park rang in my head, so I simply took baby upstairs to change his nappy and feed him his evening bottle.

During supper we hardly spoke. I kept stealing glances at him, telling myself he was the same man who had loved me in Italy and that I should give him another chance. Although I wanted him to be the one to take the lead and start the talking, I knew he wouldn't. Maybe he couldn't – just as the man in the park had suggested. It was up to me. Pushing our plates to one side instead of getting up to clear them away, I took his hand. 'Look at me,' I said, without raising my voice, 'look at me and tell me about that woman.'

His eyes met my steady gaze. He frowned, bit his lip. It was obvious he didn't want to talk but I never let go of his hand. I waited.

'I knew her before the war,' he said eventually, 'she and I used to walk out together. Mother and Father never approved of her.'

'Is she called Phyllis?'

'Oh Ines – what's the point?' He pulled his hand out of mine, leant back from me in his chair.

'The point is – we must talk. We are both very unhappy.'

'I swear she doesn't mean a thing to me.'

'Well, why?' I asked, 'Why have you been with her?' I didn't shout - willing myself to remain calm. Deep down, I knew that if I couldn't get through to my husband this evening, then I never would. 'I met somebody today who told me I should make you talk to me,' I continued.

He thumped his fist on the table, 'Which nosy neighbour have you been blabbing to? Or was it that Tiziana woman? She…'

I didn't let him finish, 'It's nobody we know… it was a complete stranger, so you needn't worry.' I waited a little and then I asked him again why he felt he needed to be with another woman. 'I want to know what I have done wrong. Tell me why I'm not enough for you anymore.'

He ran his hands through his hair. It was thinning at the top. I remembered how thick it used to be, what a problem it had been when we were trying to disguise him in the mountains.

'When I'm with Phyllis, everything seems less complicated somehow,' he said, 'as if the war hadn't happened. Like life was before.'

Hearing that was like a stab to my heart. He was more or less saying he wished he had never met me. 'So you don't love me anymore,' I whispered.

'I do love you. Of course I love you.'

'It doesn't seem like that to me.' I couldn't help it. I started to cry, silently.

'Please don't,' he said, getting up and coming over to me. He pulled me up into his arms and as he rocked me, I sobbed, 'I can't understand you anymore. You say you love me but you seem to say you were happier before the war. It doesn't make any sense.

'I love you,' he repeated, 'but it's not been easy, what with the baby and starting a new job.'

'Maybe we could go back to Rofelle and start again,' I suggested. "Maybe you could get a job there? We were happy in Italy.'

'What could I do there? There aren't enough jobs even for Italians. I thought that once I came back to England then I could leave the war behind but…' He stopped. I lifted my hands to his face and told him to keep talking. 'I can't empty my mind of what I saw.' His voice was barely a whisper.

'Talk to me, Norman. Tell me.' I took his hand and led him upstairs to our bedroom. We lay down on top of the eiderdown and I settled into his arms. At first he was very hesitant but once he started talking, he couldn't stop. I listened to the horror of what he had seen and had to do in the time we had been apart. It was like lancing an abscess that needed to be rid of its poison.

Because he knew a little Italian, he had been sent with a few 'D Day dodgers', as they had been described, to help with evacuation of Italian military internees held in Bergen Belsen after the armistice of 1943. By 1945 there were 55,000 men, women and children of different nationalities in the camp, most of them Jews.

'None of us could believe our eyes.' he said, 'We had never seen anything like it – bodies piled everywhere, stick thin bodies. Naked men and women, little children – we had to shoot the dogs to stop them eating the bodies left unburied for weeks. And the smell… even if you lit a cigarette you couldn't avoid the stench. There were creatures stumbling about – you could only describe them in that way - they didn't look like human beings anymore, they were living skeletons … We gave them our rations… We didn't understand it would kill them… They hadn't eaten properly for months and the food we gave them was too rich. And the hardest thing was not showing them our horror, our disgust at their smell, the lice, their staring eyes in their hollow skulls, trying to treat them with dignity when we just wanted to turn away and vomit…'

After a while I stopped listening and when he stopped talking and his body started shaking, I took him in my arms and soothed him like our new baby, patting his back and whispering 'there, there' while we clung together. After a long while he said 'Don't leave me, Ines. I couldn't bear it.'

That was the night I started to feel old.

I never saw the man in the park again although I looked for him and his dog whenever I wheeled Harry out in his pram. I've often wondered if he was real or if he might have been my guardian angel.

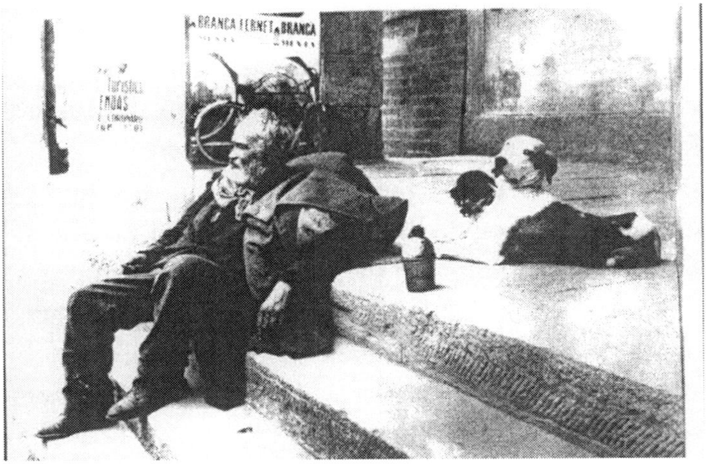
BRANCA FERNET BRANCA

Chapter 30
Late August 1999

'Why, oh why didn't she get out while she could?' Anna is on her mobile, discussing the latest entry in the diary with Francesco, who is shopping in Arezzo with Alba for the new school year.

His reply is immediate, 'Easy to say that from where you're standing now, but try to imagine yourself in those times, there wasn't the same freedom.'

'I know you're right but I still feel like shouting at her to leave him.'

'Hey - you've just told me about what he had to do in Belsen. You said you felt sorry for him. Nowadays people receive therapy for far less...' He laughs, 'if *you* are confused Anna, then think about how it must have been for her!'

'I know, I know. Anyway let's change the subject. How's the shopping going?'

He lowers his voice, 'I could do with you here right now. The little monkey keeps picking out the most hideous stuff and convincing me it's what she 'absolutely' needs for school. What do you think about pink sneakers?'

'Do they fit her? Are they sensible pink sneakers? There's nothing wrong with pink, you know. They sound much better than the brown lace-ups I used to have to wear for school.'

'Aagh! It's a conspiracy – you women are ganging up on me.'

'Just enjoy your day together. Go with the flow. See you later - ciao for now!' She smiles as she switches off her mobile, imagining the pair of them trawling the shops. Last night Alba had thrown a wobbly when Francesco cut short her bed-time story. She'd worked out her daddy was planning to spend time afterwards with Anna and clung to him, making him stay to read two more stories. They'd talked about how to deal with Alba's tantrums when he'd knocked on her door nearly two hours late and decided a shopping trip seemed a good option for one-to-one time together.

Tidying away her mother's papers, Anna thinks about Francesco's comments. He is right. It is all too easy to judge from afar and her own love life has never been exactly smooth. In fact an e mail from Will had arrived in her inbox only a couple of days previously and she nearly hadn't opened it, thinking he'd wanted to resume their relationship again. She'd breathed a sigh of relief when she'd eventually read it. After telling her his wife had collapsed and been rushed into hospital by ambulance with a suspected heart attack, he had written:

'It was the kick up the pants I needed to sort out the mess I was making of things. We're rubbing along fine now. Take care of yourself Sooty. Hope you're happy. Will xx'

As Anna has the day to herself she decides to track down Danilo again. The weather is still warm but not the same baking heat of July and early August. From the woods the noisy whirring of chain-saws is a reminder that winter is just round the corner. Woodcutters are busy at work chopping and piling up fuel for storage. On the slopes above her, the clanging of heavy bells round the necks of Chianina cattle is like a kind of music as they munch on the last of the summer pasture. Walking up here in July she had stopped to admire orchids and helleborines but they have died back now. Chicory and field scabious nod blue and purple in the breeze and as she brushes past juniper bushes, she catches the distinctive scent of their berries used to make gin. She picks her way over stones left by the latest landslide beneath the village and as she arrives at the edge of the tiny square, she is surprised to see women washing fruit and salad in the village fountain. Last time the place had been deserted except for a stray cat. By the village oven a handful of people are standing about, deep in discussion. They stop when they see her and one of the women smiles, beckoning her over. It is Sveva, the mother of little Pina who comes to Scuolaclub.

'Anna, ciao! What are you doing up here?' She speaks slowly so Anna can follow her usual garrulous Italian. 'We're having a party for *Ferragosto*. It's a little late but not everybody could make it so we postponed it until this week. Please say you'll join us for lunch.'

Anna knows *Ferragosto* is a celebration to mark the Assumption of Our Lady into Heaven, usually held on the 15th August. It's a feast day when Italians like to meet up with family and friends at the sea or in the mountains. She tells Sveva she would love to join in but apologises for not being able to contribute.

'Oh don't you worry about that - we have more than enough to eat. It's all very simple: panzanella, sausages, home baked pizza and roasted tomatoes.'

'You call that simple? Sounds like a huge feast to me.'

High quality seasonal food is important to Italians. She loves the way they share and celebrate these special days. 'I need to talk to somebody first,' she tells Sveva, 'but I'll be back to help. Thank you for asking me. *Grazie!*'

'We're lighting the old oven later but we need more wood, so maybe when you're finished you can help collect some with me.'

A good looking middle aged man approaches Sveva, a red scarf knotted at his throat, a guitar slung over his back. Sveva introduces him to Anna. 'This is my husband, Sergio. He's complaining we're not using olive wood in the oven but nobody ever did up here. Olive trees can't survive these winters. But he is a *Romagnolo* - what does he know? He's from down the valley.'

This remark is followed by laughter, banter and more heated discussion about whether Tuscany or Romagna is the most beautiful region in Italy. After shaking hands with Sergio and telling him she is not going to get involved with local politics, Anna leaves them to it and makes her way up the path alongside the church which leads to the old man's house. The door is shut but she can hear music playing inside, so she knocks. There is no answer but the music continues. She knocks again.

Grumpy old sod, she thinks, *he's probably hiding from me.*

Taking a notebook from her rucksack and a photo of her mother that she has purposely brought with her, she scribbles him a note, determined that this will not turn out to be another wasted journey.

Dear Signor Danilo,

I don't know your surname, so excuse me and excuse my poor Italian. I came to see you before but you were too busy to talk.

I would like to ask you about the war and especially my mother. This is her photo. You may remember her - she was Ines Santini before she married my father - Norman Swilland. I am their daughter.

You can contact me at Teresa Starnucci's holiday house in San Patrignano.

Anna Swilland

p.s. Please return the photo as it is an original and very special to me. Thankyou!

Pushing the note and photo carefully under his door, she knocks once more to make sure he is not in and when there is still no reply, she returns to the square where more people are gathering for the party.

'Anna,' Sveva calls, 'come and help me collect firewood and we can have a chat while we're working. The sooner Sergio gets that fire lit the better. I think lunch will turn into dinner!' Handing Anna a pair of gardening gloves to put on, she explains that they will have to be careful of scorpions in the old wood.

They take a path leading out of the village. At the edge of a copse, where piles of newly sawn holm oak lay neatly stacked, there is plenty of kindling. Suddenly Sveva stops in her tracks and clutches Anna's arm, pointing to the base of a large old oak, 'Look down there. *Che culo* ! We are very lucky!' At first Anna can't see anything but then her friend kneels down to part the grass round a clump of coffee coloured mushrooms. 'Sliced very thinly and with a squeeze of lemon and olive oil we will have a starter of carpaccio of *porcini.* Have you ever tried them?'

Anna hasn't and she wonders if there is anything Italians don't eat! She has already turned down the offer of snails that Teresa collected after the last rainfall. And then, Sveva nudges gently with her shoe at a large yellow thistle growing flat on the ground.

'This plant tastes like artichoke. We call it Carlina and it only grows high up in the mountains. But we would need many more to make a dish for today, so take this home with you and hang it on your front door, Anna. It works like a barometer: when it's going to rain, the petals close in and when it's sunny, they open wide.' She laughs when Anna yelps at the touch of the prickly thistle.

'Wrap it carefully.' Sveva breaks off two large stems of fern and wraps up the plant, telling Anna this was also how country people transported ricotta cheese, keeping it fresh and at the same time filtering excess liquid.

They continue to gather wood and Anna finds another two mushrooms which she proudly hands to Sveva, who immediately flings them away. 'These are not edible and they would give you a terrible stomach ache. Never go mushroom hunting without an expert, Anna. People die every year from mistakes. Danilo is the man, if you ever wanted to go on a mushroom hunt. There's nothing he doesn't know about plants and animals.'

'He certainly wouldn't want to go with me. Every time I try to talk to him, he avoids me.'

'He's a funny old man but he's also very respected round here. Maybe you haven't chosen the right time to talk to him.'

'It's because I'm English. In fact he told me that himself.'

'No, surely not. He fought with the English at the end of the war.'

'He told me the war was a long time ago and all best forgotten. It's most frustrating as I want to find out more about my mother's family and I think he must have known her.'

'She was a Santini, didn't you say? Quite a few members of that family moved away to find work. I think they went to France.' All the while, Sveva continues to gather up kindling, tying it into small bundles, which she loads into Anna's arms, 'let's take this wood back now so Sergio can light that fire. I'm as hungry as a wolf.'

Anna watches as the old oven is fed with some of the kindling. The rest is stacked neatly to one side. Sergio then adds thicker pieces of wood. Later, when the heat has built up he, removes the metal door sealing the oven and using a long-handled metal shovel he inserts and withdraws rounds of pizza bubbling with cheese and some of the *porcini* they have found.

'This oven is more than three hundred years old," he tells her, 'but it's damaged. We had a quote of 300,000 Lire to repair it, which we can't afford, but somehow we manage. We've patched the hole with a large stone from the river.'

She watches him extract more pizzas, the aroma of oregano and cheese making her mouth water. Suddenly there is a cluster of children around him.

'You all wait your turn,' he shouts good-naturedly. 'Anna, can you take these pizzas over to the table?'

In the meantime, into the embers he pushes a metal dish of tomatoes stuffed with breadcrumbs, parsley and garlic, followed by aubergines, courgettes and little potato cakes with fillings of spinach and wild plants gleaned from the meadows.

Corks pop into the evening air as bottles of sparkling wine are opened. As the sun slips behind the peaks, the air cools dramatically and everybody moves nearer to the oven.

As she tucks into her first delicious mouthful of pizza, her mobile rings. It is Francesco. 'Where are you?' he asks, 'we've finished our shopping, thank God! We were wondering about going to the pizzeria for supper. Do you want to join us?'

She laughs. 'I've found the best pizzeria in the area, up here in Montebotolino…hang on a moment.' She turns to Sveva, asking if there might be room for two more.

'But of course!' she replies, 'the more the merrier. Tell them to hurry though – with all these greedy children about, the pizza will be gone in no time.'

Anna warns him to come sooner rather than later and then goes across to Sergio. Together they put some slices to one side and in less than ten minutes, car headlights sweeping round the bend announce their arrival. Francesco makes his way over to her, bends to kiss her on the lips and Anna notices Sveva's raised eyebrows, thinking that soon the gossip will be all round Badia. Alba tries to pull him away. 'Is Pina here too?' she asks Sveva, 'can we sit with her?'

'She's over there on the swing, Alba…and here comes your pizza.' Sergio brings over a couple of laden plates.

'Come and sit with me over there, Papà. We can eat ours with Pina.'

'You go and sit with the children. I'll stay here with Anna.' The little girl bites her lip, throws Anna a filthy look and makes her way reluctantly over to the circle of children.

'Had a good day?' Anna asks him.

'So, so!'

'Alba playing up a bit?'

'Yep! Whoever said parenting was easy? I seem to jump over one hurdle for another to suddenly spring up before me.'

'We'll just have to give her time. She's probably a little jealous. Maybe we should try to spend less time together in the next few days?'

'But I don't want to! I've only just found you.' He squeezes her hand in the dark, looking over to Alba who is now laughing and chatting with her friends. Anna follows his gaze. 'Children are more adaptable than we imagine, you know.'

'And they are more selfish too,' he adds.

'I'm glad you said that and not me.'

They sit for a while, sipping their wine, watching the glow from the oven. Then Anna breaks the silence.
'Signor Danilo is playing hard to get again. I don't know what I've done wrong but he just doesn't seem to want anything to do with me.'
'Shall I try? Maybe he'll talk to me as he knew my father. I'll go now – what is it you say, "strike while the iron's hot"?'

She laughs and watches him walk up the alleyway to Danilo's house. A couple of minutes later he is back.

'He's definitely not in. Somebody said he left on his Vespa over two hours ago…probably down to Badia to play cards. Don't worry - we'll talk to him sooner or later.'

Sergio has begun strumming on his guitar, attracting a cluster of people round him. He starts to sing a haunting tune and a few other voices join in the chorus.

'There you are, Anna…this is definitely a song Danilo and my father would have sung during the war. Listen to the words.'

Una mattina mi sono svegliato,
o bella, ciao! bella, ciao! bella, ciao, ciao, ciao!
Una mattina mi sono svegliato, e ho trovato l'invasor.
O partigiano, portami via,
o bella, ciao! bella, ciao! bella, ciao, ciao, ciao!
O partigiano, portami via,
ché mi sento di morir.
E se io muoio da partigiano,

> o bella, ciao! bella, ciao! bella, ciao, ciao, ciao!
> E se io muoio da partigiano,
> tu mi devi seppellir.
> E seppellire lassù in montagna,
> o bella, ciao! bella, ciao! bella, ciao, ciao, ciao!
> E seppellire lassù in montagna
> sotto l'ombra di un bel fior.
> Tutte le genti che passeranno,
> o bella, ciao! bella, ciao! bella, ciao, ciao, ciao!
> Tutte le genti che passeranno,
> Mi diranno «Che bel fior!
> È questo il fiore del partigiano»,
> o bella, ciao! bella, ciao! bella, ciao, ciao, ciao!
> «È questo il fiore del partigiano,
> morto per la libertà!»

As Francesco joins in the singing, she listens to his fine voice and after a while joins in with the chorus herself, pleased she can follow the words. They tell of a young partisan bidding farewell to his beautiful sweetheart, asking her to bury him on the mountain under the shade of a beautiful flower if he should die fighting. In this way, each time anybody passes by and sees the flower, it will remind them that he died for the cause of liberty.

As the last verse drifts up into the star studded sky, there is applause, the sentiments behind the song obviously still striking a chord with these people fifty years on. And Anna finds it moving too, relating the song to events in the diaries. She feels increasingly at home in this corner of Tuscany, closer to her mother than she felt in England.

In the car on the way home, Alba seems happier too. 'That was fun wasn't it, Babbo? I wish we could have pizza picnics every night.'

'Maybe we could try and make some pizza ourselves next week,' Anna suggests.

'And try to get the oven working again in San Patrignano,' adds Francesco.

'Yay!' Alba shouts from the back, 'and we can invite Pina and the others from the Scuolaclub. It'll be a party.'

'And you can all invent different pizza toppings,' continues Anna.

'Cool!'

By the time they reach Anna's house, the little girl is fast asleep. Francesco lifts her out of the back seat and kisses Anna on the lips. '*Buona notte*! See you tomorrow!'

She watches them disappear round the corner to the *agriturismo* and then unlocks her own front door.

Climbing the stairs to bed, she feels suddenly lonely, not ready for sleep. Pulling the final pages of her mother's writing from the folder on her bedside table and flopping down on top of her bedcovers, she starts to read again.

Chapter 31
June 1949

In June 1949 we finally returned to Rofelle. It had taken longer to save up for the fares than Norman had calculated and our two babies had been born in the meantime. We were juddered and jolted about on the train, with Harry crying at the top of his little voice because he'd dropped his dinky car at Victoria station and being so preoccupied with baby Jane, I hadn't noticed. During the train journey she had grizzled nearly all the time she was awake. I had wanted her to be christened Assunta after my mother, but Norman had insisted on English Jane and I didn't have the strength to fight. But when he wasn't around I would call her Assunta and I would speak to her in Italian. And I sang to her of the mountains, deer, spindleberries in the forest and mushrooms in the meadows. I made the songs up. The words came out of my lips like birds set free. 'Shhh, baby Assunta! Mamma's here,' I would whisper, rocking her back and forth, holding her soft cheek next to mine, trying to still her crying. And little Harry would shout, 'Why are you calling her Assunta, Mummy? She's Jane...Jane...Jane...' stamping his little feet as he shouted out her name. Harry was too clever for his age, he was a miniature Norman. When I told him off, away he would scamper, sticking out his tongue at me from a safe distance. Or he'd kick my legs, the way he'd seen it done.

We travelled for two and a half tiring days in dirty carriages, with the smell of urine from used nappies and soiled clothes. It was stuffy in the carriage but I hadn't wanted to open the window because Harry was up and into everything and Norman kept disappearing down the corridor. It would have helped if he had offered to keep an eye on his son. But by now I was accustomed to doing everything by myself and nothing really mattered, for I was going home to Tuscany. The children had been sea-sick on the Channel crossing and I'd tried my best to clean them up but we were all beginning to look dishevelled. The train chugged its way through France and Switzerland and we stopped for border control before entering Italy. Up until this point in the journey, the French and Swiss guards, the vendors on the platform, they had all seemed half-dead, going about their business so seriously, so quietly. Once over the border however, I was struck immediately by the noise of shouting and friendly chatter outside the train. Pushing open the window, I sniffed the air like an animal scenting home territory. The name on the platform 'CHIASSO', which means din in Italian, made me laugh out loud. I thought the name was very appropriate. How lovely that the first city travellers should pass through in Italy should have such an honest name. The couple of hours before Milan, where we had to change trains once again, seemed to drag to ten hours. We snatched a drink at a bar on Milan station and I felt embarrassed as I stood and watched my elegant countrymen pass by. Even though the war had only been over for five years, there was a beauty and a pride to these Italians, they exuded stylishness in their well cut clothes and fashionable hairstyles that I didn't see in post-war England. I felt like the mother of a gypsy family. We had embarked on this journey clean, but by now we looked like chimney-sweeps, the soot from the steam train leaving smutty smears on our faces. Even our sandwiches tasted of coal and the toilet facilities had been totally inadequate for washing a baby and toddler.

On the next and final leg of our long journey, I fumbled in our suitcases to find the new summer clothes I had bought for Harry and Jane. I was so proud of my babies. I wanted to show them off at their best to everybody in the village once we arrived. Just before the train at long last drew into Rimini station, I pointed out the sea to Harry. The water glinted invitingly, lapping gently onto the sand, a few people already stretched out on the beach, taking the sun. How different from the pebbly shore and grey swirl of water on Hastings beach, where Norman had taken us on a drizzly Sunday last spring.

Papà was waiting on the platform. Shyness suddenly came over me, but as soon as he saw us climb down the steps, he pulled off his cap, waving it to attract our attention. He ran towards us with arms outstretched and I was his little girl again. He lifted Harry into the air, threw him up, kissed him with so much fervour that he started to cry, which then set Jane off. I was crying too by now, but mine were tears of joy. 'Where is Mamma?' I asked, looking along the platform for her. He told me she was waiting at home, that the taxi was too small to carry us all as well as our luggage up the Marecchia road and that she had stayed behind to prepare a good chicken broth. 'We've killed one of the hens specially', he added, 'and she has made trays of tagliatelle too'. He bent down to wipe away the tears from Harry's cheeks, who peeped up shyly at his grandfather, thumb in mouth.

Alberto, the bar keeper's son from Badia, worked part time as a taxi driver and Papà herded us out to his gleaming black Aprilia, which Norman greatly admired. Papà insisted Norman travel in the front while he climbed into the back with me and the babies, pulling Harry onto his knee. 'How can *nonno* hope to talk to his little grandson if he doesn't know any Italian?' he said, shaking his head at me. 'Eh, Ines? How shall we manage?' Throughout the car journey up into the mountains, he tried to teach Harry some simple words in Italian and I hoped Norman wouldn't make a fuss. '*Motocicletta*', he pronounced clearly, pointing to one of the many motorbikes spluttering past us along the route. There were far more here in Italy and Harry had fun imitating the revving sounds. Jane slept in my arms while I gazed out of the window at newly constructed houses, neatly tended meadows and beautiful mountains, seeing them with fresh eyes. When I had left, the landscape had been battle scarred, desolate and I was proud to see the resilience of my people, how they were resurrecting a new life from nothing.

'We'll stop here for a while and have a drink and you and the children can freshen up,' said Papà about an hour into the journey. But all I really wanted to do was get to the mill quickly to see Mamma again, put my arms around her and introduce the grandchildren, I didn't want the journey held up one moment longer. But Papà knew the owner of the bar on the road below Pennabilli and he wanted to introduce us and his English son-in-law who had travelled so many miles for this return visit. He was so proud of us. The wife of the owner exclaimed what a handsome young man Harry was and how beautiful and plump was the baby. 'But, signora,' she said, with hands raised in horror, 'she will catch her death in this cold, mountain air! Where are her socks? Where is her vest? Cover her up! Take this shawl and wrap her up warm.' It was surely not her intention, but she made me feel an inadequate mother. In England I always let Jane kick in her pram in our little back garden, with her chubby legs bare to the fresh air. But mountain people were wary of spring weather and waited until July and August to cast off winter clothing.

Half an hour later we were back in the car and I started to recognise all my childhood haunts. My heart beat faster and faster as we passed through Ponte Presale, where the Friday market always took place. Then I spied the huge rock studded with fossils in the meadow where our cows used to sometimes graze. Next the baker's, the cemetery of Badia, the newly built municipal hall with Italian flags fluttering proudly in the breeze, its steps flanked with geraniums spilling from huge urns. And then we were rounding a bend to take the lane down to the mill. This part of the journey seemed to last forever and ever, each bend in the road like a Purgatory until, finally, the car turned sharp right down the dirt track towards the Mill. There it stood in the afternoon sunshine, perched on its rock above the river. I could hardly wait for the car to stop; flinging open the door and grabbing hold of the children, I hurried from the car towards the mill steps. With baby Jane in my arms and Harry clinging to my skirt, I climbed the steps. I shall never forget seeing my poor mother that first time. My mamma stood there - a shadow of her self - looking tired and grey. In my shock, I nearly dropped baby. 'Mamma, mammina', I was crying as I kissed her, whilst inside I was thinking, *what have I done to you? It's my fault, isn't it? For going across the sea and leaving. Forgive me, mamma, forgive me.'*

Later on, when we were sitting round the table in the kitchen, having eaten her excellent chicken broth and

Norman and Papà had gone out to drink more wine up in the *osteria* at Rofelle, I asked Mamma if it was my fault that she looked so ill.

'Don't be foolish, Ines. The doctor says I have problems with my thyroid, that's all. I'll soon be right again after I've finished taking his medicines.' She took Jane from me and hugged her close, then bent down to touch Harry's soft curls and said she didn't want to talk about it anymore. She just wanted to enjoy the time with me and her grandchildren.

The doctor's telling lies. It's me, it's me.

Far, far away across the sea... My thoughts whispered to me, teasing me with what I believed to be the truth.

In the first days of that holiday, there was a pattern to the reaction from my old neighbours and friends. I had seen the same looks in my parents' eyes too. 'But you're so thin, Ines,' they said. That always came after the first embraces; after they'd let me go and stepped back, looking me up and down. Their faces registered shock at the state of me. I knew they were thinking how scrawny I had become, how lifeless my hair was, how my beauty had left for England on the train with me and not come back.

'Don't they feed you in Inghilterra, Ines?' commented Lucia from the farm up the road, where we had been invited to supper one evening. 'Come sit with me and I'll fill your plate. We've made pizza with courgette flowers and *stracchino* cheese. And roasted hare and boar. Eat, Ines! Give me the baby. Sit and eat.'

And Ida from San Patrignano, she left baskets of eggs, tomatoes on the vine and jars of plum jam on the door step of the mill, just like she'd done in the days before our wedding.

Now it was Norman's turn to be the foreigner and I watched how my people welcomed him, drew him into their warm circle of food and wine and love. Yes, love. That was it. That was what I had been missing back in Inghilterra.

We stayed for two weeks. Time flew by and all too soon the day arrived when we had to leave. It was so difficult. I wanted to stay but how could I? It had been my decision to leave for England with Norman in the first place. How could I even think of leaving him now and staying in Rofelle? In those days, you see, divorce was considered a huge scandal. If the young had the wisdom of the old, then I would have followed what was really in my heart and stayed in Rofelle. I have learned over the years to realise that the answers to all the questions we ask ourselves are already inside us. All we have to do is be quiet and listen. On the second Sunday of our holiday, I went to Mass in the little stone church where I had made my First Communion and later married Norman. I gazed at the cross, muttering my prayers, begging for a miracle to allow me to stay. All I could see in reply were the nails in the hands of Jesus and the blood trickling down his face from his crown of thorns. He seemed to be telling me what I knew already: that life was hard, that everybody had to suffer in some way or other. My trial was Norman and I had to stay faithful to my marriage vows.

I clung to my mother as we kissed goodbye, as if she were a piece of wreckage and I was drowning in the cold, cold English Channel. 'There's always a place for you here,' she said as she wrapped her arms around me. Yes, it was wonderful to arrive but dreadful to leave and there were tears all round.

And once again the train carried me across the miles, rocking me with imagined refrains:

I would if I could but I can't.
I would if I could but I can't.
I can't, I can't I can't, I can't , I can't...

Back in England I fell ill. I couldn't shake off my sadness. I felt constantly tired. My two babies had been born close together and both labours had been long and painful. When I eventually dragged myself to visit the doctor, I wasn't surprised when she diagnosed problems with my thyroid. In a way, I felt it was right that I too should suffer as my own mother was suffering. They were very dark times for me but my doctor was a very kind woman and she urged me to write down my feelings. 'When you feel troubled, put your feelings down on paper if it helps' she advised. And writing did help a little. Talking to Norman didn't. How many promises had he made? How many promises had he broken in our talks?

Far more than he'd kept.

In late autumn, Norman came with me to town one market day, telling me he wasn't needed at work. He was unusually playful with the children and attentive to me, offering to carry the shopping baskets. 'Don't know how you do it all on your own' he'd said, lifting the pram onto the bus. For once I felt we were a normal family.

We sat on the top deck at the front so Harry could pretend he was the bus driver. The war had been over for five years, but there were still pot-holes in the road and it was a very bumpy ride. I jiggled plump, sunny Jane about on my lap and she laughed.

'Teach me that rhyme again, Norman,' I said, 'the one about the farmer.' I was keen to learn and fit in with the English way of life. If I couldn't be a good wife then I would be a good mother and bring up my children perfectly.

'This is the way the farmers ride,' he started to sing, pulling Harry onto his leg, pretending it was a saddle. The children squealed with laughter as both of us bounced them up and down to the words. But after a while Norman's mind seemed to be elsewhere as he continued to jog Harry higher and higher, not realising he was hurting his son.

'This is the way the soldiers die, the soldiers die, the soldiers die, this is the way the soldiers die on a crisp Italian morning,' he sang tunelessly. When he stopped, Harry clambered off him and buried his head in my coat. Norman stared into the distance, 'All those scrawny mules,' he said, 'trotting up and down those rutted tracks, laden with sticks and guns.'

Trying to change the subject, I cleaned the mist off the window with my gloved hand. 'Ooh look, everybody! It's snowing. How do you say *nevischio* in English, Norman?'

'Sleet.'

'Slit,' I pronounced.

'No sleeeeet, Ines. Like the bloody sleet that stopped the tanks. Muddy ruts. Digging them out in the perishing cold. Bloody weather!'

I covered Harry's little ears with my hands and looked behind me at the other passengers. The bus was quite full now, as we approached the centre of Croydon and Surrey Street, with its market stalls.

'Don't swear, Norman,' I scolded, 'Remember 'Arry.''

'Why can't you say **H**arry?' he rebuked, 'you can say "h". I know you can. You say **h**oak trees, **h**old man…his name is **H**arry.' He emphasised the H petulantly.

'It's 'ard,' I replied, trying to make him laugh, to distract him, but he was off again, his legs still jiggling up and down although he was no longer playing the game with Harry.

'It's Hard, ' he repeated, ' Bloody hard with sleet on the hills, waking in the morning, cracking ice off sacking covers, blowing on fingers, bone cold. Bones! Bob's old bones sticking out of his trousers, stick thin scarecrow limbs.'

Suddenly the bus braked hard, throwing us all forwards in our seats. I cracked my head against the window. Harry burst out crying as he fell to the floor. I screamed as Norman dived down, shouting at the top of his voice, 'Get down everyone! Get down for cover.'

'Get up, Norman!' I pleaded, 'Arry's hurt.' Jane was crying now. A passenger came over, staring at Norman cowering on the floor. 'Are you all right, lady?' she asked, 'can I help you?'

I looked up, explaining to her and the bus in general, to the two women sitting behind us whispering behind their hands and all the rest of them, trying to look as if they weren't watching, 'No thank you. We'll be fine. He's all right. It's the war still, you see. It happens like this sometimes.'

'Get behind those rocks, in the ditch. Damn you, get down, I said.' Norman continued to rant from his place on the floor, so I handed Jane to the woman and crouched down beside him. 'Norman, get up now.

We're on the bus.' As frightened as I was by his strange turn, I spoke to him gently, as if he were a child, 'We're in Croydon. Get up – I need you to help me. *Please*, Norman!'

We got off at the next stop, even though there was still a fair walk to the market, and I crossed the road, guiding my little family, holding fast to Norman who was carrying Harry, while I clutched baby in my other arm. We waited for the next bus to take us straight home and I wondered if I would be strong enough to hold it all together.

In the meantime, Tiziana and I still continued to meet. She was the only one I could talk to. I didn't want to burden Freda and John.

'What am I going to do, Tizi?' We were sitting in her untidy living room, the children playing on a tatted rug by the fire. She'd received another parcel from Rome containing Italian biscuits and coffee and she'd added a splash of Anice liqueur to her espresso.

'I've told you often enough, *cara,* be firmer with him.'

'But how can I when he's like that? You've never seen it – he's like a child when it happens. I feel as if I've got three of them at times.'

Tiziana shrugged her shoulders, pouring another tot of Anice into her cup. 'I would have left him ages ago, I haven't got your patience.'

I knew what her answers would be but it helped to confide in her.

'What you need to do is to forget about him for a while,' she said, kneeling down to separate her boys, squabbling over a toy tractor, and smacking them hard on their behinds. '*Basta così* you two, and if I have to tell you off again, there'll be more where that came from.' Hoisting herself back onto the settee, she poured herself another coffee. 'This will make me even more *nervosa,* but who cares? You only live once.' She stirred three heaped spoons of sugar and another generous measure of the Anice into her cup and suggested, 'Tell you what, Ines, we'll go out next week to the flicks or something. Bring the bambini over here and Denis's kid sister will look after them. She's always keen to spend time alone with that boyfriend of hers. You can save a couple of bob out of your house keeping to pay her.'

So I did what she said. I sat through 'Brief Encounter', imagining Norman was Trevor Howard, crying my eyes out. It was so romantic and sad. I wasn't really crying about their doomed love affair, I was crying about mine. Tizi apologised afterwards, saying something funny, like 'Dreaming', starring Bud Flanagan would have been better but I don't think anything would have helped me at that time. Norman had been told to take leave from work to 'rest', as his employer put it, and he was under my feet all day long. He had never liked Tiziana and he was convinced we had both gone out that evening to meet men. No matter how many times I promised him we had only gone to the cinema, he didn't believe me. The beatings started again. Rofelle and our holiday seemed a life time away.

When everything got on top of me, I wrote down my thoughts or snippets of poems, like the nice lady doctor had suggested. I remembered a history lesson at school, when we learned about Etruscan women who put away their wedding sheets when their husbands died. They no longer needed them for their marital bed so they saved them, to use as shrouds when they died. To me, it was as if the Norman I had known in Italy had died and I was a widow. So I found a beautiful pillowcase that my own *nonna* had sewed for my trousseau and I wrote on that. I wrote what was in my heart, the ink blotting with my tears. Norman discovered it and we had a huge row. 'Who is he? Who is this man you are writing to?' he shouted, beating me about my face this time, so I couldn't leave the house for a week.

'Tell me, you barmy bitch,' he shouted, 'tell me or I'll hit you again. I always thought you were a loony and now I know for sure.'

I couldn't give him an answer. I didn't know myself who this man was that I had begun to dream about. I only knew it wasn't Norman.

Anna pulls out the yellowing pillowcase from its brown paper wrapping, unfolding the material to read her mother's words, the letters faded in places.

>
> Your hands are gentle hands, touching my body, silk on silk.
> They are not claws of the hawk, tearing innards from its prey.
> Your eyes are full of the light of a sun slipping down folds of mountains
> Bathing me with warmth and promise.
> Your eyes are not sparks, singeing with acrid stench, jumping from spitting fire, burning holes in my Sunday dress.
>
>
> I lie down with you under the hot August midday sun in the river's shallows,
> My petticoat hanging on branches of willow.
> Your mouth is soft, your tongue like the smooth underbelly of a tickled trout as you caress my breasts;
> You are not the frost; not the jagged spikes of wild rose or bramble
> Nor splinters from the handle of my hoe;
> Nor the viper coiled near the washing line.
> Your hands are gentle hands, touching my body, silk on silk.

Chapter 32
August 1999

At two in the morning, Anna sits cradling the old pillowcase, wishing her mother could be sitting next to her on the bed, so she can tell her how much she loves her.

There are only a few pages remaining of her story but she is struggling to keep her eyes open. Switching off her bed-side light, she falls asleep with the pillowcase in her arms.

Before even making herself breakfast next morning, she resumes reading. The date on the next page has jumped twenty years and she wonders how she can fill in the missing pieces.

Maybe she never will.

September 30th 1966
On the pantry shelves of Willow's End there is a regiment of blackberry jam. There's hardly room for more and we shall never get through it all in the coming year but when the September sun shines like this I have to be outside.

I've hurried through my morning chores, cleared the grate, laid fresh kindling and scrubbed the lino in the hall that looks so much like Italian salame. Before 10 o'clock I am out of the house. The day is mine until Jane returns from school. The curtains twitch at number twenty three across the way. The old bag will be wondering where I'm off to again. 'That foreign bit' married to Norman – that's how I've heard her call me. She's complained to him about the smell of garlic wafting from my kitchen as well. Let her complain! Back home they'd probably have muttered too, if an English woman had married one of their boys.

This morning is a little fresher than yesterday and I button up my cardigan as I hurry down the footpath. It's one of Freda's old Aran wool cardigans; a little stretched now, but I like wearing it. She was a kind woman, God rest her soul, like a mother to me, comforting me when I heard of Mamma's passing away and caring for me when I went through my black moments. I pull the rough wool closer round my middle.

It only takes five minutes to escape from the line of rabbit hutch houses. Down the footpath I hurry and when I reach the edge of the corn fields, I stop and breathe in the air, hungry for the scent of it. If I close my eyes I can almost imagine I'm back in Rofelle. The best blackberries are at the bottom of this field and my feet scrunch over the stubble of corn stalks and I can pretend I am back in Tuscany. I can pretend. Especially when the breeze rustles up a dance in the trees at the edge of the field and I look up at the billow of clouds, picturing them like the Apennines soaring above me, enfolding me.

This sun is more diluted than the August sun we enjoyed last month. Norman took us all back to Italy with some of the money Freda left. He couldn't avoid it for she had stipulated in her will that "he was duty bound to take Ines back to her home village for a long-overdue holiday". In this sheltered corner of the field, the sun does its best to shine a little warmth and I peel off Freda's cardigan. She had a good idea of what was going on between Norman and Phyllis, she wasn't soft…he was always sniffing round her. I tried to stop it. God knows how I tried.

The breeze is playing with my curls. I'm lucky, I've no grey strands. Papà had a head of black curls until the day he died and maybe I take after him. A thorn from the brambles tears at my finger and I gasp and suck the wound, blood oozing and mixing with purple blackberry juice staining my hands. It's the colour of wine at the village festa we went to last month. The men clustered round great fat flasks of strong red wine sitting on farmer Amedeo's cart, slapping each other on the back, using their hands the way we Italians do when we talk. Norman had a good amount of the wine. It was free, so he drank it greedily and he grew very drunk. He had no idea what was going on that evening.

The end of the square outside the town hall was cleared for dancing, chairs and trestle-tables arranged under the loggia in case it rained, Franco, the butcher, supervising slicing and sharing of *porchetta*. Now, as I think back, my mouth is watering at the memory of sweet meat perfumed with rosemary and garlic. All the women in Rofelle had been busy for days, mixing and cutting yellow ribbons of pasta to go with sauces of wild hare and boar. They let me help, laughing at my fumbling. 'You've forgotten, Ines, you've forgotten how to make *tagliatelle*. What do you cook back in Inghilterra. Sandwiches?'

And it's true, I had forgotten. Norman preferred his food the English way: plates piled with potatoes and meat, swimming in gravy. Nevertheless, my Italian friends let me help and I joined in with their laughter and gossip that evening and for a little while I felt I belonged again. When we had finished cooking, we sat together on hay bales, waiting to be asked to dance polkas and waltzes in the square; the young girls, modest, with eyes cast down to their hands in their laps, peeping every now and then at sweethearts.

My little hamlet would never appear on the front of glossy guide-books but that night Rofelle was a place of magic. Candles and oil lamps glowed in every niche, imbuing old stones with golden warmth. I thought back to myself as a young girl, how I'd turned up my nose at this type of festa, at the smallness of the place, the simple goodness and generosity of the people and wondered how I could ever have despised it.

Capriolo came over to ask me to dance. The years had been kind to him. He was still lean but his hair was streaked with grey, lending him a distinguished look. The women had filled me in with the gossip, telling me he'd been married for a while to a city girl from Florence but she soon tired of village life and he'd refused to leave his birthplace to go to live there with her. He was still active in local politics but his main job was on the land. I glanced over to where Norman was drinking, surrounded by other men, knocking back tumblers of wine but he was oblivious, his long face shining white in the moonlight. Jane was already on the dance floor, a young man patiently guiding her round to the music. Harry had wandered over to see what his father was up to and I saw him help himself to a beaker of wine; let him, I thought. He's nearly 19 and soon he'll be a man and off to College.

I settled into Capriolo's arms as he moved me in a waltz to the notes from Beppe's accordion. It was old-fashioned folk music; pop music by the Beatles and other groups was yet to reach this corner of Italy. The words of the songs came back to me. I sang them softly as he moved me round the square and it was as if I'd never been away. The night was warm and he had rolled up his shirt sleeves. I could feel the swell of his muscles under my fingers. As he spun me round and round, we stared deep into each other's eyes and the world beyond our space blurred. And it was at that moment I knew I had made the biggest mistake of my life all those years ago. As he danced, a lock of his unruly hair flopped down over his right eye the way it always used to when he bent over his school books in our village classroom. My fingers burned to smooth it back but I knew the eyes of the villagers, my relations, maybe even Norman and the children would be upon us. At the end of the dance I thanked him and returned to the bales. I watched the shadows of dancers move across the walls of the old stone houses and suddenly I couldn't watch anymore and I ran and ran and ran.

The road down to the mill was lit by moonlight but even in the dark I found my way there easily. As I drew nearer, the noise of the water flopping and gurgling over the stones grew louder and I leant against a rock, staring downriver towards the mill, wishing with all my heart I had never left.

Footsteps. Capriolo's voice. 'Ines?' And then his arms were round me and we were kissing.

'Someone will come along. They'll see us.' I pulled away - where we were standing, the full moon shining down on us like daylight, anybody could have seen us from the bridge.

'Come.' He pulled me down the track towards the mill, our feet skidding on the stones in our haste. He pushed open the door to the barn and, hand in hand, we went in and I was in his arms again, our kisses deeper, more urgent. We lay down on the hay and for the first time in my life I made love. We made love on the floor of a barn and for those few, sad, beautiful moments I was in Paradise. Every part of me sang and afterwards I cried in his arms.

'I should never have let you go, Ines. Maybe if we had done this before you left for England, then you would never have gone away.'

I stopped his words with my kisses and he held me tighter. We kept our eyes open and our gaze never left each other's even at the very height of our love-making. I had never felt so complete in all my life.

'Why don't you leave him? Come back here where you belong?' he said after, as we lay together.

'How can I? How can I leave my children?'

'But we love each other. Even when I made love to my wife, I was thinking of you.'

I felt jealous then. I knew I had no right, but I couldn't help it.

'They told me about her. What was her name?'

'Rita,' he said, raising himself on his elbow, staring down at me where I lay on the straw, 'but she means nothing to me.'

'There were no children, were there? Once there are children, things change.'

He shook his head. 'I shouldn't have let you leave,' he said, sitting up abruptly, his back to me.

I touched his arm and pulled him down to me again. 'Please don't spoil tonight. Just hold me.'

But we had to leave. It was gone midnight. The festa was coming to an end and we would be missed. So we dressed and he picked the straw out of my hair, helping me with the buttons on the back of my dress.

And then he smiled and, pulling a pen-knife from his pocket, he carved our names in a heart, low down on the wall near to where we had made love.

'You're a boy,' I said, 'a mad, mad boy...what if somebody sees that?'

'The only creatures to see this will be the cattle when they bend to munch on their hay and who will they tell, Ines?'

I laughed and ruffled his hair and he pulled me into his arms again. 'You are still beautiful, even after all this time.'

If the clock in the church tower on the hill above in Rofelle hadn't chimed the first notes of midnight, we would have been down in the straw again.

We left separately. When I reached the square, Norman was being supported by the sons of the owner of the little guest house where we were staying. 'This one will wake up like a bear tomorrow morning. I hope you've got some strong coffee for his head tomorrow, Ines.'

They helped me carry him up the narrow stairs and when they had gone, I undressed him and climbed into bed beside him.

I lay awake all night.

A week later we returned to England. Life resumed its routine. Autumn was upon us and I started my crazy blackberry jam making to keep myself busy. I thought I would go a little mad again, like after Jane was born. But this time, who would look after me?

In the field, the sun hides behind the clouds and I shiver, fastening Freda's cardigan again, with its old bone buttons. Just one more branch and I'll return to the house and set the preserving pan upon the stove. I pick more fruit, not caring if the thorns tear at me, just wanting this sadness to leave me. I won't ever return to Rofelle. I can't.

My only consolation is I know my love for Capriolo is not just a dream. The nausea I've been feeling has now made me certain of the life we started in the barn. I shall tell Norman it happened the night when he was so drunk. But I shall know the truth.

In my heart I long for a son. I picture how he will lean over his school books when he is older, a curl of raven-black hair falling in front of his eyes. I picture how I will gently smooth it back from his little forehead and whisper to him in Italian of how he is my special gift.

Chapter 33

Anna counts from August 1966 to May 1967 on the fingers of both her hands: nine months. Ines didn't have a son. She had a baby girl. Anna's birth date is May 15th 1967.

You're a good girl, Anna. You're my special gift. How often had her mother said those words to her in the nursing home?

Her mind fields thoughts, firing at her one after the other.

Norman wasn't my father. Capriolo was my father. I am the baby conceived in that barn. What had mother written? 'This is my inheritance to you. Do with it what you will'.

Her head is spinning. She has to get outside. Despite the rain she pulls on jeans, sweat-shirt, waterproof jacket and walking boots. Slamming the door behind her, she strides down the path to the river. The ground is cloggy underfoot, the river is full but she keeps on walking. And then she remembers the day of the storm and where she sheltered with Alba.

She quickens her pace. At the barn she undoes the wire holding the ramshackle door closed and enters. Rain splashes through the missing roof tiles and it smells musty inside, despite the sun of the past weeks. Kneeling down in the corner near their makeshift picnic table, she finds the heart scratched into the crumbling plaster near the rotten feeding trough.

DS & IS agosto 1966

She traces the letters with her finger, picturing her mother sitting there, hair undone, straw tangled in her curls, gazing at her father as he carves their initials. She can see them in the hay, making love, hear their sighs, their groans and she feels like a voyeur. Leaving, she pulls the door to and continues walking, not knowing where she is going, just following the course of the river, now more swollen with the steady fall of rain.

As she walks she tries to identify Capriolo - or DS, frowning with concentration as she racks her brain for any man who might match the initials.
Davide Santini...oh God, no! Ines's own brother!
But then she remembers that Uncle Davide had died during the war. Of course it couldn't be him.

The rain stops by the time she reaches the waterfall and she sits for a while, willing herself to calm down. The water cascades over the weir with a roar, spewing white foam into the pool below. She watches a couple of fish try to jump back up the waterfall. A grey heron with spindly legs is about to land on a log to fish for his breakfast but sensing her presence, he changes course, his large wings cumbersome as he manoeuvres his altered flight. As he soars above her head she hears the whistle of air through his wings.

Dario Starnucci.

The name comes to her, booming in her head like the announcement on a public tannoy. Blood drains from her face, her heartbeat slows almost to a stop.

Dario Starnucci. Francesco has talked about his father often enough. He was a partisan too. DS must be Dario Starnucci. The father of Francesco and Teresa is also my father.

She feels sick.

She has slept with her brother. The man she loves is her half-brother.

'*Do with it what you will*', her mother had written. But, what is she supposed to do? She walks slowly back to her house. Only it isn't even *her* house. It belongs to her half-sister, loaned to her so she could stay in Italy and be happy. And she has been happy. But nothing feels right anymore.

She lets herself in, hauls her suitcase from under the bed and tosses in items: a change in underwear, clean jeans, tops, a jacket – it will be colder in England. She checks for her passport and credit card in her handbag. All she wants now is to get away from this place, call a taxi and catch the first available plane to London. Tearing a page from one of the children's exercise books on her table, she scribbles a note to say she is returning to England for family reasons.

Then she is sick, vomiting again and again down the toilet until only bitter bile comes up. She feels ancient, wrung out, spat out and rests for a while on the bed.

She sleeps for hours, waking when the birds begin to sing. In the early light she gazes on the few possessions scattered around: heart-shaped stones collected by Alba from the river bed, the little girl's paintings, the bright tablecloth she bought from the market and she thinks they are souvenirs best forgotten.

On the journey down from the mountains to the airport, the taxi-driver tries to strike up conversation. 'My daughter, she's in England at the moment. Oxford.' He pronounces it the Italian way, emphasising the second part of the word and saying 'd' as 't'. For one moment, her teacher role wants to kick in to correct him but she lets him ramble on instead.

'She's trying to learn English but she's with all her friends from school and she's talking Italian all the time. Waste of money, I said to her mother. And she hates the food…Sorry signorina, but our Italian food is better than yours…'

He looks at her in his rear-view mirror and Anna shuts her eyes, willing him to shut up, in no mood for polite conversation. Shrugging his shoulders, he switches on the radio and puts his foot down on the accelerator. Maybe his next passenger will help him pass his time better than she has.

Rimini airport is thronging with Russian tourists on a day shopping trip, their carrier bags crammed with designer clothes and shoes. She nurses a tepid cappuccino at the bar as she waits to go through security. The big women in their tight jeans pull out flimsy blouses and bright sandals to show each other. Their words sound harsh and guttural compared with the melody of Italian. Little do they realise they've come all these air miles to buy goods manufactured especially for them and not the Italian market, that they've shopped in outlets where Italian women would never buy.

At a nearby table covered in the paraphernalia of baby's travel equipment, an exhausted young English mother sits breastfeeding a very young baby whilst trying to clean a toddler's nose. Anna picks up a toy from the floor for the little dark-haired boy and his mother thanks her, explaining that they are on their way to England to see their sick Grandpa.

The air conditioning isn't working and it's hot in the seating area. She watches a couple of *carabinieri* standing to one side, deep in discussion. Their heads swivel as they stare at a lovely young girl making her way to passport control, rolling her hips like a model on a cat-walk, their eyes feasting on her as if she were the last female they are ever going to see. Ordinarily Anna enjoys her people-watching. Down in the square in Sansepolcro she had often lingered over a cappuccino, watching scenes unfold in the piazza Torre di Berta - characters from all walks of life entering from the wings onto a stage. But today she just wants to be gone from Italy and for the day to be over so she can escape from her nightmare.

Checking the monitor to see if her flight has been called, she notes that the plane from Stansted has not even touched down yet. There's still an hour to wait. She knows she should eat something but she's not hungry. Pictures of her and Francesco in bed keep flashing into her mind. She once watched a documentary about incest, late at night on Channel 5. A boy and girl, adopted at different times by the same foster family, had ended up as a couple. They'd justified their love later by explaining that nobody had ever told them they were brother and sister. And now she is guilty of the same thing. She shakes her head to free the pictures from her brain and bends down to talk to the little boy, crying for his mother's attention. 'Would you like me to read you a story?' she asks. At least it will occupy her mind.

His young mother scrabbles around in her cabin luggage and produces a much thumbed, tatty Postman Pat story book, smiling a thank you to Anna. She starts to read to the child and he pops his thumb into his mouth, leaning against her to look at the pictures.

'Anna?' Francesco bends over her, touching her arm. She jumps up to leave, excusing herself from the young mother, leaving the little boy crying once again.

Francesco's voice is full of concern as he follows her, 'What's happened? Stop a minute and talk to me. Has something happened to your brother or sister?'

She shakes her head. She should just pretend, tell him anything, tell him Harry is in a coma in intensive care but instead she stammers, 'leave me alone.'

'Is it you then? Are you ill?'

And then she is crying.

He takes her in his arms and despite everything, she sinks into his embrace, sobbing noisily so that a policewoman approaches, '*Signore, c'è qualche problema?*'

Francesco thanks her politely and leads Anna outside the stuffy airport to a bench in the shade of a lime tree. She traces a line of obscene graffiti gouged into the wood, avoiding his gaze. 'We shouldn't be alone like this,' she manages.

'Can you tell me what I've done wrong?'

'It's not you. It's us.' She looks at him, wishing he didn't have to be so damn special.

'You're not making any sense.' He tries to take her hand in his but she snatches it away.

'I found out,' she says 'you and I...we're related.' She pauses as he pulls a face. 'You're my brother. My half brother.'

He laughs, 'What are you talking about?'

'It's in the diary. Norman wasn't my father. Your father was my father.'

He laughs again. 'Have you been at the grappa?'

She raises her voice, telling him not to make light of what she is telling him. A couple, topping up their sun-tan on the dirty patch of grass outside Departures, stare at them.

'Your father's name was Dario, right?' she asks him, 'your surname is Starnucci?'

'And so? What does that prove?'

And then she tells him what she has read about her mother's lover and the initials in the barn. 'Don't you see? Capriolo was your father – Dario – and my father too.' Getting up to return to departures, she says, 'What we've been doing is wrong. I have to go back to England, Francesco. I can't stay here with you.'

'Anna, wait!' He tries to grab her arm but she stiffens. 'All right, all right,' he steps back. 'But I think you are wrong.'

'I wish that were true.' She is crying again. She is sick of feeling sad – for her mother and now herself.

'Please come back to Rofelle with me' he continues, 'just give me twenty four hours to prove you wrong. I promise I won't touch you – but you can't just disappear like this out of our lives. Please, Anna.'

She can't make up her mind. Would it not just be prolonging the agony to stay or should she let him try to prove her wrong? The nightmare continues.

Feeling as if all the stuffing has been knocked out of her, in the end she follows him to his car. They make the journey out of the busy, scruffy Rimini suburbs and up through the Marecchia valley in silence. The sun set is achingly beautiful that evening: pinks, purples and reds melting into a silken backdrop behind the mountains. Francesco drops her at the door to the little house in the square she thought she would never see again.

'I'll fetch you just before ten tomorrow morning. In the meantime, try to rest!' he says as he waits for her to go in.

Without bothering to wash, she takes off her jeans and t-shirt and pulling up the covers on her un-made bed, she sinks into the mattress and although it is early, she falls asleep immediately.

Chapter 34

Rain falls again in the morning, a fine drizzle leaving dusty streaks on the vine leaves shading the pergola. A dramatic summer storm develops, lightning splitting the sky and a torrential downpour lasting for half an hour. Just after ten, Francesco arrives at her door. 'Buongiorno! Are you ready?' he asks.
'Where are we going?'
He taps his nose with his index finger, 'All will be revealed,' he replies enigmatically.
'I've had enough of surprises.' She picks up her umbrella from by the door but he tells her she won't need it, pointing to the blue sky that has replaced the storm clouds. Not for the first time she wonders at the extremes of this country. She follows him outside to his Fiat Panda and he opens the door for her. Just like old times, she thinks, only nothing feels the same as before.
The car bumps up the track to Montebotolino, sometimes skidding where the road still runs water from the heavy rain. In the sun, glistening raindrops cluster like jewels on spikes of *ginestra* along the verges. Steam rises from the warm earth like a stage effect and the peaks of the Mountains of the Moon are purple in the haze.
Francesco parks in the open area near the houses. 'Come,' he says, adding when she hesitates, 'trust me!' She follows him for a few metres down a

footpath indicated on the side of an outbuilding with the customary red and white way-mark. The grass is wet, her shoes are quickly soaked but it isn't cold. The rain has refreshed the atmosphere, releasing scents of flowers and grass. They stop in front of a tidy vegetable plot, terraced into the mountain side, half a dozen bee-hives in bright colours tucked against the fence. In the far corner, an old man is working, staking wayward tomato plants. It is Danilo. Francesco puts his fingers in his mouth and whistles. The old man turns round, lifting a hand in recognition.

'What are we doing up here?' asks Anna.

'You told me you wanted to talk to him – well, here's your chance.'

'It's too late now.' She turns to retrace her steps but he blocks her way, a smile on his lips. 'Talk to him. I'll wait for you by the car.'

The old man beckons for her to come and sit down. Under an apple tree, an old oak plank supported by two large stones has been made into a crude bench. 'Sit here, signorina. We need to talk.' He is nervous. He rubs his chin with a hand stained green from the tomato plants and starts to speak at the same time as she says, 'I came to talk to you before, about my mother. Twice.'

'Francesco told me…' he starts, followed by, 'you go first.'

'What can you tell me about Dario Starnucci?' she asks.

'That he was a good friend - we were in the same band of partisans, that I miss him now he's gone…'

'And that he loved my mother…' She finishes his sentence and turns to look at him but he shakes his head. 'A lot of boys were in love with your mother. Francesco told me that you think Dario is your father.'

'Yes!'

'Well, you are wrong.'

She experiences a moment of doubt and waits for him to continue but the old man is gazing into the distance. From his shirt pocket he takes out the photo Anna had pushed under his door on her last visit to Montebotolino. The black and white image of her mother stares back at her and she wishes she had never bothered to write her diary.

'Your mother was very beautiful. But very stubborn.' He touches the photo with rough, work fingers. 'I was always in love with her. Right from when we were very small and used to walk up the track to school together. I loved her when we played in the fields and later on when I was busy with the *partigian*i and she came to join us in our camp in the mountains. I always loved her.' He hands Anna the photograph. 'I knew she didn't feel for me in the same way. I was a shy young man, no good with girls. Maybe if I'd plucked up courage to tell her what was in my heart, things would have been different.'

'I don't understand.' Danilo covers her hand with his, squeezes it. 'Your mother was head over heels in love with the *inglese*. She was determined to leave and start a new life. It was hard here in the war. We had *tedeschi* living on top of us, spies everywhere. There wasn't enough food. There was no fun – it was a wretched time... I believe the *inglese* came along when Ines was ripe for romance. I tried to make her think more about what she was doing. Leaving her parents. Davide dead...'

'I know all this.'

'Ah well, you must know what I'm going to tell you next.'

She replies slowly, without conviction, realisation slowly dawning, 'What I said before - that the *inglese* was not my father and that Dario was my father.'

Danilo shakes his head, 'No, he wasn't your father.' He cups her cheek with his hand, his voice full of emotion as he says, 'I am your father.'

She stares at the old man sitting next to her, feeling the whole world has gone mad.

'Everybody calls me by my real name - Starnucci Danilo,' he continues, saying his surname first, according to Italian tradition. 'But during the war, I was known as Capriolo.'

'Then you are Dario's brother,' she manages to say, 'but why didn't Francesco tell me all this?'

'No, we aren't related and he didn't know.' He smiles at her confusion and explains. 'At least, we are not closely related. There are very few different family names in our countryside. Cousins used to marry cousins all the time; there wasn't a lot of choice.'

She looks at his face, trying to recognise something of herself in him but all she can see are the weathered, lined features of an old man. 'Why are you telling me now? Why didn't you tell me when we first met?'

He shrugs his shoulders. 'I was shocked when you turned up that day in the piazza. At first I thought I'd seen a ghost. You are very like her.'

'But I may never have found out…'

'I was angry with your mother for a long time. I couldn't understand why she wouldn't come back to me. I came to England to fetch her, you know.'

'When?'

'A long time ago…maybe more than thirty years? She told me she didn't want to make any more mistakes – she didn't want to bring more shame on her family - she had her three children to think of and she couldn't bring them away from England. She told me to forget about her.'

'Did you know about me?'

'When I came to England, she didn't want me to come to her house, so we met in the middle of a town. She arrived with a baby in a push-chair. I put two and two together but I couldn't be certain… In fact, Ines told me it was Norman's and that made me even angrier with her.'

'So, what made you decide to finally tell me?'

'Francesco came to see me last night. He was confused and upset. He told me what you had discovered in Ines's diaries and wanted to know if there could have been anything between his father and Ines. I may be a bitter old man but I couldn't let him believe something that wasn't true. I owed it to his father …as well as to you…'

He takes her hand again, 'I've had no practice at being a father. It was too late for Tina and me. I hope it's not too late to start now?'

Later on, after the three of them have toasted each other with bottles of local wine from Capriolo's store, Francesco takes Anna back down the hill. They park outside the village cemetery where the graves are protected by high walls and shaded by tall pines.

'Let me show you why it was so easy for you to think we were related.' He turns the key in the metal gate which creaks as he pushes it open. On the walls are enamelled plaques bearing the names of the dead. There are even photos, taken when they were alive, next to the inscriptions. Some show young men in army uniforms of the First and Second World Wars. There are men and women, young and old, dressed in their Sunday best. There are babies and infants. Votive lights flicker red in front of some of the memorials; faded plastic flowers and real flowers are arranged in jars, two rusted metal crosses protrude from mounds in the grass. 'Look at the surnames,' he says, taking her hand to lead her round the walls. Gori, Valentini, Santini, Starnucci and Butteri are the family names that predominate. 'In villages like ours,' he tells her, 'so remote and cut off for so many months in the winter, inter-marriage was bound to happen.'

'So we *could* be related,' she says.

'Maybe in the distant, distant past.'

She walks slowly to the corner where the Santini family are buried and peering at the photo of a young soldier, she calls Francesco over.

It is Davide, her uncle.

She has a fleeting image of her mother kneeling on the grass tending his grave, her dark hair falling round her face, arranging greenery in a jam jar. For a few, vivid moments she senses her presence, hears Ines whisper to her that she must do what her heart tells her. And then the sensation fades and patterns play upon the grass, dancing shadows cast by tall pines.

'*Andiamo*! Let's go,' she says, taking his hand.

Chapter 35
October 1999

Emerging from the church they walk beneath the avenue of plane trees to applause from friends and family showering them with handfuls of rice. Alba runs in front, her bridesmaid's dress billowing behind, bubbling with laughter as she throws rose petals into the air above the newlyweds.

Francesco pulls her close while they wait for Danilo to catch up. People from the village keep stopping Anna's father to compliment him on his newly discovered family, 'Bravo, Danilo, bravissimo! Auguri!' and he beams with pleasure and pride.

Teresa dutifully escorts Anna's brother and sister to the agriturismo pick-up. Her English family have decided to come at the last minute, curiosity getting the better of them. She doesn't mind; she has enough happiness to share around and defies anybody not to be charmed by her Italian wedding. Anna giggles into her flowers at the sight of a villager giving Jane a helpful push on her ample behind as she clambers into the back of Teresa's pick-up. The vehicle has been transformed with garlands of greenery and white ribbons. Cynthia clings to Harry's arm, her high heels totally unsuited to the cobbled path, her pink chiffon dress clinging to her, barely hiding her six month bump and Harry's smile is like a zip, unzipped wide.

Bride and groom drive down the road to the *agriturismo* in Francesco's Fiat that Harry had insisted on decorating 'English wedding style' late last night, attaching old tin cans, balloons and a wellington boot tied to the bumper. Attracted by the commotion, people come out of their homes to wave handkerchiefs, clap and cheer, 'Auguri Francesco ed Anna…complimenti!'

The railings on the steps to Il Casalone have been festooned with laurel branches, garlands of white roses and long strands of variegated ivy and Teresa and her friends from the village have been busy for days in the kitchen, banning Anna from the food preparations. The wedding meal and sharing of food is every bit as important a ritual as the nuptial mass. Tables are piled with a feast of colourful, appetising food, spread on freshly laundered Busatti linen. A warm, balmy October has followed a wet summer and so a separate round table is arranged outside on the terrace to hold a whole Parmesan cheese, cut into squares and served with sparkling Prosecco to each guest as they arrive. Teresa and her team have been busy with starters of roast peppers, courgettes and aubergines, pastries with asparagus and artichokes and melting soft cheeses, home- made cappelletti – small hat-shaped ravioli stuffed with chicken breast, lean beef, lemon zest and nutmeg - and tagliatelle, with Anna's favourite fresh tomato and basil sauce. And for the main course, Teresa carries in a platter of whole roast suckling pig served with tiny potatoes from the *'orto'*, roasted in olive oil and pungent rosemary, a salad of flowers: nasturtiums, borage and marigold petals with young dandelion leaves, wild sorrel and rocket picked by Teresa and her girlfriends from the meadows round the village. And all this is washed down with glasses of full-bodied local Sangiovese and Chianti Classico.

Jane has insisted on contributing an English tradition to the wedding. At very short notice – for the wedding has been a spontaneous affair - she baked a wedding cake before leaving England and its three tiers of columns and crafted icing draw gasps of astonishment from the female Italian guests. She confided to Anna that on the Channel crossing she had tried to slip down to the car on the deck below to check on the cake's safe being and had been soundly reprimanded by one of the crew. Before Anna and Francesco cut the cake, Danilo makes a speech. Pushing back his chair and slowly rising, he taps the side of his glass to gain attention.

'It's not the custom to make speeches at our weddings,' he begins, easing his tie a little further away from his starched shirt collar, 'but we all know this is no ordinary wedding. We are here to join in the celebrations of these two lovely people who want to spend their lives together. But, I would like to also celebrate finding my family…I hope you will all permit me this selfishness…' He pauses as the guests applaud, a few even stamp their feet and he holds up his hands, waiting for them to quieten down. When he is ready, he resumes. 'Some of you here today already know a little about my story. My older friends will also remember Ines. Ines Santini.' There are murmurings amongst the guests, some of them turning to explain to those next to them. Danilo continues and there are hisses for silence so he can be heard. 'Take a look at my beautiful daughter and I'm sure you will see Ines's likeness.' There are more comments and exclamations from the guests. Anna feels herself blushing as everybody cranes to stare. Francesco plants a kiss on her mouth and there are more loud cheers and ribald shouts of '*tanti figli maschi*' (may you have many boy children!)

'The war has been over for more than 50 years now,' continues Danilo. 'Some of you here today lived through that time, although you would probably prefer not to be reminded. I know in our school up the hill they are preparing a project and some of the children will be asking grandparents for their memories of the war. And I urge you all to be generous with your time. We should not bury our memories, even if they are painful, even if mistakes were made in those times, which caused us anguish…we must learn from them. We fought hard for our freedom, for the freedom of our children.'

More murmurings amongst the guests. Somebody shouts '*Evviva l'Italia*' and a few echo him.

Somebody else shouts, '*Evviva l'Inghilterra!*' and there is more enthusiastic applause. Danilo again holds up his hands for silence. 'It was not my intention to stand up here like the old man I am and talk about the past or to be political so, let us now all raise our glasses and make a *brindisi* to Anna and Francesco and wish them happiness. May they hold on to that happiness, keep it deep within and never let it disappear. I feel as if I am the luckiest old man alive today for somehow my Ines has come back to me …Raise your glasses everybody: to Anna and Francesco!'

There are shouts of '*Bravo! Auguri! Cin-cin!*' Anna leans over and kisses her father and he whispers in her ear. 'I have a gift for you both but you must wait until after the wedding. Today is not the right time. Come and see me soon in Montebotolino.'

Alba climbs onto his knee. The old man pinches her cheek gently between his second and third fingers and strokes her head. Later, when the tables are pushed back against the walls and the accordionist starts up his music, she even manages to get the old man to dance a polka with her.

Later, in the bed in the eaves, Francesco strokes her hair, wiping a tear with his thumb as it trickles down her cheek. 'You're weeping for Ines, aren't you?'

She nods. 'I'm so happy and it doesn't seem fair.'

'Life isn't always fair. But she's led us to each other. That might not have happened if her life had been different.'

She kisses her husband. Tomorrow she will buy a note book and start a diary… her own memory pearls.

Epilogue

Danilo died four years later, just after his eightieth birthday, but not before he was able to meet all his grandchildren. Davide, Danilo, Jonathan Starnucci was born in June 2000, at the start of a new millennium, eight months after Francesco and Anna married. Alba was over the moon with her little brother and just as excited when her twin sisters, Rosanna and Emilia, were born two years later.

To commemorate their wedding, Anna and Francesco paid for the repair of the communal oven up in Montebotolino and each *ferragosto* since, they have been asked to light the fire for the annual pizza party.

Danilo's wedding gift to Anna and Francesco was the ruined watermill along the river Marecchia - Il Mulino.

Broken-hearted that she had made a new life in England and suffering poor health, Anna's parents had almost completed the sale of the old mill to a local businessman. His plans to knock the centuries old building down in order to create a holiday park on the site were thwarted by Danilo. He managed to persuade the *Comune* to turn down the project, pointing out the importance of the listed building, as well as the real danger of flooding in that area along by the river.

Eventually, he purchased Il Mulino himself but never carried out restoration on the old building and it was in a pitiful state when Anna and Francesco embarked on their project.

Today, after extensive site visits with local architects and planners, geological surveys and successful feasibility studies, Anna and Francesco have fully restored the watermill. The original mill stones have been put back into use and once a week, Francesco produces enough grain to sell to tourists for making home-made bread. It is the venue for holidays with a difference, where real Italy can be sampled. When Anna is not busy with her growing family, she organises courses in cookery, painting and language. Francesco loves to accompany visitors on walks in the mountains, showing them the rich fauna and flora of the area. He is about to publish a field guide on butterflies and birds in the Marecchia valley. Little Davide speaks fluent Italian and English and his sisters will be brought up in the same way, encouraged to be proud of their two cultures.

The mill and the location can be seen on www.ilmulinorofelle.com, where you will be most welcome to come and visit and see for yourselves.

Acknowledgments

This story was inspired in great part by my Italian mother-in-law, Giuseppina Micheli, who fell in love with Captain Horace Petch of The Royal Artillery of the Eight Army, when they met in Urbino on 13th October 1944 and by the stories told by our friends who live in the area of Badia Tedalda, Tuscany. This stunning countryside is situated near the Gothic Line and history seems to whisper to me along every mule track. However, Never Forget is a work of fiction. Any resemblance to real personalities is purely coincidental. I would hate to think anybody might be offended by my imagination. Any mistakes that occur in historical events that I draw on in the story are purely my own.

Thank you, lovely 'Pina', for sharing your stories and letters. Grazie - Fulvio Pieghai and Roberto Marini at the Pro-Loco in Badia Tedalda - for your time and generosity in lending me photos and memoirs written by local folk. Thanks to Maureen Blundell, Liz Minister and all my writing friends. Without you…

Mummy and Daddy – Kenneth and Maureen Sutor – (who are missed each and every day), took their young family to live in Rome in the early '60's. I love you.

It goes without saying that my love and thanks go to Fagiolino, without whom I would be lost.

Bibliography

Love and War in the Apennines – Eric Newby

Manders March on Rome – d'A Mander

Mrs Milburn's Diaries (An Englishwoman's day-to-day reflections 1939-45)

Italy's Sorrow – James Holland

The Art of Falling – Deborah Lawrenson

The Voice of War – The Second World War Told By Those Who Fought It, edited by James Owen and Guy Walters

When the Moon Rises – Tony Davies

The Italian Resistance in World War II - Maria de Blasio Wilhelm

Miracle at Sant'Anna - James McBride

War in Italy 1943-1945, A Brutal Story - Richard Lamb

L'Appennino del'44, eccidi e protagonisti sulla linea gotica, a cura di Ivan Tognarini

The King's Dragoon Guards. World War 2 – Part 6

What did you do in the War, Mummy? Compiled by Mavis Nicholson.